SWEET TEA AT SUNRISE

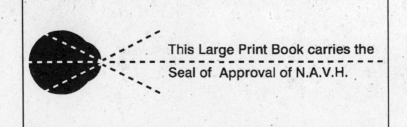

This Large Print Book carries the
Seal of Approval of N.A.V.H.

Sweet Tea at Sunrise

Sherryl Woods

THORNDIKE PRESS
A part of Gale, Cengage Learning

Detroit • New York • San Francisco • New Haven, Conn • Waterville, Maine • London

GALE
CENGAGE Learning

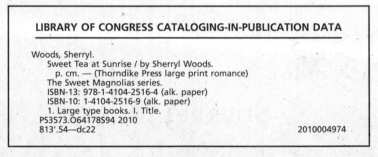

LIBRARY OF CONGRESS CATALOGING-IN-PUBLICATION DATA

Woods, Sherryl.
    Sweet Tea at Sunrise / by Sherryl Woods.
        p. cm. — (Thorndike Press large print romance)
    The Sweet Magnolias series.
    ISBN-13: 978-1-4104-2516-4 (alk. paper)
    ISBN-10: 1-4104-2516-9 (alk. paper)
    1. Large type books. I. Title.
PS3573.O64178S94 2010
813'.54—dc22   2010004974

Published in 2010 by arrangement with Harlequin Books S.A.

Printed in the United States of America
1 2 3 4 5 6 7 14 13 12 11 10

DEAR READERS,

Welcome back to Serenity for Sarah's story! The Sweet Magnolias series is all about long-standing friendships, and the one between Annie, Sarah and Raylene, despite an interruption by time and distance, is now stronger than ever.

Many of you may identify with Sarah's self-esteem issues. I know there have been times in my life when I certainly would have. And for a woman like Sarah, whose husband planted seeds of doubt in her head for many years, finding her way back to being self-confident can't happen overnight.

It seems at first glance that a sweet-talking man like Travis McDonald is exactly what Sarah needs, but will she find the courage to trust his pretty words? Recovering from years of self-doubt isn't easy, but Travis is a determined, patient man, one definitely worthy of loving.

I hope you'll enjoy their story, along with catching up with a very unexpected turn of events for Mary Vaughn and Sonny. For me one of the greatest joys of writing these books is the chance to catch up with old friends. I hope you'll feel the same way, and that you'll be anxiously awaiting the conclusion of this latest Sweet Magnolias trilogy, *Honeysuckle Summer,* in stores next month.

All best,
Sherryl Woods

1

For a few days now the same man, clad in snug denim and a T-shirt that caressed impressive biceps, had spent precisely thirty minutes in the back booth at Wharton's, lounging against the red vinyl as if he owned the place, and studying Sarah as if he found her to be the most fascinating creature on the planet. No man had looked at her like that since she'd first crossed paths with her ex-husband back in college. And even before the divorce, it had been a couple of years since Walter had regarded her with that degree of interest. It was unnerving.

Of course, a lot about her life these days was unnerving. With a whole lot of support from her two best friends, Annie Sullivan Townsend and Raylene Hammond, Sarah had finally gotten up the gumption to divorce Walter and — equally important — his entire controlling, uptight family. She'd fought to win custody of her two kids,

7

Tommy and Libby.

And, mostly in the interest of getting out of the house and doing *something,* she'd taken a part-time job waiting on tables at Wharton's, where just about everyone in Serenity congregated at one time or another during the week. It might not be making use of her degree in elementary education, but it was surprisingly satisfying. She'd discovered she had a knack for getting people to open up, a necessity in a restaurant that prided itself on being the hotbed of local gossip.

No one, however, seemed to have any idea of who the mysterious man in that back booth might be. Sarah had asked.

Just now, she'd even asked the man himself point-blank if he was new in town, here to stay or just passing through. He responded with a slow, sexy, dimpled grin that had unexpectedly sent her recently comatose libido into overdrive.

"I suppose I could be persuaded to stay if the right offer came along," he said in a low voice that hummed across her senses. "You offerin', sugar?"

Sarah was so taken aback by the flirtatious question, she scurried straight off to the kitchen to place his order. It was one thing to chat up old man Watson from the feed and grain, or the town mayor, whom she'd known since she was in diapers. It was quite another to have a man with dreamy eyes and a voice that could lure a woman straight to bed act almost as if he wanted to take her . . . well, straight to bed.

Which, of course, he didn't. She knew that. Hadn't she heard often enough about all her flaws — her weight, her disorganization, her lack of mothering skills — from her ex-husband? In retaliation for her decision to file for divorce before he had a chance to, Walter had made it his personal mission in life to see that she had not one shred of self-esteem left by the time they ended their marriage. Worse, even knowing that he was just being his ornery old self, she'd been so low that she'd taken every mean-spirited word to heart.

In the past few months, she'd worked hard to get herself back into shape. Annie had been her personal trainer at The Corner Spa, and Sarah had finally knocked off most of the weight she'd gained during two pregnancies. She had another ten pounds she'd like to sweat off, but if it didn't happen, well, she could live with that, too. Despite her success, though, she sometimes still saw herself through Walter's eyes, which annoyed the daylights out of her friends. It irked her, too, but the stream of a few years of nonstop criticism was embedded so deep, it was almost impossible to shake.

"Grace, you need to take that burger and fries to table nine," she told the owner of the old-fashioned soda fountain. The down-home cooking continued to bring in business even now that the pharmacy side of the operation was taking a hit from some of the bigger discount pharmacies in the region. In Sarah's opinion it was friendly service and gossip that had kept it afloat.

Grace Wharton eyed her curiously. "Why would you suddenly want to turn a man who looks like that and tips like a city slicker over to me?"

"Just do it, please," Sarah pleaded, not wanting to admit he made her nervous.

Grace's eyes narrowed. "Did he say something to offend you? If he did, I'll throw him out of here on his backside, attractive though that backside might be."

Sarah turned pink with embarrassment. "No, he was just joking around, that's all. You know, flirting the way some guys do. I should be used to it."

Grace observed her thoughtfully. "Seems to me you could use a sweet-talkin' stranger to put a little color back into your cheeks."

"I most definitely do not need a man,"

Sarah declared emphatically. "I just got rid of the one I had."

"Good riddance is what I say," Grace declared. "The way I hear it, all he ever did was tear you down. Now you need a fella to perk you back up. I'd think a little sweet talk would be music to your ears."

It was an oft-repeated refrain. In the month she'd been working at Wharton's, Grace had not only offered that opinion on an almost daily basis, she'd suited action to words and trotted out half the single men in town for Sarah's inspection. For all Sarah knew, this man could be the latest.

"Do you know him?" she inquired suspiciously. "The man in booth nine? Did you drive over to Columbia or Sumter or someplace and recruit him to sit in here and stroke my ego?"

Grace looked genuinely appalled by the suggestion. "Absolutely not! As if I would do such a thing. I never saw him before he turned up in here a couple of days ago," she said with obvious frustration. "He's not registered over at the Serenity Inn, either. I checked."

"Could be he's staying with friends or family," Sarah speculated.

"Might be, but it's no one who comes in here regular-like," Grace insisted. "Besides, if he were someone's guest, wouldn't they be sittin' right there with him? He's obviously on his own."

"What about Mary Vaughn?" Sarah asked. "Not only does she usually lock on to any new single man in the entire region, but she'd know if he looked at real estate."

"Sadly, since she got back together with Sonny, they take their lunch hours together . . . at home, if you know what I mean," Grace said with a grin. "Those two act like they're honeymooning all over again. Can't say I see much of either one of them. When she does come in for coffee, she's always in a rush. She gets out of here before I can get a word out of her."

"Well, someone must know who he is," Sarah said with frustration. "I asked him directly if he was new in town, and he didn't give me a straight answer." Her cheeks burned at the memory of his teasing.

Grace regarded her with amusement. "For someone who claims not to be interested in the man, you sure are determined to figure this out," she said as she picked up the plate with the burger and fries, then added another couple of meals to a tray. "You sure you don't want to take this out there yourself?"

Sarah shook her head. "You do it. I'll take

more coffee to the mayor and his buddies, maybe see if I can tempt them into putting a little ice cream on that peach pie you baked this morning."

"I declare those men are going to gain ten pounds by the end of the month, the way you talk them into having dessert every day." She shook a finger under Sarah's nose. "I don't want their wives in here grumbling at me, you hear. And George Ulster has diabetes, so don't be trying to talk him into pie and such."

Sarah grinned. "George always gets sugar-free ice cream. Howard Lewis is a widower, so nobody's going to come in here complaining about his weight, and Fred Watson's skinny as a scarecrow. It's all good, Grace."

Grace gave her a sorrowful look. "Why you'd want to hang around those old geezers when there's a certifiable hunk in here is beyond me, but there's no accounting for taste," she said, nudging the door with her ample hip and heading out of the kitchen with the three meals balanced on a tray as if it weighed next to nothing. With her round face, pink cheeks, greying hair, granny glasses perched on the end of her nose and the red uniform she'd unwisely chosen to match the decor, she looked a bit like

13

Mrs. Claus.

Sarah picked up pots of decaf and regular coffee and followed in her wake, careful not to glance toward booth nine. Something told her that a pair of sea-green eyes would be watching her, and that they'd fill with knowing amusement when Grace arrived with his lunch.

Fortunately, Wharton's was too busy for her to spend much time worrying about what he thought. She didn't even glance in his direction.

But when he rose and started toward the door, she knew it with every fiber of her being. And when he stopped just behind her and drawled, "See you tomorrow, sugar," she juggled the tray she was carrying and nearly upended two tuna-melt specials onto the black-and-white tiled floor. Bright color once again flooded her cheeks.

Before she could flee to the kitchen, he was gone, leaving her flustered and irritated in just about equal proportions.

"I don't know why he rattles me so badly," Sarah said that evening as she, Raylene and Annie sipped margaritas on the back patio at her small bungalow. She'd settled there with Tommy and Libby when it had become obvious that her marriage was all but over.

14

It was the perfect May evening in South Carolina, warm but without the oppressive humidity that would soon set in.

She'd fled to Serenity from Alabama for a break, originally intending to go back all fixed up to suit Walter's idea of the perfect wife. It hadn't taken long to realize that she'd be wasting her time trying to meet his high standards. Thank heaven her parents had had the foresight to keep this house even after they'd moved to a new retirement home on the gulf coast of Texas, apparently guessing long before she did that her marriage was doomed.

"Have either of you seen him or heard anything about him?" she asked her friends.

"Well, you know I haven't," Raylene said wryly.

Ever since she'd moved back to Serenity to escape her abusive husband in Charleston, Raylene had rarely left the house. Sarah had given her a safe haven, and in return Raylene looked after the house and babysat Tommy and Libby on occasion when the regular sitter had time off. It had been the perfect solution for both of them, though Sarah was starting to wonder just how healthy it was for Raylene to continue hiding out and pretending her problems didn't exist.

"About that," Annie began, only to draw a quelling look from Raylene that stopped whatever she'd been about to say.

Trying to broker peace, to say nothing of getting back to her own concern, Sarah said, "Focus, ladies. Who is this man? What's he doing in Serenity?"

Annie gave her an amused look. "I'm with Grace. You're showing a lot of curiosity for someone who's supposedly not interested."

Sarah scowled at her. "Well, what if he's a stalker or, even more likely, what if he's spying for Walter? I wouldn't put it past my ex to send some guy over here to try to get me all tied up in knots so I'll do something stupid that'll make it easy for him to snatch Tommy away from me."

It still stuck in everyone's craw, especially hers, that Walter had expressed interest in gaining custody only of his son — the heir to the Price family legacy, an Alabama cotton mill — but not his daughter. In fact, her lawyer, Helen Decatur, had used that very fact to show the judge why he was an insensitive, unfit parent.

Raylene looked thoughtful. "It would be just like that jerk," she said, despite the fact that she'd never personally laid eyes on the offensive Walter. She hid out in her room on the days he came to see the kids, claiming she didn't want to intrude or to say something to make the situation between him and Sarah any worse.

"Agreed," Annie said. Since she had first-hand knowledge of some of Walter's shenanigans after Sarah's return to Serenity, she spoke with even more authority. "I'll have Helen check him out. Or maybe my dad. With his store right there on Main Street, he sees pretty much everything that's going on in town. And I'll ask Jeanette to talk to Tom. She's been off for a couple of days, but she'll be in tomorrow. As town manager, Tom can check with the sheriff and see if they've been keeping an eye on anyone suspicious."

"Great idea," Raylene said, shuddering a bit. She was still spooked by the idea of strangers in town, even though she knew perfectly well that her ex was in jail.

Sarah flinched at the all-out investigation she seemed to have sparked. Maybe she'd overreacted just a little. "Are you sure we're not going overboard? Could be he's just new in town and a big flirt."

"Then we need to know that," Annie said. "It'll put your mind at ease."

"Or it'll rattle you even more," Raylene said with a grin, which was a rare enough sight to be worth noting.

"I am not interested in this man," Sarah declared forcefully.

Her friends, darn 'em both, simply laughed.

Travis McDonald sat in his cousin's kitchen nursing a cup of coffee and thinking about the pretty little waitress at Wharton's who'd been providing him with so much entertainment for the past few days. Yesterday he'd scared her so bad, she'd sent Grace over with his meal. Today she'd avoided him altogether, except for casting a few nervous glances his way. He hadn't enjoyed flustering a woman like that in a long time. Most of the women he ran across threw themselves at him, so she had been a refreshing change.

Like his cousin Tom, the town manager here in Serenity, Travis had been a college baseball standout. Then he'd gone pro and spent a few years being traded around to various farm teams before finally making it to the majors with the Boston Red Sox. It had nearly killed his Southern, blueblood family to have him playing for a team up North. The only thing worse, in their opinion, would have been if he'd signed with the Yankees.

After his career had come to a screeching

halt a couple of weeks back, when the Red Sox had released him right after spring training and no other team had come calling, the first person he'd phoned had been Tom. His cousin had invited Travis to stay until he figured out what he wanted to do with the rest of his life. They both knew that would be easier to accomplish without Travis's parents chiming in with their very vocal and usually differing opinions. There would also be relative anonymity here, since the locals were mostly fans of the Atlanta Braves and paid little attention to teams in the American League until the World Series rolled around. Travis relished the idea of a little privacy.

So far, he'd been pretty much flying under the radar here in Serenity, just the way he wanted to, while he gave his future some serious thought. He'd seen the occasional flicker of puzzlement, maybe a fleeting, vague hint of recognition, but not one single person had approached and asked for an autograph. That, too, was a refreshing change from the very public life he'd been leading.

At 29, he'd come out of baseball with a decent amount of money in the bank, no permanent ties beyond his divorced parents and a couple of well-meaning, but annoying sisters, and absolutely no sense of direction. The only thing he'd known for sure was that he couldn't get back to the South fast enough. The northern weather was too cold and unpredictable and Boston too crowded. Then, too, he hadn't especially wanted to hang around a town where he'd been dumped by its beloved sports team.

For the past several days he'd spent countless hours right here at this kitchen table talking over his options with the older cousin who'd always been a mentor to him, and with Tom's wife, Jeanette, who treated him like a younger brother, but without the nagging of an older sister.

This morning, as he'd listened to Grace Wharton try to tune in the nearest radio station from over in Columbia only to wind up with mostly static, an idea had bubbled to the surface. He could hardly wait for Tom and Jeanette to get home so he could try it out on them. It was a plan that would make good use of his education and just might satisfy his folks, plus it offered the challenge he craved.

He'd already done some digging around on the Internet and discovered that a small radio station that had virtually no signal and little programming beyond the weather and a stockpile of oldies was for sale. He'd even made a phone call to the owner and determined he could not only afford to buy it, he could buy the current owner's expertise for a few months until he got the hang of running it himself. Now all that remained was getting Tom's stamp of approval . . . or, more likely, a stern lecture detailing why he'd be out of his ever-lovin' mind to even consider such a thing.

To grease the wheels for the conversation, Travis had spent the past hour on the back patio tossing a salad and heating up the grill for the thick steaks he'd picked up at the market. He'd even set the table and uncorked a bottle of halfway decent wine in honor of the occasion. He had his favorite beer on ice for himself. The serene garden setting — which Jeanette claimed was the sole reason she'd bought the house right out from under Tom before they'd even started dating — was ideal for a good meal and some serious conversation.

An hour later, with Tom and Jeanette sighing with appreciation over his pretty basic culinary efforts, Travis launched into a description of his brainstorm. The incredulous expression on Tom's face was a little daunting, but Travis forged ahead anyway. When he'd finished, he waited expectantly.

"Are you nuts?" his cousin demanded.

Tom's reaction was pretty much what Travis would have expected from his father, so it was a little discouraging to have it coming from his cousin, whom he'd expected to be more supportive.

Jeanette, however, regarded him with obvious delight. "I think it's a fabulous idea. It's just what this town needs."

"Since when does Serenity need its own radio station?" Tom asked, his expression dubious.

"You said so yourself after that last hurricane looked as if it was aiming straight for us," Jeanette responded. "You said we needed a way for everyone in town to get up-to-the-minute information relevant to Serenity, instead of just what was going on over in Charleston or Columbia."

Tom scowled at her. "That was different."

"How so?" Jeanette inquired.

"I was just saying *someone* should do it," Tom grumbled. "I didn't mean my own cousin should come into town and throw his money away."

"Are you so sure a radio station wouldn't make money here?" Travis asked. "There's no competition, at least not close enough to matter. I'd get all the local advertising dollars."

"Haven't you heard?" Tom said. "We're in

the midst of an economic crisis. None of the businesses around here have money to throw away on advertising. They're all just trying to stay afloat."

"Which is precisely why they need to advertise," Jeanette chimed in, backing up Travis. "When did you start to sound so negative about this town, anyway?"

"I'm not down on Serenity. I'm just being realistic." He faced Travis. "Why would you want to stay here, when you could locate anywhere in the country?"

"Why not?" Travis responded. "You did. In fact, if I'm recalling correctly, you had a chance to move back to Charleston and you decided to stay right here."

Tom glanced at his wife, undisguised adoration in his eyes. "I was persuaded that someone here might make it worth my while."

"Don't blame it all on me," Jeanette said, obviously not taking his gallant words as much of a compliment. "When the town heard you might leave, they put on a full-court press to keep you here. All that flattery is what changed your mind. It certainly wasn't the salary or even my wiles."

Tom shrugged. "Okay, I succumbed to the challenge of solidifying the town's economic base," he admitted. "I decided I couldn't

23

walk away when I hadn't finished the job I came here to do."

"That's exactly what I'm looking for," Travis told him. "A challenge, and a place where I can make a real contribution to the community."

"Then I think a radio station in Serenity is perfect for you, Travis," Jeanette said. "Goodness knows, you love to talk. And with that low, sexy drawl of yours, you'd be great on the air. Every woman in town will tune in, especially if you go on the air at night."

She made an exaggerated show of fanning herself with her napkin, which drew a disgruntled look from her husband. She merely grinned and added, "And I already know for a fact that you're the hot topic of conversation in Wharton's. When I got back to work today, Annie asked me if I had any idea who the new stranger in town might be. She thought maybe Tom should have the sheriff run a check on you."

Travis chuckled, but Tom looked shaken.

"What the devil have you been doing to stir things up?" he asked Travis.

"He's been flirting with Sarah, apparently," Jeanette said, her amusement plain. "Now Annie's on the case. I tried to dodge her questions, because I know you wanted to hang on to your privacy as long as possible, but you should know Annie's not going to let this rest."

"Who's Annie?" Travis inquired.

"One of Sarah's best friends. She's also married to Ty Townsend."

"Pitcher for the Braves?" Travis asked, impressed when she nodded. "He has one heckuva fastball."

"How about we discuss your flirtatious ways and Ty's fastball a little later," Tom suggested. "Right now maybe we should put this radio idea to rest."

"I still like it," Jeanette said, giving Tom a stubborn look. "I think he'll be a huge hit."

"And who's he supposed to put on the air the rest of the time?" Tom inquired testily.

"He'll hire people," she replied.

"Are there a lot of frustrated radio deejays in Serenity?" Tom scoffed, apparently content to have this conversation with his wife without any input from Travis himself.

"He won't know until he puts out word he's hiring," she told him. "I vote yes, but since it's clear I'm butting up against my husband's superior wisdom, I'll leave you two to thrash it out. I have an early meeting at the spa in the morning."

She leaned down to give her husband a blistering kiss that made Travis's stomach

25

knot with envy. Oddly, it also brought the image of the waitress from Wharton's to mind. That probably wasn't a good thing.

Then, again, it might not be one bit riskier than this radio venture that had captured his imagination.

2

Sarah was jittery as a june bug all day Saturday. Walter was on his way over from Alabama to see the kids — well, to see Tommy, anyway — and it was the first time he'd been here since she'd started working at Wharton's. She imagined he'd have plenty to say about that. Waiting tables in a local diner didn't fit the Price definition of a suitable career. They hadn't even wanted her to make use of her degree in education, as if teaching at the local elementary school would be beneath a member of such a lofty family.

Worse, Grace had been in a bind this morning, and Sarah had agreed to cover an extra shift, so she wouldn't be at the house to break the news herself. She'd left it to the sitter and Raylene. She figured that could go one of two ways. Walter would shrug it off as one more irrational decision she'd made, or he'd come flying over here to try to drag her back home where he thought she belonged.

She was clearing tables after the breakfast crowd, getting ready for the bigger than usual Saturday lunch rush in less than an hour, when she saw Walter's gas-guzzling luxury SUV pull up to the curb. Even without seeing the driver through the tinted windshield, she knew it was Walter because most people in Serenity had adapted to the economic times with more practical cars. She sighed and prepared herself for battle.

She wasn't surprised when he pulled Tommy out of a car seat in back, but when he also emerged a minute later with Libby, she thought maybe her imagination was playing tricks on her. Walter never willingly took Libby anywhere, claiming he didn't know how to handle babies. That might have worked when she was six months old, but it had stopped being an effective excuse now that she was nearly two. She saw Raylene's hand in this. For a woman who was jumpy around strangers, she was a fighter for those she cared about. She must have come out of hiding to shame Walter into taking both kids.

"Mommy, Daddy said we could have pancakes for breakfast," Tommy announced excitedly, pushing his way inside and heading right for her. "Is it okay, even if we already ate?"

"It's fine with me," she assured him, casting a wary glance toward Walter, who was trying to slow his pace to Libby's. Once she'd learned to walk, Libby's independent streak had kicked in, and she never wanted to be carried anymore except when she was exhausted. Walter's expression radiated frustration, but to his credit he hadn't just picked her up or tried to rush her. Maybe he'd already discovered that was a sure way to get her to throw a tantrum.

Sarah met his gaze. "I wasn't expecting to see you here," she said, trying to gauge his mood.

"I wasn't expecting to find you working in a place like this, either," he said as he settled Libby in the booth next to Tommy. "I think we should talk about that."

"Not while I'm working," she said firmly, keeping her expression cheerful but unyielding. "What can I get you to drink?"

"Coffee for me," he said. "Milk for the kids, I guess. Tommy, you said you want pancakes, right?"

"This many," Tommy confirmed, holding up two fingers.

"How about one, and then we'll see,"

Sarah said. "Libby, you want a pancake, too?"

"She'll make a mess of it," Walter immediately protested.

"Not if you give it to her in little pieces," Sarah said. "I'll be back in a minute with your drinks." She escaped to the kitchen before she asked him why he'd brought them here if he was so worried about any messes they might make. She already knew the answer, anyway. Lecturing her was evidently his top priority.

When she returned with her ex's coffee and milk for the kids, he frowned at her. "Sit down so we can talk, okay? There's nobody in here."

"There will be soon, and I need to have the tables set up," she said. "Once I'm finished with that, if there's time, we can talk."

Just then Grace emerged from the kitchen, recognized Tommy and Libby and apparently guessed the identity of the man with them. "Honey, you go ahead and take a break," she told Sarah. "I can finish up with the booths, and I'll bring those pancakes out when they're ready."

"You don't need to do that," Sarah protested. "You've been on your feet all morning. You're the one who should be taking a break."

"It's okay. I've had a lifetime to get used to that. I'll bring you a glass of sweet tea, too," Grace insisted.

Sarah sighed and sat down, crowding into the booth next to her ex-husband. There wasn't nearly enough room to keep as much space between them as she'd like to. Reluctantly, she met his stormy gaze. She could barely recall what it had been like to have those bright blue eyes light with pleasure at the sight of her.

"You wanted to talk," she said mildly. "Now's your chance."

"Okay, then, what I want to know is if you're working here just to embarrass me?" Walter inquired in a strident tone that carried all the way to Grace, who was placing setups on the counter. She whirled around and gave him a hard look.

Aghast by Walter's rudeness, Sarah regarded him incredulously. "You're the only one embarrassing you," she said in a low voice. "What I do in Serenity is no reflection on you or your family. We're not married anymore."

"But it suggests I'm not paying you enough in alimony and child support," he said.

She had to try hard not to laugh at his

twisted but all-too-typical logic. "No, it suggests that I want to work and contribute to my own family's well-being."

Walter was clearly exasperated by her reply. "Then why not teach? Isn't that what you were always claiming you wanted while we were married? Day in and day out, I heard about how you were wasting your college degree."

"In case you haven't checked a calendar, it's almost the end of the school year," she said, clinging to her patience by a thread. "I've put in an application for next year, but it's too soon to know if there will be a position open."

"Well, you could wait until you hear before taking a job like this."

Sarah shook her head at his demeaning tone. "Do you happen to remember what I was doing when you and I met at college?"

"Waiting tables," he admitted grudgingly. "But we were kids then."

"And it's still a perfectly respectable job," she said. "You weren't such a snob back then, Walter. In fact, you seemed happy enough when I could give you a free burger and fries. Has living in the shadow of your family turned you into the kind of man who can't appreciate hard work, no matter what it is?"

She already knew the answer. Working for his father and living close to his family had changed him from the independent, fun-loving man she'd fallen for into someone she no longer even recognized. Every time he opened his mouth to criticize her, the words she heard were an echo of something either his mother or father had said about her. And nothing they'd ever said had been good.

He winced at her accusation, but for once he didn't bother trying to defend himself. "Okay, okay, I just hate to see you wearing yourself out when you don't need to. You couldn't keep up with the kids when you were home all the time. Now they're probably running wild because you're too exhausted to chase after them."

She doubted this had anything to do with consideration for her, but she pretended he was sincere. "Thanks for worrying, but I'm managing just fine."

"Well, you look like hell."

"Thanks so much," she said wryly, then forced a smile. She refused to rise to the bait of one dig after another. She'd finally learned it wasn't worth arguing with Walter, especially in front of the kids. She turned her attention to Tommy. "So, what do you have planned with your dad for today?"

"Daddy and me are gonna play catch," Tommy said eagerly. "Right, Daddy?"

"Right," Walter said, his eyes lighting up as he looked at his son. There was no mistaking his love for the little boy who looked just like him, with the same blue eyes and sun-streaked brown hair.

Their crooked smiles were exactly alike, too. Every time Sarah saw that smile on her Tommy's face, she thought about the man she'd fallen in love with, the one it seemed no longer existed.

"And Libby?" Sarah prodded.

"Play, too," Libby insisted, her adoring gaze on her daddy, who plainly was less than thrilled with the idea.

"That'll be fun," Sarah enthused.

"Yeah, it'll be a barrel of laughs," Walter said.

Sarah regarded him with dismay, and he had the grace to look sheepish. He ruffled Libby's golden curls. "Who knows, you could turn out to be the first girl to play in the majors."

Over my dead body, Sarah thought, but kept the thought to herself. If the outrageous idea gave Walter a rare moment of rapport with his daughter, who was she to ruin it?

Just as Grace brought the pancakes for

the kids, a few of the Saturday regulars started straggling in.

"I have to get back to work," Sarah said, leaving Walter looking flustered as he tried to deal with Libby's pancake and her demands for more syrup.

"Sure, abandon me in my time of need," he grumbled as she rose, but for once there was a spark of his old sense of humor in his eyes.

That glint made Sarah's heart catch. Walter Price had been handsome, no question about it. He still was, for that matter. But it was his sense of humor that had captivated her. When that had died, driven out by his demanding father and exasperating mother, she'd lost all hope for their marriage. That didn't mean she couldn't hope that one of these days he'd find himself again.

When Travis walked into Wharton's for lunch on Saturday, he noticed that Sarah seemed to be operating on autopilot. She never once met his gaze while taking his order. Nor did she respond when he told her she was looking mighty fine today.

He watched her as she went through the motions of handing out meals, writing tickets and making change, barely exchanging a word with any of the customers. She looked as if she were a million miles away. Wherever she was, it seemed to be an unhappy place.

Travis liked a puzzle as well as the next person, but he'd always figured the quickest way to figure one out was to ask what you wanted to know. When Sarah brought him a tuna sandwich instead of the chicken salad special he'd ordered, he snagged her hand.

"Hold on, sugar. I ordered the special."

Jerking her hand away, she looked down at the plate on the table as if seeing it for the first time, then blushed furiously. "I'm so sorry. I don't know where my head is."

"You've been looking distracted ever since I came in," he said, choosing his words carefully. Something told him she was one harsh word away from coming unglued. "Is there a problem?"

"Not really. I just made a mistake, that's all."

"Never seen you make one before."

"If you only knew," she said with an edge in her voice. "I'll get your chicken salad and be right back."

Travis decided to let her go. When she returned with his meal, he tried again.

"You know what I've been thinking?" he said, then went right on before she could walk away. "I've been sitting here thinking about how much I miss that smile of yours."

She regarded him skeptically.

Travis nodded. "That's the gospel truth," he assured her. "I count on that sunny smile. It makes people feel real welcome."

She frowned at his comment. "Sorry. It's not on the menu today."

"Any particular reason?"

Her frown deepened. "Why are you making such a big deal about this? Everyone has a bad day from time to time."

"Because it always bothers me when I see a woman looking so unhappy."

"So, what? You think you have to rush in and play Sir Galahad?"

He grinned. "Something like that. It's a curse, but that's just the way I am."

Her lips twitched slightly, as if she were fighting a smile. "Eat your lunch, Sir Galahad. I'm busy."

"Really?" he said with an exaggerated look around. He was the only customer left.

She blinked as she realized the same thing. "Oh."

"I hope everyone didn't slip out without paying," he said with feigned worry.

She did smile then, albeit with obvious reluctance. "You going to pick up their tabs, if they did? In the interest of putting a smile on my face?"

"Absolutely," he said. "Or you could just sit down here and talk about your troubles."

"With you? A total stranger?"

"Now, that's not quite right. I thought you and I had been getting to know each other for days now."

"I don't even know your name."

"Well, I know yours, Sarah. Mine's Travis. Travis McDonald." He held out his hand. Schooled with good manners, she took it, but released it almost immediately.

"McDonald?" she repeated, recognition obviously dawning as the name registered. "Any relation to Tom, our town manager?"

"He's my cousin," he admitted, then smiled. "Now, see, we're practically old friends. You can tell me anything."

"I thought men hated listening to women pour out their problems," she said, studying him curiously.

"Really? I've found it's the best way to get to know a woman. If you don't listen to what's going on in her life, how are you supposed to know how to make her happy?"

"And making women happy is what you do?"

He laughed at the innuendo in her tone. "Not in *that* way, sugar, though we could probably work something out."

She stared at him for a beat, clearly

uncertain whether he was joking or not. Finally, she chuckled. "You're outrageous."

"Just one of the words I've heard used," he admitted. "Sit, and I'll tell you some of the others."

"But I thought you wanted to talk about *me*," she said, feigning disappointment.

Travis laughed. "That'll work, too."

"Sorry. I really do have to get back to work. As soon as I get this place back in order, I need to get home to my kids. They're always upset when their daddy goes back to Alabama."

"You're divorced," he concluded.

"Yes, and a single mom of a girl who's not quite two and a boy who just turned four."

"No wonder you look a little shell-shocked. That's a heavy load to be carrying."

Her gaze narrowed. "You don't like kids?"

"I love kids, as a matter of fact. I'm just saying I know how demanding it is to raise a couple of them on your own."

"Now how would you know a thing like that?" she asked with blatant skepticism.

"Because my mama did it with me and my two sisters. My daddy, bless his heart, was worthless when it came to parenting. He was good for three things, as near as I could tell, writing checks, chasing women and telling the rest of us how badly we were screwing up."

"He sounds like a wonderful role model," she said wryly. "Are you thinking of following in his footsteps? You certainly have the sweet talk down pat."

The suggestion that he might be anything like his daddy offended Travis deeply, but she had no way of knowing that. "I certainly do hold him up as an example," he said slowly, holding her gaze. "Of what not to be."

She blinked at the heat behind his words. "Okay, then. Good for you." She stood up hurriedly. "Nice talking to you, Travis McDonald."

"You, too, Sarah," he said with more sincerity than she'd managed.

He watched her walk away, wondering at the fact that he was still fascinated despite all the complications screaming at him to stay far, far away.

Mary Vaughn Lewis couldn't recall a time in her life when she'd been happier. When she'd married Sonny Lewis the first time, she'd been after respectability and security. He was the son of the town mayor and owner of a successful car dealership. Married to Sonny, she'd believed no one would

40

ever look down on her again or bring up her less-than-respectable family.

They'd divorced because he'd tired of her taking him for granted. Or maybe because he'd tired of being second best to Ronnie Sullivan, who'd never even given her a second glance despite her very best efforts to catch his attention. It was hard to say just why Sonny had lost patience, but the divorce had been a shock just the same. She'd never envisioned Sonny leaving her. The one constant in her life had been his adoration from the time they'd been teenagers.

Only after they'd been apart for a while had Mary Vaughn realized what a treasure Sonny was. She'd found herself drawn to him in a whole new way. The passion that had been methodical the first time around had been rekindled into something that stunned her with its intensity. In their forties, they were like two kids who couldn't get enough of each other.

As much as this new side of their relationship thrilled her, it was seriously cutting into her career as a real estate agent. She'd realized she was well and truly hooked on her new husband when she chose running home for a mid-afternoon quickie over showing houses or closing a deal. Her schedule, once packed with appointments she refused to change, was now subject to her husband's timetable and the sudden impulses that might strike either one of them.

Which is why she was at home and breathless when she had a call from Travis McDonald inquiring about real estate downtown. Though she had no intention of stopping what she was doing, she couldn't keep herself from listening to his message. Since moving a property on Main Street or anywhere in the vicinity was rare, she yanked the sheet up to her chin, pushed away Sonny's roving hand and took notice, grabbing the phone out of its cradle before he could hang up.

"I have a few properties that might suit your needs," she immediately told the man on the other end of the line. "When would you like to look?"

"How's this afternoon?" he said, sounding eager. "I could meet you in a half hour."

"A half hour will be perfect," she said at once, ignoring Sonny's resigned expression. She settled the details, hung up the phone and turned to her husband. "Five minutes to dress, another five to get there. That leaves us twenty minutes. You up to the challenge?"

Sonny grinned. "You ever know me not to be?" he said, already reaching for her.

A half hour later, Mary Vaughn's hair was a bit more tousled than usual, her cheeks a little pinker, as she pulled her Mercedes to the curb. Even so, a glance at her watch told her she was right on time. Just one more incidence in her life when Sonny hadn't let her down.

At the end of May there was a frenzy of speculation in Wharton's when a SOLD sign appeared on the window of an empty space on Azalea Drive, just across the street from Town Hall and on the other side of the square from Wharton's.

Once occupied by a small newsstand that had sold magazines, cigarettes and Coca-Cola in bottles out of an old-fashioned red cooler, it had been empty for several years. The dingy front window had been covered over with curling brown paper, the once-green door was now faded and the rolled up awning was so dry-rotted it would probably crumble if anyone dared to open it.

For once, no one seemed to be able to pry even a tidbit of information from Mary Vaughn, who was usually only too eager to tell the world about the local real estate sales, especially those she'd made herself.

"Sorry, I've been sworn to secrecy," she told Sarah and Grace when they ganged up on her one morning when she stopped in to pick up a cup of coffee to go.

"Since when has that ever stopped you?" Grace grumbled with a huff.

Mary Vaughn didn't take offense. "The buyer paid full price to keep my mouth shut. What can I say? Money talks."

"Well, you'd think whoever it is would want to set off some free word-of-mouth," Grace said. "Must not have much business sense."

Mary Vaughn grinned at Sarah. "Maybe we should talk about something else. I'm hoping Rory Sue's going to move back home. Maybe she could get together with you, Annie and Raylene sometime. I think once she sees there are some young people still around, she'll feel more positive about settling in Serenity, instead of heading over to Charleston. Sonny and I are just sick, thinking about her so far away. And you should hear her granddaddy going on and on about it. Howard's beside himself."

As if Charleston were at the other end of the earth, Sarah thought. In her opinion, it wasn't quite far enough. Still, she fibbed, "We'd love to see her."

The truth was, Rory Sue had always

thought she was better than any of them, Raylene included. It didn't seem to impress Rory Sue in the least that Raylene was the only girl in town who'd had a full-blown debutante season over in Charleston, thanks to her well-connected maternal grandparents.

Like her mama, Rory Sue thought she was hot stuff because of her family, the most powerful one in Serenity. That Howard and Sonny Lewis were big fish in a very tiny pond didn't seem to faze her. It had also apparently escaped her notice that her maternal grandparents — Mary Vaughn's mama and daddy — were less than noteworthy. More like notorious for their frequent drunken brawls, if the truth be told.

"Then I'll be sure she gets in touch," Mary Vaughn told Sarah, picking up her coffee and heading for the door.

"Don't be coming back in here till you have some news you can share," Grace called after her, not entirely in jest.

"We'll find out what's going on soon enough," Sarah consoled Grace when Mary Vaughn just waved.

"Not good enough. I pride myself on knowing things first," Grace replied. "I don't understand all this secrecy unless it's going to be one of those shops that sells sex toys or something like that." Her expression turned thoughtful. "Maybe porno movies, though we have an ordinance against that, I think." She shook her head sorrowfully. "If it's not something that's going to cause an uproar, why would the owner want to keep it a secret?"

Sarah bit back a laugh because she knew Grace was serious. "I'm not sure there's a huge market for selling sex toys in Serenity," she said. "And if I were ever to consider such a thing, I certainly wouldn't put the business right here in plain view in the middle of downtown, where it'd be bound to stir up trouble. There are plenty of back alleys where a place like that might be able to operate in peace."

"Well, some people don't have your good sense," Grace grumbled. She stirred a straw around in her sweet tea, her expression despondent. Eventually she turned back to Sarah. "Maybe you could talk to Jeanette, see what she knows."

"Why Jeanette?"

"She's married to the town manager, isn't she?" Grace said, clearly warming to the idea. "If anybody knows what's going on, Tom does. He's the one on this big campaign to bring new business into downtown Serenity."

"Good point," Sarah conceded. "I'll ask her when I go over to The Corner Spa later." Of course, Jeanette hadn't been all that forthcoming about her husband's cousin, even when directly questioned by Annie, so apparently she knew how to be more discreet than the typical Sweet Magnolia. They were all pretty quick to share everything.

"If you find out anything, you call me, you hear," Grace commanded. "Don't be waiting till morning to let me know."

"I'll call," Sarah promised, then noticed Grace looking out the window again. Her expression had brightened considerably.

"Now that's real interesting," Grace said. "Just look across the street, why don't you?"

Sarah followed the direction of her gaze. There, wearing yet another pair of snug, faded jeans and a tight black T-shirt, was her mystery man, Travis McDonald himself . . . and he was walking right into that empty storefront as if he owned the place.

3

A hum of excitement stirred inside Travis as
he walked into the space that would soon
be Serenity's own country music radio station. To be honest, the task of fixing up the
space and creating a studio that would
overlook the town square was a little daunting. Right now the whole place reeked of
stale tobacco, and the yellowed linoleum
floor was scarred with burns from idiots
who'd just ground out their cigarettes
wherever they stood.

The only thing in the place worth saving
was the old red Coca-Cola cooler. It might
not serve much of a function in a radio station, but he liked the thought of having an
antique like that around. He could keep it
filled with soft drinks — bottled the old-
fashioned way if he could find them — for
the guests he envisioned putting on the air
during a morning show he'd decided to call
Carolina Daybreak. It would be a mix of

music and local news and talk, the first place people would turn to — aside from Wharton's — to find out what was going on in Serenity.

Now all he needed, aside from a significant amount of elbow grease, was the right person to sit in here and chat with residents and business folks or with anyone important who might be passing through town. He glanced across the square and spotted the person he had in mind standing in the doorway at Wharton's, staring right back at him. He waved, and the woman he'd now identified as Mrs. Sarah Price, single mother of two, ducked out of his line of sight like a scared little rabbit.

Yep, the minute he'd verbally closed the deal for the radio station, he'd decided to woo her away from waiting tables and turn her into a small-town celebrity. For days he'd watched her talking to the regulars in Wharton's in a natural way that kept thcm laughing and made them open up. He had a hunch she could get people to spill secrets faster than a skilled detective . . . and make 'em enjoy doing it. She'd bring the friendly atmosphere of Wharton's right into the studio.

Of course, the fact that she couldn't seem to string two sentences together around him

49

half the time gave him pause, but he was convinced that was an aberration. An intriguing one, in fact. For now, though, any thoughts of pursuing her for anything beyond her ability to charm potential listeners had to be put on hold. He had enough to do just getting this station on the air.

As soon as the paperwork was done and he'd finalized his plans and won the necessary approvals from the Federal Communications Commission for going on the air, he intended to sit Sarah down and have a serious conversation with her about how he could change her life.

Hopefully she wouldn't get so nervous she'd dump a pot of scalding hot coffee all over him.

For now, though, he had a lot of work to do. He walked over to Main Street to the hardware store and filled a cart with cleaning supplies. He figured he'd come back again for paint, lumber, wallboard and flooring once the whole place had been emptied out and scrubbed down and he knew what he had to work with. Maybe Jeanette would want to help him pick the colors. He liked the way her home felt — cozy and inviting — and he wanted his radio station to feel the same way. Maybe with a little less of that flowery fabric, though. He had no idea how Tom lived with that. He'd probably been blinded to it by love.

When Travis set all his supplies on the counter, the man behind it looked over the purchases. "You must be the guy who bought the old newsstand," he concluded.

Travis grinned at his assumption. "I did. Isn't anyplace else in town that filthy?"

"Not much that I know of," the man said. "I'm Ronnic Sullivan, by the way. My wife, Dana Sue, owns Sullivan's, the best restaurant in the entire state."

Amused by the heartfelt recommendation, Travis asked, "You wouldn't be just a little biased, would you?"

Ronnie pointed to a framed review on the wall that said the same thing. "General consensus," he said proudly. "You haven't been there?"

"I've pretty much been eating at my cousin's and at Wharton's," Travis admitted.

"So, you have family in town?" Ronnie said, as he rang up Travis's purchases.

"My cousin's the town manager, Tom McDonald. I'm Travis McDonald."

"Of course," Ronnie said at once. "Tom mentioned he had company. Glad to meet you, and welcome to downtown." He put the heavier items into a carton and bagged the rest. "So, what is it you plan to sell?"

The question was asked in such a cautious tone, Travis had to fight a grin. He'd heard all the speculation at Wharton's. The best, by far, had been Grace's opinion that it was going to be something lurid and inappropriate. He hated disillusioning her just yet. She seemed to enjoy working herself into a frenzy.

"I'm not quite ready to make an announcement," he told Ronnie. "I figure there's some advantage to building anticipation."

"Interesting strategy," Ronnie said with a thoughtful expression. "Are you sure you want to let people get carried away with their speculation? Next thing you know, there could be protests on the town green."

Travis did chuckle at that. "You've heard about the sex toys, too?"

"Indeed, I have," Ronnie admitted, looking intrigued. "Are they wrong?"

"Very," Travis assured him. "But let them enjoy themselves a little longer."

"Trust me, you really don't want to let Grace work up a full head of steam over this. Anything you announce after that will pale by comparison."

"I'm not worried. I think this will stir up some excitement."

"But not trouble?" Ronnie persisted.

"I can't imagine how. Tom would never let me get away with doing anything that would hurt this town. He considers its success to be his own personal mission."

"Good point," Ronnie said, looking reassured. "Let me know if you need any help fixing the place up. I know several guys who do good work — painting, minor construction, handyman jobs — for a reasonable price."

"Thanks. I'll keep that in mind."

"You need any help carrying all that back over there? I can close up for a minute and give you a hand."

"No need," Travis said, picking up the heavy box and two bags. "When it comes time for the paint and whatever else I need, I'll be back."

"Sure thing," Ronnie told him. "And don't forget to stop by Sullivan's one of these days. I'm usually hanging out there in the evening, if you find yourself looking for company."

"Will do."

Travis went back to his new space and got to work. Whenever he tired of the powerful aroma of cleaning solution, he stepped outside to breathe in the sweetly scented spring air. And more times than he could count, he caught a glimpse of Sarah looking in his direction. He wondered if she shared Grace's opinion about what he was up to, and if so, what she thought about it. One thing for sure, her curiosity was evident. He found that increasingly satisfying.

It had been two weeks since they'd discovered that Travis McDonald was the new owner of the space on Azalea Drive, but Sarah and Grace were no closer to figuring out what he had planned. The windows were still covered over with brown paper to keep out prying eyes, but it was evident that Travis had been in there every day working from morning till night. Sarah had to admit being impressed by how industrious he seemed to be.

While Sarah was curious about his plans, the whole mystery was driving Grace crazy. She was about one frenzied minute away from launching a full-scale protest on the sidewalk outside of Travis's store.

"What exactly are you going to protest?" Sarah asked her. "He hasn't done anything except fix the place up. That can't be bad."

"You mark my words, he has some dastardly scheme in mind, and I intend to nip it in the bud," Grace declared. "Nobody's that secretive without a good reason."

Sarah bit back a smile. "Grace, you're getting worked up over nothing. At least wait till he puts a sign up. I told you myself that he's the town manager's cousin. He's not going to do anything that would embarrass Tom."

"Then why won't he say so?" Grace demanded. "I'll tell you why. Because he's up to no good."

Making an impulsive decision, Sarah took off her apron. "Cover for me," she told Grace.

Looking startled, Grace asked, "Where are you going?"

"Into the lion's den," she said. "Where else?"

Before Grace could stop her, Sarah walked outside, down the block, then crossed the street. Travis was standing on the sidewalk, leaning back against the building's old red-brick facade in a nonchalant pose that belied the wary expression on his face.

"About time you came calling, sugar," he said when she drew near. "I was beginning to think you didn't care."

Immediately flustered, she almost tripped over the curb. "Oh, hush with that sweet talk," she said, moving to stand in front of him, hands on hips. "Why won't you tell people what you plan to do in here?"

"Because I don't want to," he said, his tone matter-of-fact. "Don't know of any law that says I have to announce my plans before I'm ready."

"You have to file papers with the town before you can open a business," she reminded him. "Or is Tom letting you off the hook because you're related?"

"Tom would never let me off the hook. He's a strait-laced guy. My paperwork will all be filed nice and neat when the time comes."

"Does he know what you're up to?"

"Of course."

Thoroughly frustrated by his refusal to set her mind at ease — and everyone else's for that matter — she studied him for a minute, then said, "You're enjoying all the speculation, aren't you?"

He nodded. "I'm especially fond of the sex-toy theory," he admitted with a spark of pure devilment in his eyes. "What do you think of that one?"

"I think it's crazy," Sarah confessed. "But since I know for a fact that you can be outrageous, I haven't ruled it out. Just so you know, though, Grace wants to get up a petition against it. And follow up with a protest outside your front door. I really think you're better off nipping that idea in the bud."

"Really?" he said innocently. "Just think of the publicity."

"Is that the kind you want?"

"Couldn't hurt," he insisted.

She edged closer to the door, trying to avoid getting too close to him as she did so. Something about all that heat and masculinity was way too hard to resist. She didn't want to tempt fate.

"How about giving me a tour?" she suggested. Maybe that would give her a few hints about what he had in mind. If it was something outlandish, he probably wouldn't let her cross the threshold.

Travis gave her a long, amused look, then stepped over and opened the door. "You can tell me what you think of the color scheme," he said without a hint of reservation.

Inside, to her surprise, she found the one long, narrow room had been carved up into four separate spaces, which certainly didn't look suited to retail. The largest was on the left and had the only window, which faced out on the town green and would let in plenty of light once that awful brown paper was removed. It connected to a smaller room right behind it. The entry area, no bigger than a foyer in a small home, had room enough for a couple of chairs, though the only thing in it at the moment was the old red soda cooler she remembered from her childhood. She touched it with near reverence.

"You kept this," she said, not sure why that made her so happy. Maybe she didn't think there could be anything bad about a man with a sentimental streak.

Travis was watching her with that same hint of amusement sparkling in his eyes. "Best thing in here," he said.

"What's through that door?" shc said, gesturing to the only remaining doorway off the foyer.

"See for yourself," he said, opening the door.

The back room was completely empty except for cleaning supplies and paint cans. Without a window back there, it could have been dismal, but it had been painted the same cheery yellow as the front rooms. All the trim was white enamel.

"You planning to sell the porno stuff back here?" she inquired, not entirely in jest. At least it would be out of plain sight.

"Actually I was thinking that ought to be out front," he said with a perfectly straight face. "It'll attract more customers if it can be seen from the street, don't you think?"

Sarah scowled at him. "You're not taking this seriously. Grace will stir up trouble if you don't satisfy her curiosity soon."

"Give me a timetable," he suggested. "What's soon?"

"About a nanosecond," she said. "She's on edge. She likes being the first to know things. You're frustrating her."

He gestured around him. "Do you seriously think this looks like something disreputable?"

"I don't, but I've been fooled before."

"Really? You don't seem to me like a woman who could be fooled very easily."

"How would you know?" She honestly wanted to know how he'd reached such a conclusion from a few very brief and mostly impersonal conversations. Even his outrageous flirting, she had concluded, was more from habit than anything to do with her.

"I'm a good judge of character, especially when it comes to women," he claimed. "For instance, I look at you and I see a woman who's not afraid of hard work. I see a responsible mother. And when I listen to what you have to say in Wharton's —"

"When you eavesdrop," she corrected.

He didn't seem embarrassed by the accusation. "When I pay attention," he said, giving it another spin, "I hear a woman with intelligence and wit."

His words filled Sarah with a sense of wonder. How had he managed to hit on so many of the areas in which she doubted herself? To hear that he found her to be more than adequate was a revelation. In fact, if she'd trusted him from here to the corner, his comments might have been reassuring. In her experience, though, no man who talked this smoothly was up to anything good.

Ignoring the satisfaction she took from his words, she said, "I'm just warning you, open up about your plans before Grace stirs up trouble. That'll have way too many repercussions."

"Such as?"

"People in town love Grace. They won't appreciate it if you make her look like an idiot for making a fuss, only to discover that you're planning something totally innocent. Your business, whatever it is, might never recover from that. People have long memories around here, and they look out for their own. Despite their respect for Tom, they'll see you as an outsider. You'll find yourself with a whole store full of widgets or whatever and no buyers."

He nodded, his expression sobering. "I'll keep that in mind. As much of a kick as I'm getting out of all this wild speculation, I certainly don't want to embarrass Grace."

"You almost sounded sincere just then," she said, regarding him with surprise.

"I am sincere. I like Grace. She's one of the reasons I decided to stick around Serenity. Places like Wharton's turn a town into a community."

Sarah was even more startled that he'd grasped that after such a short time. Maybe he'd fit in here, after all. She decided to try one last tactic to see if she could pry a little information out of him.

"I could always fill her in on your plans, if you just want to tell me," she offered casually. "I might even be able to swear her to secrecy for the time being."

Travis laughed. "Now, sugar, I'd put my faith in you when it comes to most things, but I've seen Grace in action. There's not a secret on earth that would be safe with her."

Oddly enough, it didn't sound like an insult the way he said it. It was almost as if he viewed her pride in spreading gossip as a good thing, even a necessary thing. That's the way most folks in town looked at it, as a frequently exasperating but much loved grapevine that kept them all informed.

"Which makes her a valuable resource, if you ask me," Sarah said, defending Grace.

"As much as it might annoy people to have their business turn into today's hot topic, at least it keeps most things out in the open. There's not a lot of secret backstabbing that goes on in Serenity."

"And how many small towns can make a claim like that?" Travis said, clearly amused by the boast.

Sarah regarded him with a narrowed gaze, not quite sure whether to take him seriously or if he was making fun of the town. "If you ask me, it's a good thing," she said.

"I couldn't agree more," he said. His gaze darkened and he reached out as if he intended to touch her, but then dropped his hand back to his side. "In fact, I'm counting on pretty much everything being out in the open before long."

Sarah puzzled over Travis's comment for most of the afternoon. How a man capable of being so secretive could want things out in the open made no sense. She'd repeated the gist of the conversation to Grace, who didn't know what to make of it, either. Now Sarah tried it out on Raylene, as they sat on the patio with their sweet tea while the kids played in the backyard.

"I swear I think it was a hint," she told Raylene. "I don't think he was trying to be cryptic at all. But what could he have meant?"

"Maybe he's a spy, or an investigative reporter and he's here to do an exposé," Raylene suggested.

Sarah regarded her with skepticism. "A spy in Serenity, South Carolina? What's he supposed to be spying on? Or exposing, for that matter? It's not as if there's a lot of dirt to dig up in a town this size. Like I told him, Grace knows most everything that goes on around here, anyway. She certainly knows more than the local weekly newspaper."

"Then I'm out of ideas," Raylene said.

"I suppose we'll all know soon enough," Sarah said with a sigh. "I think I got through to him about not dragging this out much longer." She turned her attention to Raylene, who looked drawn and nervous. "You okay? Did something happen around here today?"

If anything, her friend looked even more upset. "I had another panic attack," she admitted. "The kids were out here playing, and I was sitting here watching them, when Tommy went around the side of the house. When I called him, he didn't answer. I tried to go after him, but when I got to the edge of the patio, it was like I ran into a wall or something. I couldn't make myself take one more step. I started sweating and my hands were shaking. I finally managed to shout for him and, thank God, he came right back, but I think we need to take another look at me being alone with the kids, even for an hour or two."

Sarah could see the worry and fear in her eyes. "I have every faith that if Tommy hadn't come when you called, you would have gone looking for him."

Raylene regarded her with frustration. "You're not listening to me, Sarah. I couldn't make myself move. I couldn't!"

Sarah didn't want Raylene to see that the incident worried her. She reached over and squeezed her hand. "It's okay. Nothing happened. Tommy's fine."

"Next time, he might not be. I mean it, Sarah," she said earnestly. "I'm happy to help out with the house, but I just can't risk being responsible for Tommy and Libby. I know you're trying to be supportive, but right now the only thing that matters is the well-being of your kids."

"I know," Sarah acknowledged. No matter how much faith she had in Raylene, she knew she couldn't take a chance that it might be misplaced. "I just don't want to see you taking another step to shut yourself away here. You know this is more than some temporary thing, Raylene. Not only has it gone on for months now, but you're getting worse. You need to see someone, not for me or for the kids, but for you. Call Annie's shrink. You already know Dr. McDaniels from back when Annie was in the hospital with her anorexia. It won't be like talking to a complete stranger."

Raylene shook her head. "I know that makes sense, but I need to try to beat this on my own. I don't want my independence to be one more thing my husband took away from me."

"Hasn't it already happened?" Sarah asked in frustration. "You're already holed up here. You don't see anyone except the people we invite over and the kids and me. That's not living, Raylene."

Raylene's expression turned sad. "Believe it or not, it's better than the life I had in Charleston."

It sounded as if she were talking about more than the physical abuse to which she'd been subjected. "What do you mean?" Sarah asked. "What about all those fancy committees you told us you were on? All the fundraising you did?"

"All talk," Raylene said. "I didn't want you and Annie to know how bad things were. I couldn't serve on committees, because I never knew what shape I'd be in. You can't join those things and then never show up. Oh, I tried for the first year we were married, but then I got a reputation as someone who couldn't be counted on. I quit everything after I heard a woman telling a committee chair not to give me an important assignment because I wouldn't be around to follow through."

"I had no idea," Sarah whispered, understanding how much that must have hurt. "I'm so sorry."

"Don't be. It was my fault."

"Being abused was not your fault," Sarah said furiously. "The blame is all on that creep you married."

"I chose him," Raylene said. "And I stayed much too long, because every time I mentioned that I might leave him, my parents — well, my mother really — reminded me about all the wonderful things I'd be giving up. She didn't believe for a minute that someone from such an upstanding family and in such a respectable profession could have a mean streak. In her mind, I had this idyllic marriage, the one she should have had."

"What about your dad?"

"I never told him," Raylene admitted. "I

couldn't. It would have destroyed him, especially if he'd found out that my mother knew and advised me to stay. I'm glad he's gone now, so he'll never find out about any of this."

Sarah couldn't imagine any mother who would knowingly let her daughter stay in an abusive relationship without fighting tooth and nail to get her out of it. She'd always thought that Raylene's mother lived too much in her supposedly glorious past, that she complained too much about the pitiful life to which she'd been relegated in this little podunk town. This, though, turning her head when it came to Raylene's marital mess was truly unconscionable.

"No wonder you haven't spoken to your mother since you moved over here," she told Raylene.

"She's not as awful as this makes her sound," Raylene said wearily. "She just wanted so badly for me to have the things she didn't have with my dad."

"Material things," Sarah said with feeling. "Didn't she know those aren't half as important as love and respect? She always had that from your dad. He adored her."

"But I don't think she valued it as much as all the sterling silver that I received as wedding gifts," Raylene said. "And to be honest, at first neither did I. Thanks to you and Annie, I think I'm finally beginning to put my life back into perspective and to get my priorities straight."

"That's huge," Sarah said, giving her a congratulatory high-five.

Raylene gave her a rueful grin. "Yeah, now if my life only went beyond the boundaries of your house and this patio, everything would be just peachy."

4

Walter cursed himself every which way for mentioning to his father that Sarah had gotten a job and that the kids were spending time with a sitter. He was still struggling to make peace with it himself, and his father had finally called him on his distracted mood. Walter had told him about the situation, which was turning out to be yet another of his huge mistakes.

"You're letting a woman like that, a woman who's obviously not a good mother, get away with stealing your son!" Marshall Price accused Walter, his expression filled with disdain. "What kind of man does that?"

"Sarah hasn't stolen Tommy," Walter replied wearily. He was sick to death of the recriminations that were tossed at him every damn day since the divorce was finalized. "The custody arrangement guarantees I can see him every other weekend. Sarah doesn't object if I come more often."

"You have to see him in South Carolina," Marshall said with a sneer, as if that were akin to Timbuktu. "How's the boy supposed to learn about his legacy when he doesn't spend a minute with his family here in Alabama?"

"He's barely four. He doesn't need to learn how to run a cotton mill just yet," Walter replied for about the hundredth time. "Let it go, Dad. Maybe if you and mom hadn't been so mean and spiteful to Sarah, she wouldn't have taken Tommy and Libby and left town. I offered to buy her a house here in town, any house she wanted, but she said she could hardly wait to get away from the two of you."

Not that he didn't bear his own share of the blame. There were times when Walter felt as if he'd let his parents brainwash him about Sarah. It was interesting that she'd called him on just that last weekend when he'd been over to Serenity for a visit. He hadn't wanted to hear it, of course, but he could see now that she'd been right. His view of Sarah had started changing the minute he'd brought her home to Alabama to live.

How many times had he heard that she wasn't good enough? How many times had his mother criticized her housekeeping, her

70

social skills, her desire to teach? And, of course, the worst sin of all was that she'd gotten pregnant before they were married. They acted as if she'd done that all on her own, then treated the wedding as if it were an occasion for shame.

The real shame, of course, was that he'd let them get away with it. No, it was worse than that. It was that he'd taken up the same rallying cries. Sometimes when he looked back on his marriage, he wondered who the hell he'd been. Certainly not the man Sarah had met at college, a man so crazy about her he'd known almost instantly that she was the one he wanted to marry. He'd let his parents' nonstop criticisms erode not just the passion, but also the respect he'd always felt for Sarah.

Sadly, none of these things had occurred to him before it was too late. It was only after Sarah had gone, after the divorce was in motion, that he began to see the strong woman he'd fallen for in college. When he stopped to analyze it, which he didn't very often, he knew that was why he continued to lash out at her, like the other day when he'd criticized her taking a job in that diner. He'd heard those critical words coming out of his mouth, known how arrogant and superior he sounded, but he hadn't been

71

able to shut up.

As frustrating as it had been at the time, a part of him admired Sarah for standing up to him, defending her decision to work and defending Wharton's. He wished she'd done more of that when they'd been married. Things might have turned out differently.

"I suppose you're going over there again tomorrow with your tail between your legs," Marshall said disparagingly.

Fed up in a way he'd never expected to be, Walter stood and threw down the pen in his hand. "No," he said, drawing yet another disappointed look from his father. "As a matter of fact, I'm going over there right now."

His father seemed to take that as a good sign. "If I were you, I'd just pick Tommy up and bring him straight back here. Nobody around here would dare to take that boy away from his daddy. They'd have to answer to me."

Walter shook his head. "I'm not surprised you'd want to go that route, and you know what? It makes me glad Tommy's with his mama, because the last thing I want for any son of mine is for him to grow up to be anything like his granddaddy, thinking the whole world needs to bow and scrape to him."

The veins in his father's forehead pulsed, and his complexion turned an interesting shade of purple. "Don't you dare talk to me like that, boy! My whole life's been about you and making sure you had a legacy to be proud of. I'd think twice before mouthing off to me and throwing it all away."

"Do you honestly think I want to be trapped here in this one-horse town running a cotton mill?" Walter demanded before he could stop himself. "I had my own dream, and, believe me, this wasn't it. But I came back here because it was what you expected."

Facing down his father was something he should have done years ago, but he hadn't. Only recently had he realized why. "I figured I owed you because of all you'd done for me," he said now. "And even you can't deny that I've done a damn good job for you. I even gave you the grandson you were so anxious to have, so the Price legacy would be assured. Well, you know what? I'm done worrying about you and what you want. I'm going to start trying to figure out what I want, and then I'm going after it."

He saw his father's complexion turn ashen as he watched Walter heading for the door.

"You come back here this minute!" Marshall shouted, slamming his fist down on the desk, sending papers and a coffee cup flying.

"Sorry, Dad. I'm done dancing to your tune." Walter let that sink in, then added, "When I get back here — *if* I come back here — things are going to have to change. You're going to have to show some respect for me or I will leave, and next time it will be for good."

He walked out before his father could respond, shutting the door emphatically behind him.

Not until he was outside in the fresh air and on his way to Serenity did he think about the ramifications of what he'd done. It had felt too good to finally say all the things that had been building up ever since he'd come home with the girl he loved only to be sucked into a life he didn't want.

Unfortunately, he knew there'd be hell to pay on Monday. Marshall Price didn't take disrespect lightly. For all Walter knew he'd come back and find the locks on the mill had been changed and his house slapped with a foreclosure sign by the bank. His dad and the bank's chairman were golfing buddies. He wouldn't hesitate to do Marshall a favor, legalities be damned.

But for one glorious moment on Thursday afternoon, Walter felt like his old self, a man worthy of respect. Maybe even worthy of love. Probably not Sarah's, of course. There was too much water under that bridge. It would have to be someone else who could make him feel the way she once had . . . as if he'd hung the moon.

On Saturday morning Travis looked around his new radio station with satisfaction. Bill Roberts, the prior owner of the station, had been in here for the past week checking out all the new equipment, setting up the studio so it was ready to go on the air, advising Travis on a million details. Roberts was the kind of man who was meant to mentor. Endlessly patient, he was generous with his time and expertise. He had a wicked sense of humor, as well, something Travis could definitely appreciate.

Bill walked into the little foyer, plucked an ice-cold Coke from the cooler and settled his lanky frame into one of the two chairs. "You ready to make your big announcement?"

Travis grinned. "I should be asking you that question. Am I?"

"Seems to me everything's in place. What time's the press conference?"

Calling a press conference in Serenity wasn't exactly the same as calling one in

Charleston or up in Boston, where the sports reporters had lined up to get a glimpse of him after his signing with the Red Sox. Here, there was only the local weekly to worry about, so Travis had actually opted for inviting the entire town to the formal unveiling of the radio station. It would be another two weeks before they officially went on the air, but it was time to let the cat out of the bag. Past time, according to Grace. Given all the wild speculation lately, he was counting on a large crowd.

"Ten o'clock," Travis told Bill. "But there's one thing I need to do before we get started."

Bill regarded him approvingly. "You're going to invite Grace Wharton over for a private tour, aren't you?"

"I think she's entitled," Travis said. "She's practically worried herself sick over this. At least she'll have a fighting chance of telling a few people the news before I do."

"Smart move," Bill said. "She's definitely a woman you want on your side."

"I wonder how she's going to feel when I tell her I want to steal Sarah away from her?"

Bill chuckled. "I predict that one's not going to go over so well. You might want to call over to the military base in Sumter and

76

see if they have a spare suit of body armor you can borrow."

"You're not half as funny as you think you are," Travis said. "This could get very dicey."

"Then better to get it over with so we can patch you up before the big official announcement," Bill told him. "I think I have some kind of superhero bandages in the car from my last outing with the grandkids."

Travis gave him a friendly, one-fingered salute, then walked out the door. He figured the next half hour or so could mean the difference between kicking his new venture off with a bang or being pilloried around town. He'd spent most of his life charming women, but all of a sudden he discovered it had never mattered more. Who knew the biggest challenge he'd ever faced would be a round, older woman who looked a lot like Santa's wife?

Wharton's was packed with customers, something Travis hadn't considered when he'd come up with this plan to steal Grace away. In fact, the upcoming press conference had apparently drawn even more people than usual into town.

Still, he managed to corner Sarah by the counter. "I need to borrow Grace for maybe fifteen minutes. Can you manage on your own?"

She regarded him with alarm. "Are you out of your mind? Look at this place. Thanks to this big whoop-de-do announcement you're planning, we're packed."

"Okay, how about five minutes? It's really important." When she shook her head again, he looked around and spotted Ronnie Sullivan. He'd heard from Tom that Ronnie helped out from time to time at Sullivan's. He walked over to the counter.

"Hey, Ronnie."

Ronnie gave him a slap on the back. "You ready for your big day?"

"I think so, but I'm in a bind. I need to take Grace over to my place. Unfortunately, Sarah says she can't handle this crowd on her own. Would you mind pitching in? I just need a few minutes."

"You want Grace to have a preview of what's going to happen this morning, don't you?" Ronnie guessed.

At Travis's nod, Ronnie left his coffee on the counter and grabbed an apron from behind it. "Sarah, I'm going to pinch-hit for Grace for a bit. I'll try to keep up."

Sarah's gaze narrowed as she turned back to Travis. "How'd you pull that off?"

"Don't ask questions. Just be grateful. I'll

78

have Grace back in a jiffy."

He found her in the kitchen with a tray loaded down with meals. Fortunately Ronnie had followed him. He took the tray from Grace's hands before she had time to object.

"What the devil?" she muttered irritably as Ronnie left.

"I'm stealing you away," Travis told her. "You're going to get a sneak peek at my new venture."

All signs of annoyance immediately vanished. "Now?"

"Right this minute, before anyone else."

Her face immediately lit up with excitement. "Well, it's about time you showed some respect for me, young man!"

She hurried along beside him, looking triumphant as she walked with him across the green. Bill was waiting for them outside. Her gaze narrowed when she saw him.

"Don't I know you?" she asked, looking as if her brain were clicking through some mental photo album. She snapped her fingers. "Of course, I do. Didn't you have that radio station over in the next county? Played nothing but oldies and had a signal that wasn't worth spit."

Bill grinned. "I did indeed."

"You've been off the air for a month or so now, though."

"True."

She looked from him to Travis. Under-standing started to dawn on her face. When Travis opened the door and she stepped inside the studio, her eyes lit up. "Would you look at this," she exclaimed, her tone awestruck. "You're bringing a radio station to Serenity!"

"I am," Travis confirmed. He studied her worriedly. "What do you think? It's not quite up there with sex toys and porno."

"And a darn good thing it's not," she said, sitting down in front of one of the micro-phones. "You going on the air today?"

"Not for another couple of weeks."

"What kind of music?"

"Country."

Gesturing to the two microphones. "You planning to invite folks in to talk?"

"Absolutely."

She nodded. "I might want to give that a try one day," she admitted, clearly trying not to sound too eager. "Seems like fun."

"I think you'd be the perfect guest. You could talk about all the changes in down-town Serenity and why Wharton's has made it through all the economic ups and downs."

"Or I could tell who's been misbehaving around town," she said, her expression mis-chievous.

Travis laughed. "As long as you don't land me in a pile of you-know-what and get me slapped with a slander suit."

She frowned at his joking tone. "Don't you know by now that I never repeat anything that isn't gospel truth?"

"Does the mention of sex toys and porno in connection to this place ring any bells?" he inquired.

She waved off his remark. "I only said that because you wouldn't say what you were doing. When there's a vacuum, gossip will usually fill it."

He nodded. "Glad to know how your mind works."

"Has nothing to do with my mind," she said huffily. "It's a fact."

Travis regarded her with wonder. "Grace, you really are a town treasure."

"Hush. You make me sound like some statue on the green. I need to get back over to Wharton's before Sarah goes crazy. Everybody and their brother decided to come in for breakfast this morning before the big announcement." She grinned at him. "I hate to steal your thunder, but I might have to mention a thing or two about it when I get back there."

He feigned dismay. "You'd do that to me?"

"No more than you deserve after keeping

me in the dark for so long," she told him. "Don't fret, though. There will be plenty more who won't have a clue when they show up this morning."

"I don't suppose you could try to keep it quiet around Sarah, could you? I'd kind of like her to hear about this from me."

Grace nodded slowly. "So that's the way it is. I'd wondered. You're sweet on her, aren't you?"

"No, it's nothing like that," he said quickly, if not entirely truthfully.

"Then what is it like?" she asked suspiciously.

He hesitated, then said, "Okay, I owe it to you to tell you what I have in mind since Sarah works for you. I'm thinking of asking her to go on the air in the mornings. She's great with all your customers. She shows a real interest in their lives and they all talk a mile a minute when she's around."

Once again, Grace's eyes sparkled with excitement. "You don't have to sell me. That's a wonderful idea. She'd be perfect hosting a talk show right here in town."

"You aren't furious that I want to steal her?"

"Heavens, no! I love having her there, but her working for me was always temporary."

Travis was surprised to hear that. "Why?

She isn't planning to leave town, is she?" He certainly hadn't heard any rumors to that effect.

"No, but she's put in her application to teach in the fall. I think she's really looking forward to it."

"Then I'll just have to make her see that this opportunity is too good to miss," Travis said.

"When are you planning on talking to her?"

"I wanted to speak to you first, and now that I have, I thought maybe I'd sit down with her right after I make the announcement about the station going on the air. Will that work with her schedule at Wharton's today?"

"She's all yours right after lunch," Grace assured him. "We should be slowing down by one o'clock today, since so many people came in this morning and the rest will be over the minute you finish announcing your news. They'll want to come in and chew it over, right along with their grilled cheese sandwiches and tomato soup."

"Then I'll be by around one," Travis told her. Impulsively, he leaned down and kissed her cheek. "Thanks."

"For what?"

"Being supportive and understanding, not

83

just about the radio station, but about Sarah."

"Not a problem," she said, then gave him a dark look. "But you show one sign of hurting that girl, and you won't know what hit you."

"Warning duly noted," he said solemnly. He had the distinct feeling she was talking about a whole lot more than Sarah's future in radio.

After an insanely busy morning, Sarah was relieved when everyone disappeared precisely at 10:00 a.m. to await Travis's big announcement at the unveiling of his new business.

"Why don't you go on over there and see what he's up to," Grace suggested. "I can handle things here. Nobody's going to be setting foot in here until he's finished talking, anyway."

Sarah studied her suspiciously. "You already know, don't you? That's why he took you out of here this morning, so you could give this whole thing your blessing."

Grace beamed. "Something like that."

"And did you give him your blessing?"

"I did." She shooed Sarah toward the door. "Go on. You know you're dying of curiosity."

"You could tell me yourself and I could stay right here and help you with setups for lunch."

"Nope," Grace said adamantly. "You need to hear this straight from the horse's mouth."

"Okay, fine," she conceded eventually, stripping off her apron and going outside.

There was quite a crowd assembled on the green. She wondered if Walter had brought the kids into town for this. When he'd shown up on Thursday and announced he was staying through the weekend, she'd been startled, but not displeased. She'd never wanted to deny the kids a chance to spend time with their daddy, as long as they were here and not over in Alabama where the Prices could try to influence them against her. Though there were plenty of kids running around with balloons, she didn't spot her two or Walter.

A platform had been set up on the sidewalk in front of the new business and an older man she didn't recognize was tapping a microphone, sending ear-splitting screeches into the air. He gave the crowd a chagrined smile.

"Sorry," he apologized when he had the controls adjusted. "Nice to see so many of you here this morning."

As he spoke, Sarah heard some murmurs in the crowd. Apparently quite a few people recognized him.

He gave them a disarming grin as the murmurs spread. "I gather that those of you who didn't recognize me at first are familiar with the sound of my voice. I'm Bill Roberts, longtime host of *Top of the Morning,* and previous owner of the oldies station over in the next county."

A cheer erupted as he confirmed the guess that had been spreading through the crowd.

"Now did y'all listen real close to what I said?" he asked. "That's *previous* owner." He paused to let that sink in, then said, "And now I'd like to introduce you to the man who's helping me to retire to a life of fishing, Mr. Travis McDonald, the brand-new owner of Serenity's own radio station, WSER."

Sarah gasped right along with everyone else. That's what Travis had been up to in that building across the green? He'd been turning the building into a radio studio? No wonder Grace had sounded so excited just now.

She turned her attention to Travis, who was standing at the microphone as if he were a born public speaker. She envied him that confidence. She doubted she could have said two words without getting all tongue-tied. He just stood there calmly until the murmurs died down. Then it seemed as if his gaze sought her out. It was as if he were addressing his remarks straight to her.

"How y'all doing?" he asked. "I hope you're as excited about the idea of having a radio station here in town as I am about putting one on the air."

"What kind of music?" someone called out.

"Country," Travis said at once. "Is there any other kind in this neck of the woods?"

The news was greeted with another cheer.

"What else are you putting on the air?" a new voice asked.

"Oh, there will be plenty of local talk about what's going on around town," he assured them. Again, his gaze seemed to lock directly on Sarah.

Listening to him and feeling the way his eyes held hers, Sarah got the oddest feeling there was something significant in what he was saying, something she ought to take note of, but she couldn't imagine what it could be.

"Now here's the thing," Travis said, when the crowd had quieted. "This is Serenity's radio station as much as it is mine. If there's something you think ought to be on the air, I'm counting on you to tell me. I'm not a local, but I have ties here. You all know my cousin Tom, your town manager."

That created another buzz as people made the connection.

"Well, you can be sure I'm not going to do anything to shame him," Travis said. "For one thing, he's taller than I am, and a whole lot meaner. I try not to tangle with him."

Sarah grinned at the self-deprecating comment. She had a feeling Travis and his cousin would be an even match.

"The bottom line," he continued, "is if I'm doing something on the air you don't like, I want to hear about it. Of course, if there's something you do like, I wouldn't mind hearing about that, too." He paused, then said. "Y'all ready to see our studio?"

The question was greeted with an affirmative shout. At some indiscernible signal from Travis, the brown paper covering the window came down offering a view of a small but obviously well-equipped studio. The best part, in Sarah's opinion, was that passers-by would be able to look right in and see what was happening. And the host, of course, would be able to keep an eye on the town square where so much happened in Serenity, including the town's beloved Christmas festival, its upcoming Fourth of July celebration and so much more. It was an ideal setting for a station that hoped to be part of the community.

As Travis offered to let folks walk through for a tour of the station, Sarah walked back to Wharton's where Grace was waiting impatiently.

"So, what did you think?" Grace demanded.

"I think it's amazing," Sarah said.

"Good," Grace said, smiling a secretive little smile before walking away, leaving Sarah to stare after her in puzzlement.

Before she could figure out Grace's enigmatic reaction, the crowd from the square started spilling inside, and she didn't have another minute to think about anything until after one.

As the last of the customers left, she noted that Travis had slipped in and was seated at the end of the counter, sipping on a Cherry Coke.

"How long ago did you turn up?" she asked.

"Not long," he said. "So, what did you think of the announcement? I saw you on the square."

"I think putting a radio station right

downtown like that is fantastic. Congratulations!"

His gaze locked with hers. "You mean that?"

"Of course I do."

"You interested in being part of it?" he inquired, his tone awfully casual.

Sarah stared at him, certain she'd misheard. "You mean like a secretary or something?"

He smiled, then shook his head. "No, I mean as host of the station's morning show. I predict you'll be a local celebrity in no time. In fact, Sarah Price, if you're even half as good as I think you're going to be, this is going to change your life!"

5

Sarah did not want her life changed. Not like that. She sat on the stool at the counter in Wharton's staring at Travis McDonald as if he'd suddenly sprouted two heads. He'd said some pretty outrageous things to her over the past few weeks, but this was the craziest.

"You can't be serious," she said. "Me? On the radio?"

"That's what I said." He seemed undaunted by her shock.

"Not a chance," she told him, dismissing the idea as ridiculous. "I wouldn't have a thing to say."

"You have plenty to say in here," Travis said. "At least to everyone else. You have this easy way that gets people to open up. That's what I want you to do on the air."

"Why?" she asked, bewildered. "I mean why me?"

"Because I've been watching you. You

know how to draw people out, make them laugh, get them to reveal themselves. You'll be a natural at this, Sarah. I guarantee it."

She studied him suspiciously. "So you want me to embarrass people in town on the air?"

"I never said that," he replied with exaggerated patience. "I said you had a way with people."

"Well, if I'm so good, how come you never answered a single one of the questions I asked you? You've been coming in here for what, a month now? And I don't really know much more than your name and that you're Tom's cousin."

"And that I own the radio station that's going to make you a hometown celebrity," he reminded her.

"Well, it took until today for me to find out about that," she said. She waved off the comment. "But that's not what matters, anyway. I haven't gotten to know one personal thing about you."

He grinned one of those slow, sexy grins that made her toes curl. "Because I'm a hardcase," he drawled. "But I'm sure you could find out anything you want to know if you put your mind to it."

Sarah scowled at the remark. "Don't you imagine there are plenty of hardcases around? For all you know, you'd have nothing but dead air for a couple of hours every day. There's nothing worse on the radio than a host who's run out of questions and a guest who's clammed up. I can't just sit there and chatter away about nothing."

"Sure you can. I've seen you do it in here every single day. And if things get really quiet, you can always pump up a Toby Keith song."

"I prefer Kenny Chesney," she replied, mostly to be contrary.

"Fine. You'll play Kenny Chesney. And if you're as bad at this as you're predicting, you'll have time for some George Strait and Trace Adkins, too."

"You're not taking me seriously. I can't do this to people I've known all my life," she argued.

"All you're going to do is bring these friends of yours into the studio when they have a story to share or an event to promote," he explained. "You'll chat about it, get people excited, make them want to come. And say some celebrity comes into town, you'd get to interview them."

"We don't get a lot of celebrities in Serenity."

"Because there was no radio station for them to visit to get publicity. Now there will be. It'll be my job to make sure all these fancy New York or Nashville publicists know that we're looking for guests."

She studied him with a frown. "Did you see *Field of Dreams* a few too many times, maybe get the crazy idea if you build it, they will come?"

Travis laughed. "Personally I was a bigger fan of *Bull Durham.* My mama used to watch that on DVD at least once a year. I think that's why I grew up wanting to play baseball."

Distracted for a moment from the bigger issue, she asked, "And did you? Play ball, I mean?"

"For a while," he said, though his expression shut down. "So, what do you say? I can promise you'll make more money than you do here."

Though Helen had seen to it that Walter was generous, Sarah was not getting so much money in alimony and child support that she could afford not to consider a higher-paying job. It was just that this particular job was so far out of her comfort zone, it scared her to death. Since her marriage, she'd been even less likely to take chances than she might have years ago.

Which is all the more reason to say yes, a voice in her head nagged. *Do something outrageous for once, something risky and new. Find out what you're really made of.*

"I was hoping to start teaching in the fall," she said, clinging to the one last objection that made any sense.

"Well, I suppose if this doesn't work out the way I think it will, you could always do that," Travis said. "Unless, of course, you've already made a commitment to the school."

She shook her head. "No. I don't even know if there's going to be a position available."

"Then why trade a sure thing for something that might not happen?" he asked, then leaned a little closer and coaxed, "Come on, Sarah. Think how much fun the two of us can have starting this together."

He made it sound tempting and far more intimate than any job offer that had ever come her way. Helen would probably have a lot to say about the legalities of mixing business and personal agendas, but Sarah wasn't sure this really qualified as any kind of potential sexual harassment when right this second it felt so good.

She lifted her gaze to meet his sea-green eyes and slowly nodded, even though her heart was climbing into her throat and her palms had turned clammy. Unfortunately, she couldn't be entirely certain if that reaction was due to fear about the job or pure terror at being drawn into the world of Travis McDonald, who seemed to do disconcerting things to her common sense.

Raylene had dinner on the table when Sarah got home. The kids were in the backyard playing catch with Walter, who appeared to be showing admirable tolerance for Libby's ineptitude.

"He's making progress," Raylene noted after handing Sarah a glass of sweet tea. "I hardly had to do any arm-twisting at all today to get him to include Libby. The way she toddles around after him, hoping for just a tiny bit of attention, breaks my heart."

"I know," Sarah said. "Has he said anything about his plans? When's he going back home? He's never hung around this long before."

"He hasn't said anything to me," Raylene told her. "I get the feeling he has something on his mind, though. Maybe you should find out what it is."

"My mind's on overload as it is," Sarah said, sitting down at the table with her glass of tea. "I don't think I can take on Walter's problems."

Raylene regarded her worriedly. "What's wrong?"

Sarah shook her head. She needed to absorb all the implications of this agreement she'd made with Travis before she laid it all out there for everyone else to pick apart. "I'll tell you later. I don't want to bring it up while Walter's around." Heaven knew what he'd think of the crazy idea of her going on the radio. He might be okay with it, but she could hear his mother raising a ruckus about how unseemly it would be. She hadn't been able to completely eliminate the strident criticisms that came no matter how hard she'd tried to make peace with the woman.

"You sure?" Raylene asked.

"I'm sure. Let me get those three in here and cleaned up for supper."

She walked to the back door and called out to them. At the sound of her voice, Walter glanced up and gave her an unguarded grin that reminded her of the way he'd looked at her back in college whenever she surprised him by stopping by his dorm or, later, his fraternity house. It was a sexy, all-male smile that had once made her heart catch. Now her reaction paled in comparison to what the most innocent glance from Travis did to her. Not that many of Travis's glances were all that innocent, when she thought about it.

When Walter came inside, he leaned down and planted an impulsive kiss on her cheek that had her scowling.

"What's up with you?" she asked suspiciously.

"I just had a good day, that's all. Spending time with the kids without worrying about turning right around and heading home has been great. The Serenity Inn's not such a bad place, either."

Sarah immediately went on the defensive. "I know you think it's ridiculous to waste money on a hotel, but there's no room here."

"Hey, I wasn't being critical. The inn's fine."

She regarded him curiously. "You're being awfully agreeable this weekend. What's that about?"

He hesitated, then said, "Maybe if there's time after supper, we could talk some. I'll tell you what's going on."

"Okay."

The meal was surprisingly pleasant. Nothing the kids did seemed to faze him, not even when Libby knocked the top off her sippy cup, sending milk in all directions. In fact, he didn't utter one single criticism of Sarah or the kids. He even mustered up a couple of sincere-sounding compliments for

Raylene's cooking. It wasn't like Walter at all, or at least the Walter of recent times.

As soon as they'd finished bowls of ice cream with fresh peaches, Raylene offered to give the kids their baths.

"I'll do that," Walter said, stunning Sarah.

Raylene waved off the offer. "Let me. You can help Sarah with the dishes. That'll give you two some time to catch up."

Before Sarah could object, Raylene shooed Tommy and Libby from the kitchen.

"Well, that was subtle," Sarah said, oddly disconcerted at being left alone with her ex-husband.

"If I didn't know better, I'd think she was matchmaking," Walter said. "But she's pretty much made it clear that she's against a reconciliation."

Sarah's mouth dropped open. "Reconciliation? Where'd that come from?"

"I'm just saying she seems to be against it," he said defensively. "Not that I'm looking for one or anything."

Something in his eyes told Sarah that wasn't entirely true. "Okay, that's it," she said decisively. "Leave the dishes. We need to talk. Grab a beer or tea or something and we'll go outside."

As soon as they were settled on the patio, Walter looked around, clearly trying to avoid her gaze.

"Mind telling me why the subject of a reconciliation came up?" she finally asked. "I might have initiated the proceedings, but you couldn't wait to be divorced."

He didn't respond immediately. Eventually he sighed, then said, "I had a confrontation with my dad the other day."

She still wasn't following. "So, what? You want to get back together to spite him?"

He frowned at her sarcasm. "No, it just got me to thinking about why we split up."

"We split up because you showed no respect for me and you let your parents get away with bullying me," she said flatly.

"I know."

He spoke so softly that at first she wasn't sure she'd even heard him correctly. "You're admitting it?" she asked incredulously.

He shrugged. "I have to. It's the truth."

She sat back in shock. "Well, I'll be. That must have been some confrontation."

"It just made me see a bunch of stuff in a different light," he said. "I know it's too late for us. Not even you with your soft heart can forgive all the things I did to you." He gave her a wistful look. "Can you?"

"Probably not," she admitted.

"You left a little wiggle room in there," he noted.

She leveled a look into his eyes. "I didn't mean to. Look, Walter, if you finally see what a controlling man your father is, that's great, but I don't want any part of that life again. I'm trying to get a handle on who I am, and until I figure that out, I don't want any man trying to shape me into what he thinks I ought to be."

"I understand. You sure did get more than enough of that from me. When I think back on some of the things I said, the way I treated you . . ." He shook his head. "It makes me ashamed, Sarah. It really does."

Tears stung her eyes. "Thank you for saying that."

"I should have said it a long time ago." They sat there in amazingly companionable silence for a long time. Eventually he turned to her. "Is it okay with you if I spend more time with the kids from here on out? I'm thinking I'll try to come over every weekend and spend at least Friday night, maybe Friday and Saturday. I know that's not what the custody agreement spelled out, but there's probably a way to fix that if you don't object."

"As long as you're good to the kids — both of them — you can see them whenever you want," she said. "I have them to myself all week long. Now that I'm working, that's not as much time as it used to be, so I'll want some weekends for myself, but we can work it out so it's fair to both of us."

"Do we need it in writing? That lawyer of yours seems to like everything on paper."

"I'll speak to her," Sarah promised.

Walter stood up. "Then I'll say goodnight. I'll be by in the morning to say goodbye to the kids."

She nodded, then sat there long after he'd left, wondering at the transformation. If he truly was turning over a new leaf, more power to him. But just in case this was some passing whim of his, she thought she'd leave their custody agreement just the way it was. Maybe change was possible for some people, but she feared Walter, like the leopard, wasn't capable of changing his spots this easily.

By Monday morning the word had spread that Travis McDonald had offered Sarah a job at the radio station. It was Annie who called an emergency margarita night for all of the Sweet Magnolias, young and old, to discuss what she referred to as the insane idea Sarah had of throwing away a perfectly reliable job at Wharton's to work at a brand-new, yet-to-be-tested radio station that could be off the air in a month.

Because Raylene had flatly refused to leave the house, Annie had convinced the original Sweet Magnolias to come here. Now Dana Sue Sullivan, who owned the town's fanciest restaurant, attorney Helen Decatur and Maddie Maddox, who managed The Corner Spa which all three women owned, were seated in Sarah's living room with drinks. Jeanette McDonald, who managed the spa's personal services such as facials, massages and manicures, hadn't yet arrived.

Annie, newly married to Maddie's son, Ty Townsend, wore a worried frown on her face that even one of Helen's lethal margaritas hadn't been able to erase.

"You don't know anything at all about this man," she reminded Sarah. "He handed you some line and now you want to quit your job and become a radio star? This just isn't like you. What's Walter going to think? Did you mention it to him when he was here this weekend?"

Sarah shook her head.

"Why not?" Annie pressed. "I'll tell you why not — because you know he's going to make some big stink about it."

"Since when do you care what Walter thinks?" Sarah retorted, her determination to do this kicking up a notch. "This isn't about Walter."

"Isn't it?" Annie scoffed. "Are you telling us that on some level this isn't an in-your-face act designed to make him crazy?"

"So what if it is?" Sarah said, even though Walter hadn't once crossed her mind when she'd been saying yes to Travis. "It's not as if I'm going to be doing something disreputable that he can use against me in court." A sudden worry nagged at her and she turned to Helen. "Right? There's nothing wrong with having a local talk show on radio, is there?"

"Nothing I can think of," Helen agreed. She faced Annie. "What really has you so worried?"

Annie squirmed uncomfortably. "Okay, I mentioned all this to Ty when he called tonight. The Braves have been on a road trip so his calls don't last long, and believe me, we don't spend the time talking about the local news. When I mentioned the radio station the other day, it was the first he'd heard that Travis McDonald was settling here. Anyway, it turns out Ty knows him, or knows of him, I guess I should say. He says he had a real reputation as a ladies' man when be played for Boston. A couple of Ty's teammates have known Travis ever since he played in the minors. He called me tonight to fill me in on all this."

Sarah's mouth gaped. "Travis played for the Boston Red Sox? You're kidding me!"

"You didn't know that?" Maddie asked, looking surprised.

Sarah shook her head. "He said he'd played ball for a while. He didn't say anything about playing in the majors. I figured he was maybe on some farm team for about a minute."

"It was a little longer than a minute, according to Ty," Annie said. "It was long enough to make an impression on a lot of women in a lot of cities."

"Well, so what?" Sarah said, even though she was disconcerted by the news. "It's not as if I'm going to date him. I'm just going to work for him. Besides, maybe he's reformed and wants a chance to start fresh. Ty did."

Annie winced at the reminder of her husband's well-publicized exploits with women. He'd wound up with a son during that wild phase of his life. Trevor, in fact, was living right here with Annie while Ty was on the road with the team.

Before Annie could respond, though, Jeanette breezed in. "Sorry, I'm late. Are you talking about Travis? He just told me he'd hired you, Sarah. Congratulations!"

Maddie, Dana Sue and Helen turned on her.

"Just how well do you know him?" Dana Sue asked, radiating suspicion. "I know he's Tom's cousin, but you've never even mentioned him."

"Haven't I?" Jeanette asked with a shrug. "He's been staying with us. He wanted us to keep it quiet when he first got here. He'd had his fill of publicity."

"Did you know about the radio station?" Helen asked.

Jeanette nodded. "Of course."

"And you never said a word," Maddie said with a shake of her head. "What kind of Sweet Magnolia are you?"

Jeanette chuckled. "One who can keep her mouth shut," she suggested.

"Which is not a recommendation, as far as I can tell," Helen said. "We're supposed to be up on all the big news in town."

"And now you are," Jeanette said readily. "So, what's the emergency? Why are we all here?"

"Because some of us think Sarah's nuts for taking this radio job, especially to work with a man with the kind of reputation Travis apparently has," Annie told her. "No offense."

"None taken," Jeanette said. "But how can

he possibly have any reputation when he just got to town a few weeks ago?"

"Ty," Maddie said succinctly. "Word on the road is that Travis was a real player with the ladies when he played ball in Boston."

"Oh, so what?" Jeanette said, dismissing the assessment as unimportant. "Sarah's an intelligent woman. She's not automatically going to fall under his spell. Besides, if you want an opinion based on personal observation, rather than gossip, I think he's kind of sweet."

Sarah tried to reconcile that impression with her own. It didn't fit. Now Travis as a player? That fit him perfectly. But fair warning ought to be enough.

"Okay, I suppose I could back out," she told them. "But the truth is that I want to do something that stretches my limits, something fun. Waiting on tables at Wharton's doesn't qualify. And, if I'm being totally honest, neither does the idea of teaching kids their ABCs. I majored in education because it was a solid, safe career choice."

Raylene, who'd been silent up until now, nodded. "I think she should go for it. Sarah needs to prove to herself that she is so much more than that little Stepford wife Walter and the Prices wanted her to be."

"Amen," Sarah said.

Annie still looked concerned, but eventually she nodded, too. "Since I've been telling you ever since you got back to town that you're much more intelligent and talented than Walter ever gave you credit for being, I suppose I can't take it back now. Go for it." She shot a dire look toward Jeanette. "If Travis gets out of line, the rest of us will have your back."

Sarah laughed at the protective note in her voice. "I don't think you need to worry about that. Somebody who's a player when it comes to women isn't going to take a second glance at me."

Dana Sue reached over and squeezed her hand. "Oh, sweetie, don't sell yourself short. Obviously, he already has."

Rory Sue's visit home had been an exercise in frustration for Mary Vaughn and Sonny. She had no job lined up. Nor did she seem all that concerned about finding one. She'd flatly refused to consider anything Mary Vaughn or Sonny suggested about moving back home. Her opinion of Serenity seemed to be summed up in one oft-repeated word: boring. Mary Vaughn was at her wit's end. Sonny was even more exasperated.

"You'd think raising one child, especially

a girl, would be easier than this," he said as he and Mary Vaughn climbed into bed on Sunday evening after their precious little girl had headed back to Charleston to spend more time with her friends.

"I'm sorry we never had the boy you wanted," Mary Vaughn told him. "But you have to admit, there's something about a girl and her daddy that's special. Sometimes I felt like an outsider when you and Rory Sue would team up."

"That was true when she was nine or ten, but once she reached her teens, she didn't have much use for either one of us."

"And then we hit her with the divorce," Mary Vaughn recalled. "She never entirely forgave me for that."

"I'm the one who asked for a divorce," Sonny said. "I told her that repeatedly."

"But she knew you never would have filed for it if I hadn't done something wrong."

"Well, we're back together now, just the way she always wanted. It's not going to feel right if she's living somewhere else. It'd be nice to be a family, at least for a little while longer," he said wistfully. "One of these days she's going to get married, and then things will change forever. I want her to be happy, but I can't say I'm looking forward to that day."

"It's a funny thing," Mary Vaughn said, "but when she was away at college and you were gone, too, I still didn't feel like one of those empty nesters you read about. It all felt so temporary. Then, sure enough, you and I got back together, but without Rory Sue under the same roof, it doesn't feel quite right. I finally see what all those articles I read were talking about. It's like a piece of us is missing."

"Exactly what I was saying," Sonny said. "So, how do we get her home?"

Mary Vaughn considered the question thoughtfully, or as thoughtfully as she could with Sonny beginning to lazily caress the curve of her hip.

"I think we have to give her a little more time at her friend's place in Charleston," she finally conceded. "You know she's not job-hunting the way she should be, or if she is, she's finding out just how tough things are out there."

"I guarantee she's not too worried about it," Sonny admitted. "She knows we'll keep supporting her for as long as it takes."

"That's the thing. We can't do that," Mary Vaughn said, figuring it was going to be up to her to take the tough line. Sonny was putty in their daughter's hands. "We have to give her a deadline. At the same time, I'll give her an alternative."

Sonny's gaze narrowed. "What alternative?"

"She can come home and work with me."

"Why not with me?" he said at once. "She'll inherit that car dealership one of these days. Despite what's happened to the auto industry, we're still doing well. She ought to at least know the basics of running it."

"Can you see Rory Sue getting excited about selling cars? All she cares about is driving the latest, fanciest car on your lot. And given today's market, she's not going to make the kind of money she's expecting with that high-priced degree of hers."

"And she will in real estate?"

"She will working with me," Mary Vaughn said confidently.

Sonny finally nodded. "Okay, then, we have a plan." He met her gaze. "Now I have a few ideas of my own."

Mary Vaughn reached for him at once. "Why, Mr. Lewis, I do believe we've been thinking along the same lines." Even as she settled into her husband's embrace, she was struck by reality. "You do know, don't you, that if she comes home for good, we're going to have to start behaving ourselves around here. No more skinny-dipping in the pool, for one thing. No afternoon quickies in the middle of the living room."

Sonny looked into her eyes, but it wasn't alarm or even dismay she saw there. It was excitement.

"You're taking that as a challenge, aren't you, Sonny Lewis?"

A grin spread across his face. "You know, I am. The fear of getting caught could add an interesting edge of danger to these trysts of ours."

She laughed. "I don't know about you, but I'm not sure how much more excitement I can stand."

His touches became more intimate. "Why don't we experiment a little and find out?"

Before she could reply, Mary Vaughn completely lost her train of thought. Whatever she'd been about to say couldn't possibly be more important than the way Sonny made her feel whenever he put his mind to it. And lately, to her delight, he'd been putting his mind to it quite a lot.

6

Until Sarah walked through the door at the radio station on Wednesday after her shift at Wharton's, Travis hadn't been totally convinced she'd show up. He figured, based on what Jeanette had told him about some screwy ritual called a Sweet Magnolias margarita night, that Sarah had probably had second and third thoughts by now.

He hadn't expected his reputation with women to come into play at all, but apparently it had. He'd been tempted a couple of times to tell Sarah he'd put that life behind him, but he doubted she'd believe him, especially since he'd been flirting with her since the day they'd met.

When she stepped into the office at the back of the station, he was overwhelmed by relief. He couldn't seem to stop the grin that spread across his face.

"Well, look who's here. It's our morning deejay," he said, standing up to move the pile of papers from the seat of the only remaining chair in the cramped space. "Welcome aboard, sugar. Have you met Bill Roberts?"

She shook her head. "I did see you at the press conference, though."

"Well, Bill's the one who's going to make sure we don't go on the air and make fools out of ourselves," Travis said.

Sarah gave him a weak smile. "Then you're probably going to have your work cut out for you. This is all new to me. I'm still not a hundred percent convinced that putting me on the air makes a lick of sense."

"Travis believes it does, and that's what counts," Bill told her. Ever the Southern gentleman, he stood until she'd taken a seat. "He tells me you can charm the socks off anybody. Now instead of doing that one customer at a time, you'll be charming as many people as this station's signal can reach all at the same time."

"Oh, God," she murmured, turning pale. Her grip on the pen and pad she'd brought along tightened until her knuckles turned white.

Travis regarded her with sympathy. "Maybe you shouldn't think of it that way just yet. Concentrate on talking to one person. Everybody else, well, they're just eavesdropping."

A spark lit her eyes. "You certainly have the knack for that down, don't you?"

"Hey," Travis protested, pretending to be wounded. "Let's not start picking on the boss on your first day on the job."

"Sorry." She sounded contrite, but the glint in her eyes suggested she was anything but sorry.

Bill stepped in. "How about we go in the studio so you can see how things work? Once you have a feel for all the monitors and controls, I think you'll start to feel comfortable in there. I'm going to be around for a couple of weeks acting as your producer, so initially all you'll really have to do is interview your guests, maybe chat a little between songs. Once you're both settled in and comfortable on the air, you'll be able to handle your shows on your own."

Sarah's eyes widened with alarm. "You didn't say anything about me having to do the technical stuff," she said accusingly to Travis. "Just go on the air and talk. That's what you said."

Travis put an arm around her shoulders as he urged her toward the studio. "And that's all that matters. If ad sales keep going the way they have been for the first month, I'll be able to hire a producer before too long. First, though, I have to get an afternoon deejay on board."

"What about you?" she asked, looking vaguely disappointed. "Are you just the big-shot owner, who's going to disappear once this place is up and running?"

"Come on now, sugar. Didn't I tell you we were in this together?" he asked.

She gave him a wry look. "Men have lied to me before."

There was an edge in her voice that told him she didn't intend to put up with it again. "Those men, whoever they were, were idiots. You can trust me. I'm sticking around for the long haul."

"We'll see," she said skeptically.

"Okay, then, here's the plan," Travis began as he settled her into the comfortable chair behind the microphone. "You'll be on the air in the morning from six until noon. That's a long shift, but we're starting on a shoestring budget. I'll reduce your hours later." At her look of alarm, he added, "Your pay will stay the same."

"What on earth am I going to do for six whole hours?"

"You'll interview a couple of folks, play some music, chat about any subject that appeals to you, take a few calls. The new guy, whoever it turns out to be, will take over at noon and stay on the air until six. I'll come on then and hang out till midnight."

She stared at him incredulously. "You're planning to run a radio station with three people? Not counting Bill, of course."

"Pretty much," he admitted. "And Bill's our ace in the hole. He knows every aspect of running a station. Plus I've bought a syndicated music package that will last from midnight until you're back here in the morning. I've picked up some other programming for the weekends. I know that's a skeleton crew, and for now we're all going to be working like crazy, but hopefully I'll be able to get some other people in place in a month or so. I just need to get us up and running as quickly as possible. Then I can start focusing on expanding our staff."

"You really are nuts," she said with despair.

"Come on, where's your spirit of adventure?" he asked.

"You sound like the kid in those old movies — Mickey Rooney, I think — who used to get some neighborhood kids together and suggest they stage a play," she said.

"Hey, we're not amateurs," Travis protested. "I have a degree in broadcasting. And let's not forget about Bill. He's been in this business for thirty years or so. He knows what he's doing."

"And he's going to abandon ship," she said direly. "He just said so."

"Not until things are running smoothly and you're all comfortable," Bill assured her. "And even after I'm officially gone, I'll only be a half hour away. Travis can get me back over here on just about a moment's notice, especially if the fish aren't biting. Right now the idea of sitting out on the lake in a little motor boat with a fishing rod in hand holds a lot of allure, but my wife predicts I'll be bored to death in a month. She's probably right, in which case you're likely to find me hanging around here begging for things to do."

"And I will hire more people," Travis promised. "I just want to get this station on the air and then I'll fill whatever vacancies we have. By then I'll have a better idea of whether we need more people on-air or selling advertising or what."

"An afternoon deejay is a pretty big vacancy," she said. "What if you don't find someone in time?"

"I will," Travis said confidently.

"Or I'll fill in," Bill said. "No need to panic."

Sarah sighed. "One of us probably should. And since the two of you seem to be living in a dream world, I suppose it's going to have to be me."

Travis hid his desire to chuckle at her resigned expression. At least she hadn't bolted for the door. He'd known that hiring her was going to be a smart decision and she was already proving it.

"Let's talk about the scheduling again. That's not really an eight-hour day," Sarah said. "The salary you mentioned was for a full day's work."

"Because you'll be using the extra time to book guests and maybe even pitch in to help me sell advertising."

Her plucky attitude seemed to falter. In fact, she suddenly looked shell-shocked. "I don't know anything about selling advertising."

"You go, you schmooze, you sell," Travis said. "We're offering something brand new in this town. So far, people have been really receptive." He thought of one or two very vocal doubters, but shrugged off the encounters. "For the most part, anyway."

"It's going to be fine," Bill said, stepping in when it became obvious that nothing Travis had said had relieved her anxiety. "Right now it's all unfamiliar, but I guarantee you'll find your groove in a couple of weeks and it'll feel like you've been doing this all your life. I'm a seasoned pro and you can count on me being here to pick up any slack until this place is running like a well-oiled machine. That's a promise."

Sarah turned to him as if he'd just thrown her a lifeline. "Don't you dare leave me on my own, you hear me!"

Bill chuckled. "I wouldn't dream of it."

"What about me?" Travis said. "How come you're not turning to me?"

"Because something tells me that despite that fancy college degree, you only know a smidgen more than I do, and you're not even going to be around in the daytime."

She sounded surprisingly disappointed by that. Travis tucked a finger under her chin. "Don't worry about that. I'll be here so much, you'll wonder how you ever lived without me underfoot."

His promise seemed to disconcert, rather than reassure her. He grinned. "I told you this was going to be fun, didn't I?"

"We'll just see about that," she said, then turned back to Bill. "Start with the basics and talk real slow," she told him. "I need to take notes and then I'm going to want about a hundred hours of rehearsal time before we go on the air." She glanced at Travis. "When is that going to be, by the way?"

"July first," he said. "I'll kick things off at

midnight that night and then we'll be rolling."

Sarah swallowed hard. "That's less than two weeks away," she whispered.

Travis winked at her. "Why, yes, I believe it is, but you want to know the good news?"

"Desperately," she said.

"With the town's Fourth of July celebration only a few days away, you'll have plenty of things to talk about."

She looked as if she couldn't think of one.

"The fireworks display," he coached. "What time things are going to be happening on the green. Fireworks safety. You might want to get Grace in here to reminisce about past festivities. And on the Fourth, you'll be able to see everything from the studio and give those who aren't here a bird's-eye view of everything that's happening from the parade to the festival. I predict that'll entice even more people to town for the fireworks that night."

Her expression slowly brightened as he went on. "I can do that," she said. "I don't think I missed a single Fourth of July celebration here in town when I was a kid. I loved the parade almost as much as the fireworks."

"Then you'll have plenty to talk about, won't you?" Travis said, loving the bloom of

121

color in her cheeks as she gained confidence in herself. "Keep in mind it's going to be like a day at Wharton's, just with a whole lot of people listening in. If you focus on that, you're all set."

"This could turn out to be fun, after all," she said, already scribbling madly in her notebook.

"Isn't that what I told you?" he said.

She waved him away. "I need to concentrate."

Bill chuckled at Travis's disgruntled look. "You wanted a star. I think you've got one in the making." As they left Sarah sitting at the desk in the studio, Bill grinned. "Or were you really hoping she was going to depend on you for every little thing?"

"It might have been nice if she'd done that for maybe five minutes," Travis grumbled, even though he was ridiculously pleased to see Sarah getting into the spirit of the job so quickly.

"Want a piece of advice from a man who's been around a lot longer than you have?" Bill asked. "Be thankful when a woman's independent."

"Why is that?"

"Because the worst thing in the world is having anyone's happiness all tied up in what you can offer them," Bill said. "They need to make their own. Then you come together as equals, and what you find as a couple is just the icing on the cake."

"Isn't there a risk, then, that they won't need you at all?" Travis asked, watching as Sarah bent over her notebook, a line of concentration furrowed in her brow.

"Maybe, but I've found it's more important for someone to be with you because they can't imagine life without you than because they can't figure out how to fix a leaky faucet . . . or put together a radio show."

What Bill said made sense. Ironically Travis had never felt this yearning to be needed before. He'd never wanted permanency, figured he wasn't cut out for it, in fact, just like his daddy. After all these years of thinking he knew that much about himself, he supposed it was going to take a little time to determine why the desire for forever had stolen up on him after meeting Sarah.

"Your muscles are in knots," Jeanette told Sarah when she stopped by The Corner Spa to use the gift certificate for a massage that Raylene had given her a few days before.

"The station's going on the air in less than a week and I still don't have any idea what I'm doing," Sarah admitted. "Every time I say that to Travis, though, he just tells me everything will be fine, as if that's magically going to happen."

"He seems pretty sure of himself," Jeanette said, as she tried to knead away the tension that had settled in Sarah's shoulders. "Maybe you should trust him."

"Oh, he's sure of himself, all right. *He's* not the problem. I've heard him in the studio rehearsing and he chats away as if he was born to be on the radio. He's talking to *himself,* for goodness' sake, and he sounds perfectly natural. I try to do that and I sound like an idiot."

"But your show is supposed to be a talk show, which implies you'll be conversing with someone else," Jeanette said. "Isn't someone rehearsing with you?"

"Who?" Sarah asked. "It's not as if the station's exactly swarming with warm bodies. The afternoon guy isn't even showing up until next week, one day before he goes on the air. He has plenty of experience, according to Travis, but how can he not be hanging around the station every second to get ready? I'd be a wreck."

"Because you're new to all this. Why not bring in a couple of people just to get some interviewing practice?" Jeanette suggested. "I'll stop by and you can interview me. I'll get Tom to come by, too. And I know Maddie will volunteer. And Dana Sue."

Sarah propped herself up to meet Jeanette's gaze. "You'd do that?"

"Of course. You can even tape the interviews, so you'll have them in case somebody cancels one day and you need a last-second fill-in. You can just pop them into the tape-player or whatever and sit back and relax."

The idea was amazing. Sarah couldn't imagine why she hadn't thought of it herself. Maybe it was because she'd been so focused on filling her notebook with instructions and the calendar on her desk with scheduled guests for the first month. She hadn't even considered lining up some backup material for a crisis. That it would also give her some experience was a major bonus.

"Could you come by this evening? Or tomorrow morning? Whenever's convenient."

"I'll talk to Maddie and come back with you this afternoon, if you want," Jeanette offered. "After all, this is going to be free publicity for the spa. I think she can spare me for an hour."

Sarah's sigh of relief was heartfelt. "I think you just saved my life."

"All I did was offer a suggestion," Jeanette said. "Now in return, why don't you tell me how things are going between you and Travis?"

Sarah immediately tensed. "Me and Travis?"

"Whoa," Jeanette protested. "That brought those knots in your shoulders right back. Are you two having problems?"

"You ask that as if there's supposed to be something between us," Sarah muttered. "He's my boss. The only way this is going to work is if we keep that line very clear."

Jeanette chuckled. "Funny. He pretty much said the same thing when I spoke to him."

Sarah couldn't help the faint hint of disappointment she felt at hearing that. It might be for the best, but that didn't mean she had to like it. "Well, there you go," she said breezily. "We're both on the same page."

"Indeed, you are," Jeanette said, a funny little smirk on her face. "If denial is a page, you're both definitely on it."

"I am not in denial," Sarah insisted. "Why would you say that?"

"Because even though both of you said exactly the right thing, neither one of you looked one bit happy about it."

"So?"

"That's denial, sweetie, and the one thing I know about living in denial is that sooner or later, somebody's going to ignite a spark and all hell will break loose."

Sarah frowned at her. "Which just goes to prove that neither one of us can take a chance on playing with fire."

"Well, for whatever it's worth, I think you should go for it," Jeanette told her. "I've spent a lot of time with Travis since he got here. He's a really good guy. And you're just what he needs."

"A single mom whose life until recently was a mess," she replied skeptically. "I doubt that."

"A strong woman who's making smart decisions and getting her life on track," Jeanette corrected.

"You think this radio gig was a smart decision?" Sarah asked. "I'm leaning toward crazy."

"Let's have this conversation again after you've been on the air for a month. I predict that by then you're going to think Travis was a genius for hiring you, and that you've never had more fun in your life."

Sarah had her doubts, but she nodded. "Remind me of this in a month and we'll see which one of us is right."

In most ways, she really hoped it was Jeanette because she'd never been more excited about anything, ever. She was testing herself, trying on a whole new persona, and despite all of her anxiety and doubts, she felt darn good about it.

Travis blinked when he read the note on his desk, then started to grin. Sarah had apparently called a staff meeting for the three of them. She'd scheduled it for this morning at ten.

"You got one of these?" he asked Bill.

"I did," he said, chuckling. "She seems to think somebody needs to take charge."

Travis shook his head. "What does she think I've been doing?"

"Apparently she's not clear on that. She muttered something about keeping each other informed. She seemed pretty annoyed, to be honest. Have you done something to upset her?"

"I've barely seen her for the past week," Travis replied. "I've been out selling ad time during the day and recording spots at night."

"Maybe that's the problem," Bill suggested. "She misses you."

"I wish," Travis said, but he didn't buy it. Sarah had been strictly professional in their few recent encounters. In fact, her prim and proper demeanor was getting on his nerves, but he hadn't had time to do anything about

128

it. Probably wasn't wise to, anyway. There'd be time enough for things like that after the station was up and running in a comfortable groove. That would be soon enough for her to discover he was seriously obsessed with the idea of kissing her.

He glanced up at the clock and saw that it was five minutes before ten. Sarah breezed in the door and beamed at finding them there.

"Good. You're both here," she said. "Right on time."

"Early," Travis corrected. "You know it's usually the boss who calls the meetings."

"Well, our boss hadn't called one, so I did," she said cheerily.

Travis leaned back in his chair and studied her. Her cheeks were flushed, her hair was pulling free of a haphazard ponytail to curl around her face, and her blouse looked as if it had a streak of grape jelly on it. She looked so pretty she almost took his breath away. She caught him staring.

"What?" she demanded.

"I was just thinking how beautiful you are."

The color in her cheeks turned even brighter. "Don't say things like that."

"Why not?"

"It's inappropriate, for one thing, and it's

not true for another."

"I've never been much for propriety," he said, holding her gaze. "And it's true if I say it's true. Beauty is in the eye of the beholder, after all."

"I have half of Libby's peanut butter and jelly sandwich all over my blouse," she protested. "And I never got to fix my hair."

"Doesn't matter."

"We're getting off the subject," she said, clearly flustered.

"Sorry," Travis said innocently. "What was the subject?"

She blinked hard, then sat down behind her desk. Her prim armor fell into place. "The fact that the right hand doesn't know what the left hand is doing around here," she said. "That's the subject."

Travis frowned at that. "Meaning?"

"Meaning you've been running around all over selling ad time and I don't have a clue where you've been, what you've sold and who told you to take a flying leap. It's created some awkward situations." She leveled a look into his eyes. "I don't like awkward."

He nodded. "I get that."

"Why don't you create a list of contacts, post it with the name of whoever's going to make the call, then the outcome?" Bill suggested. Up to now he'd apparently been

130

content to watch the sparks flying between the two of them. "That way you won't have overlaps or awkward situations."

"Makes sense to me," Travis said at once, then looked to Sarah. "Anything else?"

She seemed startled to have the matter resolved so easily. "Well, no. I guess not."

"Okay, then," Travis said, standing up. He started from the room, then turned back. "Maybe this staff meeting idea is a good thing. Schedule it once a week, okay?"

"You want *me* to schedule it?" Sarah asked.

"Why not? It was your idea, after all. And, for the record, will you stop thinking of me as the boss and start thinking of this place as a partnership? We're all in it together."

She seemed momentarily taken aback by that, but of course she couldn't leave it alone. "It's your money. That makes you the boss."

"Not if I put you in charge," he countered with a wink. "Consider yourself the office manager."

Her mouth gaped as he walked away. He was almost out of the building when he heard her call after him.

"What?" he shouted back.

"Does that mean I get a raise?"

He laughed at her audacity. "If you sell

enough advertising, you do."

Before he could get half a block down the street, she was beside him.

"What if, as your new office manager, I authorize a raise?" she asked.

"You can't."

She pinned him with a look. "So, let me get this straight," she said slowly. "I have more responsibility, but no more money and zero authority?"

"Something like that," he agreed.

If he'd expected an argument, she surprised him yet again. She simply nodded.

"Just so we're clear," she murmured, and walked away.

Something told him, though, that sooner or later he was going to pay for that ready agreement.

Walter stared at the front-page story in the Serenity newspaper that Raylene had plunked in front of him on the kitchen table. The kids were upstairs napping, but he wasn't anxious to go back to the motel, so he'd opted for hanging out here. He suspected the scent of the chocolate-chip cookies she was baking had been part of the allure, more so than Raylene's usually testy company.

"What's this?" he asked, startled to see a

picture of Sarah and a guy he immediately recognized as a former big league baseball player. Some American League team, if he recalled correctly, a team not carried on local cable all that often, but big enough for the networks. Probably the Yankees or the Red Sox. Whoever he was, what the devil was he doing in a place like Serenity?

"You've been asking why Sarah's never around when you're over here to see the kids," Raylene told him. "There's your answer. She has a new job. The station goes on the air day after tomorrow."

Walter blinked at the news and tried to make sense of it. "Sarah's working for a radio station? I thought she was working in that diner."

"She was. That's where Travis met her. He hired her to work for him."

"Travis?"

"Travis McDonald."

Recognition dawned. McDonald had been a hotshot for the Red Sox, at least for a couple of seasons, then he'd been dumped when his batting average had gone down the tubes. How had a man like that hooked up with Sarah?

"Doing what?" he asked. "The woman couldn't keep our bank statement straight, so it better not be accounting."

Raylene gave him a look that took him to task for his sarcasm. "Sorry," he murmured, "but that's a fact."

"Look, I just thought you ought to know. Any questions you have, ask Sarah. I'm sure she would have told you herself, but she's been overwhelmed trying to learn all this new stuff."

"Like what?"

"Booking guests, interviewing people, working the controls on the air."

"Hold on a minute! You're telling me Sarah's going to be *on* the radio?"

"With her very own morning show," Raylene said, tapping a finger on the newspaper. "*Carolina Daybreak.* You can read all about it in the article. You should be proud of her."

Walter had no idea what to think. Back in college he'd been able to envision Sarah in front of a classroom of first or second graders, but then he'd seen how much trouble she had keeping up with Tommy and Libby and wondered how she'd manage with twenty or thirty kids. Even though it had annoyed the daylights out of him seeing her working in the local diner, he'd known she was a capable waitress. But this? Some kind of local radio celebrity? It didn't make sense for a woman who got flustered too easily.

He gave Raylene a questioning look. "You really think she can pull this off? She's not much for confrontation."

Raylene slid another tray of cookies into the oven before answering. "I do, as a matter of fact. More important, so does she. And she's not planning to be Mike Wallace or Morley Safer. There won't be a lot of on-air confrontations. And, in case you haven't noticed, Sarah's changing. She's not the timid little thing who let you and your parents walk all over her. Like I said, you should be proud. In a way you're responsible for her discovering just how strong and talented she really is."

His gaze narrowed. "Somehow I don't think you meant that as a compliment for me."

Raylene patted his shoulder. "There you go, demonstrating more insightfulness than I ever expected."

He frowned at that. "You don't like me much, do you?"

She didn't even blink at the direct question. Nor did she hesitate. "How could I? You almost destroyed my friend."

He sighed at the undeniable accusation. "And no one is sorrier about that than I am," he said quietly. "I wish Sarah nothing but the best. If this radio thing matters to

135

her, then I hope she's a huge success."

"She will be," Raylene said confidently. "But it might mean a lot to her to hear that from you."

"She stopped caring what I think a long time ago," he said candidly, then quickly added, "My own fault."

"I'm not sure a woman ever stops caring what the man she once married thinks of her," Raylene said, her expression suddenly sad. "Even when she should."

Walter studied the woman who was busying herself with a batch of cookies just out of the oven, her back to him. Though his impression of Raylene had been shaped by her bitter attitude, he saw something oddly vulnerable about her now.

"Are we still talking about Sarah?" he asked carefully.

She turned back to him, lifted her chin, her gaze steady. "Who else?" she said in a way meant to forestall any further speculation.

Walter was out of his element. His sensitive side, if he even had such a thing, floundered in the face of her response. Something told him she'd just revealed something important, but he didn't know if he should pursue it or let it drop. Because it was more comfortable, he let it go.

"I think I'll take a drive into town, see if maybe I can track Sarah down," he said, standing up. "Mind if I steal a handful of these cookies to take along?"

She gave him the kind of look she usually reserved for the kids. "Don't spoil your supper," she chided.

"Trust me, my appetite won't be affected. You going to be okay here with the kids? I'll try to get back before they're up from their nap."

"We'll be fine," she assured him. "If they wake up, we'll play inside till you get back."

It wasn't the first time she'd hinted at the fact that she didn't leave the house. He'd never questioned her about it. He hadn't figured it was his place. Now, though, he wondered.

It was just one more question for the long list he was accumulating for when he saw Sarah. Hopefully he could get through them all without getting into one of their trademark fights, because as determined as he was to stop criticizing and making judgments, his tongue still had a tendency to get away from him before his brain could kick in.

Sarah had known Dana Sue Sullivan almost all of her life. Annie, Dana Sue's daughter, had always been one of her two best friends, along with Raylcne. She'd had sleepovers at Annie's. She'd eaten at Sullivan's more times than she could count, especially when Dana Sue and Erik had been fine-tuning the menu. Back then, Annie, in the throes of her anorexia, hadn't touched more than a bite, but Sarah had savored every mouthful, then answered every painstakingly detailed question Dana Sue and Erik had about her opinion of each recipe.

Despite all that, sitting across from Dana Sue in the studio at the station made her palms sweat. There was a lump the size of a prime ribeye steak lodged in her throat. This would be the third test-run she'd taped before the official station launch, and it wasn't getting any easier. How was she ever supposed to enjoy doing a show every morning if all she wanted to do was run from the studio and throw up? Worse, so far all the guests had been people she'd known forever. What on earth would happen when she had to interview some stranger or a real celebrity?

She glanced through the glass partition into the control room and got a thumbs-up from Bill. "We're starting in one minute," he said, just as he'd told her he would for the real thing.

Her gaze darted to the clock on the wall as the second hand ticked off the time way too quickly.

"Sweetie," Dana Sue said in a commanding tone, "look at me."

Sarah's panicked gaze locked on her friend's mom. They were both Sweet Magnolias, for heaven's sake. That ought to make this easy. And maybe it would if they'd started with a margarita. Stone-cold sober, Dana Sue's familiarity didn't seem to make a difference.

"You've known me way too long to look so terrified," Dana Sue said, keeping her own gaze steady. "You were there when I tossed all Ronnie's things onto the front lawn, remember? You were there the night Annie collapsed and nearly died. We're friends, Sarah, and all we're doing is chatting, okay? Just the way we used to do around the kitchen table at my house."

Sarah gulped in a deep breath and nodded. "This is ridiculous. I should be reassuring you that I'm going to make it painless. We're just going to talk about how you started Sullivan's, the rave reviews you've had."

Bill cut in. "We're going live in five, four, three, two and . . ." He signaled for her to begin.

Swallowing hard, Sarah found her voice. "Good morning, it's *Carolina Daybreak* and I'm Sarah Price, coming to you from the heart of Serenity, right on Town Square. Today my guest is Dana Sue Sullivan, the mastermind behind Sullivan's restaurant, known all over the state for its Southern cuisine with a contemporary twist."

Once the words started flowing, her nerves seemed to settle. Dana Sue's reassuring smile helped, too. The questions, which she'd spent all last night preparing, kicked off the conversation. Dana Sue did the rest, answering with the sort of lively, self-deprecating humor that everyone in Serenity expected from this one-time rebel who'd grown up to be an innovative chef and businesswoman.

They'd taped for nearly an hour, pausing

where commercials would be inserted when the show eventually ran on the air, when Sarah looked up and saw that Travis had joined Bill in the booth. When he winked at her and gave her a thumbs-up, she nearly lost her place on her list of questions.

Something on her face must have given her away, because Dana Sue turned around to catch a glimpse of Travis, then turned back to Sarah with a broad grin. "Oh my!" she mouthed silently.

Sarah blushed. Bill's whispered reminder in her headset that she needed to wrap things up finally steadied her.

"That's it for today. I'd like to thank our guest and suggest you all stop by Sullivan's to try out the tempting new menu items we've been discussing this morning. I guarantee you won't be disappointed. I'll be back in a minute with more of Carolina's favorite music."

"And we're out," Bill said. "Good interview, Sarah."

Though his praise meant the world to her, Sarah's gaze immediately went to Travis. It was the first time he'd heard one of her tapings. The broad smile on his face said everything.

Stepping into the studio, he swept her up in his arms and twirled her around. "You were fantastic!" he said. "Even better than I was expecting."

"If I was, you can thank Dana Sue. She provided all the entertainment."

"I did not," Dana Sue corrected. "You asked all the right questions. You're a natural, Sarah. I couldn't be more proud of you. I know this was really just a dress rehearsal of some kind, but I hope you air it one of these days."

"First chance we get," Travis promised, his arm still securely around Sarah's waist. He gave Dana Sue a considering look. "You know, speaking of natural, you were great on the air. Sarah was right about that. I don't suppose you'd want to do cooking tips or something like that on a regular basis? Sullivan's could sponsor it. It would be great exposure for the restaurant. Maybe I could even get it into syndication around the state."

Sarah's eyes lit up. "Oh, Dana Sue, do it. It's a great idea."

"How often would you want it on the air?" Dana Sue asked, though she looked skeptical. "I don't have a lot of spare time."

"I'd like once a week, maybe an hour-long show for Saturday morning," Travis suggested. "You could tape it whenever it's convenient."

"I'll think about it," Dana Sue promised. "Now I have to run. The restaurant opens for dinner in a half hour. Why don't you all come over? Your meals will be on the house to celebrate the launch of the station."

Sarah wasn't sure what to say. Dinner at Sullivan's was a big deal to most people in town. Going there with Travis, even if it was mostly a business thing, would feel an awful lot like a date. Of course, Bill would be along, too.

Travis met her gaze. "How about it, Sarah? I think we deserve a celebration."

She hesitated, then nodded. "Sure."

Bill shook his head. "Unfortunately my wife's expecting me, and she hates it when I don't turn up after she's cooked. You two go and enjoy yourselves. I want to spend a couple of minutes editing this tape. We ran over by sixty seconds, and I think I know where I can cut. I'd like to do it now, while it's all fresh in my head. Then this will be ready for air whenever you need it."

"Okay, then," Travis said to Dana Sue. "Count on the two of us. We'll be there shortly."

After Bill had gone back to the control booth and Dana Sue had left, Sarah looked at Travis. "We don't have to do this. Dana Sue was a sweetheart for asking, but we both have a million things to do before the launch. I should probably get home and have dinner with the kids for a change."

Travis held her gaze. "Don't try wiggling off the hook. I don't have anything to do that's more important than taking my best on-air talent to dinner. I need to keep you happy."

The flattery went straight to her head, just like a glass of champagne. Because she wasn't used to such compliments, Sarah couldn't let herself trust it. It was smarter to treat it lightly.

"Besides Rick the Rocket, or whatever his name is, I'm your only on-air talent," she reminded him. "So I don't think I'll take your compliment too seriously."

"Hey, what am I?" he demanded.

She grinned at him. "That remains to be seen. I've heard you chattering away to yourself in the studio, but you haven't done the first rehearsal or made a single note about your program, as far as I can tell."

"Sugar, I'm relying on my charm and spontaneity to win over the audience."

"I suppose that's one way to go," she said. "I think I like my way better. At least I won't be floundering around like a fish trying to come up with something to say."

A grin spread across Travis's face. "You

ever known me to be at a loss for words?"

"No," she conceded. And that was precisely the reason she knew she didn't dare let her guard down. Because when words flowed that easily, so could the lies.

Travis knew that even a couple of hours with Sarah in the low-lit, cozy ambience of Sullivan's was probably dangerous. On his own, he probably wouldn't have issued such an invitation, at least not for a while. But when Dana Sue had offered, he hadn't been able to say no.

The past couple of weeks had been hell on his libido. All it took was one of Sarah's shy glances or the casual brush of her hand across his and he'd been on fire. He hoped like crazy it was because he hadn't been dating for a while now, because otherwise it suggested he was falling hard and fast for a woman he needed to keep at a distance. He'd figured that out in a hurry. Sarah was all about forever, and he was mostly about what felt good tonight.

During his years playing ball, finding a woman who wanted to play by those rules had been easy. He'd never once been tempted to change the rules by which he lived, the same rules that had finally forced his mother to kick his daddy to the curb.

Travis had sympathized with her, but he'd known intuitively that he was a chip off the old McDonald block. Settling down just didn't appeal to him, mainly because he knew first-hand how badly someone would get hurt if he couldn't make it last.

Yet, here he was with a forever woman, sitting down in a cozy booth, trying not to notice how soft the candlelight made her skin look or how brightly her eyes shone. Only a last-second burst of rationality kept him from sliding in right next to her, instead of on the other side of the table.

"Is this the first time you've been here?" Sarah asked him.

Travis nodded. "I've been meaning to come by, but my schedule's been too hectic ever since I bought the station. It's a nice place."

"It's wonderful," Sarah said. "And the food really is as amazing as all the reviews claim."

She studied the menu with an intensity that Travis couldn't help wishing were directed his way. She even unconsciously licked her lips a time or two, which gave a real jolt to his system. Clearly his hormones had been shut down for too long.

"What do you recommend?" he asked eventually, too fascinated with Sarah to bother looking at the menu.

"I'm having the meat loaf," she said at once. "I know that sounds ordinary, but trust me, Dana Sue raises it to a whole new level. It's one of their most popular dishes."

"Then I'll have to try it," he said, giving their order to the waitress when she came.

Now that they'd been left alone without the menus to occupy them, Sarah shifted uneasily across from him, her gaze on everyone in the room except Travis.

"Am I making you nervous?" he asked, trying to hide his amusement.

"No, why?" she asked, looking flustered.

"You just seem a little jumpy."

"My nerves are shot in general," she said candidly, then looked embarrassed by the admission. "To be totally honest, you should know that the launch scares me to death."

"Trust me, you have nothing to worry about. The shows you've taped have been fantastic. There's no reason to think you won't be just as amazing when we go live."

"You were only there tonight," she said, clearly not believing him.

"But I've listened to the other tapes," he said.

"Really? Why?"

"Because I wanted to hear your voice," he admitted before he could censor himself.

He scrambled for a less personal explanation. "I mean, to make sure you're getting the knack of doing an interview. Bill told me you were doing fine, but I wanted to check it out myself."

She looked at him as if she didn't entirely trust his response, then said, "And? How was I?"

"Stop fishing for compliments. I've already said you're fantastic. Bill's said so, too. Stop worrying."

She sighed. "You'll have to say it a lot more before I'll believe you," she said, then groaned.

"What?" Travis asked, gauging from her reaction that something had upset her.

"My ex-husband's here, and he's heading this way."

She looked so disconcerted, Travis impulsively reached over and covered her hand. "Do I need to beat him up for you?"

As he'd intended, she laughed. "I don't think that will be necessary, but you have my permission if this doesn't go well." She looked up as the man reached their table. "Hi, Walter. What are you doing here?"

"I've been looking all over town for you," he said, barely sparing a glance for Travis.

Alarm flashed in her eyes. "Is it the kids? Are they okay?"

"They're fine. Raylene's with them, and I'm heading back over there in a couple of minutes." He finally turned to acknowledge Travis's presence. "Could you give us a minute, please?"

Travis didn't want to give the man two seconds alone with her, but after a glance at Sarah, who gave him a subtle nod, he stood. "I'll be right back." He leveled a meaningful look into the other man's eyes to make sure Walter understood that he wouldn't be far away.

"Thanks," Walter said easily, then took Travis's spot at the table.

On his way to the booth closest to the kitchen, where he'd spotted Ronnie, Travis turned back to make sure everything was okay. Whatever the man was saying, he was pretty intense about it, but Sarah didn't look upset. He was surprised to discover just how interested he was in knowing what they were discussing.

"Everything okay?" Ronnie asked when Travis reached his table. "I see Walter's shown up."

"You know him?"

"We've met a time or two," Ronnie said carefully. "The first time, I wrote him off as a hot-tempered jerk, but from what I hear he's been on good behavior recently."

In Travis's experience only one thing made a man change his stripes that dramatically. "Do you think he wants Sarah back?" he asked, unexpectedly bothered by the idea.

"Maybe," Ronnie said, then gave him a consoling smile. "The good news for you is that she's not even remotely interested."

"You sure about that? They do have kids together."

"That's not enough," Ronnie said confidently.

Travis gave a nod of satisfaction. For reasons he couldn't explain, he hoped like hell that Ronnie was right.

"You have something going on with that hot-shot ballplayer?" Walter asked Sarah as Travis left them alone.

His tone grated on her nerves. "First of all, he's no longer a ballplayer," she told him, unable to keep a defensive note out of her voice. "And second, it's none of your business what I'm doing or with whom."

He frowned at her. "Don't get all worked up. I was just asking."

"Really? You weren't about to launch into a full-scale assault on my judgment?" she asked skeptically.

"No. I just came looking for you to congratulate you on the radio thing. Raylene showed me the article. It sounds like a great opportunity for you."

Sarah's mouth gaped. "That's it? That's why you tracked me down?"

He gave her a sheepish grin. "Not used to hearing much positive from me, are you?"

"Not much," she agreed. "I have to say, I'm pleasantly surprised. Actually stunned, to be honest."

"I can't blame you for reacting like that, but I want you to know that I am trying to change," Walter said, his expression earnest. "Ever since I had that blowup with my dad, I've been taking a fresh look at my life. I don't know if I'll get up the courage to make a clean break from the mill or my folks, but I want to be a better dad to Tommy and Libby and a decent ex-husband to you. No more lectures, no more fights, if I can help it."

Sarah regarded him quizzically. "What's really behind the sudden change? Have you met someone?"

"No. Haven't been looking, to tell you the truth. Of course, predictably my mother has a few candidates from among the socially appropriate women back home," he said wryly.

Sarah found herself chuckling. "Yes, I'm

151

sure she does. And I'll bet none of them are a thing in the world like me."

"Afraid not," he said. "More's the pity." He hesitated, then met her gaze. "I wish I'd appreciated you more when we were married, Sarah. I have no idea how I let things get so far off track."

"It's hard to go against the parents who've raised you and given you everything," Sarah said, finally understanding at least some of what had turned Walter into such an overbearing, critical spouse. "I probably should have called you on it the first time you started taking potshots at me, but I was already feeling overwhelmed by living in an unfamiliar place with a baby on the way. It didn't take much for me to believe I didn't measure up."

Walter shook his head. "You know, when I think about it, our problems started with the wedding. I should have stood up to my mother right then, when she insisted on a small family ceremony at home. I should never have let her get away with making you feel ashamed that you were pregnant."

Thinking back to how disappointed she'd felt when Walter had acquiesced to his mother's wishes, she agreed it had been the first step on a very slippery slope toward destroying the two of them.

"And I think the reception she held for us was even worse," Sarah told him. "Were you aware that she trotted out all these beautiful, suitable women so I'd know what you'd lost by coming home with me on your arm?"

He looked bemused. "I knew there were a bunch of old friends there that night, but I didn't know they were there to torment you."

Sarah shrugged. "Maybe they weren't. For all I know I was the one who made too big a thing of it. All those sly little comments your mother made about my background were starting to take root. It didn't require much to make me feel even more insecure." She waved off the discussion. "None of this matters now. Our marriage is over, and we're both moving on. It's all good."

To her surprise, she actually meant that. Ever since she'd started working at the radio station and preparing for the launch, the confidence she'd once had in herself had been returning, bit by bit. That Bill and Travis were both free with their praise had been like pouring water on a parched plant. She felt herself blossoming.

It didn't hurt that she'd caught Travis looking at her as though she was an attractive, desirable woman, either. Maybe those kinds of looks and the flattering talk were just part of his flirtatious charm, but it was all music to her ears. Not that she dared to let herself get too caught up in it. She was working for the man, not dating him. It was a distinction she couldn't let herself forget.

Now Walter was studying her with an expression filled with regret. "You really are getting it all together, aren't you? I'm glad. You deserve it, Sarah."

She met his gaze. "Yes, I do." And for the first time since their awful sham of a wedding, she honestly believed it.

Travis waited until Sarah's ex had taken off before returning to the table. He wasn't sure what to expect, but it wasn't the smiling woman who greeted him.

"I take it everything went okay," he said.

"We had a good talk," she said. "The first one in a long time."

"He doesn't object to you doing the radio show?"

"Not that his opinion counts, but he's all for it," she said. "Frankly, I was a little surprised by that, but I guess his parents haven't heard the news and had time to tell him he should hate the idea."

Travis regarded her curiously. "Is that what went wrong in your marriage? He was still tied to his folks by the apron strings?"

She nodded. "It was hell to live with," she said candidly. "They never approved of me, but I can see why Walter had such a hard time taking a stand against them. His dad's a powerful man, at least in their hometown. He owns the cotton mill that provides the work for many of the people in town. Walter was brought up knowing that he would take over one day. He was supposed to marry well, then ease right into the role of big man around town. Instead, he turned up with me."

Travis regarded her with shock. "What's wrong with you?" he asked incredulously.

"According to Mrs. Price, there was very little right with me. My clothes, my hair, my social graces. All lacking. Worst, of course, was that I was already pregnant."

"I assume she'd figured out that her son had something to do with that," Travis said.

"Actually I don't think she much liked thinking about how it happened," she said, grinning. "It was enough of an embarrassment that it had. Of course, that didn't stop them from wanting to raise Tommy to follow right along in his daddy and granddaddy's footsteps. I suspect Walter's parents would have been holding a party on their front lawn to celebrate my leaving except for the fact that I took Tommy with me."

"They sound like awful people," Travis said, hating that she'd been through all that.

"They were just . . ." She hesitated, then said, "I suppose they were just traditional."

"They were snobs," Travis corrected. "And people with as much breeding as they apparently thought they had don't make other people feel small and insecure."

She gave him a surprised look. "How would you know a thing like that?"

"How much do you know about Tom's family, the McDonalds?"

"I know he's from Charleston, but that's about it."

"Well, the McDonalds, despite some financial setbacks and misbehaving through the years, rank pretty high up there in Charleston social circles. My daddy was a black sheep, but I still grew up around all that highfalutin nonsense. I was told on more occasions than I can count that McDonalds don't do this or McDonalds don't do that." He grinned. "Which, of course, made it all the more essential that I do all of those things."

"You broke the rules?" she asked with feigned surprise. "I can't imagine such a thing."

"Broke a few that hadn't even been written, because folks thought it went without saying," he said. "I liked shocking people. I figured it was my obligation to stir things up, keep them from getting too stuffy. It also took some of the heat off my daddy, who had a tendency to be the center of a lot of gossip."

"Why was that?"

"Let's just say he has a well-developed appreciation of women, and they tend to reciprocate. It caused no end of embarrassment to the family in general and to my mother in particular."

There was an expression on Sarah's face he couldn't quite read. He had a feeling it had something to do with what she'd heard about him.

"Before you ask," he said, deciding on a preemptive strike, "some say I'm a chip off the old block."

Though she looked startled by his admission, she leaned closer, studying him intently. "Are they right?"

"They were," he said candidly.

"Were?"

"Let's just say I'm finding the straight and narrow a lot more appealing recently."

"Any particular reason?"

He loved that she had absolutely no idea that she might have anything to do with his recent desire to transform himself. And since he wasn't sure he could stick to his resolve, it was probably best that she not figure it out.

"Time for a change," he said with a careless shrug.

"Maturity?" she suggested.

He laughed. "You never know. Maybe so."

He hoped not, though, because that would imply that he'd be able to control this increasingly powerful desire to take Sarah straight home to bed and make love to her till it was time for the station to go on the air. He was hoping like crazy he'd succumb to that desire — that they both would — before his freshly minted conscience kicked in.

8

Rick the Rocket was drunk. Oh, he did a pretty good job of covering it for the first five minutes he was in Travis's office, but he wasn't a good enough actor to hide it any longer than that.

Travis exchanged a look with Bill, then took a deep breath. "You're fired," he said, not hesitating for a single second over the decision.

The middle-aged man looked as if he was still trying to recapture his youth in a wrinkled T-shirt from a heavy metal group that had long since faded into oblivion. His shabby jeans were about a hundred wash cycles past trendiness. He regarded Travis with confusion.

"Fired? Why?"

"You're drunk," Travis said with exaggerated patience.

"So what?" Rick asked, looking genuinely bewildered. "I'm not on the air till tomorrow."

Travis shook his head at the poor logic. "And I'm not taking any chances."

"But you heard my tapes, man," he said. "I'm good."

"You were," Travis conceded. "But I have no way of knowing whether you were drunk or sober then, or what you'll likely be tomorrow."

"This blows," Rick said. "How are you gonna replace me before tomorrow?"

"Not your problem," Travis told him. The headache was his, and most likely Bill's. He'd seen the subtle nod indicating that Bill was well aware of the cost of firing Rick with so little time before the station's launch. Bill's fishing would be on hold until further notice. "Look, even though you haven't worked a single day, I'll give you a week's severance for your trouble. I think that's generous under the circumstances."

"Where am I supposed to go now?" Rick asked. "I gave up a job to come here."

"Maybe you can get it back," Travis said. "I'll call the station and tell them things didn't work out."

Rick was already shaking his head. "I burned that bridge, man."

"Then I'd suggest rehab," Bill said quietly, speaking for the first time. "Now's the perfect time for you to get your act together. I remember you when you first hit the air in Columbia a couple of decades ago. Your morning show rocketed straight to the top in the ratings. That's how you got your nickname, right?"

"I was something," Rick acknowledged with absolutely no hint of humility. "Still am."

"How long have you been away from Columbia? Ever since you got serious about drinking, I'll bet," Bill guessed. "How many other stations have there been? Two? Ten? Each one smaller than the one before?"

Rick regarded him with blurry-eyed animosity. "They didn't know a good thing when they had it. You hicks here are no better."

"Maybe not," Bill said, "but we're giving you the best advice you've probably had in years. Clean up your act."

Travis nodded. "You do that, come back here with proof you're sober and we'll talk. I agree with Bill. That's the best advice anyone will ever give you."

Rick stood up, wove a little trying to get his bearings, then let loose with a stream of profanity that topped anything Travis had heard in the locker room, even after a humiliating loss.

"That's it," Travis said, escorting him from the office. Fortunately Rick was too wobbly to put up much resistance.

He drove the deejay over to the Serenity Inn, rented him a room for the night and told him to sleep it off. By the time he got back to the station, Bill was filling Sarah in.

She turned to Travis with wide-eyed panic. "You fired the afternoon deejay the day before we go on the air? Are you insane?"

"Which part of drunk as a skunk did you miss?" Travis asked. "I wasn't about to risk putting him on the air."

"Maybe he only drinks when he's not working," she suggested.

"To all intents and purposes, this meeting was work," Travis told her. "He was three sheets to the wind for it."

She sighed. "Okay, I know you're right, but that's hours of airtime that has to be filled."

"And I'm going to fill it," Bill said. "For now, anyway. The fish haven't been biting worth a damn anyway."

Sarah's obvious relief mirrored Travis's.

"I'm going to owe you for this," Travis told him.

"You're doing me a favor," Bill insisted. "I've barely been home lately and my wife is already sick of me. That doesn't bode well for the peaceful retirement I was envisioning."

"I'll find a replacement as soon as I can," Travis promised him.

"No rush. Next time, check more references. I guarantee you the ones Rick gave you were only of people anxious to have him gone. You dig a little deeper, say, where a prospective employee worked a couple of jobs back, and you'll get more unbiased feedback. I imagine his old station in Columbia would have given you an earful. Also wouldn't hurt to pay attention to the trajectory of a man's career. Sometimes you can tell by the size of the stations if he's heading up or sliding down."

"Lesson learned," Travis said. He turned to Sarah. "So, other than panicking over this minor little crisis, are you all set for tomorrow?"

Sarah nodded. "Grace is going to be my first guest. I think we can count on her to keep things lively."

"Just try to keep her from spreading any gossip we can't substantiate," Travis warned.

"We're going to stick to talking about the Fourth of July traditions here in town," Sarah promised. "I won't let her get off track."

Travis regarded her skeptically. "Won't

that be like trying to corral a wild mustang?"

"I'm up to the challenge," she assured him.

"Okay, then, I propose we all take the rest of the day off. I'll be back here at midnight to sign us on and will stay through the night, along with the engineer, to be sure we're not having signal problems. Sarah, you'll be here early in the morning?"

"At least an hour before showtime," she promised. "Given how nervous I am, it could be even sooner. I doubt I'll sleep a wink."

"Try," Bill encouraged her. "You'll want to be rested. It's important to start off with a lot of energy, especially in the morning. People like to leave the house feeling upbeat."

"I figure we'll all be operating pretty much on adrenaline tomorrow," Travis said. "I try not to let myself think about it, but I have a lot riding on this."

"Your investment's safe," Bill assured him. "Your ad revenue's solid, even better than I anticipated. Serenity was obviously ready for something like this."

Travis looked toward Sarah, thinking about how much she was counting on him being right about *her.* "The money's the least of it," he said quietly.

Bill immediately understood. "No worries on that front, either. Your talent is highly professional."

Fortunately, Sarah seemed to have no idea they were talking about her stake in the station's success. In fact, for the past five minutes, she'd been totally engrossed in the notebook in which she wrote down a hundred little reminders a day. Going over them seemed to soothe her.

"I'd suggest a toast," Travis said, "but given how I came down on Rick for drinking, it's just as well I didn't bring over any champagne."

"Diet Coke suits me just fine," Bill said, lifting one of the half-dozen cans he seemed to go through in a day.

"Works for me, too," Sarah said, lifting her own can.

Travis popped the top on another one and tapped cans with his team. "Then here's to a successful launch and many more years together," he said. His gaze caught Sarah's and held.

Eventually she blinked and looked away, but not before he'd caught the flash of confusion, then the glimmer of hope in her eyes. It was the hope that scared him, because as much as he was starting to want more with her, he wasn't the least bit sure he had what it took to make it happen.

The Voice of Serenity, WSER, went on the air at 12:01 a.m. on July 1. Sarah and Raylene sat up to listen to it. When Travis's low, sexy drawl came over the airwaves, Sarah felt a thrill wash over her that had little to do with the station's official launch. It was all about that amazing voice and the heat it stirred inside her. Judging from Raylene's rapt expression, she wasn't immune to it either. He was, indeed, one sweet talker.

"Now that's a man who could get me out of this house," Raylene said, a poignant note in her voice.

Sarah immediately forgot about the station and Travis, and regarded Raylene with concern. "I know you're only half-joking," she said, seizing the opportunity. "Maybe it's time to think about seeing Dr. McDaniels."

Raylene was already shaking her head before Sarah completed the thought.

"I know you think you have to beat this on your own, but staying locked up in here the way you do, it's not good, sweetie," she continued despite Raylene's stubbornly set expression. "I get that a part of you is still scared that your vile ex-husband is going to come over here after you, but those days are over. He'll never lay a hand on you again. In fact, once he finishes that pitiful excuse of a jail sentence they gave him for beating you, if he's smart he'll move across the country. I swear, if he hadn't had all those connections, he'd never have gotten a plea deal like the one they gave him. Once he's out, he should thank his lucky stars and head for someplace they've never heard of him."

"Rationally, I know all that," Raylene admitted. "But I can't seem to make myself step across the threshold of the front door." Her expression sober, she said, "And I've been meaning to talk to you about that. I love taking care of Tommy and Libby, but even though I only do it once in a while, I worry that they could slip out of the house and I wouldn't be able to chase them down."

"They adore you, and you're only alone with them for a little while when the sitter's late or I'm in a bind. I'll make sure they understand that they can't go outside. The point is, though, that you need to do something to change what's going on. For your own sake, Raylene. Don't let this drag on. You're missing out on life."

"Look, this is my problem," Raylene said.

"We need to rethink this whole arrangement, Sarah. I probably should find some little apartment of my own, where I can hide out and not let my fears impact anyone else."

"No," Sarah said flatly. "You're going to remain right here. And if staying with the kids for even an hour worries you, we'll find another way to handle that. But I will keep pushing you to see Dr. McDaniels. Annie and I both will go with you. Or maybe she'll even come here, at least at first. Will you at least think about that?"

Raylene nodded, though with obvious reluctance. "In the meantime, I'd rather think about *him,*" she said, gesturing toward the radio, where Travis continued to drawl out the next best things to sexy sweet nothings that could be sent over public airwaves.

Sarah sighed as she listened. "He does have a way about him, doesn't he?"

And increasingly, it seemed, he was practicing that sweet-talking technique on her. She wondered if they'd invented a vaccine that could protect her against it, because she knew with every fiber of her being that sooner or later, if she let herself believe even half of what he said, she'd wind up getting her heart broken.

On the Fourth of July, every business on Main Street was draped with red, white and blue bunting. American flags flew all around the square and in front of the Town Hall. The sidewalks were jammed with families eagerly awaiting the start of the annual parade. Heat seemed to roll off the sidewalks and streets in waves, but there was a hint of a breeze and the sky was pure summertime blue.

On the green, vendors were already setting up with arts and crafts and food. The aroma of hot dogs and hamburgers on the grill filled the air. Given the soaring temperatures predicted, the snow cone and ice cream booths were going to do a brisk business. Sarah's favorite had always been the icy snow cones with syrups in every color of the rainbow and then some. It took her forever to decide between orange, cherry, lime and root beer. Then she'd spend the rest of the day regretting the ones she hadn't chosen.

Barriers set up outside the studio kept the area in front of the station relatively clear, so Sarah could see everything happening on the green. She'd also be able to describe the parade as it passed by, just like those big-time announcers who were on TV for the annual Macy's Thanksgiving Day parade in New York or the Rose Bowl parade in Pasadena on New Year's Day.

Not that the Serenity Fourth of July parade was in the same league. Local veterans marched in rag-tag fashion. The ones who could fit into them wore their uniforms. A couple of area high school bands and majorette groups were interspersed with floats dreamed up by local businesses.

Traditionally, Wharton's had the most lavish float, a flat trailer that this year was going to be decked out like the pharmacy's soda fountain. They'd even re-created an old-fashioned jukebox which would be playing the same rock 'n' roll music available inside the restaurant. A few high school kids, dressed up in sixties attire they'd borrowed from their parents or even grandparents, would dance as the float made its way along the route through town.

Inside the studio, Sarah was almost as excited as she had been two days ago, when Grace had joined her on the air for her first show. She gulped, though, when Travis walked into the studio and sat down opposite her.

The second they went to a commercial,

she asked, "What are you doing here?"

He winked at her. "I thought I'd help out with the commentary on the parade."

She frowned at that. "Don't you trust me?"

"Of course I do, but having two of us in the booth will make things livelier. That is the way they do it on television, you know. Listeners will love hearing us bantering about what's going on."

"I suppose."

"You're not scared of being all alone with me in this cramped little space for a couple of hours, are you?" he asked, a taunting note in his voice that Sarah couldn't ignore. "I promise I'll stay on my side of the desk, unless, of course, you'd prefer me to cozy up next to you."

"You don't scare me, Travis," she said emphatically, wishing it were true.

He grinned. "Good to know. Now, I hear the first band, so we need to get ready to go live, sugar."

She scowled at him. "I know that." Somehow she managed to keep the same sour note out of her voice as she told the audience, "We're back live from Serenity's Town Square, where I can already hear the Serenity High School marching band. They should be coming into view any second now."

"I'm anxious to hear them," Travis chimed in. "I understand they won the state band competition last year in their division."

Sarah regarded him with surprise. That hadn't been in her notes. Nor was it written down on anything in front of Travis, as far as she could tell.

"They won back when I was in school here, too," she said, suddenly carried back to the day of their triumphant return. "It just proves a school doesn't have to be huge to have a competitive band if they have a dedicated band director. Mike Walker has been director here for nearly thirty years now." She glanced out the window and caught a glimpse of the band's red-and-white uniforms turning the corner. "Here they come now, everyone. They're going to stop right in front of the grandstand to play our national anthem. Let's listen in."

She hit a switch to the microphone Bill had installed on the grandstand. It wasn't exactly a top-notch sound system, yet it was clear enough to capture not only the sound of the band but also the clear, rich voice of Annabelle Litchfield, who was singing the words of the anthem.

Sarah waited until after the last note had played and the cheers had quieted before killing that microphone and turning to her unexpected cohost.

"What did you think, Travis?"

"That little girl sure has one sweet voice," he said. "I've heard there's talk she wants to try out for *American Idol.* She wouldn't be the first Carolinian to have big success on that show, now would she?"

Once again, he'd caught Sarah by surprise. She wasn't sure why she'd dismissed his dedication to preparation. Probably because she hadn't seen any evidence of it firsthand, but clearly he'd done his homework. She was impressed.

"You seem to know quite a lot about our local talent," she said. "How about filling us in on the first float? It just made the turn onto Main Street."

The local nursery had decorated a trailer like a backyard vegetable garden. A low picket fence around the edge added charm and made it safe for the three people on board. A woman, dressed in shorts and a tanktop, held a watering can, while two young children pretended to pull weeds and toss them into a wheelbarrow. Shock registered when Sarah realized the woman was Annie and the kids were Tommy and Libby. Annie pointed out Sarah through the window of the studio, and Tommy and Libby waved wildly. Though she couldn't hear their voices, they were clearly shouting, "Mommy!" She waved back, thrilled by the surprise.

Apparently Travis had figured out what was going on, because he told listeners all about the float, then added that the cutest kids in town, the children of his cohost, were aboard the float.

A few minutes after the float passed the grandstand, Annie brought Libby and Tommy to the sidewalk outside the station, where they again waved to catch Sarah's attention.

Travis announced a commercial break, then told her, "Go outside and say hello. You have a couple of minutes, and I'll cover if you don't get back before we're back on the air."

She didn't even hesitate. "Thanks. I won't be long."

She ran outside and scooped up the kids, giving them a tight hug.

"Did you see us?" Tommy asked excitedly. "Did you? It was a surprise."

"It certainly was," she said. "And you were wonderful. You did a great job. I'm so proud of you." She glanced up at Annie. "How'd you get talked into doing this?"

"I was supposed to help with the spa's

float, but then the nursery was in a bind. They had a great idea, but the family that was supposed to ride on the float bailed. Maddie agreed to loan me out, and we decided to borrow your kids."

"Why not hers or even Helen's?" Sarah asked.

"Helen's little girl is riding on the Sullivan's float with Erik, and Maddie's kids are on the spa's. I probably should have asked, but I thought it would be a great surprise."

"It was. I wish Walter could have seen them."

"Oh, he did. He's around here someplace. He was snapping pictures like crazy."

Just then Walter rounded the corner and made his way toward them. Tommy ran for him, shouting, "Daddy, did you take our picture?"

Walter laughed as he scooped up her son. "I probably took a hundred of them," Walter said, then winked at Sarah. "I'll bring some prints over for you."

"Thank you," she said, surprised that he didn't seem bothered that the kids had been on a float. Although efforts had been made to make sure they were safe, usually he'd be pitching a fit about the dangers. "What do you think your parents will have to say when they see the pictures?"

He frowned. "It might be best if they don't see them. I'll get a half-hour lecture on how they've demeaned the Price name."

"I was sort of expecting that from you," she admitted.

"New leaf," he told her, holding her gaze. "I told you I'm thinking for myself these days, and all I could think today was that they looked like they were having a blast."

"Me, too," she said, relieved by the changes she'd seen lately in his overall attitude. "I need to get back inside. I'm working." She turned to Annie. "Thanks for the surprise. It was a great one."

"See you at the house later," Annie said. "Why don't you invite Travis along to the barbecue? Tom and Jeanette will be there. I think Mom and Dad have invited half the people in town. Then we'll walk back to the green later to watch the fireworks."

"I'll think about it," Sarah said, then hesitated. "What are we going to do about Raylene? I've tried to talk her into going, but she's flat-out turned me down."

"Me, too," Annie said. "But I'll try again."

Sarah ran back inside and nearly collided with a tall, willowy woman who was literally perfect from head to toe — perfectly highlighted blond hair, designer sunglasses and

176

a halter-top sundress that showed off per-fectly tanned shoulders. She even had the perfect pedicure on display in sandals that had probably cost more than Sarah made in a month. Mariah Litchfield, if she wasn't mistaken — Annabelle's mother.

"Thank you again," Mariah said to Travis as she backed out of the studio. Her voice was as sugary as a mint julep and twice as seductive. "I just had to run right over and thank you in person for the sweet things you said about my daughter."

"Every word was the gospel truth," Travis told her. He gestured toward the blinking on-air sign that was signaling the end of the commercial break. "Gotta go, sugar. You stop by again sometime."

His low, sexy tone and the invitation he'd uttered hit Sarah like a blow to the stomach. It all sounded so familiar. Even though she'd known deep down that she wasn't anything special to Travis, she'd hoped otherwise. Damn the man, she thought, then bit back a sigh that would be way too telling. No, the fault was hers for taking one word he'd ever said to her seriously. He was just a big ole flirt, a label he'd never even tried to deny.

Unaware of her turmoil, he caught sight of her in the doorway of the studio and smiled his trademark grin, the one that set off butterflies. "Welcome back, sugar. We're on the air in five."

Reminding herself that she was a professional now, she took her seat, plastered a smile on her face and got through the final half hour of the parade, exchanging banter with Travis as if there weren't a thing in the world wrong.

The instant the show ended, though, and Bill replaced them on the air, she bolted from the studio. She grabbed her purse and would have torn out of the building if Travis hadn't blocked her way.

"Where's the fire?" he asked, regarding her with a puzzled expression.

"I have someplace I need to be," she said tightly.

"Away from me, I'm guessing," he said, his gaze holding hers.

"Not everything is about you, Travis. I'm going to a barbecue with my kids and my friends."

"I know. I'm going, too. I figured we could ride over together. Carpooling is good for the environment, right?"

Dismay crept over her. Annie had said she should invite him, so she'd assumed if she didn't, he wouldn't be there. Obviously Jeanette and Tom had thought to include him.

"As if you give two hoots about the environment," she mumbled.

Travis regarded her with confusion. "Mind telling me what got your knickers in a twist? You were fine an hour ago."

"That was before I heard you and Mariah Litchfield," she blurted, then could have kicked herself. Now he'd think she was jealous, which she wasn't. She was annoyed. There was a difference, or at least she thought she could make a strong case that there was.

A spark lit his eyes, making them dance like sunlight glimmering on the lake. "You're jealous!" he gloated.

"I most certainly am not. I just thought you had better sense than to flirt with a woman who's almost old enough to be your mother."

He seemed to be having a very hard time keeping a straight face. "Sugar, I enjoy flirting with a pretty woman, no question about it, but I draw the line at going one bit further with married women. And, for the record, Mariah's not anywhere close to being old enough to be my mother. A big sister, maybe, but that's it."

"Whatever," she muttered. "If we're going to Dana Sue and Ronnie's, let's go."

"You gonna drive or should I?"

"I will," she said. "That way, if you get on my nerves, I can run off and leave you there."

He laughed. "Something tells me that the likelihood of me getting on your nerves is about a thousand percent. The only real questions are how long it will take, and which of my many flaws will tick you off?"

"At least that's one thing we can agree on," she said, enjoying the sight of Travis trying to cram his long legs into the passenger side of the little VW bug she'd had since before her marriage. It wasn't the ideal car for two kids, but she loved it, and it was hers, free and clear. She'd happily left that monstrous SUV Walter had wanted her to drive back in Alabama for him to fill with gas about every ten minutes.

"Sorry there's not more legroom," she said.

Travis gave her a considering look. "You don't sound sorry. You sound as if you're enjoying the fact that I might be miserable and uncomfortable."

She met his gaze, her expression as innocent as she could possibly make it. "Oops! Caught me."

His gaze narrowed. "Are you really sure you want to taunt me, sugar?"

She hesitated, as if giving the question careful consideration, then nodded. "Actually, I think I do. It's satisfying. I like knowing I can get under your skin, the same way you get under mine."

"Okay, then." Before she could blink, he managed to turn sideways in the seat, reached out to cup the back of her head and sealed his mouth over hers. She gasped, which was a huge mistake, because he deepened the kiss. Her pulse scrambled. Her heart raced. And every single sane thought flew out of her head.

Instead, it was all about the fire licking through her, the faint stubble on his cheeks from being at the station just about 24/7 for the past couple of days, the fresh scent of soap, the way the soft cotton of his T-shirt felt when she bunched it up in her fist, his heat radiating out toward her already overheated body.

The initial anger behind the kiss gentled. He tasted and savored. She trembled and stopped fighting it. If she'd been capable of clear thought, she might have rated it as the best kiss of her life.

When, at last, he slowly released her, he looked into her eyes. His were like a storm-tossed sea now.

"Just so you know, I have no interest in

kissing Mariah Litchfield," he said quietly. "You're the only woman in Serenity I've kissed, the only one I'm interested in kissing. And before you can say hell will freeze over before I kiss you again, let me assure you that you're wrong. This will happen again, sugar."

"Oh," she whispered, not sure what to make of his fierce tone.

"And also, just so you know, I am not one damn bit happy about that," he added. "It complicates things. Work. My life. All of it."

"I know," she said, her own annoyance gone in the face of his admission. "Maybe you're wrong. Maybe this was like a one-time thing because you were exasperated with me and you thought I was jealous." She nodded, pleased with her analysis. It made sense.

He chuckled, but there was a bitter note to it. "Yeah, that's it. You keep believing that, sugar."

She had to, she thought, because she didn't dare let herself believe anything else. Not even for a minute.

9

Ever since he'd started spending every weekend in Serenity, Walter had been getting nonstop phone calls from his mother complaining that he was never around. He'd translated that to mean that she was ticked off that he hadn't been available for any of the women she'd picked as prospective replacements for Sarah.

On Thursday afternoon when he saw his parents' number on caller ID on his cell phone, he sucked in a deep breath and reluctantly answered.

"Hello, Mother."

"Well, it's about time you took one of my calls," she said with a sniff.

"I've been busy at the mill and spending time with my children."

"As long as you're not getting involved with that woman again," she said, then gasped. "Oh my God, you aren't, are you? Surely you have more sense than that."

He sighed. "Mother, you won. Sarah's out of my life. Why can't you let it alone and at least remember that as the mother of your grandchildren, she deserves your respect. Now tell me what's on your mind."

"I just wanted to make sure you're free for dinner tomorrow night."

"You know I'm going to Serenity tomorrow night," he said, his impatience returning at once.

"Just this once couldn't you stay here? This dinner's important."

"Why? I'm sure it's because there's someone you want me to meet."

"Actually you already know her."

Dread settled in his stomach. "Oh?"

"Yes," she said cheerfully. "I convinced Patricia Warren to join us."

She'd caught him completely off guard with that one. It was the last name he'd expected to hear. "Why the hell would you do that?" he asked, bewildered.

"The two of you were engaged before you met that little tart at college," she said evenly. "She was always more suitable for you."

"In your opinion," Walter said slowly. "Not in mine. Patricia and I were over long before I even met Sarah."

"She still loves you."

184

"She told you that?" he asked incredulously. "I doubt it. I'm pretty sure she hates my guts. She was picking out silverware and china by the time I had the gumption to call things off. It was yet another situation that I allowed to get out of hand in an attempt to please you and Dad."

"She's forgiven you," his mother assured him. "I've been able to help her see that you were young and immature back then, that you didn't know what you wanted."

"Actually I had a very clear picture of what I didn't want — Patricia. Mother, we were a very bad match then, and we'd be an even worse match now. Forget dinner. I'm going out of town, as planned."

"I will never forgive you if you embarrass me like that."

"Emotional blackmail isn't going to work. You set this up, you can deal with the fallout. Tell her I had to see my children. That, at least, is probably more truthful than anything you told her to get her to agree to this farce."

"Why are you being so hateful? I'm just trying to help you get your life on track."

He realized with a blinding flash of insight what he had to do, what he should have done years ago. "Mother, if my life's going to get on track, I'm the one who'll have to put it there. Dad can't do it. Neither can you. And I'm increasingly convinced that it will never happen here."

"Walter Price, what are you suggesting?" she demanded with genuine dismay.

"I believe I'm saying that my future is in some other city, in some other job."

"You can't be serious!"

He hesitated for less than a second, then said, "You know, I think I am. About time, wouldn't you say? Don't worry about breaking the news to Dad. I'll tell him before I leave tonight."

"Tonight? You're planning to pack up and leave for God knows where tonight?"

"No time like the present," he said, his resolve building. "I'll let you know where I am once I decide what's next for me."

"You were always too impulsive," she accused him. "You never thought things through. If you had, you would never have married that woman and ruined your life."

"My life will only be ruined if I stay here one more day. 'Bye, Mother. I do love you."

He hung up before she could say anything that might change his mind. To his astonishment, instead of feeling panicked over his decision, for the first time since he'd left college and come back to Alabama, he could actually breathe again.

■ ■ ■ ■

Sarah was sitting on the back patio with a glass of sweet tea when she heard a car pull into the driveway. She'd spent a lot of time on her own in recent days trying to make sense of that kiss Travis had planted on her and the regret he'd expressed about doing it . . . or even wanting to.

Now, every time she saw him, she felt even more awkward. Apparently he did, too, because he seemed to be going to extremes to avoid her. They only communicated by Post-it notes left on their respective desks.

A few minutes after she heard the slam of a car door, Walter came around the side of the house. Thankfully, his arrival no longer had the power to stir all her insecurities.

"I thought I'd find you out here," he said. "Any more of that tea?"

"Sure." She stood up, then took a closer look at him. There was something different about him, but she couldn't put her finger on it. "Everything okay?"

"Better than okay," he said. "Bring me that tea, if you don't mind, and I'll explain."

She returned a few minutes later with a full pitcher and another glass. She poured his, then added some to her own glass before meeting his gaze. "What's going on?"

"I've left home," he announced. "For good, I mean. Quit my job at the mill, too."

She stared at him in shock. "You're kidding me. How'd that happen?"

"It doesn't matter really. You should know, though, that I have plenty of savings in the bank. This won't affect your alimony or child support, at least not in the short term."

"That's not the first thing that came to mind," she said honestly. "All I can think about is how stunned your parents must be."

"I left Dad ranting and raving about how he'd never take me back at the mill. I hung up on Mother before she got too worked up."

"Oh, my." She glanced at him. "Is this somehow going to turn out to be one more thing that's my fault?"

He laughed at the question. "More than likely."

She nodded. "Good to know, in case they decide to come gunning for me."

They sipped their tea in companionable silence for a while. Eventually, Walter said, "Sarah, I'm really sorry I didn't do this sooner. We might have had a chance, if I had."

"You had to do it when it was right for

you," she told him. "I never asked or expected you to do anything this drastic. I always understood you felt you had an obligation to your family."

"My first obligation should have been to you and the kids. I should have seen that making a break was the only way to save us, to save myself. I spent way too long trying to do what my parents expected of me. What kind of man does that?"

"One who loves his parents and feels indebted to them," she said. "What now? Do you have any idea what you want to do or where you'd like to live?"

"Someplace closer to Serenity, I think. Maybe even here, so I can spend more time with Tommy."

Sarah stilled, but even before she could react, he was saying, "Don't make anything out of that. I meant to say Libby, too."

"But she's still an afterthought, isn't she?" Sarah said wearily.

"I don't want her to be. I love her. I'm just not sure how to deal with a little girl. I was a roughhousing kid. I had to be to fit in. Otherwise, I'd have been the kid who lived in the big house on the hill, whose parents held the power to fire the other kids' moms or dads. I didn't have sisters. Libby's so delicate, even now, it scares me."

Sarah smiled despite herself. "Trust me, she's not all that fragile. She has the Price will of iron."

He chuckled. "More's the pity, huh?"

"I don't know," she said thoughtfully. "I think maybe it'll be a good thing when she grows up and starts dating."

"She's not dating for at least thirty years," Walter said in a horrified tone.

"You may be forced to rethink that," Sarah told him, amused by his dismay. "Otherwise the two of you are doomed to butting heads."

"Well, at least it's not going to come up overnight," he said. "Maybe I'll have time to get used to the idea." He turned to face her. "How would you feel if I stick around town, or at least someplace nearby?"

"I think it will be great for you and the kids," she said honestly. "But I will ask you to do one thing for me. Don't tell Tommy and Libby until you're sure it's going to work out, okay? Find a job, figure out where you're going to live and then tell them. I don't want them to get their hopes up and have it not work out."

"Fair enough," he said, then stood up. He bent down and brushed a kiss across her forehead. "Thanks. I'll be in touch."

"Good night, Walter, and congratulations!"

"For what?"

"The first day of the rest of your life."

He laughed. "It is, isn't it? I'll be damned."

After he'd gone, she waited for regrets to roll over her. Regrets that they hadn't stuck it out. Regrets that it was too late for the two of them. Instead, though, all she felt was relief that Walter had made the break before he'd wasted a lifetime.

After greeting all the regulars, Travis settled into his usual booth in the back at Wharton's. Coming here wasn't half as much fun now that Sarah was no longer working here. In fact, lately he'd been coming by, grabbing a couple of to-go orders, then taking the food to the station for both of them.

Sarah, sadly, didn't seem to appreciate the gesture. In fact, since the kiss, she'd been giving him a wide berth. He told himself that was the way it needed to be, that in fact it was the way he'd intended to play it, but it annoyed the daylights out of him that Sarah seemed to agree. He was not unaware of the irony.

Today, though, he'd agreed to meet Tom for lunch. Since the station had gone on the air, they'd hardly had five minutes to catch up. Unfortunately, it seemed his cousin was running late, which gave Grace the perfect excuse to slide into the booth across from him.

"So, have you asked her out yet?" she inquired.

Travis regarded her blankly. "Who?"

"Sarah, of course."

"She works for me. It would be inappropriate for us to date." He sounded so darn self-righteous it was unnerving. A few months ago appropriate behavior would have been the last thing on his mind.

"Then what the dickens were you doing kissing her on the Fourth of July?" Grace demanded.

Travis was pretty sure he'd never blushed in his entire life, but he could feel the heat climbing into his cheeks now. "What kiss was that?"

"In the alley behind the station," Grace said impatiently. "The two of you were all jammed up inside that teeny little car of hers, kissing the daylights out of each other. Or would you have me believe the quarters were so tight, you accidentally locked lips?"

"What were you doing in the alley? Were you spying on us?"

"I have better things to do than spy on people," she said with a huff. "But I do keep my eyes open. How do you think I know so much?"

Travis debated whether to dismiss the incident as momentary insanity, pretend Grace needed to have her eyesight checked, or just deny ever being anywhere near that alley.

"Cat got your tongue?" Grace prodded.

"Okay, I'm not going to deny the kiss," he said eventually. "But it was a one-time thing. It doesn't imply there's anything going on between me and Sarah. Please don't start spreading it around town that the two of us are involved. It would just embarrass her."

She studied him intently, then nodded. "Okay, say I forget about what I saw. Will you tell me why on earth you're *not* dating?"

"We work together. It's as simple as that." He figured sticking to his story was the only way to get everyone to believe it. Maybe even he would buy it eventually.

Grace rolled her eyes. "So, kissing a coworker, employee or whatever, that's okay? But not dating?"

Travis chuckled at her interpretation. He could hardly defend his logic. "No, the kiss was a mistake."

"Didn't look like it to me, but what do I

know?" she said with a shrug.

"Quite a lot," he said. "But this time you got it wrong. Let it go, okay?"

She shook her head, her expression filled with disgust. "Some people don't have the sense the good Lord gave a duck." She stood up. "I'll bring your soda and a coffee for Tom. Maybe he'll believe this nonsense you're selling."

She stalked away just as Tom arrived and slid into the seat she'd vacated.

"Why's Grace in such a sour mood?"

"She didn't like my answers to her questions."

Tom regarded him blankly. "Do I want to know more?"

"I don't think so." He hesitated, then said, "Can I ask you something?"

"Of course."

"How the hell do women's minds work? I thought I knew. I mean, I've dated probably a hundred different women over the years. Learned something from every single one of them, but I have to say when it comes to how they think, I'm at a loss."

"Are we talking about Grace or Sarah?" Tom asked.

"Sarah, of course. I kissed her. I know I shouldn't have, but I did. The thing of it is, she kissed me back. Now she's avoiding

194

me." He shrugged. "Or I'm avoiding her. It's hard to tell. We're communicating by little notes left all over the office."

"Have you called her on it?"

"No," Travis admitted.

"Why not?"

"I'm thinking maybe it's better this way. Why take chances that we'll be tempted to kiss again? Maybe even a whole lot more?"

Tom shook his head, his lips quirking in amusement. "And you think *she's* sending mixed messages? What about you?"

"Guilty," he conceded.

"Let's cut to the chase. Are you attracted to her?"

"Yes."

"Are we talking about the kind of attraction that could lead to something more, or a one-night-stand attraction?"

"She's not a one-night-stand kind of woman," Travis said. "It would make it easier if she were."

"Glad you see that," Tom told him.

"Then you can see why she scares me to death. I don't do the hearts and flowers, forever stuff."

"Bull," Tom said. "Ever since you hit your teens, you've been using the excuse that you're just like your daddy to avoid making a commitment. But down deep you want exactly what I have with Jeanette. I know you do."

"I might want it," Travis conceded, "but I'm bound to screw it up."

"How will you ever know that unless you try?"

"Come on," Travis scoffed. "I can't imagine a day without flirting with every woman who crosses my path. It's who I am. Wives, even girlfriends, tend to frown on that kind of thing."

"Not if you've made them feel secure. Not if they know there's a difference between all that casual talk and the real thing that you save only for them."

"I want to believe that," Travis said. "I really do. But Sarah's not that woman. She has just about zero self-confidence, thanks to her ex-husband. If I say boo to another woman, it'll freak her out. It's already happened. When I joked around with Mariah Litchfield at the station, Sarah overheard me and got a little bit crazy."

"Only because she doesn't know yet where *she* stands with you," Tom insisted.

Travis sighed. "Maybe that's the real problem. *I* don't know where she stands with me. Until I figure that out, I need to keep my distance."

Unfortunately, he feared he'd be constitu-

196

tionally incapable of keeping his distance for long. Teasing Sarah, putting a flush on her cheeks, keeping her off-kilter was all more fun than he'd had in ages.

"You just stop that right this second," Sarah said to Travis after he'd taunted her with yet another flirtatious remark suggesting that he found her attractive.

The station had been on the air for two weeks now. There had been glitches behind the scenes and on-air flubs, but for the most part WSER was a hit with the residents of Serenity. Grace kept it tuned in all day long at Wharton's.

Sarah's working relationship with Travis, uneasy in the first days after *the kiss,* had returned to something that passed for normal. He bantered. She tried to ignore it. Mostly, it was innocent, but the flirting had started to creep back in, and her nerves were once again jittery every time they were in the same room. She really had to get a grip. The only way to do that was to set boundaries.

"If I were of a mind to, Travis, I could sue you for sexual harassment if you keep saying things like that," she told him, even though she was struggling to keep a straight face. A part of her liked the teasing that made her feel like a desirable woman. She was trying hard to tame that part of her.

"But you won't," he said confidently.

"Oh, and why is that?"

"Because you love it when I tease you."

"At least you admit you're teasing," she said, fighting to hide the disappointment she felt at the acknowledgment.

He gave her a long, considering look that made her pulse jump. "You so sure about that, sugar?"

"Of course, I am." Because every time she allowed herself to think for a single second that he might not be, she heard Walter's critical voice in her head telling her she was too fat, a lousy mother or whatever other hurtful thing he could think of to say. Not that he'd said anything remotely like that recently, but the old wounds were still there. Until she underwent some magical extreme makeover in her own head, she'd continue to see herself that way.

Up until that moment, Travis had been lazing back in an old office chair that he'd apparently found in some thrift shop. He rose as if he had all the time in the world, his gaze locked on her face. On her mouth, if she wasn't mistaken. She trembled as he took a step closer, and then another.

"What are you doing?" she asked, trying

to slide her own chair backwards in the cramped space of the studio.

"Just a little experiment," he said.

Sarah scrambled around behind her desk. "Don't even think about it. We've already done a whole lot more experimenting than we should have."

His eyes flashed at the challenge. "Are you talking about that nothing little kiss on the Fourth of July?" he inquired.

"It was *not* a nothing little kiss," she said, then could have yanked her tongue out for making such a revealing statement.

"I'm thinking I can improve on it," he said with quiet intensity, already reaching for her. "Like this, maybe." His lips grazed her cheek. "Or this?" He found her mouth, then settled there for just a beat. He sighed.

"I haven't been able to think about any- thing but this for two weeks now," he said, sounding exasperated with himself. "I think I need to make sure I'm remembering right."

His lips found hers again.

It was the kind of sweet, heady kiss that women dreamed of, wove entire fantasies around. It was confident and tender, de- manding yet gentle, possessive and intrigu- ing. Just enough to lure, not so much that it set off warnings. It was the kind of kiss

Sarah had forgotten was possible. The kiss in the car had been good. This one was amazing!

As her blood heated and her body swayed, she lost all sense of indignation and most of her common sense. The only thing that mattered was this man's mouth on hers, reminding her that she was all woman. For a few fleeting seconds, she was even able to imagine that she was beautiful.

When Travis finally stepped away — way too soon and not nearly soon enough — she was dazed. And maybe just a little bit enchanted.

When he gave her a cocky grin and left her standing there, with at least a half-dozen passersby on Azalea Drive staring in the studio window, she covered her face in her hands.

Enchanted, she thought to herself. That had to be it, because otherwise what had just happened here was totally insane. They could not keep kissing and calling it an experiment or a mistake or anything else. Kissing this good, however it started out, was pretty much bound to lead to a whole lot more.

10

Sarah was sitting at the kitchen table, staring glumly into space, when Annie walked in, looking suspiciously like some sort of avenging angel. Sarah's gaze immediately narrowed. Annie on a mission was never good.

"Did I know you were coming over?" she asked her friend.

"You should have," Annie said, her expression grim. "Where's Raylene?"

"Playing a game with the kids in the living room," Sarah said distractedly, then glanced at the clock. "Or maybe getting them into bed." She shrugged. "I'm not sure."

Annie just shook her head. "I'll get her. My mom, Maddie, Helen and Jeanette will be here any minute. You could start making margaritas."

Sarah regarded her with confusion. "What's going on?"

"We're having an intervention," Annie replied.

"With Raylene?"

"No, with you."

Annie walked away before Sarah could think of a single thing to say. She didn't need an intervention. She hadn't done anything of which she was ashamed, wasn't engaging in any irrational behavior. . . . Oh, sweet heaven, they were coming here because of the kissing!

"Are the kids asleep?" she asked when Raylene followed Annie into the kitchen, her expression as bewildered as Sarah's had probably been earlier.

"Out like little angels," Raylene confirmed.

Sarah whirled on Annie. "In that case, just so you know, I resent this. I do not need an intervention," she said fiercely.

"Tell that to someone who didn't catch you kissing the daylights out of Travis McDonald in plain view of anyone who happened to be on the Town Square this afternoon," Annie said. "There I was, walking down the street with my husband, who was in town for about fifteen minutes because of the All-Star break, and what did we see but the two of you locking lips. Even Ty was shocked."

Sarah rolled her eyes. "I doubt that. I'm sure he's seen people kissing before and, assuming you were overjoyed about him being in town, he's probably even been doing a fair amount of kissing himself."

"Not the point," Annie said, blushing.

Raylene's eyes lit up as she listened to the exchange. She immediately turned to Sarah. "You kissed Travis?"

"He kissed me, if you want to be technical," Sarah admitted. "But, yes, there was kissing."

"In the studio?" Raylene asked, turning back to grin at Annie. "With that humongous window?"

Annie nodded. "See why somebody needs to straighten her out in a big fat hurry? I swear if Ty hadn't had to go right back to Atlanta, I would have insisted he have a talk with Travis."

Raylene once again faced Sarah, her eyes twinkling merrily. "Maybe you should have drawn the blinds."

"That is so not the point," Annie said.

"If it ever happens again, I'll be sure to do that," Sarah promised Raylene, her tone wry. "But I'm pretty sure this was a one-time thing." Since they obviously hadn't heard anything about the other kiss, it was best to keep quiet about that. It might suggest a pattern, and Annie was already pretty worked up as it was.

"You haven't made the margaritas," Annie said, already opening cupboards to find the glasses.

"I don't even know if there's tequila," Sarah responded, not budging. This was Annie's impromptu show. She didn't intend to help her out one little bit.

"How can a Sweet Magnolia not have tequila?" Annie said, rummaging in the pantry and then emerging victoriously with a half-full bottle. "Found it."

"There's probably no frozen limeade," Sarah said. Maybe without margaritas everyone would have their say and leave. She could just sit stoically and listen, perhaps nod from time to time.

"Of course there's limeade," Raylene said, plucking a container from the freezer. "I put it on the grocery list myself. Walter picked it up when he shopped last weekend."

Annie whirled in Raylene's direction, openmouthed with shock, her attention at least momentarily diverted from Sarah and Travis and their very public kiss. "Walter's doing your grocery shopping? What's that about?"

Raylene shrugged. "Ask Sarah. He belongs to her."

Sarah frowned. "Walter does not belong to me, not anymore. The short version is that he quit his job in Alabama and is looking for something nearby, so he can spend more time with the kids. He's staying at the Serenity Inn full-time now."

"And the hits just keep on coming," Annie said, looking dazed. "Are you okay with that?"

"It's going to be great for the kids, so I'll manage," Sarah said. "And to be honest, we're getting along a lot better now than we did when we were married. He's even helping out around here, which explains the trip to the grocery store. He's trying to make himself useful, something he never voluntarily did while we were together."

"Does he want you back?" Annie asked, clearly indignant at the idea.

"Not that he's mentioned," Sarah said. "The subject of reconciliation did come up once, but we both dismissed it as an absurd idea."

"Are you so sure about that?" Annie scoffed. "Men never say what they want, but women always know. Does he want you back?"

Sarah shook her head. "Not an option," she said flatly.

"Well, thank God for that." Annie's gaze narrowed. "Does his presence have anything to do with the kissing between you and Travis? Were you trying to prove something to Walter? Or to yourself?"

"Absolutely not. I'm telling you it was just one of those things that happen."

The back door swung open again and Dana Sue, Maddie, Helen and Jeanette walked in carrying bags of chips and a sealed container that doubtless held Dana Sue's spicy guacamole. With luck, the bags also held some of Dana Sue's famously tempting appetizers, and Sarah could keep her mouth stuffed with those so she wouldn't have to answer any more questions.

"I'll bet I know what this is about," Jeanette said as soon as they were all settled around the kitchen table with their drinks. "Half the town is talking about the smoldering kiss between Travis and Sarah today."

"Oh, God," Sarah whispered, burying her head in her arms for the second time that day.

"How did I miss that?" Helen asked. "I have to stop going to the courthouse. I swear I never hear anything good over there, and I certainly never see anyone kissing."

Maddie patted Helen's shoulder sympathetically. "But you do good things. That's more important than being up-to-date on the local gossip."

Dana Sue's worried gaze settled on Sarah. "Do you need to talk about what happened?"

"To be honest, I'd like to forget about it," Sarah told her, then gestured around the table. "That doesn't seem likely, at least tonight. And if Jeanctte's right that everyone is talking about this, I may never be able to show my face in town again."

"Oh, hogwash!" Dana Sue said. "Sweet Magnolias don't worry about a little talk. We thrive on it. Right, girls?"

"To be honest, I wasn't so thrilled when Cal and I were at the center of all the gossip," Maddie contradicted. "And Bill and I before that."

"But that's the point," Dana Sue said. "Gossip comes and goes. Tomorrow it might be all about Sarah and Travis, but by this time next week, it'll be somebody else. Annie, sweetie, you ought to know that as well as anyone. Nobody mentions a thing about Ty's tabloid scandals anymore."

Annie groaned. "Gee, Mom, thanks for reminding me of that joyous time in my life."

"I'm just saying that this is nothing for

Sarah to worry about," Dana Sue said.

Annie frowned at her mother. "I'm not worrying about the gossip. I'm worried about *Sarah*. She's obviously being taken advantage of by this player." She turned to Jeanette. "No offense."

Jeanette laughed. "Hey, nobody's trying to deny that Travis has a past. He owns up to it himself."

"Which makes him absolutely, positively the worst possible choice for Sarah. She's sweet and naive and vulnerable," Annie declared.

Sarah scowled at her friend. "Thanks for the vote of confidence. You make it sound like I'm seventeen, and not all that smart to boot."

"Oh, face it, you *are* an innocent when it comes to this kind of thing," Annie said. "And you're ripe for a rebound relationship. Which would be all well and good, if you weren't destined to get hurt with this particular man."

"I don't think a kiss, albeit a very public one, indicates a thing in the world about a relationship," Sarah said. "We're coworkers. Actually, he's my boss. That's our official relationship. End of story."

Helen's eyes lit up, her barracuda attorney instincts kicking in. "Sexual harassment? I'll sue him if you want me to."

"There was a lot of mutual consent in what I saw," Annie admitted grudgingly.

"Doesn't matter," Helen replied. "I can make a case. Sarah, is that what you want? If I even threaten to take him to court, it'll put a stop to this once and for all."

Sarah had tired of the discussion. She stood up and looked around the table. After her two margaritas, everyone was starting to look a little fuzzy. "I do not want to sue anyone. I can handle this, whatever it is. I do not want to discuss it to death, either. I'm going to bed. I have to be on the air at the crack of dawn, and I do not want to have a raging headache while I'm trying to be all perky and informative."

She leaned down and gave Annie a fierce hug. "I love you for caring so much, but let it go. If you can't do that, then stage an intervention with Travis. I might even enjoy being there for that."

The diabolical gleam that immediately lit Annie's eyes was not reassuring.

"I was joking," Sarah told her flatly. "Really. No more interventions, period, okay?"

"But —"

"None," Sarah said emphatically, then had another thought. "And don't send your husbands after him, either." She waited for the nods of agreement that were awfully slow in coming. "Okay, then. Good night, everyone."

She hoped her departure would put an end to the discussion of the kiss, if not to the entire gathering. Judging from the low murmur of voices she could hear long after she'd checked on Tommy and Libby, taken a shower and climbed into bed, the rest of them still had plenty to say.

She wondered if she ought to call Travis and warn him, but decided against it. He was a worldly, macho guy. He could defend himself. Then, again, he'd probably never stirred the wrath of a group of women like the Sweet Magnolias before.

Travis hung up his phone, shook his head in bemusement and went looking for Sarah.

"I just had a call from Annie Townsend," he told her. "She seems to think I should stay away from you."

Sarah regarded him with an innocent expression he didn't quite buy. "Did you put her up to that?" he asked.

"Of course not," she said, though there was a twinkle in her eyes that suggested she knew more than she was admitting.

"How about . . . ?" He glanced at a message slip. "Helen Decatur-Whitney? You know her, too, right?"

A little of the color drained out of her face then, but she gave him a confirming nod.

He gave her a sour look. "Yeah, she wanted to warn me about sexual harassment at work. She said she'd be happy to talk to me about the law. She's another friend of yours, right?"

Sarah nodded.

He waved more pink slips in her direction. "I've also had calls from Dana Sue Sullivan and Maddie Maddox. Hell, even Tom's wife called. I haven't returned any of those calls yet, but since they were all at that barbecue on the Fourth, something tells me all the calls have something to do with you. What did you do, sic the whole damn town on me?"

Her lips twitched, her expression turned guilty and then she chuckled. "Sorry. Actually I told them all to lay off and leave you alone."

"Well, obviously they didn't listen."

"Not my fault. You're the one who kissed me in plain view of the whole stupid town. This is the consequence. You've created a public uproar."

He shook his head wearily. "And here I thought I was kissing a mature woman who was capable of saying no if she didn't want me to."

"I am. I was," she said, clearly flustered. "They're just a little overly protective."

"Do I need to hire a lawyer?" he asked, not entirely in jest. "Or a bodyguard?"

She laughed, then sobered and shook her head. "I think you're safe, but you might want to put a lid on the kissing."

He gave her a belligerent look. "And what if I don't want to?"

She blinked at that. "You'd risk a lawsuit just to kiss mc?"

"The sane part of me would like to think I know better. The part that's itching to kiss you right this second suggests otherwise." The admission made his palms sweat. He'd known putting himself within a few feet of temptation every single day wasn't smart, but he'd done it anyway. "I need to get out of here."

He was almost out the door when Sarah spoke. He turned and met her gaze.

"Travis, I'm not going to sue you," she said solemnly.

Heat spiraled through him. It wasn't just the promise. It was the hint he could swear he heard that she wanted him to do it again. She'd left the damn door open. He could see it on her face.

Travis wanted nothing more than to walk back to her desk, pull her into his arms and test her on that, but he didn't. He just gave her a jaunty, careless salute. "Good to know, sugar. I'll keep that in mind the next time I have an urge to play with fire."

Mary Vaughn had been feeling queasy all morning, but her lunch plans with Rory Sue were too important to cancel. She intended to convince her daughter that she belonged back in Serenity working for her in the real estate business. They'd make an outstanding team. Rory Sue had her gift of gab and her steely determination.

She'd tried out her strategy on Sonny last night and he'd helped her fine-tune it. He wasn't going to be at lunch because he tended to cave in the second Rory Sue turned her big ole tear-filled eyes on him.

Unfortunately, when Mary Vaughn walked into Sullivan's, she saw that her daughter was with her granddaddy. She had to fight the desire to yell at Howard for intruding. How could she, though, when she knew how much he and Rory Sue adored each other?

"I wasn't expecting to see you," she said, leaning down to give her father-in-law a kiss, then brushing another one across her daughter's cheek.

"Sorry to crash the party," Howard said. "But I haven't seen nearly enough of our girl during this visit. I was afraid she'd get out of town before we had a chance to spend any time together."

"Well, if I have my way, she'll come home for good," Mary Vaughn said.

"Mom, you know I don't want to live here," Rory Sue said with disdain, then regarded her grandfather apologetically. "No offense. I know this town means the world to you, but it's boring."

"That depends on what kind of excitement you're looking for," Howard said.

"I agree," Mary Vaughn said. Her agreeing with anything Howard said was rare enough that both he and Rory Sue stared at her. She decided to stick with her plan.

Regarding her daughter with an unyielding expression, she asked, "Tell me this, have you found a job yet?"

"I've only been out of college a couple of weeks," Rory Sue said airily. "Give me a break."

"Actually, it's been a month. How hard have you looked?" Mary Vaughn persisted. "I know you. You're hanging out with your friends over in Charleston and probably haven't set up a single interview."

"I've had two interviews," Rory Sue said triumphantly.

"Did either of them look promising?" her granddaddy asked.

"One woman called back, but I said no. The pay was lousy."

"Entry level pay usually is," Howard said. "You have to work for a while before you make the kind of money you'll need to live in a city like Charleston."

"Daddy said he'd help me out with rent," Rory Sue said.

Mary Vaughn frowned. Sonny hadn't mentioned a thing about that to her. She'd thought they were together on getting Rory Sue back here. She wondered just which of her many wiles Rory Sue had used to win that concession from him.

Undaunted by the setback, she forged ahead. "Okay, let me spell this out for you," she told her daughter. "If you want to live in Charleston, you have until the end of the month to find a job and a place to live. And don't be counting on help from your daddy and me. Whatever he agreed to give you toward your rent is no longer an option."

Rory Sue's gaze immediately shot toward Howard.

"Nor will you let your grandfather subsidize your living expenses," Mary Vaughn added, shooting a forbidding look in his direction. For once, Howard didn't argue with her.

Her daughter immediately pouted. "That's not fair."

"That's the real world," Mary Vaughn said sternly.

"And what if I don't meet these deadlines of yours?"

"Then you'll come back here and work with me. When you've saved up enough, if you still want to give Charleston another try, you'll have the financial means to do it."

"I think that's a great idea," Howard enthused, once again startling Rory Sue by agreeing with her mother.

Just then the waitress brought their meals. Mary Vaughn took one whiff of Howard's rare steak and nearly gagged. She leapt up and ran for the ladies' room, ignoring Howard and Rory Sue's shocked expressions.

A minute later, when she'd thrown up and her stomach felt more settled, Rory Sue came into the restroom.

"Mom, are you okay?" she asked tentatively. "I'm sorry if I upset you."

"I'm better now," she said, splashing some cool water on her face. "It's not your fault.

It must be a touch of the flu."

Rory Sue gave her a knowing look. "Or you're pregnant," she said quietly.

Mary Vaughn stared at her in shock. "At my age? That's insane. Why would you even think such a thing?"

"Because I've seen the way you and Dad are all over each other," Rory Sue said. "It's weird. I don't even know why you'd want me home. I'll just be in the way."

"You could never be in the way," Mary Vaughn insisted. "Having all of us together again, at least for a little while, it's all your daddy and I want."

"You're not going to feel that way once there's a new baby in the house," Rory Sue said. "Not unless you expect me to babysit all the time, which I am not going to do. I have a college degree. I need to have a real job."

Mary Vaughn hid a smile. "Isn't that exactly what we've been discussing? Real estate is a real job."

"You know what I mean. A job in my field, on a career track."

"If you find a job like that, you'll hear no more complaints from me," Mary Vaughn assured her. Her stomach rolled over again. "Oh, crap," she murmured, as she threw up again.

When she emerged from the stall, Rory Sue had a damp paper towel ready for her. "I have some mouth spray in my purse, if you want it."

"Yes, thanks."

Rory Sue's eyes sparkled as she handed the mouth spray to Mary Vaughn. "I'll bet you fifty bucks I'm right," she said. "About you being pregnant, I mean."

No way, Mary Vaughn said to herself, her knees suddenly wobbly. She walked back into a stall and sat down. It couldn't be.

Then she thought of the day she'd sold that space downtown to Travis McDonald. She and Sonny had been in a rush. Too much of a rush to worry about a condom? More than likely.

"Damn, damn, damn," she murmured, stunned. She was forty-three. Her daughter was twenty-one. And it appeared there was a very good chance she was about to have a baby. For a woman who thought she had her future all mapped out, wouldn't that be a kick in the rear? As for Sonny, he'd probably run around town gloating or have a heart attack. It was hard to know for sure just what his reaction would be.

"Don't you dare say a word to your grandfather or your father about this," Mary Vaughn told her daughter. "I need to know for sure before I get anyone else all stirred up."

"You can pick up a home pregnancy kit at Wharton's," Rory Sue said, her eyes alight with mischief.

"And have the whole town discussing it by nightfall? I don't think so. I'll have to take a run out to one of the big discount stores."

"I can do it, if you want," Rory Sue offered, suddenly solicitous. "Then if anyone happens to see me, they'll just assume I've gotten myself into trouble. Again. They'll never in a million years think it's for you."

Mary Vaughn knew there was a downside to that. If someone did see Rory Sue with a pregnancy test and assumed the worst, Sonny or Howard were bound to hear about it. Right this second, she preferred that possibility to the reality she was facing.

"Go," she said. "And please hurry. I'll deal with your grandfather, and then meet you back at the house in an hour."

Rory Sue started from the restroom, and then came back to give her a hug. "It'll be okay, Mom. No matter what happens." An impish grin lit her face. "And a baby brother or sister might be cool. Embarrassing, but cool."

Mary Vaughn sighed. Embarrassment was the least of it.

11

Sarah finished her show on Friday morning and uttered a sigh of relief. It had been a very long week. Not only had there been the now-infamous kiss and the fallout from that, but Travis had been in a weird mood ever since the Sweet Magnolias had ganged up on him. She didn't know quite what to make of it.

Now, for instance, he was lounging behind his desk in his usual laid-back posture, but something about the pose told her he was anything but relaxed. He looked moody and edgy. It didn't help that his gaze seemed to be fastened on her.

"Is something wrong?" she asked finally.

"Not a thing," he claimed.

"Then why are you staring at me like that?"

His lips curved slightly. "Because you're prettier than staring at the walls of this place."

She rolled her eyes. "Whatever."

He was instantly on his feet, which had her instinctively pulling back. The last time he'd gotten a glint like that in his eyes and moved that quickly, he'd kissed her and stirred an uproar.

"Come on," he said, holding out his hand.

"Where?"

"Trust me."

The problem was, she didn't know if she could. Okay, maybe what she really didn't know was if she could trust him . . . or herself.

He frowned at her hesitation. "What's the problem?"

"I just want to know where we're going," she said, balking at just taking off impulsively. "I have kids. I have responsibilities. I can't just take off whenever I feel like it."

"I wasn't thinking of taking off on a Caribbean cruise, though the idea does hold some appeal," he said, regarding her with amusement. "I need fresh air. You look about as jumpy as I feel, so I figured you do, too."

Sarah bristled. "If I look jumpy, it's because you make me nervous. You're unpredictable."

Naturally he looked a little too pleased by that, but he refrained from comment. He continued to hold out his hand. "Come on, sugar. I promise not to do anything you don't invite me to do."

"I hate to admit it, but that's not especially reassuring," she told him, still holding back.

His smile spread at her revealing comment. "In that case, it could be an interesting afternoon. We'll take my car. It has more room than that little toy thing you own."

The voices of six Sweet Magnolias sounded an alarm in her head. In the end, that's what decided her. It was a Friday afternoon, blue skies and sunshine beckoned, and she was feeling a little reckless. She might not trust Travis entirely, but she did know he'd meant what he said. Nothing would happen that she didn't want to happen.

"Okay," she said eventually. "Give me a minute to call the house and make arrangements with the sitter."

He nodded. "I'll bring the car around front and put the top down."

She held up a hand. "Just so we're clear, this isn't a date."

"Whatever you say," he said agreeably. "Call it a business conference, if it makes you feel better."

She nodded. "That's good, because Helen was very clear about what you can and can't do when it comes to anything related to business, right?"

He nodded solemnly. "Very clear. She spelled out the legal parameters of sexual harassment in terms even I could understand."

Somehow, she wasn't entirely reassured, but she nodded. "Okay, then. I'll meet you out front in five minutes."

"Which means fifteen, if I know anything at all about women and their primping," he said with exaggerated resignation.

Sarah beamed at him. "Why would I primp if it's not a date? What you see is what you get."

The fact that he didn't seem one bit put off by that disconcerted her more than the invitation had in the first place. She wished like crazy she could see herself through his eyes, because what she saw in the mirror was still colored by Walter's nonstop criticisms. Even if she trimmed down to a svelte 110, had her hair styled by the best of the best in a New York salon and wore designer clothes, on some level she'd still feel like a frumpy, overweight housewife who couldn't do anything right. Not even Walter with all of his apologies and well-meant attempts to put things right had been able to dispel fully the effect of years of verbal abuse.

■ ■ ■ ■

With the top down on his very expensive red sports car and Sarah by his side, Travis should have been able to relax, but he still felt off-kilter. He'd gone on dates with supermodels that had been less stressful. Being with Sarah, knowing that she was unlike any other woman he'd ever known, that she wasn't someone he could toy with and toss aside, made him edgy. He didn't want to hurt her. Unfortunately, he couldn't seem to make himself leave her alone, either.

Driving to the park seemed like a safe enough option. At this time on a summer day, it was crawling with moms and kids and older retirees out for an afternoon stroll. The swans were gliding across the lake. Ducks were following anyone who looked as if they might drop a few crumbs for them. It was a completely tranquil setting that usually soothed him.

Of course, that was when he was here in the evening alone, going for a run around the perimeter of the lake, or even accompanied by Tom, who knew how to keep quiet when the occasion called for it.

When he stopped the car, Sarah glanced over at him, looking vaguely disgruntled.

"We're going for a walk? In this heat?"

"Yep." He gave her a considering look. "Unless you'd like me to check us into the Serenity Inn for an afternoon of hot, sweaty sex."

She swallowed hard, but didn't look away. "I thought we'd ruled that out."

"Sugar, I never rule anything out. So, what's it going to be?"

"We'll walk."

"Too bad," he said cheerfully. "However, if you keep up and don't complain about everything, I'll buy you ice cream at the end."

She looked mildly intrigued by the offer. "All the way around the lake?"

He nodded. "It's only a mile. No big deal."

"Are you hoping to sweat another five pounds off me?"

He frowned at her. "Why would you ask me something like that? There's nothing wrong with you the way you are. Women are more attractive when they don't look like skinny little scarecrows."

She didn't look as if she believed him. Travis shook his head. "Boy, that husband of yours must have been a real piece of work," he muttered.

"He was just being honest."

"He was being a jerk," Travis said.

"You didn't see me when I first got back to town," she argued.

He stopped in his tracks, put his hands on her shoulders and looked straight into her eyes. "I might not have seen you then, but I can see you now. My eyesight's twenty-twenty, and you look damn good." He dropped his hands and backed off a step before he made the mistake of kissing her again just to prove the attraction was real. "A little too good for a man who's supposed to be remembering that this is not a date and that sex is out of the question."

Her mouth curved slightly at that. "Thanks."

She sounded so pleased by that paltry little compliment, he wanted to track down Walter Price and slug him for putting such a dent in her self-confidence.

He slung his arm over her shoulders and nudged her with his hip. "Come on, Sarah, let's relax and enjoy the scenery."

They strolled along like that, the silence companionable. Sarah seemed to be oblivious to the stares aimed in their direction, but Travis wasn't. He knew with gut-wrenching certainty that this walk, like the kiss, would be the talk of the town by nightfall. Which probably made it one more mistake that would wind up causing both of them grief. Somehow, though, he couldn't seem to make himself regret it.

About a hundred yards before they reached the ice cream vendor, Travis broke the silence. "I'm thinking two large cones with chocolate and vanilla swirled together. What about you?"

Her eyes sparkled with mischief as she looked up at him. "You're having two large cones?"

"Hey, I could handle it, but I meant one of those for you."

"Make mine small," she said.

"Is that because it's really all you want, or because you'll feel guilty if you eat a large one?"

"I'll feel guilty," she admitted.

"Well, I'll feel guilty if I have a large cone and get you only a small one, so you're just going to have to humor me this time."

She seemed to struggle with herself for a heartbeat, then shrugged. "Well, if I have to, I have to."

He grinned. "That's the spirit."

He bought their cones and they walked to an unoccupied bench in the shade. Watching Sarah run her tongue around the soft ice cream was almost his undoing. He hadn't heated up that quickly in months. He blinked and looked away.

228

"Thanks," she said eventually.

"For?"

"The whole afternoon. I never take time for myself like this anymore. If I have spare time, I think I should be home with Tommy and Libby. I'd forgotten that quiet pleasures can be good for the soul."

"Absolutely," he agreed. "And you'll be a better mom to your kids if you've taken some time to relax. You'll have more patience."

"I know you're right, but that guilt thing kicks in and I run straight home."

"It has to be tough being a single mom," Travis said thoughtfully. "I know it was for my mother, and she had a lot of support."

"Now that I'm back here, I have plenty of support, too," Sarah said. "Raylene, whom you haven't met yet, she's staying with me and she adores the kids. She pitches in around the house, too. The situation's a little complicated, but I love having the company. And, of course, you know how the Sweet Magnolias like to meddle in my life."

"First hand," he agreed. "They're a scary bunch."

"Not once you really get to know them. They're just protective." She sighed. "Then there's Walter."

"Your ex-husband," he said, his tone disparaging.

"He's not as bad as you've probably heard," she said, jumping to his defense in a way that stirred Travis's annoyance.

As if she sensed his disapproval, she quickly added, "Oh, he *was* awful, believe me. That's why I left Alabama. Lately, though, he's gotten away from his parents' influence and he's almost human again, the way he was when we first met back in college."

Travis tensed. "With all this self-improvement, are you planning to give him a second chance?"

"No," she said with conviction.

"But you said he's more like the man you met, which means he's more like he was when you fell in love with him, right?" Travis persisted, not quite sure why he wanted so badly to pin down her feelings for the guy.

"That doesn't mean I'll ever forget how he was after we were married," she said. "Our marriage was broken beyond repair. It's not as if it could be fixed at this late date. I don't think I could ever trust him not to revert to that kind of behavior. At least, it's not a chance I'm willing to take."

She sounded dead-certain about that, but

in Travis's experience women could be fickle. And men could be slick. If Walter Price wanted her back and set his mind to winning her over, it just might work. There were two kids to consider, too.

Maybe he really did need to take a step back, not just for Sarah's sake, but for his own as well. Why put his heart on the line for the very first time for a woman who might not be free of her past?

Of course, that was the sensible, self-protective side of his brain talking. He usually ignored it.

And, as he looked over at Sarah, saw the concentration furrowing her brow as she tried to keep up with her melting ice cream, and felt his libido kick in, something told him this was going to be another one of those times.

On Saturday evening, Travis and Tom settled into comfortable chairs on the patio after dinner, beers in hand. Jeanette had driven to Charleston with Maddie and her kids to see a movie, leaving the two of them with a rare guys-only night.

"I need to start looking for my own place," Travis said. "I've been intruding on you and Jeanette long enough."

"It's fine. You're not around at night,

231

which gives us time together when we need it. You don't leave your dirty socks and underwear all over the house, so Jeanette's not complaining."

Travis grinned. "That's her standard for a houseguest?"

"Pretty much. She's a low-key kind of woman these days. And she's very big on family, now that she's reconciled with her parents. She even tolerates my folks and, believe me, they got off to a very rocky start."

Travis didn't have to feign his shock. He knew how impossibly stuffy Tom's folks could be. "Jeanette must be a saint," he said mildly.

"Tell me about it," Tom said with feeling. "Look, if you find your own place, fine, but there's no rush about it. We're not going to need that room for a nursery for a while."

Travis turned to find his cousin with a broad grin on his face. "Don't tell me! Jeanette's pregnant?"

Tom nodded. "It caught me by surprise, too. We'd been talking about it. We'd even decided to start trying, but it took, like, fifteen seconds apparently."

"That's those potent little McDonald guys," Travis said. "They're great little swimmers."

Tom's expression sobered. "Which should be a warning to you."

"Not to worry," Travis replied. "My guys are not allowed in the pool. There will be no unprotected swimming. I'm not sure the world needs any more McDonalds from my side of the family."

"That's crazy," Tom said. "I've seen you with your sisters' kids and with all the children running around at the picnic over at Dana Sue's on the Fourth of July."

"I love kids," Travis admitted. "But I don't think I'm cut out to be a father."

"Because your dad was so lousy at it, I assume," Tom said.

"To be fair, he was a lousier husband than he was a father," Travis said. "Other than disagreeing vehemently with just about every decision I ever made, he wasn't all that bad as a dad. In some ways he was just an irresponsible, overgrown kid himself."

"My father certainly wouldn't take top honors in a daddy competition, either," Tom reminded him. "But I'm hoping I learned from his mistakes." He fell silent for a minute, then said, "That reminds me of something I've been meaning to talk to you about."

"Oh?"

"Cal Maddox and I have started a Little

League program in town. It was just a couple of teams last year, but there were so many kids who turned out this spring, we really want to add more teams so all the kids will have a chance to play a fair amount instead of warming the bench half the time."

"And you want me to coach one of them," Travis guessed.

"If you're willing and have the time," Tom confirmed. "You'd be great at it. And it would give you another way to become a part of the community. What do you think?"

"Count me in," he said at once, immediately excited by the idea. "The radio station can sponsor the team, too. It'll be good PR."

"We haven't actually had sponsors so far," Tom admitted. "Cal and I have just picked up the financial slack when it comes to uniforms and equipment."

Travis frowned. "Well, I could do that, too, but it seems to me it increases community involvement to have businesses participate. That's the way it worked back home," he reminded his cousin. "How about I try to find a few other sponsors? How many teams are we talking about? Four? Six?"

"Let's say four for the rest of this season," Tom told him. "You sure you want to take on trying to drum up sponsors, when you're trying to get a new business on solid ground?"

"I'm out soliciting for advertising, anyway," Travis said with a shrug. "I can always offer a package deal . . . ads on the radio station in return for team sponsorship. It'll be an introductory win-win all around."

Tom regarded him with surprise. "You might have a knack for the whole broadcasting thing, after all. You're actually thinking like a smart, creative businessman."

Travis grinned. "Thanks for the grudging support."

"You know I support you. I just thought you were taking on too much in an area in which you had absolutely no experience."

Travis's grin spread. "Do you actually know what my degree is in?"

Tom looked flustered by the question. "No. I figured physical education, maybe. Wasn't that the plan when you left for college?"

"Sorry, pal. It was always broadcast journalism. I thought if my name got big enough, I could wind up calling games on TV once I retired. I even did a couple of nights on the air with the team's local radio guys in Boston when I was out with a sprained wrist last season."

Tom appeared to be genuinely impressed. "Well, why on earth didn't you pursue that when the Red Sox let you go?"

Travis shrugged. "I thought about it, but then I realized I'd be on the road constantly and a part of me wanted more than that. I love the game, but I hated sleeping in hotel rooms night after night, not even knowing where I was half the time. I wanted a place to call home. To be honest, it surprised the heck out of me that I felt that way. I hadn't been here with you more than a week when I realized I'd found it. And once the radio deal started to fall into place, well, it seemed like fate."

"Who knew?" Tom said, his expression still disbelieving. "Okay, then, you'll find the sponsors for our teams and take on coaching the older kids. You'll be a real role model for them."

"Who's been coaching the older kids up till now?"

"Cal."

"Then he should keep doing it," Travis insisted. "I'd like to take on the little kids, teach 'em to love the game along with working on the basic skills. That's what's lacking for too many of these kids. They get into sports because their dads are trying to relive some childhood fantasy. They never get to play just for fun."

Tom shook his head. "You're just full of surprises. It's okay with me. I'll run it by Cal."

"That only gives you three teams, though. Who's going to take over the fourth?"

"Cal's trying to get Ronnie Sullivan to do it, but he has to ease him into the idea. Ronnie's business has taken off, and he likes being available in case Dana Sue needs him to pitch in at Sullivan's. Cal's had him helping out regularly, and he figures in another week, he can point out that Ronnie's at the ballfield all the time anyway, so why not just take on his own team?"

"Smooth," Travis said approvingly.

"Once he says yes, we can schedule more games," Tom said. "There are half a dozen teams in neighboring towns in each age bracket."

Travis thought of Sarah's little boy. Just four, he was a little unsteady on his feet, but in Dana Sue's yard on the Fourth of July, Travis had seen his enthusiasm for throwing a ball around and even swinging some lightweight little bat someone had given him.

"What about T-ball?" he asked. "Maybe I could organize a couple of teams for that, too. We'd just need a few dads to keep order, since they're not exactly going to be skilled players at that age."

To his surprise, his cousin regarded him with immediate suspicion. "Any particular reason you'd want to do that? It wouldn't have anything to do with Sarah Price's boy, would it?"

"What if it does?" he responded defensively.

"Don't play games with her," Tom warned. "And you definitely don't want to involve her children in them, especially if you even think you could wake up one morning and decide Serenity's not for you."

"An ironic thing to say coming from a man who'd once intended to use this town as a stepping-stone to bigger and better things," Travis said testily. "Look, the only game I'm interested in is T-ball. I told you I knew right away I wanted to settle down here, and I meant it."

Tom still looked worried. "And Sarah's part of that?"

Travis nodded slowly. "It's entirely possible that she could be."

"Well, all I can say is be careful, because if you do anything to hurt that woman, you'll be dealing with the wrath of the Sweet Magnolias."

"Trust me, I've already had one brush

with them." Travis described the fallout from the kiss. Tom was chuckling by the time he'd finished reciting all the different angles they'd used to come after him.

"Then you obviously know they're the most loyal, intimidating group of women on the planet," Tom said. "I'm married to one of them, but only because there was consensus from the group that I passed muster. Like I said, you don't want to mess with them, okay?"

Tom sounded so serious, Travis had to fight the desire to laugh. Then he thought of the evidence he'd seen of Jeanette's fiercely protective streak, Annie's guard-dog belligerence and the way Helen had threatened him with a sexual harassment suit, and it wiped even the faint beginning of a smile from his face.

He supposed the good part of what Tom was telling him was the confirmation that Sarah really did have fiercely protective backup. From what he'd been hearing about her marriage and what he'd seen of her skittishness around him, she needed it. He felt better knowing she had women who were there for her. He'd always had male friends, guys he hung out with, and some — like Tom — to whom he could tell anything. He understood the importance of friendships.

In the case of the Sweet Magnolias, he just had to make sure he didn't do anything more to tick them off.

12

Sarah was starting to settle into a routine at work. Once she was off the air, she'd have a quick lunch, which was sometimes supplied by Travis along with a few flirtatious remarks that she basically ignored. Then she made phone calls to schedule guests for upcoming shows. If there was time after that before she needed to be home, she'd make a few calls to potential sponsors or straighten out the office. Or she'd update the master schedule she'd created on a giant erasable board so that she, Travis and Bill weren't approaching the same potential guests or advertisers.

For a woman whose household was generally chaotic, discovering that she could keep things at the station on track had been a revelation. Certainly Travis didn't bother with details. Bill was better, but he had less to organize. Used to years of being on the air alone and simply talking to listeners, he didn't book a lot of guests. Nor was he covering more than a handful of accounts.

Sarah had also taken Travis at his word and called regular staff meetings for the three of them so they could plan shows and brainstorm ideas. She'd even pestered Travis to buy a file cabinet so they could keep neat folders on their advertisers. Of course, the folder for accounts Travis handled tended to be stuffed with Post-its, while Sarah's held detailed notes and even scripts for the commercials she or one of the others recorded.

She was alphabetizing files after Travis had haphazardly stuffed things back into a drawer, when he came up behind her. He didn't have to say a word. Her whole body went on high alert the second he even walked into a room. The faint citrus scent that lingered on his skin after shaving was like an aphrodisiac. She automatically wanted to turn and bury her face in his neck and breathe deeply.

"Can I help you?" she asked without turning around.

"I wanted to talk to you about something," he said. "Let's take a break and go get some coffee."

"I don't have time for a break," she said automatically. Turning him down for the most innocuous things had gotten to be second nature. It made it easier to say no when he tossed in a request for anything that sounded remotely like a date.

"I don't think I asked if you had time," he said testily.

She did turn then and frowned at him. "Travis McDonald, are you ordering me to take a break?"

He returned her challenging look. "Why, yes, I believe I am."

She might have argued with the man, but she knew better than to fight with him when he was in this particular mood. He rarely pulled rank on her, but when he did, she found it exasperating. Most of the time she believed they worked as partners. Maybe not financial partners, but two people who were attuned to anything that was good for the station. She basked in the respect he showed for her opinions. That meant more than the flattery he doled out without thinking.

Despite her annoyance, she forced herself to respond with indifference. "Okay, then. You're the boss."

"Wharton's okay?" he asked, obviously still miffed.

"If that's where you want to go."

He gave her an equally exasperated look.

"Are you planning to be a pain in the butt while we're there?"

"I believe I am."

He shook his head. "Okay, then. This should be fun."

They crossed the square in silence, Travis walking a few paces ahead of her as if he were some sort of royalty and she his subservient minion. Trotting to keep pace, though, would only make her feel more foolish, so she deliberately dawdled. If it hadn't been against the law to pick the flowers on the green, she'd have paused to do just that.

At Wharton's, he held the door until she got there, then walked to the closest booth and sat down. Sarah slid in across from him, then folded her hands primly on top of the table and waited.

"Are you trying to tick me off?" he asked. "You look like a kid who's waiting outside the principal's office expecting to be punished."

"Really? I thought I was behaving like a dutiful employee, eagerly awaiting the word from on high."

His scowl deepened. "What is wrong with you?"

She sucked in a deep breath, then decided to tell the truth. "I don't like your attitude."

"Since when?"

"Since about fifteen minutes ago, when you started treating me like some low-level employee you get to order around just because you're in a snit."

"I hate to tell you, but I'm having trouble keeping it straight. How am I supposed to treat you?"

"Not like this."

"And not like a woman I'm attracted to," he countered.

"Yes, not like that." She actually understood a little of his frustration. She got confused from time to time herself. Finally she said wistfully, "How about friends? Couldn't we act like friends and coworkers who respect each other?"

His expression softened. "You mean instead of me trying to bulldoze over you or seduce you, depending on my mood?"

She allowed herself a smile. "Yes, that would be an improvement."

"Okay, I'll try," he promised. "To be honest, I'm not used to having to sort through all these tricky dynamics. Most of my relationships have been pretty straightforward. I played ball with — and for — a bunch of men. Believe me, I didn't want to sleep with any of them. I dated a lot of high-profile women who wanted to sleep with me. The distinctions were pretty clear-cut."

"None of those women were friends?"

"Not a one."

"That's sad."

He shrugged. "Probably, but it worked out fine for me at the time."

"Maybe we should agree that we both need to be more patient when the lines get a little blurry," she suggested.

"Or we could agree to sleep together and get that out of the way," he countered, his expression boyishly hopeful.

Despite herself, Sarah couldn't help laughing. "Not in the cards." It was so easy for her to say that when he was being deliberately outrageous. Had he looked for even an instant as if he'd meant it, she wasn't sure she could have laughed off the suggestion.

"You're tough."

She was surprisingly pleased by the comment. No one had ever thought she was tough before. She'd mostly been a pushover. "Thank you. Now what is this very important meeting all about?"

He stared at her blankly, then shook his head. "I have no idea."

"You have no idea," she repeated slowly. She regarded him incredulously.

He shrugged. "I just wanted a few minutes alone with you and all of a sudden it turned into this big deal," he admitted, looking sheepish. "Sorry. If you need to get home, go ahead."

She probably should have done exactly that, but suddenly she didn't want to. Instead, she frowned at him. "You have to be kidding me. After all this, the least you can do is to buy me a burger and fries." She tilted her head thoughtfully. "I believe I'd like a chocolate milk shake, too."

"I can do that," he agreed at once. He signaled to the teen who'd replaced Sarah as a part-time waitress and placed the order, then turned back to Sarah. "We're okay?"

"We're okay," she confirmed.

In fact, if they were any more okay, she'd be dragging him straight home to bed, which was exactly why she needed to keep little outings like this to a minimum.

Travis hadn't been over to Charleston to see his folks since being released by the Red Sox. The frequent phone calls, especially from his mother, had been awkward enough. Lately, though, they'd taken on an unexpected tone of urgency. When his mother insisted he drive over on the weekend for lunch, he finally acquiesced. Clearly there was something on her mind.

Since he couldn't see her without fitting

in a visit with his father, he made arrangements to meet him for dinner. It promised to be a fun-filled Sunday, he thought sarcastically as he reluctantly headed across the state.

After the divorce, his mother had moved into a condo that required less upkeep than the house she'd always despised. After years of living with McDonald family heirlooms, she'd fought tradition and decorated with a clean, modern look that left Travis cold, but somehow suited her sophisticated style. Rather than the massive flower arrangements they'd always had at home, she accented rooms with a single, dramatic bird of paradise in a heavy crystal vase, or a few tulips artfully arranged in a bouquet.

When he arrived, she welcomed him with a kiss on the cheek.

"We'll eat right away," she said, leading the way directly to the dining room, where the table had been set for two. "I know you're having an early dinner with your father, and I wouldn't want to hold you up."

Travis flushed. "Sorry, but I could only get away for the day. The radio station is taking up a lot of time, even when I'm not on the air."

"And I want to hear all about it," she said, though she didn't sound particularly eager.

248

Mostly, she sounded distracted, and oddly upset.

"Mother, what's on your mind? Let's deal with that first. Maybe then you'll be able to enjoy your meal and actually listen to anything I have to say."

She looked faintly embarrassed, but she didn't deny that her mind was elsewhere. "There *is* something you need to know," she said.

She sounded so somber, his gut twisted into a knot. Was she about to tell him she was ill? Or, God forbid, dying? "Mom, are you okay?" he asked worriedly. He might not be the most attentive son in the world, but he did love her.

She looked startled by the question. "Me? I'm fine. It's your father."

Travis was puzzled. His father had sounded particularly exuberant on the phone. "He's not sick, is he?"

"Not unless you count losing his mind as being sick," she said bitterly. "You need to be prepared for tonight."

"Why? Did he get a bad toupee or something?" His father had been unapologetically bald as far back as Travis could remember, even before the style had become popularized by younger male celebrities shaving their heads.

"Worse," she said. "He's gotten engaged."

The news wasn't half as shocking as her reaction to it. "And you don't approve," he surmised.

"No one approves."

"Why?"

"Because he's engaged to Mimsy Phelps's daughter, that's why."

Travis didn't even try to hide his dismay. "Trina? Dad is engaged to Trina Phelps? She's my age."

"A year younger, actually. I suspect tonight's dinner is all about you breaking bread with the happy bride-to-be and giving the couple your blessing."

"My God," Travis murmured. "Does Dad know that I used to date Trina?"

"It may have slipped his mind," she said. "But I doubt it. He seems to be in a particularly rebellious mood these days."

"Is this some kind of midlife crisis or something?" Travis asked, though he knew better. His father had always pushed the limits when it came to women. The more inappropriate the relationship, the better. Marriage hadn't stopped him. Divorce had only given him license to take his philandering ways more public.

Across the glass-topped dining room table, his mother set down her sterling silver fork — one of the few treasured heirlooms she'd kept — and looked him in the eye, her expression earnest. "You have to stop him."

"Me? When has Dad ever listened to me about anything? And how am I supposed to discuss this with him if he brings Trina along to dinner?"

"I'm sure you can make him see how wrong this is, even if she's there. Appeal to her good nature, if nothing else. Heck, seduce her yourself. You found her attractive enough once upon a time."

"Mother!"

"Well, something has to be done. and I'm at my wit's end. He won't listen to a word I say."

Though it should have gone without saying this many years after their divorce, Travis felt compelled to point out, "Dad is no longer your problem."

"Technically, no, but God help me, I've always had a soft spot for him. It pains me to see him acting like a fool. The whole town is talking about this. If it were just some passing whim, that might be one thing, but marriage? It's absurd!"

For all of its growth in recent years, Charleston essentially remained a small town when it came to a certain social set.

The McDonalds had their place and, despite the long-ago divorce, what his father did might still reflect badly on his mother. At the very least, Travis could see how it would cause her embarrassment.

"I'll do my best, Mom, but don't expect miracles. Dad's done whatever he wanted for a long time now."

"Well, this girl is going to take him for every penny he has, if he's not careful," she declared. "You mark my words. Why else would she be with him?"

"Maybe for the same reason you once were," he said carefully. "Maybe she really does love him."

"Oh, hogwash!" she said dismissively.

"I can't believe it's about money," he said. "Doesn't her family have buckets of it?"

"Not since the recession came close to wiping them out. The word at the club is that Mimsy's broker invested in some very bad things, then took off to God knows where. I doubt they're poor as church mice, but they don't have the unlimited resources they once did."

"And Dad does?" He had no idea what his father's net worth might be these days. He'd always had a tendency to act as if money grew on trees.

"For all of his profligate ways, yes. He's

smart when it comes to financial matters, and nobody's going to push him into bad investments."

Travis was beginning to see why she thought there might be a problem. He just had no idea what he could do about it. "Mom, he isn't going to appreciate either of us meddling in his life."

"I don't give two hoots whether he appreciates it," she said fiercely. "Fix this, Travis. I mean it. Otherwise, I'll never be able to hold up my head in this town again."

Travis tried to keep any hint of pity from his expression, but, truthfully, pity was what he felt. Because despite every humiliation, every angry word they'd exchanged and years of divorce, his mother was still as in love with his father as she had been on the day they'd wed. He even wondered if, on some level, she hadn't always expected him to come back to her once he settled down and tired of chasing every pretty woman who crossed his path.

He gave his mother's hand a quick squeeze and promised he'd do what he could, then deliberately changed the subject, telling her all about the radio station, singing Bill's praises for all he'd done and mentioning Sarah only in passing.

Unfortunately, the second Sarah's name

crossed his lips, his mother regarded him with a penetrating look. "She's special, isn't she?"

"Why would you think that? I barely mentioned her name."

She smiled. "Which is exactly what gave it away. Are the two of you dating?"

"No. She won't go out with me." He heard the grumpy note in his voice and grimaced. It was way too telling.

"Interesting. She's obviously very smart. That's the best way I know to keep a man fascinated."

"She's not playing some game with me, Mother. We're a bad match. I'm too much like Dad."

"Oh, hogwash," his mother said for the second time in a few minutes. "You're nothing at all like your father. He indulges his weaknesses. You never have."

She was wrong about that. "I dated every available woman who came my way while I was playing ball," he countered.

"And never promised one of them anything, I imagine. You played fair."

"Of course."

"That alone differentiates you from your father. He never played fair. He shouldn't have married me."

Travis was surprised by that assessment.

"Why not?"

"He was nowhere near ready to settle down."

"But he chose you just the same."

"Only because I was pregnant with you."

Travis had figured that out years ago, so her words didn't come as a shock.

"I should have had sense enough to say no," she continued, "but I wasn't quite strong enough to face having a child on my own. Plus, I knew he cared about me. I thought I could turn his affection into love. Women are extremely foolish when it comes to that sort of thing, you know. We all believe we can change men into being exactly what we want."

"Sarah's not like that. She's not the least bit interested in changing me." He had to wonder if that wasn't why he found her so fascinating. She simply didn't have the same kind of feminine guile he'd seen so often in other women.

"Maybe because she's the first woman who can see what's in your heart, rather than the bad-boy public image you've worked so hard to cultivate."

"Or maybe because all she sees *is* the public image, and she doesn't want any part of it," he countered. "It doesn't matter. We're not dating, much less involved."

But even as he tried to summarize their relationship and put it into a safe, familiar compartment, he felt an odd sense of dismay stealing over him. Could he really have the missing piece of that perfect picture he'd described for Tom . . . a new career, a welcoming community, a home *and* the right woman, one suited for the long haul? He'd have to give that some thought.

First, though, he had to see if there was any chance he could save his father from whatever crazy path he was on.

Travis met his father and Trina in a small, informal seafood restaurant known mostly to longtime Charleston residents and hidden away from tourists. The waterfront setting and ambience were decidedly casual, but the chef was first-rate and the prices matched. Greg McDonald enjoyed the contradiction.

He stood when Travis crossed the dining room, then gave his son a hearty slap on the back.

"You're looking good, Dad," Travis said, meaning it. His father was tall and trim with a golf-course tan that accented his blue eyes. His classic bone structure worked well with the bald look.

Travis then turned to Trina, who looked

vaguely uncertain about what reception to expect.

"You must be good for him," Travis told her, hoping to at least start off putting her at ease until he had a better sense of where things stood. He'd decided on a strategy on the drive over, but he'd wait to make sure it was the best way to go.

"I try to be," she said, looking relieved. "How are you, Travis? It's been a long time."

"My senior year of college, as I recall. You were a junior." He emphasized the latter and saw his father flush.

"Travis!" he said, his tone filled with warning.

Travis turned an innocent look on his father. "Did I say something wrong?"

"Obviously your mother has filled you in," Greg said. "Even though I asked her to let me tell you. Yes, Trina and I are getting married. I hope you'll be happy about that."

"I'm not the one who needs to be happy," Travis said.

His father looked slightly taken aback. "You mean that?"

"Look, I can't honestly say I'm not surprised, but beyond that, it's none of my concern. If this is really what you want, Dad, I wish you well. You, too, Trina."

"Thank you," she said, taking his words at

face value.

His father still didn't look convinced. "I'm sure you have more you want to say."

"Nope," Travis said. "You're a smart man. Smart enough to take care of all the legalities, I'm sure."

Trina's expression froze. "Legalities?"

"A prenup, that sort of thing," Travis said. "I'm sure you want that, too, Trina. You don't want Dad taking advantage of your family's wealth, or vice versa. If you two love each other, it's only fair to keep the whole money thing out of it, right?"

"Actually we don't want to start our marriage with some piece of paper that suggests we're already thinking about how it might end," Trina said.

Travis reacted with feigned surprise. "Really? I mean, I get that it takes the edge off the romance and all, but people in your financial world have to be responsible and practical, don't you think, Dad?"

Greg McDonald looked disconcerted, though it was hard to tell whether it was due to Travis's mention of a prenuptial agreement or Trina's obviously agitated response to the suggestion.

"Could we stop talking about money and just enjoy the evening?" Greg suggested, giving Trina's hand a squeeze. "There's plenty of time to worry about all that."

Travis decided to let it go. He was pretty sure he'd made his point. "When's the wedding?" he inquired.

"I'd like to get married as soon as possible," Trina said.

There was an unattractive hint of desperation in her tone, though Travis was sure she meant only to sound eager.

"Possibly in the fall," his father said. "Or maybe after the first of the year. I want Trina to have the wedding of her dreams."

She leaned over and kissed his cheek. "I keep telling him he's all I need, but he doesn't believe me."

"I do," Travis said. In fact, he was just about a hundred percent certain she'd be pushing for a quickie wedding in Vegas before the night was out. Things must be really tough for the Phelps family these days, and she was the designated savior. That much was clear to him, if not to his father. Too bad he couldn't pull Greg aside and have a real heart-to-heart with him. Surely he wasn't entirely blind to what was going on.

Travis managed to choke down his meal, but he could hardly wait to get away from the happy couple. He rose as soon as they'd all finished their coffee.

"I have a long drive ahead of me," he told them. "Dad, I'll speak to you tomorrow."

"Sure, son," Greg said distractedly, clearly engrossed in Trina, whose hand seemed to be wandering somewhere out of sight under the table. Travis shuddered.

By the time he climbed into his car, he fully understood his mother's concern. For all of his years of playing an irresponsible bachelor, Greg McDonald had always been smart enough to avoid falling into any sort of feminine trap. Now it seemed the trap had been sct and baited, and he was barely one step away from getting caught. It just proved that even the mightiest player could fall.

Travis had a hunch there might be a lesson in there for him, too.

13

Sarah reluctantly loaded the kids into the car late on Sunday afternoon for a barbecue at Tom and Jeanette's. She had a feeling she'd been invited primarily because of Travis. Jeanette was still conspiring to throw the two of them together, despite Sarah's repeated claims that she wasn't interested.

Of course, maybe she was reading things into the invitation. All of the Sweet Magnolias were supposed to be there, including Annie. Annie was also bringing her stepson, Trevor. There was even a chance Ty would make it over from Atlanta, if his home game ended early enough. The team had Monday off, so he'd promised to try. Along with Maddie's kids and Helen's little girl, the younger generation would be well represented, so it would be fun for Tommy and Libby.

Because the backyard at Jeanette's had been turned into a spectacular garden, the kids and the men had been relegated to the front lawn to play. Libby and Tommy were welcomed, and immediately joined in the impromptu game of T-ball being played.

"We've got 'em covered," Tom assured her. "Go on inside. The women are in the kitchen or maybe out on the back patio. We've been told to stay out from underfoot."

Sarah glanced around, looking for Travis, but saw no sign of him. To her surprise, however, Walter was there. He waved a greeting but didn't come over.

"Two questions," she said, pulling Annie aside when she walked into the kitchen.

"I'll bet I know one of them," Annie said. "Walter's here because he and my dad have suddenly become pals. I have no idea why."

Jeanette apparently overheard them, because she grinned at Sarah. "And I'll bet I know the other question. You want to know why Travis is missing."

Embarrassed, Sarah flushed. "I never mentioned his name."

Jeanette pinned her with an amused look. "Oh, then what was your question?"

She held up the salad she'd brought. "Where do you want me to put this?" she asked.

"On the table on the patio," Jeanette said. "And even though you didn't ask, I'll tell you that Travis is in Charleston. He might make it back by dessert. He already knows the big news anyway."

Her hint that the evening was more than a casual get-together took the edge off the news that Travis wouldn't be here. Annie and Sarah both regarded Jeanette with curiosity.

"There's big news?" Annie said.

Jeanette nodded. "But nobody finds out until later. I worked too hard on this meal. I want everyone to give it their full attention."

Sarah's gaze went to a plate piled high with burgers ready for the grill. If she knew anything about the men in this crowd, Tom had made those. "Yes, I can see how you've slaved."

"And Sarah brought the salad," Annie said. "And I brought corn on the cob. Mom brought appetizers, Helen and Erik brought dessert. What exactly did you do, Jeanette? Open the packages of hamburger rolls?"

"Very funny," Jeanette said. "I cut up lots and lots of veggies, which are steaming in little foil-wrapped packets on the grill at this very moment. I also opened bags of chips. It was very tedious."

"You poor thing," Annie said, slipping an arm around her shoulder. "We feel for you. You probably need a margarita."

Jeanette shook her head, her cheeks turning pink.

Annie's gaze immediately shot to Sarah's. "No margarita."

"You're pregnant," Sarah guessed at once. It was the only thing that ever kept a Sweet Magnolia from their favorite drink.

The color in Jeanette's cheeks deepened. "No comment. I promised my husband we'd make this announcement together." But even as she spoke, the protective hand resting on her stomach told the story.

"Then let's get this party started," Annie said. "I'll carry out the rest of these bowls. Sarah, you round up the kids and the men."

Just as they went outside, Ty showed up. After scooping Trevor into his arms for a smacking kiss on the cheek, then releasing him, Ty dragged Annie off for a private greeting. She was flushed when they finally returned, and turned even redder when they were greeted with applause and taunts.

"Hey, I don't get to see my husband that often," she retorted, linking her arm possessively through Ty's. "I intend to make the most of every minute. Deal with it."

An hour later, with the sun dipping below the horizon and the garden awash with a golden glow, Tom stood up and pulled Jeanette to her feet beside him.

"We have news," he said, his adoring gaze on his wife. "Jeanette and I are having a baby."

Just as he made the announcement, Travis came through the gate, grabbed a beer from the cooler and slipped into the chair next to Sarah's. She turned and caught an odd expression on his face, even as he lifted his bottle in the air to join in the toast proposed by Cal Maddox.

Sarah frowned. "You don't look very excited about their news," she said, noticing that though he'd gone through all the right motions, something about his reaction was off.

"I am," he insisted. "I know how thrilled Tom is, and I couldn't be happier for them."

"Then what's going on? You don't look that happy."

"Nothing worth talking about," he said moodily.

"Come on, Travis. Don't put a damper on their big moment."

"How am I doing that? I just got here. I toasted them. What else am I supposed to do? Should I dance a little jig?"

She studied him with a puzzled expression. "Now you sound ticked off. What's that about?"

"If I am, it's because you're making a big

production out of my mood. I had a lousy day. Dealing with my folks is never a picnic. Seeing the two of them reminds me of why I've always been determined to stay single. Lately I'd almost forgotten how messed up relationships can get."

His words cut right through Sarah. It wasn't as if she'd ever looked far enough into the future to imagine a life with Travis. Not really. But apparently on some subconscious level, that hope had been buried inside her. Now he'd snatched it away fairly emphatically. If he'd truly reconsidered ever settling down, then what was she supposed to do with all these unvoiced feelings he stirred in her? Trying to figure it out depressed her more than she wanted to admit.

"Did something in particular happen today?" she asked, not quite able to make herself let it go.

"I spent the afternoon trying to calm my mother down because my father intends to marry a girl I used to date in college," he said. "Is that twisted enough for you?"

She blinked at his response. "Okay, that must have been a little unsettling," she admitted slowly. "Do you still have feelings for this woman?"

He looked horrified at the thought. "Good God, no! That's not the point."

"Then what is? Are you worried about getting along with your new stepmommy?" she asked, deliberately injecting a teasing note into her voice.

To her relief, his lips twitched. "I hadn't thought of that. We got along well enough years ago."

"I'm sure," Sarah said wryly. "Look, at this stage of your life, what your father does has nothing to do with you."

"I know that, but it does affect my mother. She's all worked up over this. She expects me to fix it."

"How are you planning to do that?"

"I've already planted a few little seeds about the importance of a prenuptial agreement. That definitely spoiled the glow for the bride-to-be."

"You think she's after your father's money," Sarah concluded, less shocked than she probably should have been. Maybe her own marriage had turned her into a cynic, after all.

"Seems like it."

"Can't your father look out for himself?"

"I always thought so, but after watching him tonight, I'm not so sure. Men can be fools in the hands of the right woman."

"Is this more philosophy from the man who intends to remain single?"

"Based on fact," he said.

"Based on the facts as you've observed them," she contradicted. "I daresay there are many relationships in the world you haven't seen. And if you want to take a look at one a bit closer to home, who would you say was the fool in my relationship with Walter, me or him?"

He scowled at the question, his gaze drawn to Walter, who was ignoring Libby's pleas to be picked up. "Something tells me I should go with a no comment on that one."

"Then I'll answer it myself. I was the idiot," she said. "I allowed him to demean me for way too long."

"And even now that you've seen the light, you still let him get away with it," Travis said.

When Sarah would have objected, he held up his hand. "I've seen it."

"You've hardly ever seen us together," she argued defensively, even though she knew what he was saying was true.

"Can you deny that there have been times when you'll be saying and doing all the right things and the next time we talk you start questioning yourself?"

"Possibly," she conceded.

"Well, every single time when I've asked

you about the doubts, it's gone back to some conversation you've had with Walter."

"You're wrong," she said. "He's been better."

"Better doesn't mean it never happens," Travis countered. "Shall we get him over here and see how long it takes him to intimidate you?"

Sarah sighed, because she knew Travis was right. Walter could still send her into a tailspin. "No need for that," she told Travis. "I'm working on it. I swear I am."

"If it weren't for your kids, I'd do whatever it took to get him out of town," Travis said. "Having him here is not good for you. Watching the way he can still tie you up in knots makes me crazy."

She was startled by his vehemence. "Why?"

"Because you're better than that. Everyone knows it except you. I don't know what it's going to take to give you back your confidence. Maybe you need to be the one to tell him to leave or at least to straighten up and treat you with respect."

"Honestly, Travis, he really has been trying. Most of the time we've been getting along okay, and when he does slip up, I'm standing up to him. Can we drop this, please?"

"Is that because you still want him in your life?"

"Not for myself, no," she said adamantly. "That really would be self-destructive. But you said it yourself, I have to find some way to deal with him for Tommy and Libby's sake. They adore him."

"I can see that," he said, nodding in their direction. Libby kept trying to scramble up into Walter's lap, but he systematically set her back on her feet. He was clearly exasperated, though he seemed to be trying not to let it show too plainly.

Travis finally stood up and crossed the lawn in long strides. He scooped Libby into the air and set her on his shoulders. She was giggling and pulling his hair as he returned to the chair next to Sarah's. Walter's face flushed at the unspoken rebuke in Travis's actions, but he kept silent.

"I'll take her," Sarah offered.

"Not a chance," Travis said, sitting Libby on his knee. "This little girl is all mine, and I'm going to tickle her until she screams for mercy." Libby dutifully squealed, the happy sound carrying across the lawn and earning another scowl from Walter.

"You're deliberately baiting him," Sarah said, trying to figure out why he'd bother. Was it some macho, territorial thing? She doubted it had anything to do with her, and probably not much to do with Libby.

"No, I'm doing what he should have done," Travis said flatly. "I'm spending a little time with his daughter. Watching her beg for his attention was starting to break my heart."

Though he made the comment in a flip tone, Sarah saw something in his eyes that stunned her. There was a real undercurrent of fury there that made her glad she'd never crossed Travis. For the first time, she realized that for all of his easy-going ways, he'd make a daunting enemy.

Mary Vaughn had known officially for a week now that she was pregnant, but she still hadn't gotten over the shock. Not only had the three home pregnancy tests that Rory Sue had bought confirmed it, but so had her doctor. The hoped-for possibility of some kind of fluke, of not one but three false-positives had been ruled out. She was going to have a baby in about seven months. Oh, sweet heaven!

Now she had to tell her husband. She couldn't put it off any longer. She'd decided to do it over dinner at Sullivan's tonight. At least if Sonny passed right out, there'd be people around to help with CPR.

She'd spent all day Monday in a nervous daze. Even her clients had commented on the fact that she didn't seem to be herself. Now she'd yanked everything out of her closet trying to find the perfect outfit for telling Sonny he was about to become a daddy again. Unfortunately, despite years of priding herself on her sense of fashion, she had no idea what to wear for an announcement that huge.

She finally opted for a simple black dress with a low-cut bodice. Not only was it a dress she probably wouldn't be able to fit into in a few weeks, the display of cleavage might distract Sonny from the full shock of her news.

She arrived at Sullivan's fifteen minutes ahead of time. She started to order a glass of wine to calm her nerves, then realized she couldn't. That left her with a bad case of jitters and too much time on her hands.

When Sonny walked in, she tensed, even though the sight of him made her stomach all fluttery. Sometimes it hit her just how handsome he was, and just how lucky she was that he'd taken her back. He stopped several times en route to the table to speak to people, which gave her more time to study him, more time to panic.

"Hey, darlin'," he said, dropping a discreet

kiss on her cheek, then sliding into the booth next to her and giving her knee a much more intimate squeeze. "You look fabulous. What's the occasion? I thought we were just grabbing a bite to eat."

Mary Vaughn swallowed hard. "There's something we need to talk about," she said, her voice choked.

Sonny gave her a quizzical glance, then noticed her club soda. "What's with the fizzy stuff? Don't you want wine?"

"Not tonight."

"A beer?"

She shook her head.

He studied her with a narrowed gaze. "The only time I've ever known you to turn down a drink was when . . ." His voice trailed off and his eyes widened with shock. "Holy crap! Are you pregnant?"

So much for the big announcement, Mary Vaughn thought, almost giddy with relief. She nodded, watching carefully for a clue about his reaction. He'd gone very still and just a little pale beneath his tan.

"Sonny? Are you okay? Are you in shock?" She picked up his glass. "Here, drink some water."

He blinked and stared, his gaze going immediately to her stomach, then back up to meet her eyes. "A baby? We're going to have

273

a baby? How? When?"

She finally felt herself relaxing. At least he didn't look horrified. A little bewildered, but not horrified.

"The usual way," she told him, grinning. "And I think I can pinpoint when." She reminded him about the afternoon she'd sold the space that was now the radio station. "The doctor figures I'm due in about seven months."

Finally a full-fledged, genuine smile broke across his face. "This is the best news I've heard in I don't even know how long! Are you okay? I mean, it's not a problem that you're . . ."

"Old?" Mary Vaughn offered wryly. "We'll probably want to do some additional testing later on, but the doctor says I'm healthy and everything should progress without a hitch."

Sonny yanked his cell phone out of his pocket. "We need to tell Rory Sue."

She covered his hand. "Put that away. Rory Sue already knows. She was here when I had my first episode of morning sickness. She figured it out before I did. She even went out and bought a bunch of home pregnancy tests for me."

"How'd she take it?"

"You know, at first she seemed a little

thrown, but since then she's kind of gotten into it. Ever since the doctor confirmed it last week, she's been bugging me every day to tell you."

"You've known for a week?"

She nodded. "Don't be mad. I needed to get used to the idea, I guess. Figure out the best way to tell you. The amazing part is that I never had to say a word. You just knew."

"Wild guess," he insisted. "I never really imagined . . ."

She squeezed his hand. "I know. Neither did I, but it's okay, right? You're happy?"

"I can't even imagine anything that would make me happier."

"It's going to mean middle-of-the-night feedings and changing diapers and pre-school, then science fairs, and eventually all that teen angst. Do you think we're up to dealing with all that again?"

"Hey, we can do anything. We did it before."

"Yes, but that was over twenty years ago."

"Doesn't matter. We'll get help, if we need it."

Mary Vaughn saw the excitement in his eyes, the love that shone whenever he looked at her. "Do you have any idea how remarkable you are, Sonny Lewis?"

"I do when you look at me like that," he said quietly.

"I'm sorry it took me so long to figure it out," she told him, not for the first time.

"Darlin', now's all that matters. And you and me, we're having a baby! It just doesn't get any better than that."

Even though he was on the air until late at night and rarely got to sleep before two in the morning, Travis found himself waking to listen to Sarah in the morning. Lying in bed with the sound of her sweet voice washing over him was torture. If he closed his eyes, he could imagine her right here beside him, the two of them intimately tangled together in the hot, sweaty aftermath of sex. It was starting to drive him a little nuts.

Then, again, lately everything was getting on his nerves. Tom and Jeanette were so happy, it was hard to be in the same room with them. His father was stubbornly going ahead with his wedding plans. And his mother had stopped bitterly complaining and now spoke in the resigned tone of the recently bereaved.

The only thing he could think to do that would change his circumstances was to move out of Tom and Jeanette's and into a place of his own. In sheer desperation, he'd even considered a move to the Serenity Inn, but that suggested a lack of permanence, something he thought might impact the way people viewed the radio station. After all, why support a business when the owner wasn't even a real part of the community?

He spent several days with Mary Vaughn Lewis looking at town houses and the few condos that had sprung up outside of town. They had the advantage of being new with little need for upkeep, but to his surprise, he realized he wanted a real home. He wasn't sure why he yearned for a house, when up until now any four walls would do.

After the tenth walk-through listening to Mary Vaughn chat up granite countertops and walk-in closets, he finally said enough. "This isn't what I want," he told her.

"But you said you wanted something small with no upkeep," she said, regarding him with bewilderment.

"I know. It's not your fault. I guess I didn't realize what I wanted until I spent so much time looking at what I don't want. These little cookie-cutter places aren't doing it for me."

"You want a house," she concluded. "I can do that. Do we need to go through another process of elimination, or do you know what kind you'd like to see?"

He laughed because she said it so cheerfully, without the faintest hint of impatience or resignation. "You're a trouper, you know that?"

"So they tell me, but I hope you'll make a decision before I go into labor seven months from now."

He regarded her with surprise. "You're pregnant? What's going on in this town? Is it catching? Jeanette is, too."

She laughed. "I know, but at least she's not going to be as old as the grannies most of the other kids have. I should not be having a baby at my age."

"But you're ecstatic, just the same. I can tell."

"Actually, I am, and Sonny is over the moon. I think Howard would have posters printed up with the announcement, if we let him."

"Don't let him," Travis said. "It'll give Tom ideas. Jeanette's already worried he's going to come on the air at the radio station one day to announce it. She's made me swear I won't let him near a microphone."

"I think it's kind of sweet the way all these men are so excited. I doubt they'd feel that way if they were the ones with morning sickness, though. Which reminds me, if we're going to look at houses, we should get to it.

My morning sickness tends to kick in around noon, which means this baby is going to be as perverse as his or her granddaddy."

"We can wait and start tomorrow," Travis said.

"Nope. I want to show you two houses right now. They're at opposite ends of the spectrum in terms of style. Your reaction will give me some idea of what I need to zero in on."

The first was in a new development on the outskirts of town. Though the lots were large, the houses overwhelmed them. All of the trees that might have offered shade or charm had been ripped out during construction. Travis refused to even leave the car.

"This isn't it," he said, waving her on.

"Okay, then, we'll stick to Serenity proper. How do you feel about Tom and Jeanette's house? I sold it to her, you know. In fact, she stole it right out from under Tom, and he didn't utter a single protest. That's when I knew they'd wind up living there together."

"I love their house," he admitted, "but I doubt they'll let me have it."

She chuckled. "But you do like the cozy little cottage style?"

He nodded. It felt like a real home, not like the mansion he'd grown up in or the sterile places he'd lived while he'd played ball. He wanted a house where he could envision raising a family, which was ironic since he had no intention of ever having one.

"Then I know just the place," she said, "but I won't be able to show it to you until tomorrow. The owner's still living in it, and I need to schedule appointments a day in advance. She hates being there when people are walking through. She says it makes her sad to think of moving away."

"Then why is she going?"

"Her son's made arrangements for her to move to an assisted living facility closer to him. Even though she hates the idea, she doesn't want to fight him on it. Of all her family, he's the only one who lives nearby. She tends to listen to him."

Travis bristled. "He shouldn't be forcing her to do something if she's going to be miserable."

"She's eighty-two. Managing a house is getting to be too much for her. It's sad, but that's reality," Mary Vaughn said. "Do you still want to see the house tomorrow?"

He nodded. "Where will she go when we come by?"

"To play cards at the senior citizens' center. She and her friends play gin rummy."

At least she was still active, he thought. And had friends. In her eighties, that was something.

He told Mary Vaughn to schedule the appointment for ten-thirty, then vowed to tell Sarah about the senior center. Some of the members might make great interviews. Heck, maybe he'd go by himself. They could even do a remote from the center one day, he thought, excited about the idea. He'd never really known his own grandparents, so he liked listening to the older generation talk about the way things used to be.

As he headed for the station, he thought about the way he was becoming a part of Serenity bit by bit. He cared about the community. He liked the people in it. It should have felt like home, or the way he'd always imagined home should feel.

However, even he knew something was missing. Worse, he suspected it was more than just owning a house. And he was very much afraid that even though that something might be within reach, he wasn't going to be brave enough to try to grab it.

14

Travis fell in love with the cozy little three-bedroom house that Mary Vaughn took him to see in the morning. On a tree-lined street in an older neighborhood, it boasted a screened-in side porch that was shaded by a giant oak, a brick-paved driveway and planters spilling over with bright flowers on either side of the front steps.

The house itself was filled with comfortable, if somewhat shabby furniture, but the colors were bright, and every available surface was covered with framed photos. On the mantel a wedding photo, clearly taken years ago, showed a man and woman whose eyes sparkled with mischief despite the solemnity of the occasion.

"What's her name?" he asked Mary Vaughn, gesturing toward the picture.

"Elizabeth Johnson," she said. "She likes to be called Liz."

"She looks like a real pistol."

"She certainly was in her heyday," Mary Vaughn confirmed. "She led protests against segregation and challenged everyone she knew to do the right thing. Serenity wasn't as slow to come around as some cities in the South, and that was partly due to Liz. She took her maid to lunch at Wharton's and practically dared Grace's mother-in-law, who ran the place back then, not to serve her."

It sounded to Travis as if it would be a real loss to Serenity if she moved away.

"Want to see the rest of the house?" Mary Vaughn asked, a sparkle in her eyes. "I have a surprise for you out back."

He was figuring there'd be some sort of humongous gas grill or something, but it turned out to be a tiny guest cottage, just one bedroom with a bath and a kitchen that consisted of the basics — a small stove, refrigerator and sink.

"So, what do you think?" she asked him. "Isn't it perfect? You could use it for guests, or as a rental."

The whole property was perfect, but somehow Travis couldn't see himself making an offer. It would feel too much like snatching this remarkable woman's home right out from under her, especially when he knew she wasn't anxious to leave.

"It's definitely the best house we've seen, but I need to give it some thought," he told Mary Vaughn.

"It won't be on the market for long," she warned him. "Not even in this economy. The asking price is reasonable. It's been priced to sell."

"I don't question that," he said. "It sounds more than fair."

"Then tell me your reservations. Maybe I can help."

"Thanks, but I need to work through this on my own. Just let me know if another offer comes in before I get back to you. Can you do that?"

"I'll do what I can, but I'm obligated to take any offers to Liz."

"I know that, but if I tell you I might be willing to top such an offer, then you'd be obligated to get back to me, right? It would be in her best interests."

She studied him curiously. "Travis, what's going on? If you like the place that much, why not put in a bid?"

"You'll just have to accept that I'm not quite ready," he said, not sure he could explain it himself.

He left her staring after him, then drove to the station, where Sarah was winding up her show. The second Bill took over and she left the studio, Travis caught her.

"I need you to come with me," he said. "No questions for once, okay?"

She regarded him with bewilderment. "What's going on?"

"There's somebody I want to meet and I want you along. It's not a ploy or a date or whatever else usually gets your hackles up. Okay?"

"I guess," she said, grabbing her purse and leaving the station with him.

"Are you planning to give me any clues at all?" she asked as he drove through town.

"Nope. Just keep your eyes and ears open."

The Serenity Senior Center was a small pink-brick building on a grassy lot. It had white columns and a portico in front and white shutters on the windows. Ironically, it had once been a funeral home, but the funeral home had outgrown the space and built a much larger facility a few blocks away.

Inside there were two front parlors on either side of the door. One was book-lined and filled with comfortable chairs. A flyer posted next to the doorway listed upcoming programs that would be offered, including a lecture series by professors from a nearby community college. The other room had been set up with card tables, and even now there were a dozen or so seniors playing canasta, bridge and gin rummy at the different tables.

"Why are we here?" Sarah asked, glancing curiously around the foyer, which had a faded Oriental carpet on the floor and a table that had been polished to such a shine that the vase of hydrangeas sitting in the middle reflected in the wood.

"I'm looking for Elizabeth Johnson. Do you know her?"

"Everyone in town knows Liz," she said at once. "She's right over there. She's playing cards with Flo Decatur — that's Helen's mother — and two people I don't know."

She directed his gaze across the room to a woman with snow-white hair that curled softly around her lined face. Her blue eyes sparkled alertly as she studied her cards, then snatched up the previous player's discard and triumphantly declared, "Gin" as she spread her cards on the table.

"Not again," another woman at the table moaned. "I don't know why we even bother playing. You always win, Liz."

"Well, of course I do. I pay attention to the game, instead of Jake Cudlow over at the next table."

The other woman flushed. "Will you keep

your voice down, please? You're embarrassing me."

"You're an embarrassment to yourself, Beverly," Liz countered. "If you're interested, just invite him to dinner and stop ruining our card games by not concentrating."

Travis chuckled. "You know, it's really amazing," he said, lowering his voice. "I saw an old picture of her as a young woman and got this idea in my head of what she'd be like now. She's exactly the way I expected her to be — feisty and full of life. Do you actually know her? Can you introduce us?"

"Sure, but I'm not sure I understand why."

"I'm not a hundred percent sure myself. I just know I want to get to know her. I'm also thinking she'd be a great guest for your show. She must have an amazing perspective on the history of Serenity." Travis had forgotten to keep his voice low as he said this, and he saw the object of his speculation gaze right at him.

"I may be old, young man, but I still have excellent hearing," Liz called out to him. "And just so you know, I don't go all the way back to the days of the slaves, and that's when this town was founded." She beckoned to him. "Come over here."

Travis grinned at having been caught talking about her. "Yes, ma'am."

Liz's gaze assessed him from head to toe. "You're that boy who bought the radio station, am I right? I recognize your voice. You have quite a way about you on the air."

"Thank you."

She turned to Sarah. "Don't hang back there, Sarah. It's been a long time since I've seen you, but I'd know you anywhere. You look just like your mama did at your age."

She introduced the two of them to her companions, then turned back to Travis. "I gather you wished to speak to me. Any particular reason?"

"As I was telling Sarah, I thought perhaps you'd like to come to the station one day and talk about your memories of Serenity."

"And? You have something else on your mind, too, don't you?"

Travis needed more time to decide if he could trust his instinct on the rest. "I do, but let's start with the show, if you're willing."

"Oh, there's nothing Liz likes doing more than talking," her friend Beverly chimed in with a wicked glint in her eyes. "Isn't that right, Liz?"

"True enough," Liz said, clearly not offended. "Whom will I be talking to? You, Sarah?"

Sarah nodded. "I would love it."

"Perhaps, if you're finished with your card game, we could have lunch at Sullivan's and discuss the topics the two of you might cover," Travis suggested. "Do you have the time, Liz? May I call you that? Or would you prefer Mrs. Johnson?"

Liz's eyes twinkled. "Liz is perfectly fine. Something tells me the two of us are going to become great friends. It's been a long time since I had a man your age courting me."

"Their loss," Travis said. "Would the rest of you like to join us?"

"Wouldn't dream of intruding," Beverly said. "Liz was always a bit selfish when it came to keeping her men to herself."

"Besides, Beverly has her eye on Jake Cudlow," Flo Decatur countered. "She's hoping he'll invite her out for ice cream after he finishes this hand of bridge."

"Another time, then," Travis said, giving Beverly a wink. He leaned closer and whispered, "Good luck with Mr. Cudlow."

Liz Johnson drew herself up to her full five-feet-two-inches and walked out with him and Sarah. Though she carried a cane with a silver handle, she clearly didn't rely on it.

In the parking lot, she took one look at

Travis's bright red convertible and her eyes lit up. "You are going to put that top down, aren't you?" she asked eagerly.

"If you'd like me to," he told her.

"It's the only reason to have a convertible, don't you think? Seems a waste not to have it down." Her expression turned nostalgic. "My late husband had a convertible when we met. We used to take a spin in it every evening. I think that's why I married him, because I loved that car so much."

All the way to Sullivan's, she regaled them with stories of her courtship and the rides they'd taken in Henry Johnson's baby-blue convertible with its white top.

Though Travis encouraged her to sort through a variety of topics they could discuss on the air, Liz kept slipping surreptitious glances his way. At the end of the meal, she put her napkin down on the table and looked him in the eye.

"Okay, young man, what is this really about? You're not trying to butter me up so I'll lower the price on my house, are you?"

Sarah's gaze shot to him. "You're buying her house?"

Travis flushed guiltily. "I looked at it this morning, but I haven't put in an offer." He regarded Liz apologetically. "And I swear to

you this was only about meeting you. When
Mary Vaughn was telling me about your
circumstances and then I saw your property,
I had this crazy idea, but I wasn't sure it
could work. Now I'm convinced it can, if
you'll just hear me out."

Liz regarded him with suspicion, but she
nodded. "I'll listen."

"First, let me be sure I have my facts
straight. Your son wants you to move to an
assisted living facility?"

She made a face. "True enough."

"And you don't want to go."

"Of course not. My friends are here, but
he does have a point. The house is getting
to be too much for me. And the rest of the
family is scattered. He's the closest, but he's
in Columbia. It's inconvenient for him to
be driving back and forth over here every
time I sneeze."

Travis hadn't planned to do something
this impulsive without giving the matter
more thought, but since Liz had called him
on having ulterior motives, he had little
choice but to float the idea here and now.

"Would you consider staying on in the
guest house?" he blurted. "I'll buy the
property, but you'll continue to live there
for as long as you choose. Rent free, of
course."

Sarah stared at him in shock. Liz's eyes immediately filled with tears.

"Why would you even suggest such a thing?" Liz asked, but the hopeful note in her voice told him she desperately wanted to believe the offer was sincere.

"It just seems wrong to make you leave your home when you're not ready to do it," he said. "I'm sure your son's heart is in the right place and he's looking out for your interests, but when Mary Vaughn filled me in, none of it set right with me. Then, when I saw the guest cottage, it seemed to me there was another solution." He met her gaze. "If you're interested."

Liz's frail hand covered his. Only a faint tremble gave away how moved she was by his suggestion. "Young man, I think you may be the most generous, kind-hearted person I've ever met, but I think we both need to take some time to think about this. We've just met. By morning you might regret being so impulsive."

"I won't," Travis said flatly. "But if you want some time, take all that you need. You'll want to speak to your family, too, I'm sure. Why don't Sarah and I take you home, and then I'll stop by tomorrow morning and we can discuss this some more."

She nodded. "That's a very sensible plan,"

she said. "Just don't be too late. My card game starts at ten."

Travis chuckled. "I'll be there by nine," he promised. "We wouldn't want Beverly or Flo to have time to stack the deck."

"As if they could put one over on me," Liz said with a sniff.

At the front door of her house, she turned to Sarah. "This young man of yours is a keeper," she said. "Don't let him get away."

Sarah sputtered, but to Travis's relief, she managed not to correct Liz's impression.

"A keeper!" he gloated as they walked back to the car. He slanted a meaningful look in Sarah's direction. "I hope you were taking notes."

"You just offered to let the woman stay in her own home," she began.

"The guest cottage," he corrected.

"The point is, she's understandably besotted. She can't see beyond the superficial sweetness to the wicked soul underneath."

"I do not have a wicked soul," he said indignantly. "Come on, admit it. I'm trying to do a nice thing."

She sighed. "Yes, you are. I just wish I could figure out what's in it for you."

"Maybe I'm just after karmic brownie points," he suggested.

"Maybe," she said, though she studied

him with a narrowed gaze. "But I don't think so."

The truth was that Travis wasn't entirely sure why he'd done it, either. Maybe in some weird way he was trying to fill his prospective new home with a family . . . without any of the messy complications of actually having to marry someone.

"It was the most amazing, totally selfless gesture I've ever seen," Sarah reported to Raylene that evening. "You should have seen the sparkle hc put into Liz's eyes when she realized she might not have to leave her home, after all."

"Maybe he just did it to impress you," Raylene suggested cynically. "After all, he did invite you along to witness this burst of generosity."

Sarah shook her head. "Nobody would make a grand gesture like that just to get a woman's attention. After all, he's going to be stuck with having Liz as a neighbor. He has to be doing it because he thinks it's the right thing to do. And it *is* the right thing. It's remarkable."

Raylene regarded her knowingly. "And you are impressed, right? So it's served that purpose, too. In fact, I'll bet if he'd asked you on a date on the way back to the station, you'd have found it impossible to resist."

"Don't be ridiculous. I know better than to date Travis. He flirts with any female who's breathing, Liz Johnson included."

It was true, though, that she'd seen an unexpected side of him today. She'd already figured out that he was far more than a shallow player whose only goal in life was scoring with the next woman who crossed his path. She even knew that beneath his flirtatious ways, he was a decent man. But if he turned out to have real substance — kindness and generosity — she might find the attraction she felt for him impossible to resist. Raylene was right about that.

Just then Annie tapped on the back door and walked in with Trevor in tow.

"My boy here wants to play with Tommy and Libby, if they're up for company," Annie said.

"They're in the living room looking at a video," Sarah told him.

"Great," Annie said. "I'll get him settled and be right back. Don't talk about anything juicy till I'm here."

The instant Annie was gone, Sarah scowled at Raylene. "Do not mention any of this to her, okay? She'll just jump to all sorts of wild conclusions."

"You mean the same ones I jumped to," Raylene said dryly. "But I get it, you don't want to have to defend your claim that you're not falling for him."

"I am so not falling for him," Sarah said, keeping her voice low.

"Falling for whom?" Annie inquired, slipping back into the kitchen. She looked from Raylene to Sarah and back, then sighed. "Do I even need to ask? You're talking about Travis. Sarah, sweetie, please tell me you are not giving him so much as a second glance. You know what Ty said. And surely you remember the ruckus that kiss stirred up."

"He's a player, blah-blah-blah," Sarah dutifully repeated. "Yes, I get it. My guard is up. I've refused to go on a date with him, not that he actually asks me on dates."

"Then why were you at lunch with him today at Sullivan's?" Annie asked. "My mother couldn't wait to tell me."

"Did she also mention that we were with Liz Johnson, interviewing her about being a guest on my show?"

Annie frowned. "No, she didn't mention that."

"See?" she said triumphantly. "It was work. Not a date. Now can we talk about something else, please? Doesn't Ty have another stretch of home games soon? Are you going over to Atlanta this time? It must feel like a honeymoon when you finally see him in person. You two practically lit up the backyard with your glow at Tom and Jeanette's."

Annie's eyes sparkled. "Yes, and without Trevor this time. It's just a three-day home stand, so Dee-Dee and her husband are going to come down here and keep Trevor for the weekend. It will be exactly like having a honeymoon," she said with a dramatic sigh. "Three whole days to ourselves!"

"And a few thousand baseball fans," Raylene chimed in.

Annie frowned. "They don't get to come home with us. And I like sitting in the stands with the other wives and having Ty look up there as if there's not another soul in the whole stadium."

"No pangs when you see the groupies hanging out trying to catch the attention of the players?" Sarah asked carefully.

It was a groupie — Dee-Dee — who'd gotten pregnant with Ty's son. That fleeting and complicated relationship had nearly torn them apart.

Annie's expression sobered. "Not anymore. Ty and I are solid. I really do believe that." She grinned. "And I think he knows now if he so much as looks at some groupie, I will cut off parts of which he is exceedingly fond."

"Yes, that should keep him in line," Raylene agreed with a chuckle.

"Now that we've covered what's going on in Annie's life and in mine," Sarah said with a pointed look at Raylene, "let's talk about you."

Raylene immediately stiffened. "Not this again."

"Yes, this," Sarah said emphatically. "You can't spend all your time with the babysitter, me and the kids for company. You need to socialize. You missed Tom and Jeanette's big announcement. In fact, you miss all the parties that aren't here. You're way too young and attractive to settle for some bizarre kind of spinsterhood."

"I socialize all the time," Raylene said defensively. "People are constantly running in and out of here."

"But you're hardly likely to meet an available man," Annie protested.

"Who says I want to?" Raylene countered. "Besides, Walter's here every time I turn around. He's available."

Sarah blinked. "Walter? I thought he was out job-hunting every day."

Raylene shrugged. "He has been. There's

298

not a lot available, so when he finishes, he stops by here to see the kids."

"Is he bothering you?" Sarah asked worriedly. Walter was not the most sensitive man in the universe, and Raylene was pretty vulnerable these days.

"No. He just needs somebody to talk to. I listen."

Annie frowned as she listened to the exchange. "He's not, I mean you're not . . . interested?"

Raylene looked genuinely shocked. "In each other? No way. He's just lonely. I'm always around to be a sounding board. That's it. Half the time I don't even think he listens to a word I say. He just has to work through things aloud."

"Now that sounds familiar," Sarah said, unable to keep an annoyingly bitter note out of her voice. "He never listened to me, either." She regarded Raylene earnestly. "But you'd tell me if he's bothering you, right? I want him to spend time with the kids, but he should be doing it when I'm here."

"It's not a big deal," Raylene assured her. "Honestly."

Annie didn't look entirely satisfied. "Which still doesn't address the fact that you need to deal with your problem, Raylene. Last time I saw Dr. McDaniels, I mentioned what was going on —"

Raylene scowled. "Did I ask you to do that?"

"No, but I wanted to get some idea if there's help for agoraphobia. I know we've all been dancing around saying it out loud, but that is what's going on here. Anyway, she says there are things you can do to get past this, but obviously she can't even say if that's what you have unless you meet with her."

"I'll think about it," Raylene said.

"That's what you always say," Annie protested with obvious frustration.

"Because it's always true. I do think about it. When I'm ready to talk to her or anyone else, I'll let you know."

"But —" Annie began.

Raylene stood up. "I'm going to bed."

"It's not even six o'clock," Sarah argued. "Don't run off just to avoid discussing this."

"Yeah, well, it's been a long day," Raylene said. "You two enjoy yourselves. I'll see you in the morning, Sarah. I'll check on the kids."

"We should probably go in there ourselves," Annie said. "It's been quiet for a while. There's no telling what they're up to."

"You go," Sarah said. "I'll put together some supper. Salad okay for you?"

"Sure," Annie said.

"I have spaghetti for the kids. That ought to be good and messy."

Annie laughed. "That's why you're the fun mom. You don't care if they have to have yet another bath before bedtime."

"We can always take 'em out back and hose 'em down," Sarah said, not entirely in jest. It was amazing that now that she was working, she actually didn't mind the kids' messes the way she once had. "So, no objections to the spaghetti?"

"Not when you put it like that," Annie said, then gave her a pointed look. "And once these kids crash, you and I are going to continue that conversation about Travis. I'm not entirely convinced you're as immune as you say you are. I sense you're weakening."

Yeah, Sarah was afraid of that, too.

15

Travis was right on time for his appointment with Liz Johnson in the morning. When he walked in the door, he was struck by the same sense of rightness that he'd felt the day before. This house, the arrangement with Liz, suited him.

It didn't hurt that this morning the house was filled with the aroma of homemade chocolate chip cookies, his favorite.

"You baked," he said, sniffing the air appreciatively.

"Never knew a man yet who could resist my chocolate chip cookies," she said. "We'll talk in the kitchen."

After he'd pulled out a chair for her at the kitchen table, she poured cups of tea for both of them, then passed a plate of cookies fresh from the oven.

"Any second thoughts?" she asked, studying him intently.

"Not a one," he assured her. "Did you talk

to your family?"

"They want to meet you," she said with a chagrined expression. "I gather they want to be sure you're not planning to take advantage of a senile old lady."

Travis laughed. "You're about as far from senile as anyone I've ever met."

"Still, at my age, I suppose it pays to be cautious. I can't argue that."

"Neither can I," he said, not taking offense. "When are they coming?"

"The troops will rally this weekend," she told him. "Think you can handle it? I'm counting on you to help me persuade them that this is the perfect solution for me."

"I've handled being shouted at by a mob of angry fans when I struck out in the bottom of the ninth," he told her. "I think I can deal with your family."

Liz gave him a sharp look. "Just so you know, I'm only doing this to humor them. If it were just me, I'd say yes right this second. I've been around a long time. I know when someone's a crook and when they're a decent human being. I liked you the second I set eyes on you, and that was even before you made this crazy proposition of yours."

Her faith in him was gratifying. If only Sarah were as easily swayed. Heck, if only *he* believed he was so praiseworthy. "I promise I'll do my very best to convince them I'm trustworthy," he said.

"Sunday dinner's at half-past one," she said. "Bring Sarah. She makes a good impression."

He winced at the command. "I'm not sure Sarah will be available. She and I aren't involved, so I don't keep tabs on her schedule when she's away from the station."

She waved off the claim. "Well, the two of you will be involved. Saw that straight off. Might as well start acting like it. And you'll look more respectable if you're with a lovely young woman."

"You don't think I'm respectable enough on my own?" he asked, not even trying to hide his amusement.

"I'm not the one you need to impress. Charlie's a lawyer. He doesn't trust anybody. He's going to think you're after my money no matter what I say. The whole situation will seem less fishy if you have a lady friend."

"Then I'll do my best to get Sarah here," he promised.

"Just so you're prepared, I'm inviting Mary Vaughn and Sonny, too. Might as well have the paperwork on hand once I get a stamp of approval from the kids. I don't believe in wasting time. Once they get away from here and start comparing notes, who knows what they'll think up to insist I go through with moving to that assisted living place."

"But you're pretty confident they'll go along with this, aren't you?"

"Like I said, they will once they've seen you for themselves. I love my children, but they all have busy lives. I think they'd turn me over to just about anyone if it let them off the hook. Still, they have to go through the motions of looking out for me. I can't be sure they won't have second thoughts later. I'm not taking any chances."

"Doesn't it bother you that all they really care about is any inconvenience to themselves?"

"I've been painting them in a bad light," she said apologetically. "They do care about me. Up till now, I've been able to live my life without answering to anybody. Once I hit eighty, though, it occurred to them I might be slowing down. Not that they had any evidence of that. One of them probably read an article somewhere that cited a bunch of statistics about mental capability decreasing after a certain age. It wouldn't take much to get them all stirred up."

She said it with a wry expression that

impressed Travis. "You have a pretty clear view of what's what, don't you?" he said.

"I spent my whole life seeing things for what they were, even when everybody around me wanted to ignore the obvious. No reason to stop doing that now," she told him. "Now let me wrap up the rest of these cookies for you and grab the package I put together for the senior center and you can give me a ride over there."

"I'd be happy to," he said.

She gave him a penetrating look. "Will driving me places from time to time be a nuisance?" she asked candidly. "I don't take my car far these days. I might think my reflexes and my eyesight are just fine, but there's no sense taking chances I might be wrong."

"Absolutely not," he assured her. "I'm happy to take you wherever you need to go if I'm around."

She shook her head, her expression bemused. "You don't look like any saint I ever envisioned, but you surely must be one."

"Not likely," he said, then leaned down to whisper, "but if you wouldn't mind mentioning that opinion to Sarah, I'd appreciate it."

"She's a sharp girl. She'll see it for herself."

"I don't know," he argued. "She doesn't see too clearly where I'm concerned."

She gave him a penetrating look. "And that really matters to you?"

He took a moment to give the question the consideration it deserved. "More than I ever expected it to," he admitted eventually.

"Then just leave it to me," she said decisively. "Fixing your love-life will provide an interesting challenge. I haven't had one I could sink my teeth into for a while now."

She sounded so enthused about the project, it gave Travis pause. He'd never needed anyone meddling in his relationships before, but something told him if he was going to have someone on his side, Liz was the best possible advocate.

Sarah was trying hard to ignore Travis's presence, even though it was almost impossible in the cramped office space they shared.

"If you're not actually working, why don't you go away?" she finally said testily. "You're just sitting there staring at me. You seem to have turned it into some kind of hobby. It's getting on my nerves."

"I'm thinking," he claimed.

"About?"

"You," he said, then gave her a beguiling

smile, "and how I can get you to agree to do something for me."

She sat back, regarding him with suspicion. "What kind of something? If it's work-related, all you have to do is tell me to do it."

He crossed over and sat on the corner of her desk, his knees nudging hers. "That's the thing. It's not work-related. It's personal."

"I will not go on a date with you," she said firmly. "I thought we'd established that."

"Not a date, either," he said.

Her gaze narrowed. "What then?"

"Liz Johnson has invited both of us to Sunday dinner."

"Why? You didn't lead her to believe we're having some kind of relationship, did you?"

"No. In fact, I told her precisely the opposite."

"Then why does she want me there with you?"

"To help me make a good impression," he said, his expression sheepish.

Sarah chuckled. "Really? On whom?"

"Her kids. It seems I need to pass muster before they'll let her stay on in the guest house, just yards from my evil clutches."

"They're wise to be cautious," she said.

"Hey, I'm a good guy."

"Mostly," she conceded. "But I meant in general. After all, a lot of men who made the kind of offer you made would have an ulterior motive."

"Well, I don't."

"I actually believe that."

"So, you'll help? You'll come to dinner?"

She made a show of hesitating, even though she already knew she'd wind up giving in. What he wanted to do for Liz was a really sweet thing. "I hate to take time away from the kids on the weekend," she said.

"Let Walter step up. It would be a refreshing change."

She frowned at his sarcasm. "Why do you dislike him so much? You really don't even know him."

"I've seen the aftereffects of what he did to you," he said flatly. "Never mind. I don't want to get sidetracked by that discussion. It's a couple of hours. If you don't want to do it for me, think about Liz. This matters to her. She really wants to stay on here, and this is the only way she can do that. She needs our support to pull it off."

When he put it that way, how could she say no? "Okay, I'll do it. Just don't start acting all territorial and weird on me. I'll call you on it."

"Wouldn't dream of it," he said, though the twinkle in his eyes belied his solemn tone.

She frowned at him. "I mean it, Travis, don't try taking advantage of the situation."

He sketched an exaggerated cross across his chest. "You have my word," he told her.

So far his word had been good enough. In fact, it suddenly occurred to her that when push came to shove, Travis was more reliable than many of the men she knew. It came as an eye-opening revelation that despite all the flip words and iffy reputation, he truly was someone she could count on. She'd have to give that some thought one of these days, preferably when she wasn't feeling particularly vulnerable.

It was probably for the best, too, if she didn't do it while they were half-pretending to be a couple. She might be tempted to start believing in the illusion.

Mary Vaughn knew that the sale of Liz Johnson's house to Travis depended on what happened at this Sunday dinner she'd pulled together, but for the life of her she couldn't entirely figure out the dynamics.

For one thing, Sarah Price was supposedly with Travis in some capacity that wasn't entirely clear. Liz Johnson's children, most of whom had been in school with Mary Vaughn and Sonny, seemed to be regarding Travis with distrust and each other with barely banked hostility.

"This is fun," Sonny muttered under his breath when an awkward silence had dragged on a little too long. "Why are we here again?"

"Because if this goes smoothly, I'm going to get to close the deal for the house this afternoon. I have the paperwork in the car."

"Is it going smoothly?" he asked. "Because you sure couldn't prove it by me."

Mary Vaughn shrugged. "Me, either, to be honest, but it's too soon to throw in the towel."

"What we obviously need is some excitement to break the tension," Sonny said.

In the car business, Sonny was an expert at making jovial chit-chat. Mary Vaughn nudged him. "Talk to Charlie. See if you can get him to relax instead of sitting there scowling at Travis."

"I'll do my best," Sonny said.

He'd barely turned in his chair when Mary Vaughn gasped and clutched her stomach.

"Sonny!" she said urgently, her voice tight with anxiety.

He turned back, took one look at her and

turned pale. "Is it the baby?"

Unable to speak, she nodded, terrified by the cramping sensation in her stomach. Whatever was going on, it wasn't good.

Sonny was on his feet at once. "Folks, I'm afraid you'll have to excuse us. Mary Vaughn's not feeling well. I need to get her to the hospital."

"I'm pregnant," she explained. "I'm so sorry to spoil the dinner. Liz, thank you for including us." The polite words were barely out of her mouth when she gasped again as what felt like a powerful contraction hit her.

She looked toward Sonny for reassurance. He scooped her into his arms at once. "Stay calm, sweetheart. I'll have you at the hospital in no time."

Travis immediately came around the table. "I'll drive you," he told Sonny. "You need to sit in back with Mary Vaughn and keep her calm."

Sarah was right beside him. "Take Sonny's car. It's an SUV. It'll be more comfortable than your convertible," she told Travis. "I'll follow in your car, so you'll have a way to get back home later."

Mary Vaughn hated being in the center of so much commotion, but her fear was greater than her embarrassment. "Please hurry," she whispered. "I can't lose this baby. I just can't." Even though she was only nearing the end of her first trimester, she'd started envisioning her life with this new baby to raise. Sonny was counting on it even more than she was.

"You're not going to," Liz assured her, her voice calm, her expression comforting as she gave Mary Vaughn's shoulder an encouraging squeeze.

But even with Liz's reassuring words echoing in her head, it wasn't until Sonny had settled her in the backseat with her head in his lap that Mary Vaughn began to calm down. Travis was driving at a speed that probably would have made her dizzy had she known what it was. All that mattered, though, was that they reached the emergency room in record time.

Sonny carried her inside, barking orders at nurses, orderlies and doctors until she was in a cubicle with half a dozen people dancing attendance. Only then did she see the panic in his eyes.

Even so, he clung to her hand and kept reassuring her that it was going to be okay. His soothing tone belied the anxiety she could read in his expression.

Finally a nurse took him gently by the shoulder and guided him from the area. "Let us do our jobs. She's in good hands."

Mary Vaughn barely heard the buzz all around her, but the pain eventually stopped and she felt herself relaxing. Gazing into the doctor's eyes, she finally had the nerve to ask the question that had been on her mind since that first awful pain had struck.

"Am I going to lose the baby?"

"Not if I can help it," he assured her. "What happened today wasn't unusual, but at your age this is a high risk pregnancy. Add in the fact that your blood pressure's running quite high and you're already at risk for preeclampsia. I'm going to recommend bed rest to see if we can control the blood pressure."

Bed rest didn't sound so bad, especially if it meant the baby would be okay. "For how long?"

"That depends. It could be a few days or a few weeks, or it could be for the remainder of your pregnancy. We don't want to take chances."

Mary Vaughn just stared at him. She couldn't imagine being confined to bed for a day, much less six months. Worse, though, was the thought of not carrying this precious baby to term.

"Let's get your husband back in here and talk about what needs to happen next," he said.

Sonny listened intently to everything the doctor said, then nodded. "Not a problem."

"Six months," she said, overwhelmed by the thought. "How will I manage?"

"We don't know for sure if it will need to be that long," the doctor reminded her. "Let's take this one day at a time and see where we are in a few days."

Sonny gave her an encouraging smile. "And if it turns out to be longer than a few days, Rory Sue will stay home with you. I've already called her. She's on her way."

"We can't ask her to sit around the house all day taking care of me," Mary Vaughn protested.

"Yes, we can," Sonny said flatly. "And she'll help you out with your real estate business, just the way you planned, so you won't be fretting about that."

"But she needs training," Mary Vaughn objected. "She's not qualified to work on her own."

"Which is why she'll do the legwork and you'll close the deals from home," he said. "We'll make this work, sweetheart. Nothing is going to happen to you or our baby. That's a promise."

He sounded so confident that she finally let herself relax. If Sonny made a promise, she could count on it. Resting her hand protectively on her stomach, she finally fell asleep knowing she and her baby were in good hands.

After the unexpected commotion at Liz's dinner on Sunday and the rush to the hospital, Travis and Sarah had driven home in silence. Only when they were a few miles from her house did he turn to her.

"That was something, wasn't it?" he said, still shaken. "Do you think the baby will be all right?"

"Sonny says the doctor is very hopeful," Sarah responded. "I didn't even realize Mary Vaughn was pregnant."

"She'd mentioned it to me when I started house-hunting. She's so excited about it. I'd hate to see something happen."

"Bed rest, especially if it turns out to be for the duration of her pregnancy, is going to make her crazy," Sarah said. "I can't even imagine such a thing, and I'm not half as hyper as Mary Vaughn. You were very good to jump in like that and offer to drive. Sonny, for all of his determination to stay calm for her sake, looked like he was about two seconds from coming unglued."

Travis nodded. "I know. No way could I take a chance he'd wrap the car around a tree trying to race her to the hospital. If it had been up to me, though, I'd have called an ambulance."

"With a volunteer squad, it can take too long. Unless it's an accident or somebody's critical, we have a tendency to just head for the hospital on our own."

"But at least the EMTs would know what to do."

"Stop fretting over it," Sarah told him. "Everything went just fine, thanks to you and Sonny."

"I think we need to campaign on the air for a fulltime rescue squad," Travis persisted. "I don't ever want to be in a position like this again."

"Go for it," she encouraged. "But you might want to discuss the budget realities with Tom so you don't wind up pitting yourself against your cousin."

He nodded. "Good point." He turned and met her gaze. "I'm going to stop by Liz's and fill her in. Want to come, or should I drop you off?"

She glanced at her watch. "I should get home," she said.

He pulled to a stop in front of her house a few minutes later. "I'm glad you were there today, for all of it. Thanks."

She smiled. "It was definitely an interesting afternoon. I hope everything works out

317

the way you want it to for the house."

Travis nodded. He should have let her go then, but instead he found himself reaching out and putting a hand on her arm.

"Sarah?"

Startled, she met his gaze. Before she could do or say something that would stop him, he leaned across the console and kissed her, just a quick brush of his lips over hers.

"Thanks again," he murmured, resisting the idea of kissing her again, resisting the need that was humming through him.

"Sure," she said, obviously disconcerted.

She left the car slowly, so slowly that he wondered if she wanted him to ask her to stay. As she walked toward the house, he saw her lift her hand and touch her fingers to her lips. It was a fleeting gesture, so brief he easily might have missed it, but it told him everything he needed to know. Her feelings for him were growing, just as his were for her.

And one of these days they were going to have to do something about them . . . if they dared.

For the better part of a month after Mary Vaughn's trip to the hospital and Travis's tender kiss, Sarah was more skittish than ever around the station. She knew with a hundred percent certainty that she was in serious danger of falling for a man who was all wrong for her.

If she'd only been dealing with her own emotions, she might have been able to keep things in check, but Travis seemed to have sensed some kind of shift as well. He'd been asking her out just about daily. Regular as clockwork, he'd linger around the studio while she was on the air, then suggest lunch or a walk to get ice cream or a cool drink at Sullivan's. Not even the fact that she'd turned him down every single time seemed to daunt him.

When she brought Tommy out for T-ball at the urging of Jeanette and discovered that Travis was coaching the team, she almost turned right around and walked away from the field. Travis caught her before she could reach her car.

His eyes locked with hers, he asked, "Running away, as usual, sugar?"

Sarah bristled. "Of course not."

"Then why'd you leave without signing Tommy up to play?"

Tommy regarded Travis with curiosity. "Play ball?"

Travis nodded. "Yep, that's what we're going to do. Every Saturday."

Tommy turned his precious little face up to look at her. "Can I, Mommy? Please?"

Just as Travis had clearly anticipated, there was no way she could say no now. "Of course you can play," she told her son, saving her scowl for Travis. He returned it with a perfectly innocent expression.

"Oh, don't give me that look," she said sourly. "You knew exactly what you were doing."

"Giving your son a chance to spend some time outdoors with kids his own age learning to play a game?"

"Manipulating me to spend more time around you," she corrected, then conceded grudgingly, "And that other stuff, too, I suppose."

As they strolled back toward the field, Tommy spotted another boy from their block. "Mommy, can I go? I wanna play with Jimmy."

Since they were only a few feet away, she let him go, even though it left her alone with Travis.

When she would have walked off and left him, he caught her hand. "Hold on a sec. Mind telling me why I make you so nervous? I could have sworn we were making progress."

"Progress toward what?"

"Building some kind of a relationship," he said.

Her gaze narrowed. "We can't have a relationship."

"Because?"

She scrambled for a believable excuse. "Because we work together. You're my boss. I don't think we should muddy the waters by having any kind of personal relationship. Didn't we establish all this months ago when I first came to work for you?"

"That's all very politically correct," Travis agreed with a twinkle in his eyes. "Helen must have coached you. Only problem is, you're fibbing. I scared you to death long before I hired you. Why? Be honest with me."

Sarah took a deep breath and blurted out the truth. "Because you're just playing a game with me. You're no more interested in me than Brad Pitt is."

Travis lifted a brow. "You know Brad Pitt?"

"Stop it. You know what I mean. I won't let you make a fool of me."

"You mean the way your ex-husband did?" he asked quietly. "That's what this is really about. You still believe no man could possibly find you attractive or want to be with you. I think we both know that I am attracted and that I do want to be with you, so please don't compare me to him."

"You're nothing like Walter," she admitted. For one thing, Travis only said nice things about her. Even when there was something she didn't know, he didn't demean her because of it. Still, she knew her own limitations. Walter had drilled them into her head, and not even his recent apology had taken away the sting of those hurtful words.

"Do you trust me?" Travis asked, his gaze intense.

She hesitated, then conceded, "Yes."

"Then why can't you believe that when I ask you out it's because I really want to spend time with you?"

He sounded so sincere. She wanted desperately to believe what he was saying, but she couldn't shake the memory of all the times Walter had made her feel self-conscious or inept or fat. Why would this man who could have any woman, a man who'd dated supermodels, for goodness' sakes, be interested in *her*?

When she didn't answer immediately, Travis regarded her with regret. "Walter really did a number on you, didn't he? Even though you defend him now and claim he's been on good behavior since he moved here, you can't forget the past."

She could hardly deny it. "I've been working really hard to get my act together," she began, only to have Travis cut her off.

"There's nothing wrong with your act, dammit! Get it through your head that the guy is a jerk. Or, if you insist, he *was* a jerk!"

"That doesn't mean he wasn't right about a lot of things."

"Such as?"

"I'm overweight. I'm disorganized. I struggle every single day to do the right things with my kids."

As she spoke, Travis's expression grew increasingly incredulous. "Have you looked at yourself in the mirror lately? You're beautiful. You may not be model-thin, but what man really wants that? I want someone with curves in my arms. And I know for a fact how organized you are. Your shows are scheduled well ahead of time. Your desk is neat as a pin. You even keep me on track at the station with those little Post-it reminders about calls I'm supposed to make. To be honest, I don't think the place could run without you. As for your kids, they seem perfectly healthy, happy and normal to me."

She wanted to tell him that looks were deceiving, but a part of her wanted to soak in all that praise like a sponge that had been left too long without water. "Is that really how you see me?"

"It's not just how I see you," he declared. "It's the truth. Surely your friends have told you all that."

"Sure, but I figured they were biased. Maybe you are, too."

He laughed. "I'm not biased. I'm infatuated, and one of these days, if you'll actually go out on a date with me, I'll prove it to you." He stroked a callused finger along her cheek. "But right this second I have a whole bunch of impatient kids over there with the attention span of gnats. I need to get to work."

Resisting the urge to put her hand over the spot he'd touched on her cheek, she nodded. "Go."

"We'll finish this conversation later," he promised. "In private."

In private. Somehow those two simple words carried a whole lot of meaning. Just thinking about being alone with Travis Mc-Donald made Sarah tremble with anticipation in a way she hadn't for a very long time. Maybe he was right about one thing. Maybe it was time she took a giant leap of faith — not in him, but in herself.

16

Travis had been playing things Sarah's way from the beginning. Other than a few stolen kisses, he'd pretty much kept his distance. Though he'd risked repeated rejections and uttered a string of invitations for the kind of things he thought she might be willing to accept — coffee, a drink, ice cream — he decided it was time to start asking for what he really wanted: a chance to prove how well-suited they were.

Of course, he'd accumulated a lot of evidence that the direct approach didn't work. She turned him down with such regularity that *no* was usually on her lips before he could fully form his request.

That left him with trying a more subtle, sneaky approach. Prevailing on Tommy's love of playing ball had seemed to be the most likely tactic. Though the groups he'd put together were informal and mostly too young to play in any kind of skillful fashion,

Tommy clearly loved every second he played. That meant Sarah was at the field Saturday mornings like clockwork. It was evident there was nothing she would deny her son. And since Walter had moved to town and spent part of most weekdays with Tommy, he mostly left the weekends to Sarah. Travis figured that could work to his advantage.

A week after the first practice, he had two groups of kids on the field, with a couple of the dads helping out. It was mostly barely organized chaos, but the boys were having a blast, and so was Travis. He loved seeing kids so excited just to be playing what they thought of as a big-boy game. The skills and rigid rules could come later.

Batting was, quite literally, a hit-or-miss thing. Running the bases was a challenge, since some of the boys tended to be distracted by the sight of mom or dad on the sidelines. Even so, at the end of the hour, Travis was enthusiastic with his praise.

"Okay, kids, how about pizza, just like we do after the older boys play?" he asked.

A chorus of cheers greeted the question. Many of these same kids had tagged along with Mom or Dad after their older brothers played ball and already loved the tradition.

"Moms and dads, any of you who want to

come along, I'll see you in ten minutes at Rosalina's. The pizza's on me." He turned to Sarah, who was hunkered down in front of Tommy, having a conversation that obviously wasn't going the way she wanted. Tommy's expression was mutinous.

"Is there a problem?" Travis inquired, joining them.

"I was trying to explain that we need to get home," Sarah said. "Libby's there with Raylene, and I don't like to leave them alone for more than an hour."

Travis had figured out that Raylene had some issues, but everyone was careful to dance around them. He hadn't pried. "How about letting Tommy come with me? You can go home and pick up Libby and join us."

"Yes, please, Mommy," Tommy said, seizing on the offer. "I'll go with Travis."

Just then Annie appeared with Trevor, who'd turned out for this week's practice. Travis had a hunch she was there mostly to keep an eye on Sarah, or more specifically *him* and Sarah. She'd made her distrust of him evident more than once.

"Or Tommy can go with us," she said, her expression all innocence as she offered an alternative Sarah was bound to seize. "We're going for pizza, too."

As Travis could have predicted, Sarah immediately looked relieved. "Are you sure, Annie?"

"It's not a problem," Annie insisted, turning a triumphant look on Travis as if she'd figured out exactly what he was up to.

"Okay, then," Travis said, giving in gracefully. "I'll see you there."

Once he reached the family-owned Italian restaurant, though, he made sure the table at which Annie was seated with the two boys was too full to accommodate Sarah when she arrived with Libby. Travis gestured for them to join him in the two seats he'd managed to save.

After casting a resigned look toward her friend, Sarah slipped into the chair he was holding for her. He leaned down to whisper, "You had to know I was going to win round two."

Her startled gaze met his. "Round two?"

"Annie took the first round," he said.

"I had no idea there was a game," Sarah said.

"It's been going on since the day we met," he told her, enjoying the blush that spread across her cheeks. "Now tell me what kind of pizza you like."

"Pepperoni for me," she said. "Plain for Libby."

"Perfect. I already have you covered. See how well I know you?"

"Lucky guess," she said. "Don't most people like either plain or pepperoni?"

He grinned. "Some of us like a little more spice. I've added a few jalapenos to mine."

Though the table was too noisy to pursue a private conversation, Travis managed to find any number of excuses to brush his fingers along Sarah's arm, touch her shoulder or look into her eyes. By the end of the meal, she was obviously disconcerted, but she didn't hop right up at the first opportunity and flee. He figured that was progress.

Or maybe it had something to do with the fact that Libby had crawled right into his arms and settled there. She was now fast asleep, snuggled against his chest.

Sarah looked at the two of them and shook her head. "I'm going to have to talk to her about falling for the bad boys."

"Maybe you should take lessons from her, instead," he suggested. "She obviously feels safe with me."

"I know better. Do you realize there are at least three single moms in this room right now who'd like to rip out my heart because I'm sitting here with you and they aren't? Why not go for the easy score?"

"Because easy doesn't interest me. You do."

She regarded him with confusion. "Why?"

"I'm starting to feel a little like I have to keep proving myself, to say nothing of needing to justify the way I feel about you. How do I love thee and all that. Do you really need me to count the ways?"

"It might be helpful."

"I thought I did a good job just last week of countering all those negatives that obviously play on some reel in your head. Didn't you believe even one word of that?"

To his shock, her eyes filled with tears before she looked away. "Sarah," he said quietly, tucking a finger under her chin and forcing her to look at him. "What's wrong? What did I say?"

"That's just it," she whispered. "You say all the right things, everything I want to hear. It scares me."

"Why?"

"Come on, Travis. Everyone knows what a player you are. You flirt with any female who still has breath in her. How can I possibly believe that you truly mean what you say to me, when the only other man in my life, the man who married me and fathered my kids and probably knew me better than anyone, always said the exact opposite whenever he got the chance? Even now, when he's apologized and swears he's reformed, he can't resist taking a potshot from time to time. He didn't even think I could cope with being a waitress at Wharton's, for goodness' sakes."

"I thought we'd established that Walter is an idiot."

She almost smiled at that. "But he's an idiot who knows me pretty well."

"No," Travis said fiercely. His voice must have startled Libby, because she stirred in his arms. He rubbed her back until she sighed and fell back asleep.

Travis lowered his voice. "Maybe Walter knew who you were when he was belittling you every second of the day, though I have my doubts about that. But for sure he doesn't know the woman you've become. You're building a new life for yourself. You're strong, and God knows you're independent."

She did smile then. "You make that sound like a bad thing."

"Not bad, just exasperating," he said, grinning at her. "You're very hard on my ego."

"Really?"

More than anything else he'd said, *that* was what pleased her. Go figure, Travis thought. "Yes, Sarah," he said solemnly. "If any other woman on earth had told me no as often as you have, I'd have given up and moved on."

"Why haven't you done that, then?"

He sighed. "I honestly don't know."

"It's probably just the challenge," she said.

He skimmed the back of a finger down her cheek. "I don't think so, but I do think I'll go a little crazy if I don't get to figure this out."

Her gaze narrowed. "How?"

"Go out with me on an honest-to-goodness date. We can get dressed up, drive over to Charleston or stay here and go to Sullivan's, whatever you want. Just you and me, spending a quiet evening together. Despite the amount of time we spend together, we don't really know each other. Don't you think we owe it to ourselves to at least do that much?"

"We probably won't have anything to talk about," she said, looking flustered.

He chuckled. "I'm not worried. I talk for a living. So do you."

"If I say yes, you'll probably lose interest."

The excuses just tripped off her lips, but he was ready for them.

"I would think me losing interest would make you happy," he said. "Assuming you're telling the truth and have no interest in me,

332

it'll be sort of a put-up-or-shut-up evening."

She frowned. "I'm not putting out for you."

He chuckled at her misinterpretation of his meaning. It definitely told him the direction of her thoughts. "Did I say anything that remotely implied sex was part of the evening?" he asked.

"With men like you, dating always leads to sex eventually."

"Dating usually leads to sex with anybody," he countered. "Assuming it works out well." He held her gaze. "And it's going to work out very, very well with us. I can tell."

She blushed. "One date, and you promise you'll stop pestering me?"

"One *bad* date and I'll stop pestering you," he agreed. "If this goes the way I'm anticipating, there will be more pestering and more dating. So, how about it? It's time to stop listening to Walter's voice in your head and test the wings of the new you, don't you think?"

Before she could answer, Annie once again appeared, her timing sucking as usual.

"What are you two talking about?" she asked cheerfully, jamming a chair in between them as Trevor and Tommy climbed up on adjoining chairs and reached for the remaining slices of pizza on the table.

"No more," Annie told them, drawing scowls, though neither boy retreated. Clearly they planned to wait for her attention to be diverted before grabbing the leftover pizza.

Annie turned back to Sarah. "What's up?"

"Sarah was just agreeing to go out with me," Travis told her, all but daring Sarah to contradict him.

Annie scowled. "Really?" She cast a meaningful look in Sarah's direction. "Are you sure you want to do that?"

Normally that look might have intimidated Sarah, but apparently she'd had enough of being bullied because she immediately turned to Travis. "When?"

Trying not to look as triumphant as Annie had at her earlier victory, he said, "Tomorrow night?"

Sarah nodded. "Seven o'clock?"

"That works for me." He stood up, eager to leave before she changed her mind.

"Um, Travis," she said, regarding him with an amused expression. "Are you planning to give me back my daughter?"

He'd gotten so used to holding Libby, he'd almost forgotten he had her. "Sure," he said, transferring her back into her mother's arms. He felt oddly bereft when she was gone. That was a new feeling, he thought.

He would have walked away then to ponder the unexpected reaction, but he paused long enough to lean down and whisper in Annie's ear. "Don't you dare try to change her mind. She needs this."

He heard Annie's indignant gasp, but he left before she could challenge him. He hoped if she took even a couple of minutes to think about his words, she'd see that he was right. Ever since her divorce, Sarah had been petrified to try again. It was time she tested herself at dating and it might as well be with a man who genuinely cared about her. Whatever happened between the two of them down the road, at least she would have taken the first step toward moving on with her life. This time it would be toward a full life, rather than the sheltered existence she seemed willing to settle for.

That afternoon when Travis went for a run with Tom, he told his cousin about his success in getting Sarah to agree to a date. "Now I just have to pray that Annie Townsend doesn't talk her out of it," he concluded.

Tom glanced over, his expression serious. "Travis, swear to me this isn't a game with you."

Travis tried to rein in his indignation. Surely his own cousin should know him better than that. "I told you it's not," he said testily. "Sarah's great. We click on a lot of levels, if only she'd admit it."

Tom still looked concerned. "You're honestly ready to think about settling down?"

Travis regarded him with impatience. "I bought a radio station here and I'm working my butt off to make it successful. I'm in the process of buying a house. What other evidence do you want that I'm here to stay?"

"I'm not questioning your commitment to Serenity, just to sticking with one woman. It's one thing to play the field in a place like Boston, but around here, it's not a good idea."

Travis stopped in his tracks, which brought Tom to a halt a couple of feet ahead of him. His cousin turned back. "What?"

"Here's the deal. I like Sarah. I'm attracted to her. She's not a thing in the world like all those women you were talking about in Boston. They knew the score. Despite having been married, Sarah's still naive. She's vulnerable in a way that gets to me. I want to protect her. I want to show her just how amazing she is. And if everybody would stop interfering —" he gave Tom a pointed look "— or busting my chops, I think I could be good for her."

A slow smile spread across his cousin's face. "Okay, then. Point taken." He slapped Travis on the back. "Good luck."

Travis's gaze narrowed. "You mean that?"

"Of course, I do. Nothing would make me happier than to have you right here in Serenity, married and settled with a family. As the only males in our generation of McDonalds, we're more like brothers than cousins."

Travis swallowed hard. "Married and settled with a family," he echoed, suddenly unnerved. "I never said I was ready for that. I mean, I've thought about it, but come on, Tom, we haven't even been on a real date yet."

He was prepared to defend his position when Tom glanced over his shoulder.

"Uh-oh," he murmured.

"What?"

"Here comes trouble," Tom said.

Travis regarded him blankly. "Trouble?"

"Annie, and she's evidently on a mission."

"We could probably outrun her," Travis suggested, only partially in jest.

"And then hear about it till our dying day," Tom said.

Before Travis could decide whether to risk

her wrath, Annie joined them.

"Jeanette told me I'd find the two of you here at the lake," she said.

Travis frowned at Tom. "Your wife's gone over to the other side?"

"I warned you the Sweet Magnolias stick together," Tom said, his amusement plain.

Annie, however, did not look the least bit amused. She scowled at Travis. "We need to talk about this date you're planning with Sarah."

He faced her squarely. "I don't think we do. I asked. Shc said yes. She's an adult, who knows her own mind. Stop treating her like some fragile piece of glass."

"That's the thing," Annie said. "She is fragile."

Travis lifted a brow. "Obviously you don't know the same woman I do. She's been through a lot, no question about it, but she's coming out of it stronger than ever. She'll be even tougher once she starts making her own decisions about things, instead of listening to her friends."

Annie blinked at his fierce response. "It almost sounds as if you respect her."

"Well, of course I do," he said incredulously. "Why wouldn't I?"

His vehemence seemed to rattle her. "I just thought you were taking advantage of her. You know, the poor little divorcée could use a sexy man to throw a few compliments her way, take her to bed, that kind of thing."

"That's insulting," Travis said. "To Sarah and to me."

Annie glanced at Tom, who was listening silently. "And you think he's being honest?"

Tom nodded. "Believe me, I've had a similar conversation with him. I live with a Sweet Magnolia. I'm not taking any chances on hearing about it forever if he messes with Sarah's head."

Annie seemed to be considering Tom's response. Finally she nodded. "Okay, then. I'll back off." She waved a finger under Travis's nose. "But if I get the idea that you're playing a game with her, there will be hell to pay."

Travis chuckled. "Duly noted."

After she'd gone, Travis breathed a sigh of relief. "Did you deal with this kind of stuff when you were dating Jeanette?"

"Worse," Tom said. "I had Cal, Ronnie and Erik on my case. They were sent by their wives, of course."

"Then I guess I better call on my A game," Travis said. "Anything less and I'll probably be run out of town."

"Now you're getting the picture," Tom said. His somber expression suggested he wasn't kidding.

Saturdays and Sundays were two of the biggest days in the real estate business. Weekends were when people had the time to go shopping for new homes. And here Mary Vaughn was, stuck not only at home, but in bed. It was the third week since the incident at Liz's and the doctor still wanted her to stay put. It seemed her blood pressure was still running too high to suit him.

She'd never been more frustrated in her life. The one activity which might have distracted her — sex — had been forbidden for the time being.

"Why don't I go to the video store and rent a bunch of movies?" Sonny suggested, clearly at his wit's end. He hated watching movies at home.

"Whatever," Mary Vaughn said, not the least bit interested.

Sonny kept trying. "I'll pick up some popcorn and a big tub of ice cream, too."

"And then you can sit here and watch me get big as a house," Mary Vaughn replied grumpily.

"Darlin', I don't know what you want me to do," he said, finally letting his frustration show. "How about cards? We could play gin rummy, if you want to, or poker."

"The only kind of poker that's any fun is strip poker," she said. "And what's the point of that, when we'd just have to keep our hands to ourselves?"

"The library's open for another hour," Sonny said. "How about I get you some books? You're always saying there's never enough time to read. Now's your chance."

"I need to be selling houses. That's what I need to be doing," she countered glumly.

"Well, that's out of the question, at least for the moment," Sonny said.

Amazingly, he kept his cool, but Mary Vaughn regarded him with dismay. "I know I'm being a bitch. I'm just frustrated."

"Understandable," he said. "Nobody likes being confined to bed." He got a wicked gleam in his eyes. "Unless they can do something interesting while they're there."

"Well, we can't," she snapped.

"I know that, darlin'. I was just sayin' . . ."

She reached over and squeezed his hand. "I know what you were saying. I'm sorry. I'm just in a miserable mood, and I'm taking it out on you because you're handy. Tomorrow, when Rory Sue comes back to stay, I'll probably be driving her to distraction, too. How are we going to survive six months of me being so horrible?"

"You're not horrible," he said. "Ever. And

341

don't worry about Rory Sue. You'll be teaching her the ropes of the real estate business," Sonny said.

"You know she's not interested," Mary Vaughn said, not happy about that either. Rory Sue had made it plain she'd do it because of the circumstances, but her heart wasn't in it.

"Well, she's still going to have to learn," Sonny declared. "Come on, darlin', can't you see how this is all going to work out for the best? We'll have our girl here for the next few months. She'll help you out with your business and around here. She'll make a little of her own money, for a change. Maybe that'll be just what it takes to get her to decide to stay here in town for good."

"Or else she'll be so sick of me, she'll flee the second the baby's born," Mary Vaughn said, unable to stop this gloomy mood of hers from infecting every word she uttered.

"Now that's enough of that," Sonny said, then nudged her to move over. He stretched out on the bed beside her. "Now there's no law that says we can't sit here and snuggle like we did when we were teenagers. Put your head on my shoulder and close your eyes."

"We did a lot more than snuggle when we were teenagers, Sonny Lewis," Mary Vaughn said, but she did close her eyes.

It was amazing how safe she felt with this man. More amazing was how desperately she wanted to make love with him. That desire still had the power to overwhelm her. It hadn't been there the first time they were married. Now, though, it was killing her to be this close and do nothing about it.

"I wish we could . . . you know," she said, her voice thick with frustration.

"Me, too," he said. "But this is nice."

At one time Mary Vaughn had shuddered at the thought of anything between a man and woman being *nice.* She equated that with boring. She wanted excitement, passion, even a little danger. She'd craved the attention of the bad boys, Ronnie Sullivan back then being the town's prime example.

Now, though, listening to Sonny's heartbeat, feeling his arm wrapped securely around her shoulders, nice took on a whole new meaning. Maybe, for a few months anyway, it would be enough, especially if she kept reminding herself of the stakes. At the end, she and Sonny would have what amounted to a miracle baby, a real testament to the depth of their love the second time around.

17

"I can't go out with Travis!" Sarah announced, emerging from her room after two hours of trying to find the perfect thing to wear.

Raylene merely nodded. "Okay, don't go."

Sarah stared at her in dismay. "You didn't even ask why I couldn't go," Sarah replied, frustrated at not getting any argument from her friend.

"Because I assume you're a mature, rational adult who has her reasons," Raylene said, then grinned. "And not some flighty teenager who's about to tell me she has nothing to wear."

Sarah heaved a sigh and flopped into a chair. "Well, it's true. I don't have anything to wear. Sometime when I wasn't looking, I apparently lost a few more pounds. Nothing fits. Nothing flattering, anyway. I can't just wear the same old slacks and blouses I wear to work. Besides, they're baggy, too."

"Then go shopping in my closet," Raylene suggested.

"What's the point? You're skinny."

"So, my friend, are you. Stop whining." She gave Sarah an encouraging look. "At least try on a couple of things. Those fancy dresses I paid a fortune to buy ought to be seen out in public. They've been shut away in a closet for too long."

Sarah opened her mouth to suggest that Raylene ought to be the one wearing them, but her friend's scowl kept her quiet.

"Don't even start with that," Raylene said fiercely. "Just find a pretty dress, so you can knock the man's socks off."

"The goal is to have him keep his clothes on," Sarah protested, though the thought of Travis wearing nothing made her mouth turn dry.

Raylene gave her an incredulous look. "You have to be kidding me. Even I want that man's body, and I've taken a vow of celibacy."

"I didn't say I didn't want his body," Sarah retorted. "I just meant that I don't intend to let things go that far." She gave Raylene one last chance to take back her offer. "Are you sure it's okay for me to try on something of yours?"

"Try it on. Wear it someplace fabulous,

and if you have even half a brain, let the man strip it off of you. Somebody in this house needs to start living again."

Sarah stared at her with surprise. "You don't sound at all like Annie. She thinks this whole date is nuts."

"Maybe because she hasn't seen the way your face lights up when you talk about Travis," Raylene said. "I have. After coping with Walter, you deserve to have the time of your life with a guy who treats you decently, and if Travis can give you that, I'm all for it."

"He could also wind up making me miserable."

Raylene shrugged. "That's life. It doesn't come with guarantees. Walter made all sorts of vows, yet he still made you miserable." She grinned wickedly. "And I'll bet you never had any of the highs with him that you'll have while things are good with Travis. You have to take some risks. Otherwise, you're not living. You're existing."

Again, Sarah opened her mouth, only to have Raylene regard her with another quelling look. "Not talking about me," Raylene said flatly. "Now, scoot and try on some clothes. You can put on a fashion show for me."

Though she still wasn't convinced that she'd fit into anything Raylene owned or that she'd have the nerve to wear something with a designer tag that cost more than she made in a month, Sarah went into her friend's bedroom and opened the closet door. Her gaze immediately went to a sapphire-blue sundress that matched the color of her eyes. It was stunning in its simplicity.

Her hands actually shook as she took it off the hanger, then held it up in front of her. Her complexion immediately looked rosier, and her eyes seemed even larger. Stripping off her shorts and T-shirt, she slid the soft-as-silk fabric over her head and let it drift over her body. The bodice caressed and emphasized her breasts. The skirt skimmed her hips and swirled at her knees. It fit as if it had been custom-tailored for her. It was the kind of dress that could be fancied up with the right jewelry or made more casual with a summery scarf or wrap.

Sarah stood in front of Raylene's mirror, staring at herself with shock. Her hair was a mess and she didn't have on so much as a hint of lipstick, but she actually looked radiant. And even more startling, she was thin! The vision actually overrode Walter's voice at last. She could hardly deny the evidence right in front of her.

Swallowing hard, she walked back into the

living room and stood hesitantly in front of Raylene. She knew her friend wouldn't hold back. Whatever she said, it would be honest.

Raylene's eyes lit up. "You look amazing," she said softly. "That dress never looked half that good on me. The color is perfect for you. What do you think?"

"I fell in love with it before I got it off the hanger. I can't believe it actually fits," Sarah admitted.

"It fits like a dream," Raylene assured her. "Try some more."

"But I love this," Sarah said, fingering the fabric.

"Why stop with one? I'm betting you'll have more than one date. You might as well have the outfits all picked out."

"But I shouldn't be raiding your closet for an entire wardrobe," she protested.

Raylene waved off her argument. "Those clothes represent nothing but bad memories for me. I only brought them over here after Paul was locked up because they were too nice to toss, and I didn't have the strength to box them up and give them away to someone who'd look as fabulous in them as you do. Take whatever you want."

She gave Sarah an imploring look. "Please, Sarah, do this for me. It makes me feel better knowing they're being worn by someone who matters to me. After all you've done for me, it's the least I can do for you. It'll make me feel like a fairy godmother."

An hour later, Sarah had a half a dozen dresses they'd agreed were meant for her. "Now I can't decide *which* dress to wear," she told Raylene.

"But you have to admit, that's a much nicer problem to have," Raylene said with a grin.

Sarah laughed. She hadn't felt this excited about a date since her very first one with Walter. She hadn't felt this good about herself since back then, either. Maybe she really was about to have a whole new beginning. Hopefully, though, the ending would be a lot happier.

Travis and Sarah had agreed to have dinner at Sullivan's, rather than driving over to Charleston. He'd been relieved when she said that was her choice, because he'd taken one look at her in a blue dress that bared her shoulders and clung to her curves and come very close to swallowing his tongue. He was pretty sure he didn't belong behind the wheel of a car on a long drive, not the way he was fighting the temptation to touch her.

"You sure do clean up pretty," he'd murmured in what had to be the understatement of the century.

As inept as the compliment had been, she beamed. "Thanks," she said in a shy voice that was barely above a whisper.

At the restaurant, heads turned when they arrived. Alerted by the hostess, Dana Sue came dashing out of the kitchen even before they were seated and demanded that Sarah twirl around and show off her dress.

"Sweetie, you look absolutely beautiful. Tell me where you got that dress. It definitely wasn't here in town."

Sarah chuckled. "You'd be surprised what's available in Serenity if you know where to shop."

Dana Sue looked bewildered by the comment, as was Travis.

"Raylene," Sarah told them. "It seems she has an entire wardrobe of things she doesn't want to wear."

"Well, she couldn't have chosen anything more perfect for you," Dana Sue said. "Now what can I bring you to drink? Champagne? Wine?"

"Iced sweet tea," Sarah said. She glanced pointedly at Travis. "I need to keep my wits about me."

Travis gave her a rueful look. "Hey, I'm totally trustworthy."

"In what universe?" Sarah teased.

Dana Sue laughed. "So, two sweet teas?"

"I suppose so," Travis said. After she'd gone, he said, "Do I really scare you that much?"

"No, I scare me. I haven't felt like this in a long time, kind of giddy and out of control."

The uncensored, totally vulnerable admission made Travis's heart do an odd little stutter-step. "Sarah Price, what am I going to do with you?"

"Probably not what you'd like to do," she said, again catching him off-guard with another daring display of her heretofore unknown wicked sense of humor.

Travis laughed. "You really are full of surprises tonight," he said, just as his cell phone rang. Annoyed, he yanked it out of his pocket, intending to shut it off, when he saw that it was Tom. His cousin would only be calling if there were some kind of emergency. He knew how important this date was.

"Excuse me," he said to Sarah. "I have to take this." He punched the talk button. "This better be good."

"How about the fact that your father showed up here with his fiancée looking for you?" Tom said. "Is that good enough?"

Travis sighed. "Where is he now?"

"On his way to Sullivan's. It seems he and the bride-to-be have an announcement that can't wait."

"And you told them where to find me? Are you nuts?"

"Believe me, I tried to send them away, but Greg was having none of it. Since he was getting on my nerves, I figured the best thing was to let you deal with him. I'm guessing you have about five minutes to make a run for it."

"Thanks for the heads-up," Travis said, then cut off the call.

Sarah studied him intently, then asked, "What's wrong?"

"It seems my father's on his way over here with his fiancée."

"You don't look happy about that. Is it because he's here or because he has his fiancée with him?"

"Both, to be perfectly honest," he said. "Care to sneak out through the kitchen with me?"

Her jaw set stubbornly. "After he's come all this way? That would be rude."

"This is going to be awkward and unpleasant," he warned her.

"Only if you want it to be," she said. "I want to meet your dad. I'll be able to see for myself if you're anything like him." Her expectant gaze went toward the front door.

Travis just shook his head and waited. Less than a minute later, his father strolled in with Trina on his arm. Travis glanced at Sarah and noted that her jaw had dropped.

"She's . . ."

"Younger than me," Travis supplied. "In fact, she and I went out back in college. I thought I'd mentioned that."

"You did, but I guess it didn't really register."

There was an oddly worrisome expression on her face as she watched the couple cross the dining room, but Travis didn't have time to question her about it.

"Hello, son," his father said jovially. "Sorry to interrupt your evening, but we wanted you to be the first to know our news."

"You should have let me know you were coming," Travis said. "As you can see, I'm on a date."

Sarah put a hand over his and smiled at the couple. "It's okay. Join us. I'm Sarah Price."

To Travis's dismay his father beamed at her and took the invitation at face value.

"Don't mind if we do," he said, pulling out a chair for Trina. "Sarah, I'm Greg Mc-

353

Donald, and this is Trina Phelps."

"We just couldn't wait to fill you in," Trina said, beaming. She actually slid her chair closer to his father's and clasped his hand. She drew in a deep breath and then announced in a triumphant tone, "We're having a baby."

This time it was Travis's jaw that dropped, though Sarah looked a little shell-shocked as well. So much for worrying about a prenuptial agreement, Travis thought. These two were now going to be tied for eternity.

"You'll have a little half-brother or sister," Trina gushed. "Isn't that fabulous?"

"Fabulous," Travis muttered. Even as he spoke, he heard the sound of the trap snapping closed, his father now firmly ensnared. His mother's heartache was about to get much, much worse.

The rest of the evening passed in a blur. By the time he and Sarah had been left alone, his mood was sour.

"You weren't very pleasant to them," she said accusingly.

"Because that little witch did this deliberately," he said, drawing a shocked look from Sarah.

"What do you mean?"

"You can't be that naive. The last time the three of us were together, I was encouraging my father to get a prenuptial agreement drawn up. Now this? I'm more convinced than ever that she's after his money."

"He really looks as if he loves her," Sarah said.

"He's besotted," Travis said succinctly. "He's always besotted with one woman or another. It never lasts. Usually, though, they've been more age-appropriate, and he's always had his eyes wide open when it comes to the gold diggers."

As soon as the harsh assessment crossed his lips, he saw something in Sarah's expression shut down.

"What's wrong?" he asked, determined not to let his father's visit or his own sour mood destroy the evening.

"How many times in your life have you been *besotted,* just like your father?"

"Never," he said at once. "At least not until you."

"Come on. You've always been a self-admitted player."

"It's not the same thing," Travis said, though he could see exactly why she might think it was. "Come on, Sarah. Neither of us knows what's going to happen tomorrow. We're dating. We're trying to figure out where this could go. It's the first time I've cared about anyone enough to even think beyond a single date."

Her expression remained bleak. "How can I believe that?"

"Because I've never lied to you," he suggested. "Not about my past, not about anything."

He thought for a minute he'd reached her, but he could see the second that doubts started crowding out facts.

"This was a mistake," she said softly. "I'm sorry. I need to go." She slid out of the booth. "Stay. Finish your dessert. I'll catch a ride home with someone."

Travis's temper kicked in. He wasn't sure if his exasperation was directed at his father for showing up, at Sarah for having so little faith in him, or himself for believing that they might have a real chance.

"You came with me," he said quietly. "I'll take you home. And don't you dare create a scene. It'll be bad for the station if the two of us are seen fighting in public."

Her eyes, which had been dull with resignation, now sparked with fury. "That's what you care about? That we don't do anything that will reflect badly on the station?" Despite her scathing tone, she did lower her voice. "Maybe everyone was right about you, after all, Travis. I thought you had integrity and depth, but now I have to question that if your only concern is for your precious public image."

"It's the station's image that concerns me," he corrected. "And since that's where you're employed, I'd think you'd worry about it, too."

She sighed and closed her eyes. "Okay, you're right. Let's just go, please."

They made the drive to her place in silence. By the time he parked in the driveway, his temper had cooled. He turned to her, hoping maybe she'd cooled down, too.

"Look, I'm really sorry about how this turned out. If only my father hadn't showed up —"

"If he hadn't showed up, I might not have seen what you're going to be like in a few years."

Travis was horrified by her assessment "Bite your tongue. I'm not going to be anything like him." He considered his pursuit of Sarah proof of that. Since meeting her, he'd started believing himself capable of making a lifetime commitment. Of course, his father had once thought that, too, when he'd married Travis's mother. Travis wanted to believe when he promised forever, it would mean just that.

Sarah continued to regard him with skepticism. "What is it they say — past behavior foretells future behavior?"

Though her words cut right through him, he managed to keep his voice calm. "If I believed that, I wouldn't be here," he said quietly. "I would have picked a different town, a totally different lifestyle and a different kind of woman."

Something in his voice must have reached her, because her hand on the door handle stilled, and she actually looked at him for the first time since they'd left the restaurant. "Meaning?"

"Serenity's the kind of place a man can build a real life with a wife and kids, the kind of life that will last," he said with feeling. "You're the kind of strong, complicated woman who's worth having for the long haul, not some easy one-night stand. Whatever else you believe about me, please believe that's how I see you."

She seemed to be letting his words sink in. Eventually, she said, "You almost sound as if you mean that."

"Because I do. Trust me, Sarah, I might have flirted with you from day one, but I thought long and hard before I pushed you to go on a real date with me. I needed to know it was right, not just for me, but for you. I wouldn't have asked if I thought it was a given that I'd wind up hurting you."

He dared to reach over and touch her cheek, felt the surprising dampness of tears on her skin. It was like a knife twisting inside him. "Just think about what I said, okay? Don't rule us out because of one bad date."

"You said you'd stop pestering me if the date was bad," she said with a hitch in her voice.

"I changed my mind. I think it'll take at least a couple of bad dates before we know anything for sure. What do you say?"

She lifted her watery gaze to his. "I'll have to get back to you on that."

He nodded. "I'll be waiting."

And, amazingly, he knew he'd wait forever, if he had to, because Sarah was definitely worth waiting for. He'd never been more certain of anything.

Things had not been going well with having Rory Sue back home. She was bored to tears by the real estate books Mary Vaughn had given her. She wasn't interested in any kind of lessons on the subject either. Her list of complaints about being back in Serenity was endless.

"Mom, I'll happily bring you meals, take care of the house, get you to doctor appointments, whatever you need, but I don't want to be a real estate broker," she told Mary Vaughn emphatically.

"Why not?" Mary Vaughn asked in frustration. "You'd make a good living. I certainly have, haven't I?"

"Sure, but you worked really, really hard. You barely had any life after Dad left."

Mary Vaughn regarded her daughter with impatience. "What do you have against hard work? That's how most people support themselves or their families. They don't do it by sponging off Mommy and Daddy forever. Did your father and I ever lead you to believe that was an option?"

"Daddy was willing to help me out with rent in Charleston till you had to go and stop him," she said, a whining note in her voice that sent a chill down Mary Vaughn's spine.

"That's not how you learn to be responsible, Rory Sue," Mary Vaughn said flatly. For once she was not going to cave in just to keep peace with her daughter. "It's about time you make your own money and live within your means. Either you learn the real estate business and help me while you're here, or you're going to be very short on funds."

"What about just helping out around the house?" Rory Sue asked. "Aren't you going to pay me for that?"

"What are you, twelve and in need of an allowance?" Mary Vaughn stared at her incredulously, wondering when her daughter had become so selfish and entitled. "You're helping out around here because you're family and that's what families do. They pitch in during a crisis."

"Well, that just sucks," Rory Sue retorted, flouncing out of the room just like she had when she was a teenager who hadn't gotten her way.

"Get back in here right this second," Mary Vaughn shouted after her. "I have some papers that need to be delivered this afternoon."

"Call a courier," her daughter replied.

Mary Vaughn counted to ten, then dialed Rory Sue's cell phone, the only thing she was likely to respond to.

"What?" her daughter snapped.

"You may be twenty-one, but you are still my child and you will treat me with respect."

"Or what? You'll send me to my room?" Rory Sue asked sarcastically.

Off the top of her head, Mary Vaughn actually couldn't come up with anything threatening enough to scare Rory Sue when she was in this belligerent mood. Before she could think of a thing to say, she heard a door slam, then the low murmur of Sonny's voice, followed by Rory Sue's defiant tone.

Within minutes, a contrite-looking Rory Sue walked back into the bedroom, a scowling Sonny on her heels.

"I'm sorry," she murmured, though she didn't sound terribly convincing. "Where are those papers and where do they need to go?"

"They're right here," Mary Vaughn said, handing them to her. "And they need to go over to the new radio station on Azalea Drive. They're for Travis McDonald."

For the first time all afternoon, Rory Sue's eyes lit up. "Travis McDonald the baseball player?"

Mary Vaughn regarded her with surprise. As far as she knew, her daughter had never shown much interest in sports. "He played for the Red Sox, yes. Do you know him?"

"Only that he's a hottie," Rory Sue said. "What's he doing in Serenity?"

"His cousin's the town manager," Mary Vaughn told her. "Travis bought the old newsstand, turned it into a radio station and now he's buying a house. Or at least he will be if I can get these contracts signed today."

"I'll make sure he signs them," Rory Sue said, suddenly sounding a lot more eager. "I'll wait around to make sure he does."

She snatched up the envelope and took off, leaving Sonny and Mary Vaughn staring after her.

"I don't like that gleam in her eye one little bit," Mary Vaughn said.

Sonny looked blank. "Why not? Everything I hear about Travis is good. Maybe it'll do Rory Sue good to be interested in a man here in town."

"Not if he's already involved with Sarah Price," Mary Vaughn reminded him, her tone dire. "You saw them at Liz's. Since then, Jeanette's filled me in. Apparently Travis is pretty serious about her."

"Then he won't give Rory Sue a second glance," Sonny said.

She regarded her husband with a pitying look. "Have you ever known our daughter not to go after whatever she wants? We'd better start praying she takes an instant dislike to Travis or vice versa, because anything else is going to stir up more trouble than this town has seen since I went after Ronnie Sullivan."

Judging from the horrified expression on Sonny's face, he finally got exactly what she was talking about.

18

Sarah still couldn't figure out how an evening that had started with so much promise had ended up such a disaster. Something about seeing Greg McDonald with a woman young enough to be his daughter had triggered every negative thought she'd ever had about herself. She hadn't been able to hold on to Walter, whose father had been devoted to his shrew of a wife for thirty-five years. How on earth could she hope to keep a man whose primary male role model was a man who had apparently chased anything in skirts most of his adult life?

Oh sure, Travis claimed he hated the way his father had lived his life, but he also acknowledged that some thought they were just alike. What was she supposed to believe? Even Travis didn't seem to be a hundred percent certain that he'd made a successful transformation from the player he acknowledged having been during his baseball career.

More important, how could she risk not only her own heart, but her kids' affections on a man who might be gone tomorrow? They were having a tough enough time dealing with the divorce. They didn't need to become attached to a man who'd only end up leaving them.

On Monday she hoped to finish her show and get away from the studio before Travis turned up. Surely he would be considerate enough to allow her to make her escape and avoid an awkward confrontation.

Then, again, she should have recognized he was a determined man who'd stated very clearly that he didn't want things between them to be over. Naturally he turned up, not just at the station, but in the studio a half-hour before the end of her show. What was she supposed to do, cause a scene on the air? After the way he'd worried the night before about the damage a public argument might cause, an on-air battle was out of the question. Even she could see that. Should she go to commercial and try to kick him out? Neither option seemed like a good one, so she settled for ignoring him.

"Hey, sugar, did you watch those country music awards being handed out last night?"

he queried on-air, forcing her to reply.

"You know, I didn't haven't a chance," she said, shooting him a look that would have withered a man with less ego. Travis was clearly unfazed. "I was busy."

"Out having a good time?" he asked, a wicked gleam in his eyes.

"Not so much, as a matter of fact. Did you want to talk about who walked away a winner at the awards show? Or were you hoping to pry into my private life?"

"Oh, sweet thing, I know all about your private life," he said in a low, sexy tone meant to stir the imagination.

"You most certainly do not," she snapped before she could stop herself. Nothing like treating the folks of Serenity to their lovers' spat, she thought, humiliated. What on earth was he thinking by taunting her like this?

Travis, darn him, chuckled. "Our Sarah seems a little on edge this morning," he told the audience. "I wonder what that's about."

"Be careful or I'll tell them," she retorted, locking her gaze with his in a dare-me expression. She'd had just about all she could take of this on-air game he was playing. If he wanted to spark fireworks, she was more than ready for them.

Just then the phone lines started lighting up. She stared at the little blinking lights in

366

dismay, terrified of who might be calling in and what they were likely to say. Travis clearly had no such qualms. He punched the first line.

"Good morning. You're on the air with Sarah and Travis," he said cheerfully as if this were an everyday occurrence.

"Didn't I see the two of you at Sullivan's last night?" the female caller asked.

To Sarah's ears, it sounded a lot like Mariah Litchfield, whose flirtatious exchange with Travis had stirred her jealousy back on the Fourth of July. Leave it to her to try to stir up trouble now.

"Looked to me like you were on a date," the caller who might be Mariah said. "With another couple, in fact."

Sarah could feel the color rising in her cheeks. If she could have reached across the desk at that moment and strangled Travis, she would have. He'd deliberately started this. Now the whole town was going to know their business. And what they didn't know, they'd most likely make up.

Travis laughed. "There you go. You caught us," he said.

"Did you all have a fight?" the woman asked. "Things looked cozy enough while I was there."

Sarah decided the game had gone on long

enough. "Hon, Travis and I don't have a thing in the world worth fighting over, except deciding whether to order the catfish or the meat loaf. He's just in here this morning trying to cause a commotion. It must be just about time for them to start counting our listeners for the ratings or something."

She cut off the call to avoid further observations, but Travis immediately punched another line.

"Sarah, it sounds to me like Travis has gotten under your skin," the next caller said. "Maybe you two need to kiss and make up."

"Sounds good to me," Travis said. "What do you say, Sarah?"

"You don't want to know what I have to say to that idea," she muttered, then glanced at the clock. Thankfully, it was just seconds away from noon. Bill was already waiting in the control booth to take over.

"Okay, folks, that's all for *Carolina Daybreak* on this Monday morning. I hope you'll join me here again tomorrow when my guest will be Coach Maddox, who's going to talk about the summer baseball program here in town. There's still time to get your little ones involved, and there's plenty you can do to support the program."

"Actually I'm going to be the one talking

about that," Travis interrupted. "The coach's schedule got jammed." He winked at Sarah. "So come on back here first thing tomorrow, folks. Sarah and I will be fussing at each other again, I'm sure."

Sarah punched the button to take them off the air, then glowered at Travis. "That was totally unprofessional."

He didn't seem to be even a tiny bit intimidated or even worried by her comment. "But it was fun, wasn't it? The phone lines haven't lit up like that since we went on the air. I'm thinking we should make this a regular thing. You and me crossing paths in here will have people talking."

"Over my dead body," she snapped.

He gave her a bland look. "Do I need to remind you who owns this station?"

"Do I need to remind you that I can quit?"

The threat seemed to take the wind out of his sails for about a nanosecond, but then he shook his head. "But you won't."

"Oh, why is that?"

"Because, let's face it, sugar, you have more fun on a bad day with me than you have on a whole string of good days with anyone else."

It was true, dammit, but she was not going to admit it. Travis got her adrenaline pumping in a way no other man ever had.

"What happened to worrying about the station's image?" she asked, unable to keep a plaintive note out of her voice.

He grinned. "Well, that's the thing. It occurred to me that the two of us fussing and fighting on the air might stir up the kind of talk that could positively affect ratings, just the way you said. It'll all be in good fun."

She frowned at that. "That's how you see it? The two of us arguing is just for fun?"

He gave her an innocent look. "Well, if we can actually work out a few of our issues along the way, so much the better."

"We're only likely to do that if we bring in a mediator," she said. "Or a shrink."

He nodded. "Something to think about."

She stared at him indignantly. "Are you crazy? I was joking."

Just then she noticed Rory Sue standing in the foyer looking absolutely fascinated. Since she probably couldn't hear what was being said in the soundproof booth, her awed expression had to have something to do with Travis. Rory Sue was a lot like her mama in that way. She found bad boys fascinating.

"Your public awaits," Sarah said, gesturing toward Rory Sue. She was determined not to pay one bit of attention to the twinge of jealousy nagging at her to stay put. "I have to go. I have ads to sell this afternoon."

"Stick around. Let's have lunch," Travis said, not even turning to see who was waiting.

"Not if I were starving," she said, exiting the booth, nodding at Rory Sue as she grabbed her purse and then taking off before she did what she really wanted to do, which was lock lips with the maddening man who was turning her emotions inside out.

Travis might have gone after Sarah, but the tall, long-legged young woman in the lobby blocked his path.

"I have some papers for you," she said. "They're from my mom, Mary Vaughn Lewis. She says they're important. I'm Rory Sue, by the way. You could look them over while we have lunch, if you have the time."

Travis had enough experience to know she was offering more than lunch. In another lifetime, he might have been interested. She was thin, in the willowy way of a super-model. Her long hair had been stylishly cut to look perpetually tousled. Her lips were glossy and invited kisses. The smoky makeup she wore around her eyes might have been seductive in a bar in Boston, but it seemed way overdone compared to Sarah's fresh-faced, wholesome appearance.

"No time," he said. "I'll look these over this afternoon and get them back to your mother. How's she feeling, by the way?"

"Miserable and cranky," Rory Sue said.

"I imagine it's tough being stuck on bed rest. Tell her I'll drop these off later. Nice to meet you."

There was no mistaking his words for anything other than a dismissal, but she didn't budge.

"Maybe we could have a drink one night," she said. "I'm going to be bored to tears while I'm stuck here looking after my mom. My dad will take over in the evening, though, so I'll be able to get out of the house and have some fun."

"Thanks, but I don't think so."

"You're not married," she said. "I checked. You're not even engaged, so what's the problem? It's a drink, not a commitment. Come on, Travis. Keep me from going stir crazy while I'm here."

He realized he wasn't even tempted to take her up on the offer. "I'm seeing someone," he said.

Even though he didn't mention Sarah's name, she caught on at once. Her eyes widened.

"Sarah?" she said incredulously. "Then

you weren't just kidding around on the air? There's something going on between you two?"

"There will be," Travis said with determination.

"Going out with me could make her jealous," she suggested.

Travis chuckled. "Now, would that be fair? Certainly not to you."

"Hey, I'm a big girl. I'm willing to take my chances."

"I don't think so. You tell your mama hey, okay?" He went into the office and shut the door firmly behind him. He had a feeling that she stood there debating with herself about whether to follow him, because it took a very long time before he heard the station's outer door close.

Now he just had to figure out how to get these papers back to Mary Vaughn without crossing paths with her daughter.

Walter wasn't one bit happy when he discovered that Travis McDonald was hanging around his wife and kids. Okay, his ex-wife, but that didn't mean he didn't have a duty to see that she didn't bring lousy influences into Tommy's life.

He'd seen them together once or twice, then heard the two of them on the air the other day. There'd been enough sparks flying that there was no mistaking the chemistry they had. He'd tuned in again the next day, and it had been more of the same. He'd finally cut off the radio in disgust. He couldn't imagine why he hadn't recognized what was going on the day Travis had practically snatched Libby away from him just to show him up at that barbecue.

When he stopped by the house after another fruitless day of job-hunting, he dismissed the sitter, poured himself a glass of tea, then sat at the kitchen table to wait for the kids to wake up from their naps. A few minutes later, Raylene appeared.

"I thought I heard you come in." She frowned. "You look annoyed. What's that about?"

"Have you been listening to Sarah's show?"

"Every morning," she said. "Why?"

Before he could answer, her expression changed. A grin tugged at her mouth. "You're talking about what's happening between her and Travis."

"Of course. What's she thinking? Those two are making fools of themselves in front of the whole town."

"It makes for downright sexy radio, if you ask me."

"She's a mother. It's inappropriate."

"Trust me, Tommy and Libby are oblivious to the nuances. They just like listening to mommy on the radio."

"The sitter lets them listen?" he demanded irritably. "That has to stop."

Raylene studied him with a knowing look. "Don't tell me you're jealous, Walter. It's a little late, isn't it? You're the one who drove Sarah away."

"I am not jealous. I'm just worried about the influence a man like that could have on my kids. Believe me, I've looked him up on the Internet. He cut quite a swath through the female population of Boston and beyond. Sarah's no match for a man like that."

"There you go, once again selling Sarah short," Raylene said. "Your ex-wife is a match for any man. You'd have seen that if you hadn't been so busy listening to your mother and father cut her down."

Walter retreated at once. "I can't argue that, but come on, Travis McDonald? Why would he be with a small-town girl? A guy like that's looking for one thing from a woman."

"Maybe it's because he's chosen to live in a small town," Raylene suggested. "Obviously he likes the lifestyle and the people. He especially seems to like Sarah."

"Well, I don't have to approve of it," he grumbled.

Raylene sat up a little straighter and looked him in the eye. "Don't you dare interfere in this, Walter Price. You hear me? It is none of your business."

"My kids —" he began.

"Are perfectly fine. They adore Travis, especially Tommy."

Walter's gaze narrowed. "Meaning?"

"Just that Travis is coaching a bunch of the littler kids in T-ball. You knew that."

He had, but it hadn't really mattered before. Now that he knew there was something going on between McDonald and Sarah, well, that was different. He'd stayed away from the ball field because Saturdays and Sundays were the days Sarah got to spend more time with the kids.

Not this week, though. When Saturday rolled around, he intended to be front and center so he could see the situation first-hand. And then he'd do whatever needed to be done. No hotshot ex-ballplayer was going to stand in as daddy to his kids.

When Walter arrived for T-ball practice on Saturday, his already sour mood worsened. Tommy was gazing at McDonald with something that looked a lot like hero worship. And there was Sarah sitting in the bleachers with Libby, a similar love-struck expression on her face. It was enough to make him want to break things, though he told himself it had nothing to do with jealousy. It was just that a man shouldn't be replaced in his own son's life.

He was about to cross the field and yank Tommy out of the game when Ronnie Sullivan appeared, his expression jovial enough but his stance suggesting he was all set to intervene if Walter intended to cause trouble.

Walter had an okay relationship with Ronnie, but he knew better than to get him riled up. He was one very protective man. Walter had figured that out on the night they'd met, when that meddling daughter of his had called Ronnie to intercede in an argument Walter was having with Sarah. Walter had known that night that his marriage was over. Ronnie had been there to help point out the obvious, and to keep Walter's temper in check. When he'd calmed down, he'd been grateful for that.

Sarah wasn't the same here in Serenity. Surrounded by friends, she didn't waver in the face of his criticism the way she once had. She stood up to him. He'd tried to pacify her by going to a counseling session, but it had been a complete waste of time. He'd refused to go again. Not long after that, she'd filed for divorce and that barracuda attorney of hers had worked the court to see to it he had only limited access to his kid.

Okay, kids, he amended. He knew it drove Sarah nuts the way Libby seemed to come in second with him, but the truth was that sometimes he didn't know what to make of his daughter. An only child, he'd grown up with a lot of expectations heaped on his back. Just like his father, he'd always thought he'd have sons who could take over the family business in Alabama. Libby had been a disappointment, so he'd focused all his energy on molding Tommy for that role. Not that there was much molding to be done to a kid who was barely out of diapers.

Lately, though, even after cutting the ties with his father, Walter felt the weight of years of parental expectations on his shoulders. The Prices had a position of respect back home. Tommy should be ready to take over there someday, if that's what he wanted. Outside influences — not Sarah and certainly not Travis McDonald — had no place in that decision.

He took another step toward the field, trying to evade Ronnie, but the older man didn't budge.

"Don't," Ronnie said. "Tommy's having a good time out there. Don't create a scene and spoil it for him."

Just then Sarah joined them, pushing Libby in a stroller. Walter saw McDonald staring their way as well. That look stirred his temper.

"I'm here to see my boy," he said angrily. "What's the big deal?"

"If you want to watch Tommy play, it's fine," Sarah assured him.

"What if I want to take him out after?"

Sarah regarded him with confusion. "Why is this suddenly so important? You've known about these games for weeks now, and you've never shown up before."

"But I didn't know you and the coach had the hots for each other until this week," he said.

Something in his tone had Ronnie taking a step closer, but Sarah just met his gaze evenly. "*That* is none of your business," she said flatly. "Not that it's even true."

"Oh, please," he scoffed. "There can't be a person in this town who hasn't heard the two of you seducing each other on the radio." He turned to Ronnie, seeking an ally. "You've heard 'em, right? Would you want your wife acting like that in public?"

Ronnie's expression remained neutral, but Sarah's eyes flashed with fury. She actually stepped right up and got in his face.

"Don't you dare criticize anything I do ever again, Walter Price," she said, her voice low, but emphatic. "You don't have the right."

Walter took a step back. "Okay, okay, you're right. It's none of my business. I was just thinking about your reputation."

"My reputation is none of your concern, either," Sarah said.

"It is if it affects the kids."

"Do you know who you sound like right now? You sound like that mean-spirited mama of yours," Sarah told him. "I thought you'd vowed to put that kind of nonsense behind you."

Walter flinched at the accusation. Even as he spoke, he'd heard the same kind of criticisms coming from his mama, and wanted to take it back. "I'm sorry," he said, meaning it.

Sarah drew in a deep breath and tried to stare him down. Eventually she said quietly, "Look, if you want some time with the kids today, it's okay with me. You can take Tommy for pizza with the team after. He loves that."

"I'm not taking him to spend more time

with McDonald," Walter said flatly.

"You will if you want the afternoon with him," Sarah said just as firmly. "This is about what Tommy likes to do. It's not about you and some petty contest you think you're in with Travis."

"Okay, fine," he said grudgingly. "I'll ask Tommy what he wants to do."

She met his gaze, then glanced down at the stroller. "What about your daughter? Libby's here right now. I know she's missed her daddy."

Aware that both Sarah and Ronnie were watching him intently, Walter reluctantly bent down and picked up Libby.

"Daddy," she said, smiling happily and patting his cheek.

When he didn't say a thing, her smile faded. Big blue eyes stared at him solemnly, waiting. He had no idea what to do or say under the weight of all those unspoken expectations.

Then Libby sighed and rested her cheek against his chest and something shifted inside him. This little girl he hadn't wanted and didn't quite know how to handle trusted him. Nothing else mattered, not the silly argument with Sarah or his jealousy of McDonald. None of it.

Suddenly, out of nowhere, came an overwhelming need to protect Libby, to be the kind of father she deserved. Tears filled his eyes. He blinked them back, ashamed of the emotion they represented, especially out here in public, practically in front of the man who was trying to take his place in his family's life.

It was Sarah who touched his cheek. "It's okay, you know. She's your little girl. She always will be."

He regarded her with dismay, struck by the full depth of the mess he'd made of his life. "How the hell could I have ignorcd her the way I did?"

Sarah regarded him with sympathy. "Conditioning, I think. Your parents doted on Tommy because he represented the future of their precious business, or so they thought. You just followed their lead. Maybe now you'll see what a blessing your daughter is, too."

Just then they were joined by McDonald, whose gaze was fixed on Sarah and filled with real concern.

"Everything okay?" he asked quietly.

She returned his gaze in a way that told Walter more than words ever could have. She was in love with the guy. He had a hunch she didn't even realize it herself, but he recognized the look. Once upon a time, she'd looked at him just like that . . . and he'd tossed that love aside.

"Everything's fine," Sarah told McDonald. "Right, Walter?"

He couldn't seem to find his voice, so he merely nodded.

Travis gave him a look that spoke volumes. It was part warning and all possessiveness. Walter knew without a shadow of a doubt, if he wanted to take on Sarah over anything, he'd have a real fight on his hands.

Amazingly, he realized he was less intimidated by the other man than he was by the woman he'd once bullied at every turn.

It seemed today was a turning point in the way he regarded the two women in his life — Libby and Sarah. Regrets about the past were useless. But from here on out, he vowed to show them both the respect they deserved.

19

Travis hadn't heard anything of what Walter had been saying to Sarah at the ball field on Saturday, but from the look on Ronnie's face, he'd sensed that none of it was good. Although Sarah had apparently handled the situation and kept it from spinning out of control, it grated on his nerves that she'd had to. He'd wanted to rush in, but he was wise enough to know he'd probably be making matters worse, especially in light of the way she'd leapt to Walter's defense on the occasions when he'd criticized the way her ex-husband had treated her in the past.

On Monday he was still stewing over the scene at the ball field when Bill got off the air and joined him in the office. There would be a few hours of syndicated programming before Travis went on the air tonight.

"Problems?" Bill inquired.

"Just leftover annoyance," Travis told him.

"Good show today, by the way."

"Thanks." Bill hesitated, his expression tense. "I know it's been crazy around here the past few weeks and I hate to bring this up, but are you having any luck finding a replacement for me?"

Travis regarded him with alarm. "Are you getting tired of helping out? I know you'd planned to be completely retired long before now, but I thought you were content to be back on the air."

To Travis's relief, Bill visibly relaxed.

"That's the thing," Bill said, looking sheepish. "Now that the station's no longer my responsibility and I can just be a radio personality the way I was back in the beginning of my career, I'm happier than I've been in years. If you want me to stay on permanently, I'd like to do it."

Travis was so delighted by the news, he almost embarrassed them both by jumping up and hugging the man. "Want you to? Nothing would make me happier. I think we have a great on-air team with you, me and Sarah. And you've brought a lot of listeners with you, to say nothing of knowing this area in a way that I don't. I predict our ratings are going to be real solid, especially for a station just getting off the ground. The kind of input you can give me about running this place is invaluable, too. Don't think I don't appreciate that."

"I totally agree that we're a great team," Bill responded. "And I'd hate not being around for the celebration when those first numbers come out."

"How about a contract?" Travis offered. "One year? Two? As long as you want."

Bill shook his head. "I don't need a piece of paper. Let's just say I'll stay as long as it's working, and shake on it. It's not as if I'm trying to lock in a long-term career at this stage of my life. If things change, though, I'll give you plenty of notice. I won't leave you in the lurch. You do the same for me. Let me know if you need to make a change."

Travis was ecstatic over this turn of events. "This is great. It's exactly what I'd been hoping you'd decide."

Bill's gaze narrowed with suspicion. "Had you even been looking to find somebody else?"

Travis shrugged. "Honestly, no. I thought maybe as long as I didn't mention it, you wouldn't notice you'd been filling in for a very long time."

Bill laughed. "One more thing, if you don't mind me butting in. When are you going to hire a full-time advertising salesman? It's getting way too busy around here for you and Sarah to spend time chasing new accounts and keeping in touch with the old ones. It's enough that you have to record the spots when you're not on the air. You're going to be in demand for all sorts of events now that so many people are tuning in. You need more help, at least behind the scenes."

"I know," Travis admitted. "The work keeps piling up, but the days aren't getting any longer."

"Especially when you've been showing up to be on the air with Sarah on a regular basis," Bill said slyly. "Is that calculated for ratings, or is that the only way you can get the woman to spend time with you?"

"A little of both," Travis admitted. "But it's mostly because I can't seem to stay away from her. She, however, seems quite adept at avoiding me."

"Because your reputation precedes you?" Bill guessed.

"That's definitely part of it." Travis waved off the topic. "None of that's your problem. Any suggestions for the ad job?"

"As a matter of fact, yes," Bill said. "I've run into a guy who just moved to town. He was with a family company. He has loads of sales experience, but there aren't a lot of openings around the area, not for someone with his qualifications."

Travis got a sinking sensation in the pit of his stomach. "Who is it?"

"Walter Price," Bill said, and immediately held up his hand to forestall Travis's objections. "Before you say no, just hear me out. He's experienced. His kids are here in town, so he's not going to take off for a better opportunity."

"He's also Sarah's ex-husband and he treated her like dirt. Still does, from what I saw just this weekend." Travis shook his head. "I'm not hiring him. Right now, we have a good team running this place. We all get along." He grinned, thinking of the regular on-air and private spats he had with Sarah. "Mostly, anyway. Adding Walter to the mix would be a disaster. I'd kill him inside of a month." He paused. "Or Sarah would."

"Maybe you should ask her what she thinks," Bill suggested.

Travis shook his head. "No way. Have you already talked to him about this? Did he plant the idea so he could get close to Sarah again?"

Bill shook his head adamantly. "Absolutely not. It was nothing like that. We just ran into each other at Wharton's and had a cup of coffee together. He didn't even know I worked here or that we might be thinking about hiring someone. *I* didn't even know if you'd be interested in adding to the staff."

"Hiring a salesperson makes sense. Hiring Walter Price is out of the question."

"Your station. Your decision," Bill said, letting it go.

Travis nodded. "Thanks for understanding."

The next day he posted the job on the station's Web site and mentioned it to Grace Wharton and Ronnie Sullivan. He figured that would be enough to get the word out. With any luck, though, it wouldn't reach Walter Price.

To Sarah's relief, Tommy's T-ball game on Saturday morning was uneventful, especially compared to the week before. After hearing about the commotion while she'd been in Atlanta with Ty, Annie took up a protective position at Sarah's side this week, but Walter stayed away.

"Are you taking Tommy for pizza after the game?" Annie asked curiously.

"Sure," Sarah said. "He really loves it. Why?"

"I thought maybe you were avoiding Travis."

Sarah grinned. "It's hard to avoid Travis. He's in my face just about every single day. I'm sure you've heard that he's been joining me on the air. It seems our conversations are sparking listener interest. The switchboard goes wild the second people know he's in the studio."

"If he bothers you, kick him out," Annie said, as if it were a simple matter.

"His station," Sarah reminded her, as he'd told her often enough. "Besides, we do have fun, even if he does make me a little crazy."

"Crazy, or hot?" Annie inquired.

Sarah flushed. "Okay, that, too."

Annie's expression turned thoughtful. "You know I've been worried all along about him playing games with you, but now I have to wonder."

"Wonder what?"

"Are you playing games with him just to stroke your battered ego?"

"Don't tell me you'd feel sorry for him if I were," Sarah said.

"No, but I would warn you that you're playing with fire. When it comes to games, I imagine Travis McDonald plays by different rules."

Sarah made an elaborate show of fanning herself. "Don't I know it!"

Annie's mouth gaped. "Sarah Price, what's

happened to you?"

"Maybe I'm just figuring out that I'm a sexy, desirable woman, after all."

"Well, hallelujah for that!" Annie said sincerely. "Just be careful, okay?"

"Hey, careful's my middle name," Sarah said, though lately she was beginning to wonder if maybe it shouldn't be changed to reckless, because when it came to Travis, good sense seemed to have flown out the window.

The T-ball players along with their coach and several moms and dads had barely been seated at Rosalina's when the door opened and Rory Sue walked in. Just as her mother might have a few years back, she was dressed to get attention in short shorts that showed off her endless legs and a halter top that emphasized the rest of her assets. Sarah regarded her with dismay.

"What's she doing here?" Annie asked Sarah in an undertone.

"Watch and learn," Sarah replied.

Rory Sue immediately zeroed in on Travis, though she took her time sauntering over to his seat across from Sarah. The better to give everyone a full view of her considerable charm, so to speak. Though there wasn't a vacant chair, she grabbed one from a nearby table and pulled it up close to his, then leaned against his arm. Travis tried to scoot away from her, but the table was too crowded.

"Oh, boy," Annie whispered. "Shades of Mary Vaughn going after my dad."

"Exactly," Sarah said, tamping down the streak of jealousy that made her want to rip the girl's perfectly highlighted tresses right out of her head.

"I have to give Travis credit," Annie said. "He seems immune."

"For now," Sarah said direly. "Come on, though. He's human. She's throwing herself at him. Given his past history, how long do you think he'll resist?"

At precisely that moment, Travis shoved back his chair, apologizing to the people who'd been sitting on either side of him. Two seconds later, he'd jammed another chair between Sarah and Annie.

"Save me," he muttered with heartfelt emotion.

"You're a big boy," Sarah said, though she was relieved to see that he hadn't yet snapped up the bait. "Surely you've handled predatory females before."

"I have," he agreed. "But usually in Boston, I could rest assured I wouldn't be running into them every five minutes."

"That is the downside of a small town," Annie agreed. "I know how I'd feel if Dee-Dee lived here and Ty was bumping into her every time I turned around. It's hard enough when she's here visiting Trevor."

Travis regarded her with feigned annoyance. "Focus, ladies. I'm the one with the immediate problem. Her mother's my real estate agent, I can't offend Rory Sue."

Sarah chuckled. "Sure you can. It won't stop her, though. She'll just take it as a challenge."

"Then what am I supposed to do?"

He sounded and looked so genuinely bewildered that Sarah took pity on him. "Here's a thought," she said slowly, wondering if maybe she hadn't gone just a little bit insane with jealousy, after all.

She twisted in her chair, made sure Tommy was distracted at the next table and Libby asleep in her booster seat, then put her hands on either side of Travis's face and kissed him with everything she had in her and then some. It was the kind of bone-melting, stolen-breath kiss that pretty much destroyed every last ounce of resolve she had where he was concerned. Obviously whatever this game was between them, she was all in. Judging from Travis's momentarily stunned response and then the way he took charge of the kiss, he was pretty much leaping in, as well.

Though she knew almost nothing by the time the kiss ended, not even her own name, she did know that whatever happened from here on out, she could no longer deny how she felt about Travis. She was head-over-heels, pants-on-fire in love with him.

And if anyone tried to mess with her man — specifically Rory Sue — they'd have a real fight on their hands. Maybe Dana Sue would coach her on getting the best of a predatory female. She'd certainly had plenty of experience with Mary Vaughn.

Travis was pretty sure it would be a couple of hours before he could stand without embarrassing himself after the kiss Sarah had planted on him. The second they'd surfaced for air, she started scrambling to gather up Tommy and Libby. She barely spared him a glance as she headed for the door.

He turned what was probably a dazed look on Annie. "What just happened here?"

Annie grinned at him. "I'd have to say that Sarah was staking her claim."

He nodded slowly. "That was the impression I got. Why'd she run off?"

"Because despite her very bold move, I'm

sure there's a part of her that's absolutely scared spitless that you might not return her affections."

"I've been chasing her since the day I hit town," he said.

"Seriously?"

"Well, no, not at first," he admitted.

"Then how's she supposed to know you're serious now?" She leveled a hard look into his eyes. "You are, aren't you?"

"Very serious," he said solemnly, knowing he'd have a battle on his hands if he even hinted otherwise.

"Then you might want to go after her," Annie said. "Because just about now I imagine she's having second and third thoughts about what just happened here. Plus she's probably worrying herself sick that Tommy might have seen the kiss."

Travis was on his feet in a heartbeat. He found the waitress, stuffed a bunch of twenties in her hand to pay for everyone's pizza and headed for the door. To his astonishment, Rory Sue tried to intercept him.

"Told you it would work," she gloated.

He regarded her with bewilderment. "What are you talking about?"

"You don't think that kiss came out of the blue, do you? It was because of me. Sarah figures I'm trying to steal her man, so she made sure I knew to steer clear."

"Aren't you?"

She laughed. "Well, of course I am, if you're willing, but I'm not stupid. I figured out which way the wind was blowing back at the station the other day. You made it plain enough. I also knew everybody in this town, Sarah included, would think I was just like my mama was when she was fighting an uphill battle to get Ronnie Sullivan's attention. There's a big difference between us, though. I know when to cut my losses. It took my mother a little longer to figure out the man she really belonged with was my dad."

"So you turning up here today was some altruistic act to kick things between Sarah and me up a notch?"

She nodded. "And maybe a little test to be sure I hadn't gotten it wrong," she admitted.

Travis shook his head. "I don't think I'll ever understand women."

Rory Sue gave him a pitying look. "You're a man, poor thing. It's not in the cards that you'll ever fully understand us. Now run along and catch up with Sarah. Something tells me you can capitalize on that kiss if you hurry."

"Thanks. I owe you," he said and took off.

He made it to Sarah's house in less than ten minutes. Her car was back in the driveway, but when he knocked and rang the bell, no one answered. Finally he walked around to the back, where he found Sarah sitting all alone on the patio. She glanced up at his arrival, but her expression was wary.

He dropped down into the chair next to hers.

"Kids inside?" he asked.

"Raylene's getting them down for their naps."

Satisfied that they were alone and likely to be that way for a while, he said, "That was quite a show you put on back at the restaurant."

"I thought it might get Rory Sue to back off." She pinned him with a look. "That is what you wanted, isn't it?"

"It's only part of what I want."

"What's the rest?"

"You," he said quietly. "I want you. After that kiss, I'm thinking maybe that's a possibility, after all. What do you think?"

"I think maybe we're both confusing lust with something else," she told him. "It's been known to happen."

"Sugar, I've always been real clear on the difference. I've probably been in lust with one woman or another since my teens.

You're the only one with whom I've ever wanted more."

There was no mistaking the faint spark of hope that lit her eyes before she looked away. "You talk a great game, McDonald."

"It's not just talk, and I'm definitely not playing a game."

She didn't look as if she was buying it.

Travis tried again. "Come home with me," he suggested. "Tom and Jeanette have gone to see his folks in Charleston. We'd have the house to ourselves."

"Wouldn't that pretty much be proving my point?" she asked. "All you want is to get into my pants."

He had to fight a smile at her determination to act blasé about it. "I'm thinking if we get the lust out of the way, we'll strip things down to what's really going on between us."

She laughed at that. "A very convenient strategy, if you ask me."

"Well, at least it's a strategy," he said. "Do you have a better way to figure things out?"

"Time," she said at once.

"In other words, you want me to jump through hoops, proving my intentions are honorable." If any other woman had suggested putting him to a test, he'd have walked away. With Sarah, he understood

398

why she needed him to prove himself. He met her gaze. "Okay, but you have to play fair with me."

"I always play fair," she said with a touch of indignation.

"My point is that you have to open your heart to the possibilities. You can't hide from me. We start doing things together, hanging out like this, whatever." He grinned. "Maybe even kissing from time to time."

She nodded slowly. "That seems reasonable."

"We could seal the deal with a kiss," he suggested. "Nothing too dangerous, of course. Just a little peck on the cheek, maybe."

She looked vaguely disappointed by that. "I suppose."

"You coming over here, or should I come there?"

Her lips twitched at that. "Your move, McDonald."

"Okay, then," he said, rising to his feet and crossing to her chaise longue. Instead of the promised peck on the cheek, however, he nudged her legs to the side and sat down beside her, then leaned forward very, very slowly. He braced his hands on the back of the chaise on either side of her, then paused just a hairsbreadth away from her mouth and waited. Their breath mingled. Her eyes widened. She nervously licked her lips. Only then did he cover her mouth with his. He took his time about it, tasting, savoring, persuading until her lips parted.

When he finally pulled away, he decided it had been a very satisfactory beginning, but only a beginning. He wanted much, much more, and he intended to have it very, very soon.

For the second time that day, Sarah ran away right after Travis had kissed her. She needed to catch her breath, needed to be sure he couldn't see just how desperately she wanted more. He'd take advantage of that, and she wouldn't be able to stop him . . . wouldn't *want* to stop him. For a woman who wanted guarantees, the only thing these kisses guaranteed was that she was putting her heart at risk.

Inside, she leaned against the kitchen counter and sucked in great gulps of air, then splashed her overheated face with cool tap water. She was drying her face with a paper towel when she heard the back door open and close.

"I thought you'd left," she said, regarding him nervously.

Travis held her gaze. "Did you really

want me to?"

"No," she admitted. She swallowed hard, then said, "Why don't you stick around and have dinner with us? We're just doing burgers on the grill. Raylene's made potato salad and cole slaw. It'll be pretty casual."

"You sure?"

"I may not be sure about a lot right now, but dinner's fine," she said. "I think I can control myself for a couple of hours, especially with chaperones." She hesitated, then said, "We'll be eating inside."

"Even though it promises to be a nice night?"

She debated hedging about the reason, but too many people knew. Besides, his reaction might give her a clue about whether he was as kind and open-minded as she thought he was.

"It's Raylene," she explained. "You need to know that she gets these panic attacks if she tries to leave the house. It's why she doesn't keep the kids for long. She worries they'll slip outside and she won't be able to make herself go after them." She gave him a challenging look. "Don't make too big a deal out of it, okay? I'm telling you so you won't embarrass her."

Travis looked offended. "I'm not an insensitive jerk, you know. I already had some idea there was something going on with her. I'd wondered why she didn't seem to come to any of the other places I'd seen you with your friends. People have said some things, but I wasn't sure they were right. Gossip gets a lot of stuff wrong, so I try not to pay too much attention to it."

Sarah frowned. "Like what? What do they say about her?" she asked, immediately defensive on Raylene's behalf. The idea that people might be talking insensitively about Raylene or even making jokes about her situation incensed her.

"Simmer down. They're not criticizing. They say that her ex-husband abused her."

"True," she admitted. "Even I don't know all the details of how bad it was, but it must have been pretty bad. Her husband's in jail now. He negotiated some kind of plea deal, thanks to his family connections. He got off way too lightly in my opinion."

"And you think that's why she has these panic attacks if she goes out?" Travis concluded. "He's not out of jail already, is he?"

"Not yet. Even so, I'm pretty sure her fear of him coming after her one day is what's keeping her locked up in the house. Annie and I have tried to convince her to get help. Unfortunately, she thinks she can fix the problem on her own." She shrugged. "I guess she'll ask for help when she gets tired of being stuck in the house all the time."

He regarded her with undisguised admiration. "You're a terrific friend to have taken her in."

"There was never a question about it. She needed a safe place to come to," Sarah said simply. "But I'm not sure I'm doing her any favors by not pushing her harder to get professional help."

"Whatever kind of problem a person has, they need to be ready to solve it. You can't do it for them."

"I suppose."

"Will me being here be a problem for her?"

The question showed exactly the kind of compassion and understanding Sarah had hoped for. "No, Raylene loves having company," she assured him. "It's the outside world that seems to scare her. You'll see. She's great. I don't know what I would have done without her, really. She takes care of the house, and the kids absolutely adore her."

Travis still seemed worried. "How about this? I'll run home, take a shower and change. That'll give you time to let her know I'm going to be around for dinner."

When Sarah started to protest that it

wasn't necessary, he held up his hand. "Look, I'm not just unexpected company, I'm a man she's never met before. After what she's been through, strangers could throw her."

Again, she was overwhelmed by his thoughtfulness. "I appreciate your concern, but she's been very anxious to meet you. She feels as if she already knows you. And, at the risk of giving you a swelled head, I'll tell you that she's one of your biggest supporters when it comes to me."

Travis's expression lit up. "Have you been talking about me, sugar?"

Sarah rolled her eyes. "Some, but that's not why. Raylene listens to your show. You'd be surprised just how much you reveal about yourself on the air."

He grinned. "So she's a fan! Then all the more reason for me to put my best foot forward. Want me to bring back ice cream, while I'm at it? Maybe a strawberry-rhubarb pie? This morning I heard Grace say she'd gotten some in today."

"I don't give two hoots whether you get freshened up, but I'm all for you bringing back pie and ice cream," she said eagerly. She'd been so careful about her diet for so long that she could allow herself an occasional treat like this.

He gave her a lingering, speculative look. "Think that might earn me another kiss?"

"Some things you should do for the pure pleasure of making someone else happy," she chided.

"Exactly. And a kiss would make me very happy."

"I'll keep that in mind," she promised.

As he left, she stood there staring after him, wondering just how wide she was going to open the door to let him into her life. Right this second, though, she was *almost* persuaded that moments like the ones they'd shared today were worth just about any price she might wind up paying.

20

Mary Vaughn had sufficient pull to arrange for the closing on Travis's purchase of Liz's house to take place at home. Sonny helped her dress, then carried her into the living room in the morning and settled her on the sofa despite her protests that she was perfectly capable of putting on her own clothes and walking a few hundred feet.

"Not on my watch," he said, just as Rory Sue appeared with a tray laden with juice, a pot of herbal tea and toast.

"All this and breakfast, too," Mary Vaughn said, impressed with her daughter's sudden attentiveness. Then she took a closer look at what Rory Sue was wearing. It was a summer dress with a deep-V neckline that showed off a little more cleavage than was called for. Mary Vaughn regarded her suspiciously. "Are you all dressed up because Travis is coming over?"

"What if I am?" Rory Sue said, immediately defensive.

Sonny had apparently taken another look at their daughter, because he frowned. "That dress is a little revealing, don't you think?"

"I'm not sixteen, Dad. There's nothing wrong with this dress. Every fashion magazine is showing dresses just like this one."

"This is daytime in Serenity, not nighttime in Vegas," he retorted, an edge of fatherly outrage in his voice.

Rory Sue looked taken aback by his very vocal disapproval. Sonny, more than anyone else, could cut right through her bravado. Her face fell. "You really don't like it?"

Mary Vaughn squeezed his hand meaningfully. He glanced down at her, then said more calmly, "I didn't say I didn't like it or that it isn't flattering, hon. I just don't think it's appropriate for a business meeting, okay?"

Rory Sue turned to her mother. "Mom?"

"Your father's right. You don't want to give Travis the wrong impression about the kind of woman you are, do you?"

"Trust me, Travis isn't even likely to look at me," Rory Sue responded in a resigned tone. "He's all about Sarah these days. Not that I'm ready to throw in the towel just yet. I'm not sure Sarah's smart enough to know how lucky she is."

Sonny frowned. "That's not a very nice thing to say about a friend," he said.

"Sarah and I are barely acquaintances, Dad. She, Raylene and Annie were like these mini Sweet Magnolias back in high school. They were seniors, and I was only a lowly sophomore. They all stuck together. I was an outsider."

"How can you say that?" Sonny said. "You were one of the most popular girls in school."

"When it came to guys, yes," Rory Sue said. "But I didn't have a lot of girlfriends."

"I'm sure they'd love to see more of you," Mary Vaughn said, knowing exactly what it felt like to have plenty of male companionship but no real friend to confide in.

Until she'd gotten to know Jeanette, who'd brokered peace with the other Sweet Magnolias, Mary Vaughn hadn't had a lot of women friends, either. Now at least Maddie and Helen tolerated her, and Dana Sue had stopped looking at her as if she were pond scum. Not that they'd ever once invited her to join one of their Sweet Magnolias gatherings, she thought with resignation. She supposed that would be asking too much after the way she'd gone after Ronnie. At any rate, it made her sympathetic to what Rory Sue was feeling.

"I spoke to Sarah myself a while back," she told Rory Sue. "I mentioned you'd probably be around, and she said they'd be glad to include you when they get together. You just have to make an overture."

Rory Sue frowned. "I made an overture. Unfortunately, I made it to Travis right in front of Sarah. I don't think she'll want me as a pal anytime soon."

"Oh, sweetie, I'm sorry," Mary Vaughn said. She also knew what it was like to be an outsider in this close-knit town. Her family background had been troubled, and all that most people felt for her was pity. Only after she'd married Sonny had she finally started to feel as if people in Serenity respected her. She'd lost that when she'd lost him, and it had taken a long time for her to win it back on her own merits. In the end, though, that had been sweeter.

"We'll think of some way to fix things," she promised Rory Sue. "Right now, though, we need to focus on this closing. Have we received all the papers?"

Rory Sue nodded. "I checked everything against your list twice."

"And the attorney for Liz and the bank knows to come here?"

"I told his secretary," Rory Sue confirmed.

"It's all good, Mom."

Sonny leaned down and kissed Mary Vaughn. "Satisfied, worrywart?"

"I'm just not used to not being in control," Mary Vaughn lamented.

"Well, get used to it," Sonny said, his hand resting on her stomach. "Because once this little one gets here, you and I won't be in control of anything for at least eighteen years or so."

Although the prospect of that flat-out terrified Mary Vaughn, Sonny seemed ecstatic. It was probably a good thing that one of them could roll with whatever lay ahead.

Travis had dreaded crossing paths with Rory Sue at the closing, but to his surprise, she was all business. She was obviously Mary Vaughn's second in command and demonstrated a clear understanding of most of the paperwork and details. He was impressed.

Best of all, everything went without a hitch. He and Liz signed what seemed like hundreds of documents and he turned over the cashier's checks he'd brought from his bank, but in the end when Liz handed him the keys to her house, he felt as if she were bestowing a great gift on him.

"Thank you," he said, surprised to find

that he truly felt emotional. Though he'd had plenty of places of his own since college, some of them pretty pricey and sophisticated, this was the first real home he'd actually owned.

"Feeling like a grown-up?" Rory Sue teased, startling him with her insight.

"Something like that," he admitted.

"I don't suppose you'd like to go celebrate," she said, then glanced quickly toward Liz. "You, too. This is a big day for both of you. I'd love to take you to Sullivan's for lunch."

"What a lovely thought, Rory Sue," Liz said, giving her hand a squeeze. "But I still have a lot of straightening up to do in the guest house. It's not easy consolidating all those years of accumulated memories into a small place."

"And I need to help her," Travis said. "But thanks for the invitation, Rory Sue. How about we celebrate when your mom's up and around again? We'll have a big housewarming at my place."

Rory Sue hid her disappointment well. "Sure. That'll be great."

"And I'll definitely be ready for a party by then," Mary Vaughn said. "I'm already way past stir-crazy being confined to the house like this."

Liz regarded her sympathetically. "I was on bed rest with my first child. Had the exact same problem with spiking blood pressure, in fact. I remember what it was like. Why don't I come over with a couple of my friends to play cards one afternoon a week? Would that be okay? I know we must seem like a bunch of old fogies to you, but the company would provide a distraction."

"I would love it," Mary Vaughn said, sounding touched. "You'll have to be very patient with me, though. I've never had much time to play cards."

"We'll teach you everything you need to know," Liz promised.

"Watch her, though," Travis teased. "Word at the senior center is that Liz plays a cut-throat game of gin."

"I play to win, no question about it," Liz said unrepentantly. "What's the point, otherwise?"

Mary Vaughn laughed. "I'm all about winning. I'll give you a run for your money."

Liz gave a nod of satisfaction. "Suits me. Flo Decatur's the only one who can beat me regularly, but she doesn't play nearly as often as I'd like. She's real attached to Sarah Beth, that sweet little granddaughter of hers. You should see the two of them with their heads together. It's the cutest thing."

Liz stood up and linked her arm through Travis's. "Okay, young man, let's go home." She turned back and winked at the others. "It's been a long time since I've been able to say something like that with a handsome man at my side. I could get used to it."

"I know I'd go home with him in a heartbeat," Rory Sue said.

Travis's head snapped around to look at her, but her expression was totally innocent. She merely winked at him, then walked them to the door and waved as they left.

In the car, Liz turned to him with a frown. "That young lady is interested in you. I hope you're not doing anything to lead her on," she scolded. "I happen to know you care about Sarah."

"I do, and believe me, Rory Sue knows that."

"Knowing is one thing," Liz said. "You might need to slap a *hands off* sticker on your backside to make things crystal clear."

Travis started to chuckle until he saw that Liz was totally serious. "Don't worry. She's not going to come between me and Sarah."

"I hope you're right about that," Liz said direly as they pulled up in front of what was now his house. "Now help me around back," she said. "I have things to do."

"I told you I'd help," Travis said as he

walked with her.

"I don't need you pawing through my things. Go on over to the main house and get yourself settled. Then you can come over at five for a drink to celebrate, if you have the time. I'll invite Sarah, too. I want to see for myself how the two of you get along. Our Sunday dinner was cut short by Mary Vaughn's untimely contractions, so I couldn't form a clear picture of what's going on with you two."

Travis regarded her worriedly. "You're not seriously planning to meddle, are you?"

"Heavens, no. I have enough to do without worrying about your love life, young man. I'll be inviting my own beau to join us." Her expression turned thoughtful. "And maybe a few others."

Travis chuckled. "I should have known you'd have a man on the line."

"Well, of course, I do. Keeps things lively. Not that I want to live with one again, but every now and again I can use him to open jars and carry things."

Travis bent down and kissed her cheek. "You are a pistol, Liz. I'm so glad we're going to be neighbors."

"We're going to be *friends*," she corrected. "I insist on it."

"You'll get no argument from me. Call

me if you need anything. Otherwise, I'll see you at five."

"Don't be late. I like my martinis perfectly chilled, and I hate to start without my guests."

Travis watched until she was safely inside, then walked over to step into his first-ever home. Even without furniture and with the walls bare, it felt welcoming. Something told him, though, it wouldn't feel a hundred percent like home until he could convince Sarah and her kids to share it with him.

The invitation to Sarah to have drinks with Liz pretty much came out of the blue. She showed it to Annie and Raylene when she went home to lunch. The handwritten note was on thick vellum in a strong, cursive style. The old-fashioned, formal touch struck her as more of a command than a casual invitation.

"Why do you suppose she wants me there? I hardly know her."

"Travis closed the deal on her house today. Maybe she's hosting a celebration," Annie suggested.

Raylene shook her head. "You two seem to have forgotten that Liz lived in the same block I did when I was a kid. I've known her all my life. She's interested in everything that goes on around town, especially when it comes to romances. This is all about getting Sarah and Travis in the same room so she can get the lay of the land for herself."

Sarah blinked. "You're kidding. She's meddling?"

"I'd lay odds on it," Raylene said. "Be prepared to answer a whole lot of questions about your relationship."

"We don't actually have a relationship," Sarah protested.

Raylene and Annie exchanged such disbelieving looks that Sarah felt compelled to defend her claim.

"Not like you're talking about anyway. We haven't . . . you know."

Annie chuckled. "I doubt even Liz wants the details about *that*."

"Don't be so sure," Raylene said. "Look, stop analyzing why she wants you there and just go. Do you have any idea how many people in this town would be thrilled to get an invitation from Liz? She's practically a legend. And her parties, even the simplest ones, are memorable. She was known for doing some pretty outrageous stuff in her prime."

"Raylene's right," Annie said. "Go and have fun." She grinned wickedly. "Maybe Travis will invite you next door to view his etchings."

"Travis has a radio show to do tonight," Sarah reminded her, though she had to admit to a tingle of anticipation at the possibility that he might try to get her alone in his new place. Lately, being alone with him was just about all she could think about.

A few hours later, wearing another of the dresses from Raylene's closet, she arrived on Oak Drive to find that most of the parking spaces were already taken. Apparently Liz's gathering had drawn quite a crowd.

Sarah was crossing the back lawn when Travis materialized at her side.

"Where'd you come from?" she asked. "I thought you'd already be at Liz's."

"I waited for you. I thought we should make an entrance together. It'll make Liz happy."

"Then she *is* matchmaking," Sarah said, resigned.

"Pretty much, but then we're already a match, so she doesn't have much work to do."

Sarah didn't have the energy to debate the point for once. Instead, she merely asked, "Doesn't it bother you that we're going to be on display?"

"Why should it?" he said easily. "Relax. We'll have a drink, maybe some cheese and

417

crackers, and then we can sneak away and do far more fascinating things at my place."

"I thought you hadn't bought any furniture yet. Isn't that what you told the company out on the highway to get them to advertise? You said you'd have a whole house to furnish soon. They figured you'd be spending enough to underwrite the cost of a few ads. At least that's what they told me when *I* tried to sell them ads." She gave him a chiding look. "Of course, I wouldn't have wasted my time if you had bothered to put a note on our chart about meeting with them."

"Sorry," he said, though his guilty look was very fleeting. "The strategy worked, didn't it? They bought a whole package of thirty-second ads. And I did buy one thing on the spot."

"Oh?"

He grinned wickedly. "A great big king-size bed."

She laughed. "Optimistic that you'll find someone to share it, aren't you?"

"Oh, sugar, I know I will. In fact, I've already picked her out. It's just a matter of time."

Sarah sighed over his super-sized ego. Unfortunately, though, that's what she figured, too.

■ ■ ■ ■

It had been two months and Walter still hadn't found a job, not in Serenity, not within a fifty-mile radius. Searching had been an eye-opening experience. He was overqualified for much that was available, not that he wouldn't have taken anything at this point, but those hiring for even the most menial jobs questioned whether he would stay long enough to make it worthwhile training him.

With a degree in business, a shortage of executive positions and too many people at that level out of work, he was competing with people whose qualifications and work experiences were more varied than his own.

And yet the prospect of going back to Alabama and asking for his old job back was too humiliating to contemplate. He refused to get sucked back into a world dominated by his parents.

"So, what are you going to do?" Raylene asked him one afternoon when they were sipping iced tea at the kitchen table while the children napped.

Walter found these quiet conversations to be oddly comforting, though he certainly wouldn't have described Raylene as a relaxing person. She was usually edgy and critical and blunt. Surprisingly, he appreciated the fact that she spoke her mind, even when he came out wanting.

"I'll keep looking," he told her now. "I may have to go farther afield though. I think my prospects will be better in Charleston or Columbia."

"Or you could swallow your pride and apply for the sales position at the radio station," she suggested innocently.

"Not a chance in hell," he said fiercely. He was not going to Travis McDonald, hat in hand, and asking him for anything. He'd heard about the job on the very day it had been listed, but he'd known even trying to arrange an interview would be a complete waste of time.

Raylene shrugged. "Suit yourself. I thought staying near your kids was what mattered most."

"It is."

"Well, then?"

"Look, you know perfectly well that Travis and I don't exactly see eye to eye on a lot of things."

She smiled. "You mean Sarah."

He shrugged. "Pretty much," he admitted. "I've heard he blames me for really messing her up, making her think she's not good enough."

"Well, duh. Isn't that exactly what you did?"

"Not intentionally," he said, though he couldn't deny that had been the effect of not only his nonstop criticism, but the barrage of negativity from his parents that he'd failed to stop. "I admit I was a lousy husband. I should have taken her side, instead of jumping on the bandwagon when my parents went after her."

"Yes, you should have," Raylene agreed without hesitation. "But there's nothing to say you couldn't try to make up for it now. You still have a tendency to point out something negative whenever you're around her. Surely you've noticed all the good things she's accomplished."

He regarded her wearily. "I know it's a habit I need to break, and I am trying, but I don't see why anything I say matters anymore. We're divorced. Sarah doesn't give two hoots what I think."

"Oh, she's a lot stronger now, no question about that, but I know that every time she gets close to really believing in herself, especially as a woman, it's your voice she hears in her head, and every single doubt comes stampeding back."

"After all this time?" he said incredulously.

"That's ridiculous."

"I agree, but it's true. Think about this. When you're having a bad day or something doesn't go your way, whose voice do you hear in your head? Your mother's or your father's, right? Even when you know how wrong they were or when you resent the way they talked down to you, you can't shake all those years of criticism."

Walter realized she was exactly right.

"Look, here's the bottom line, Walter. When a woman loves a man the way Sarah loved you, it gives that man power. He can use it to build her up or to tear her down. We both know which way you went. Words can hurt, especially when they're repeated often enough by someone you love and respect. If you care about Sarah, if you ever cared about her, fix the damage you did so she can move on. You owe it to her. Do that, and maybe Travis will look at you differently."

He got what she was saying about Sarah, but the mention of Travis stirred his temper. "I don't give a damn what Travis McDonald thinks of me."

She gave him a wry look. "You should, if you want the best available job in town."

Unfortunately, she had a point. "I'll think about it," he conceded eventually.

"Think fast. That job's not going to be available for long. I happen to know you could have the inside track if you'd eat a little crow."

"Meaning?"

"Sarah told me that Bill had already recommended you. Travis has a lot of respect for his opinion."

"And Sarah? What does she think?" he asked, not wanting to get his hopes up.

"Ask her yourself. Personally, I think she'll want it to work out so that you'll be able to stay close to the kids. She always puts them first."

"You said Bill recommended me. I'll bet Travis told him to forget it, didn't he?"

"He did, but when Sarah spoke to him, he said he'd reconsider if you showed signs of taking responsibility for what you'd done to her. The man will do pretty much anything she wants."

Walter regarded her with exasperation. "And you know all this how? Eavesdropping?"

"I don't have to resort to eavesdropping. People like me. They tell me things." She grinned. "Even you've revealed a lot more than you realize. Now, fix this, Walter. Not just before it's too late for you to get this job, but because it's the right thing to do for Sarah. She needs it so she can move on to the life she deserves."

"With Travis, I suppose," he said.

"Possibly. That's up to her. I just want her to have the option of reaching for anything and believing she deserves it."

"You're a good friend."

"So they tell me."

"When are you going to get out of this house and grab a life of your own?" He knew Sarah believed Raylene was agoraphobic, scared of what awaited her in the outside world. He wondered if the panic really ran that deep, or if she'd just grown comfortable and complacent where she was. What would it take to motivate her to try to change? The nagging of her best friends certainly hadn't worked.

Her grin faded at his question. "Not your problem," she said stiffly. "I need to check on the kids."

He snagged her hand. "You've been a friend to me, so I'm going to try to return the favor. See a shrink, Raylene. Stop hiding out before it's too late. You don't want to wake up one day years from now and realize your entire life has passed you by. You say Sarah deserved better than what she got from me. Well, you deserve better than this. Staying locked up inside this house is letting that miserable ex-husband of yours win."

She looked genuinely taken aback by the mention of her ex-husband, but before she could respond, Walter stood up. "I'll check on the kids. You sit here and think about what I said."

His opinion probably didn't matter a whole lot to Raylene, but something told him if he did manage to get through to her, he might become a hero in Sarah's eyes. He'd like to have that feeling again.

21

Travis, darn his hide, had Sarah blushing furiously as they wound up another morning of *Carolina Daybreak*. He seemed to take great pride in getting her all flustered on the air by saying the most outrageous things. Today, without actually saying it, he'd managed to suggest to the entire community that she was tired because she'd been out cavorting with him the night before. He never actually crossed a line and lied, but he was a master of suggestive innuendo. Listeners clearly thought their love life was a whole lot more interesting than it was.

As soon as Bill had gone on the air in the control booth, Sarah scowled at Travis. "Why do you do things like that? You know perfectly well what people are going to think."

He grinned without the slightest hint of guilt. "Yes, I do."

"Does it occur to you that you might embarrass me?"

"That's half the fun," he admitted. "I love seeing you get all flustered."

"Well, what if Walter decides I'm making a spectacle of myself on the air and decides to sue me for custody of Tommy and Libby? Will it still be all innocent fun for you, then?"

Travis's expression sobered at once. "He wouldn't dare."

To be honest, Sarah didn't think he would either, but it wouldn't do to let Travis know that. "He might," she said direly. "Are you going to explain to my kids why they have to leave Mommy?"

"I'll beat him to a bloody pulp before I allow that to happen," Travis said.

He sounded so grim, she backed off. The last thing she wanted was to have Travis and her ex-husband brawling on the town green. "I don't think that'll be necessary," she said. "I'm just saying you need to think about the consequences before you say some of this stuff."

"One of the consequences I'm hoping for is that me talking about the two of us often enough will get *you* to believe we're destined to be a couple." He grinned. "Who knows, you could go crazy one day and seduce me."

"Don't count on it," she said, hoping her tone was firm instead of filled with the quivering anticipation his words had set off inside her.

He perched on the corner of her desk, his knees crowding her. "How about we talk about this some more over lunch at Wharton's? You can fill me in on what you think is appropriate and what's going too far."

It almost sounded as if he really wanted to know. Before she could utter her usual refusal, she found herself nodding. "Okay."

Travis regarded her with a startled expression. "Was that a yes?"

"Don't push me," she told him. "I could change my mind. Let's get over there before it gets too crowded."

He stood up, grinning, then signaled to Bill with an exaggerated thumbs-up. "She said yes," he mouthed.

Beside him, Sarah rolled her eyes. "To lunch," she said before Bill announced to all the world that the question had been something else entirely.

At Wharton's, most of the regulars had already claimed their booths, but there was one left in the back. As they walked toward it, the mayor winked at Travis. "Good show today." His buddies seemed to concur.

"They just enjoyed it because they think

you got the better of me," Sarah grumbled at the demonstration of masculine support. "Men in this town stick together."

"Come on, sugar, everybody in town knows it's you who's got me twisted in knots," he replied.

"As if," she murmured, grabbing a menu and burying her head in it as if she didn't already know it by heart.

When Grace appeared to take their order, she was grinning from ear to ear. "I swear I can't get a thing done in here when you get to going on the air. I haven't had so much fun listening to two people courting since back when Dana Sue and Ronnie were shooting off sparks all over town."

Sarah gaped at her. Courting? That's what Grace — and most likely everyone else in town — thought was going on? Oh brother. It was already worse than she'd thought.

Once Grace had gone, she studied Travis to see if he was finally beginning to understand the risk of his on-air games. He didn't appear to be the least bit fazed.

"You did hear what Grace said, didn't you?" she prodded.

"Which part?"

"People think we're courting."

Travis met her gaze evenly, his expression about as serious as Sarah had ever seen it.

He didn't look upset. In fact, he appeared totally calm and relaxed.

"Haven't you figured it out before now, sugar?" he asked. "Courting is exactly what we're doing."

"I'm not," she said at once, then blinked. "Are you?"

A smile played on his lips. "I am."

She sat back in her seat, her heart hammering. *Well, I'll be,* she thought. She'd thought she understood all about Travis playing a game on the air. It was second-nature to him, but this? He was actually serious? That was an entirely different kettle of fish.

"Are you sure?" she asked, earning a full-fledged grin.

"Very sure."

"Well, you need to stop it," she told him. "My divorce is barely final. I can't be thinking seriously about another man, especially you. A game's one thing. I'm a lot rusty at those, but I can probably handle it. Courting? I am not ready for that."

He laughed. "Why especially me?" he asked.

She waved off the ridiculous question. "Because you're you."

He feigned confusion, though he had to know exactly what she meant.

"You mean because I'm tall?" he asked.

"No."

"You don't like dark hair?"

"Oh, stop being ridiculous. You know who you are, *what* you are."

"Oh, we're back to me being an irresponsible player again, is that it?"

"Hey, I didn't pin that label on you," she said defensively. "You came to town with it."

"And I think I've done a pretty good job of trying to live it down," he said quietly. "Have you even seen me look at another woman besides you?"

"Mariah Litchfield," she said at once.

His brows shot up. "We had one conversation in the studio, and it was about her daughter's singing."

She realized she was on thin ice with that one, so she moved on to a more recent example. "Rory Sue," she said.

"*She* looked at *me*," he corrected. "I haven't given her the time of day."

She honestly couldn't deny that's the way it had seemed, at Rosalina's anyway. She still wasn't quite ready to let it go, though.

"Well, I have no idea whom you see in your spare time," she retorted, aware that she was losing her very best argument for continuing to keep him at a distance.

"I have almost no spare time," he said. "And every minute of what I do have is spent trying to persuade you to give me a chance. I could probably give you an accurate accounting of every minute over the next week, if that will help. I'll keep one of those charts you love so much."

She scowled at the ridiculous offer. "Will you just stop it, please? You don't have to account for your time with me."

"Apparently I do."

Sarah sighed. She wasn't going to win, no matter how hard she tried. He talked faster and had the skill to spin just about anything to his own benefit.

Fortunately, before she needed to come up with some quick-witted reply, she looked up and saw Walter heading in their direction, a determined expression on his face. For once, she was almost glad to see him. That reaction was startling enough to keep her from worrying about Travis for a half second.

"You looking for me?" she said, then slid over to make room for him.

The instant Travis realized whom she was speaking to, his expression turned sour.

"You two have met," she said a little too cheerfully, then fixed her gaze on her ex-husband. "Is there a problem with the kids?"

"No, I was actually hoping to talk to you about something," Walter said.

Though she'd usually rather be tortured than left alone with Walter, she immediately nodded. "Travis won't mind leaving us alone, will you? I'm sure Grace can fix your order to go."

Travis scowled and didn't budge.

Beside her, Walter squirmed uncomfortably. "Actually, I'd like him to stay," he said, then glanced across the table. "If you don't mind."

Since Travis had shown no sign of leaving anyway, it was a moot point.

Walter cleared his throat, then met Travis's gaze. "I know you and I have gotten off on the wrong foot. You've probably heard a lot about all the things I did wrong while I was married to Sarah, and I can't deny a one of them. I'm trying to do better by her." He turned to Sarah with a hopeful expression. "You can see that, right?"

She realized now where this was going. She didn't want to sabotage him, so she nodded. "You have been trying harder."

"The bottom line is that I love my kids and I want to stay close to them, but the way my job hunt has been going, I'm going to have to think about moving over to Charleston or Columbia." He leveled a look into Travis's eyes. "Unless you'll at least consider interviewing me for your sales position."

Sarah knew what it had taken for Walter to swallow his pride just to ask for a chance, especially with Travis. A glance across the table told her that Travis understood it, too.

Travis turned to her. "Sarah? How do you feel about this? You, Bill and me, we've been a team from the beginning, so you have a say in this, too. You say no, and we stop this right now."

She met Travis's gaze evenly and repeated what she'd told him in private when she'd first heard about the job opening. "I think you should talk to him," she said sincerely. "Walter's more than qualified for the job. He'd be great for the station. As for him and me getting along, we can manage to be civil, right, Walter?"

"I promise there will be no friction," he said, then ventured a grin. "I imagine Sarah will be the first to call me on it if I get out of line."

Travis didn't look entirely convinced by their show of unity, but he nodded. "I'll see you at two-thirty at the station. I'm not making any promises, but we'll talk and see how it goes."

Sarah could feel the tension go out of

Walter's body and realized just how badly he wanted this to work out.

"Thank you," he said to Travis. "Now I'll leave the two of you to your lunch."

He'd barely walked away before Grace appeared with their meals. "I didn't want to interrupt. Things looked pretty serious over here."

"Just a friendly chat," Travis said, clearly disappointing Grace, who'd obviously been hoping for fireworks.

After she'd gone, Sarah reached across the table and squeezed his hand. "Thank you for agreeing to see Walter. I know it took a lot for him to ask. Walking away from his family's business and being out of work has been humbling for him."

Travis nodded. "I got that. In fact, that's what decided me. It takes a certain amount of courage to go to someone you know dislikes you and ask for a chance." He studied Sarah intently. "I know you said you could handle it, but are you sure it'll be okay for you working with him?"

"We'll make it work," she said with resolve. For Tommy and Libby's sake, she couldn't do any less.

"If I overhear him saying one thing to cut you down, he'll be booted out the door," Travis warned.

"And I'll be holding the door open for you," she promised.

His apparent anxiety faded. "You had me worried for a minute. I thought maybe you were mellowing toward the man."

"I'm mellowing. I'm not nuts," she said.

It was a relief to figure out that she actually understood the difference.

Walking back to the station, Travis reached for Sarah's hand, half anticipating that she'd yank it right back. When she didn't, he took it as another sign that maybe she was starting to get used to the idea of them as a couple.

The shocking part was how content he was with the simple act of holding her soft, delicate hand against his calloused skin. He'd always moved directly past the hand-holding stage — or even the kissing stage — to get to more intriguing intimacies. Because of Sarah's reticence, he was coming to appreciate the foreplay.

"This feels like courting to me," he said casually. "How about you?"

She glanced up at him, a twinkle in her eye. "Could be."

"Can you live with that?"

"I'm starting to get used to the idea," she admitted.

Travis would have danced a little jig right there in the middle of the square if he hadn't spotted his mother steaming toward the door of the radio station. Her arrival couldn't mean anything good.

"Who's that?" Sarah wondered when she saw the woman opening the door to the station.

"My mother," Travis said with an air of resignation. "You may want to run for your life."

"Why?"

"Because something tells me she's not here for the grand tour of the station."

"Oh?"

"It's bound to be about my father. It's *always* about my father. From the time I was ten, when he had his first very public affair, she has vented about his behavior to me."

"Even when you were just a kid?" Sarah asked, looking shocked.

"She thought I could shame him into walking the straight and narrow."

"What a horrible position to put a child in!" Sarah said indignantly. "She should have been trying to shield you from what was happening, not putting you into the middle of it."

Travis nodded. "I couldn't agree with you

more. At least that might help you to see why my father and I have this strange sort of love-hate relationship. I was taught to judge his actions at an early age. Then people started comparing me to him. Until recently, I had no idea whether I could be a decent husband or if I even wanted to try."

"And you know now?"

He met her gaze. "I do," he said solemnly. "At least I'm going to do my best not to be like my father. If and when I make that kind of commitment, it will be because I know with everything in me that I can make it work."

"So, what do you think your mother wants from you now?"

"My guess is she's heard about the baby and she expects me to fix things."

Sarah looked justifiably bewildered. "How?"

"Beats me." At the door to the station, he pressed a quick kiss to her forehead. "Go on home. There's no reason for you to get dragged into this."

"But I have some paperwork to do."

"You won't get it done with my mother ranting for the next hour," Travis told her.

"I could provide backup," she offered.

He chuckled. "Nothing I'd like to see more than that, but no. It's my family drama."

"You've been dragged into mine," she reminded him. "Walter will be here at two-thirty."

"Yet another reason for you to leave," he said. "Go home and take a nice long bubble bath. Thinking about that will get me through the next couple of hours."

"If I stay in the tub that long, I'll shrivel up like a prune."

"You only need to promise you'll do it in order for me to get the picture," he assured her. He closed his eyes. "Yep, there it is. The image I was hoping for. Very sexy!"

Sarah laughed. "You're a little crazy, you know that, don't you?"

"Does that bother you?"

She reached up tentatively and touched his cheek. "Not half as much as I expected it to."

It was a rare night when all of the Sweet Magnolias — young and old — could get together these days. All of them had busy lives and too many of them had young children. Apparently, though, Raylene had spent the day organizing it.

"I was going a little stir crazy for some adult company," she admitted sheepishly when Sarah got home. "I called everyone, and they all said they'd come. While the kids were napping, the sitter ran to the store and picked up everything we'll need. She's taking Libby and Tommy over to Annie's and will watch them and Trevor tonight."

Sarah was startled and pleased that Raylene had taken the initiative. She wasn't entirely sure what it meant, though. Was Raylene ready to take the next step and ask for help? Rather than pressing her, though, she merely asked, "You haven't already made the margaritas, have you?"

Raylene looked genuinely horrified by the suggestion. "Absolutely not. That's Helen's job."

"Whew! I'm glad you remembered that. And the guacamole?"

"Stop worrying. Dana Sue's making it. I know the pecking order in this group. Those two and Maddie have a practically lifelong system. I'm not about to tamper with it. I'm just glad they've welcomed us into the margarita-night tradition."

"Isn't that the truth," Sarah said.

That night, she repeated the same thing when they were all gathered together. "Do you know how rare it is to have two generations get along as well as we all do? I feel so blessed."

Annie feigned a scowl. "It's easier for you.

You don't have to bare your soul in front of your own mother."

Dana Sue sat up a bit straighter. "Do you have secrets, young lady?"

Annie chuckled at her mother's exaggerated indignation. "You bet I do, and they will never come out in front of this crowd."

"Now that's a fine thing to say," Maddie said. "You're married to my son. I want to know any secrets the two of you might have."

Annie blushed and tried to avoid Maddie's gaze.

"Oh my gosh, you're pregnant," Sarah blurted without thinking. "How long? Does Ty know?"

Annie whirled on her, her stunned expression giving away the secret even before she demanded, "How on earth did you figure it out? I only found out today after using about four different home pregnancy tests."

"Then it's true?" Maddie asked, even as Dana Sue sprang up and ran to hug her.

Then Maddie and Dana Sue were embracing. "We're gonna be grandmas," Dana Sue exulted. "Can you believe it? Not that we're not already, because of Trevor, but this will be ours, together, if you know what I mean."

Annie shook her head. "This is exactly why I wasn't ready to tell you yet. Suddenly it's all about the grandmothers, and not one bit about me."

"Oh, of course, it's about you," Sarah said, giving her a hug. "You're going to have a baby! This is so exciting. You never did say, does Ty know?"

Annie shook her head. "Since it's still pretty early, I wanted to see the doctor and get final confirmation. Then I'll tell him in person. The team will be home this weekend, though, honestly, if I make the mistake of trying to tell him on the day he's pitching, it'll probably go in one ear and out the other. All he can think about is the opposing team and his notes on the batters and whether his stupid fastball is losing some of its pace."

Maddie gave her a sympathetic look. "I remember days like that. I've never known a kid to concentrate on a game the way he did. Cal says that's how he knew Ty was going to be great."

"Well, as long as I get my timing right, he'll only be concentrating on me," Annie declared. "I've already bought the lingerie to be sure of it."

Maddie and Dana Sue clapped their hands over their ears. "Too much information," Dana Sue said.

Annie gave her an amused look. "Mom,

how exactly do you think we made this baby?"

"I try not to think about it," Dana Sue told her. "And you really do not want to ask your father that question. As much as Ronnie loves Ty, he still has mixed feelings about his baby girl being married."

Raylene had been fairly quiet during the excitement, but she regarded Annie with surprising longing. "This means a baby shower. Please let me plan it, okay?"

"It's way too soon to be thinking about a baby shower," Annie said. "Let me at least grow a bump before we even start talking about a shower."

"But when the time comes, you will let me plan it?" Raylene persisted.

"Sure," Annie said, though she looked puzzled by her insistence. "You okay?"

"I'm fine," Raylene said, but there were tears welling up in her eyes. She tried to brush them away, but Sarah caught her.

"Raylene, what is it?" she asked quietly as the others went back to talking.

Raylene just shook her head. "Not now. Leave it alone, okay?"

Sarah backed off because she looked so distraught, but the minute everyone had left, she cornered Raylene in the kitchen. She gestured toward a chair. "Sit down and tell me what had you so upset earlier."

"Just forget it, please. It's over and done with."

"Not if it still has the power to make you so sad. Tell me."

Raylene sat down and closed her eyes. Tears leaked out and spilled down her cheeks. In all the months she'd lived with Sarah, in all the times they'd talked about the past, tonight was the first time Sarah could recall her crying. When she'd arrived, she'd been defeated, then eventually angry, but sad was something new. It gave Sarah a sick feeling in the pit of her stomach.

"Raylene?" she prodded more gently.

"The last time," she began in a halting voice. "When Paul hit me that last time, I was pregnant. I was only as far along as Annie, more than likely." When she opened her eyes, they were filled with despair. "That night I lost the baby."

"And that's why you finally left him and came home," Sarah concluded.

"Hurting me, that was one thing, but our baby," she whispered, her voice breaking. "How could I stay after he killed our baby?"

"Oh, sweetie," Sarah murmured, gathering her close. "I'm so, so sorry."

"No," Raylene said fiercely, pulling away. "Don't be sorry. Not for me, anyway. It was my fault. I put my baby at risk."

"You were living with a monster," Sarah said.

"But I knew what he was and I didn't make myself leave," Raylene said. "I should have gone the second the doctor told me I was carrying a child, but stupid me, I thought maybe Paul would be happy about it and maybe we'd finally have a real marriage. Instead, he was furious. It was the worst argument we'd ever had. How can I ever forgive myself for letting that happen? I'm the one who didn't deserve to go on living."

Suddenly it all came crystal clear for Sarah. "And that's why you've stayed shut up inside this house, because you don't think you should have a life of your own. It's more than just being afraid of Paul. You've been punishing yourself all this time."

Raylene shook her head, then said, "I guess. Maybe. I don't know. I can't seem to sort it all out."

The admission was all it took for Sarah to make a decision. "Then it's time to talk about all this with someone who can help you. I'm calling Dr. McDaniels in the morning."

"No," Raylene said. "I'll do it."

Sarah studied her doubtfully. "You will?"

"I promise. I'll do it soon."

"Tomorrow would be good," Sarah pressed.

A fleeting smile touched Raylene's lips. "Does Travis know what a nag you are?" she asked.

"Actually he does."

"And yet he still cares about you," Raylene said, feigning astonishment.

"Why not?" Sarah retorted. "You do."

"Right this second, not so much," Raylene insisted, but the sparkle was back in her eyes.

Maybe, Sarah thought, Raylene was finally ready to take the next step toward reclaiming her life.

22

After spending the afternoon first with his mother and then with Walter, Travis could have used a drink . . . or ten, but instead he had his show to do. Since thinking about Sarah had gotten him through the awful confrontation with his mother and the reasonably civil, if awkward, meeting with Walter, he decided to keep her front and center while he was on the air.

"Ladies and gentlemen, I'm going to dedicate this pretty little ballad by Mr. George Strait to my morning cohost. Sarah, this is just about how far I'll go to prove my love to you."

No sooner had the song begun than his private line lit up. He knew even before glancing at the caller ID who it was.

"What do you think you're doing?" Sarah asked, sounding scandalized.

"I'm courting you," he said mildly. "I thought we'd established that."

She sighed heavily. "Do you think maybe you could do it a little more privately?"

He chuckled at the frustration in her voice, but she had left the door open for more. That was something. "Have dinner with me Saturday night at my place," he said. "You agree to that, I won't say one more word about you on the air tonight."

"I think there are probably too many loopholes in that promise, but okay," she said. "I'll deal with one crisis at a time."

"Seven o'clock?"

"We could settle the details when I see you tomorrow," she said.

"I think I'd like to pin this down while you're in an amenable mood."

"Seven is fine."

" 'Night, sugar. Nice to know you listen in when I'm on the air."

"I can't help it. I never know when you're going to set off a fire I'll need to put out."

"Gotta run. George is just about finished up. I think this time I'll go with Brad Paisley's "Waitin' on a Woman," 'cause it seems like that's what I've been doing ever since I hit town."

"If you say that on the air, our date's off," she warned.

"Oops," he said unrepentantly as the hit song began playing. "The microphone must have been open."

"You enjoy taunting me entirely too much," she accused.

"Yes, I do," he admitted. " 'Night, sugar. Sweet dreams. I'll see you in the morning."

He smiled as he ended the call. That little interlude might have been brief, but it had surely wiped away all the lingering frustration from dealing with his mother and Sarah's ex-husband.

Though talking with Sarah the night before had improved his mood, unfortunately the effect didn't last through his phone call to his father first thing in the morning. Truthfully he had no idea what he could possibly say to Greg to get him to rethink his disastrous plan to marry Trina now that there was a baby involved, but he'd promised his mother he'd try.

"I assume your mother's been to see you," Greg said, his tone resigned.

"How'd you guess?"

"Because she's always run straight to you. What I can't figure out is when you're going to refuse to get involved. Our lives are not your problem."

"Believe it or not, I actually get that, but for once I happen to agree with Mom." He decided to be blunt. "Trina's after your money, Dad. Remember, I've known her a lot longer than you have. If I didn't believe it before, I certainly do now that she's tried to seal the deal by getting pregnant."

"You know, son, you and your mother have never given me half enough credit. Don't you think I can read a woman like Trina, after all the experience I've had over the years?"

"Then why on earth are you marrying her?"

"Because that's what men in my generation do. If we create a child, we accept responsibility for it. Why do you think your mother and I married? That's what has her in a tailspin, you know. She recognizes that there was only one other time I let things go this far, and it was with her. In some twisted way, until now she took a certain amount of satisfaction in thinking our relationship was unique."

The announcement wasn't news to Travis, but it still rankled that his very existence had thrown these two mismatched people together.

"Look, I'm not saying you shouldn't be responsible, just that you don't need to marry Trina to take care of your baby. We might all have been better off if you hadn't married Mom."

"Maybe I'm hoping for a second chance to get it right," Greg said quietly. "I was a lousy father to you. I wasn't around. I let your mom put you in the middle of all our drama. I was — and still am — a terrible role model. I'd like to do better this time. Maybe this old dog can finally learn a few new tricks."

Travis heard the sincerity in his voice. He certainly couldn't argue with the sentiment. "And you and Trina? How's that going to work?"

"I know what you're asking," he said. "We understand each other. I know what she wants and needs from me. She's terrified of being poor. She wants to hang on to her respectability. She's grateful to me for giving her that."

Travis was incredulous that his father would settle for so little in return. "And that's enough for you?"

"You really don't want me to get into the rest, do you? I'll just say she makes me feel young again, and leave it at that."

"Enough said," Travis told him. The last thing he needed to hear about was his father's sex life with a woman he used to date himself.

"Tell your mother she needs to move on," Greg said. "No matter what I've done over the years, no matter how many times I've told her that we were through, for some reason she's held out hope that was going to change. It's not."

"Have you ever told her that in so many words?" Travis asked.

"Too many times to count," Greg said wearily. "Your mother doesn't hear anything she doesn't want to hear. Not from me, anyway." He hesitated, then said, "I'm sorry. Now I'm doing what I accused her of doing, using you as my go-between. Forget my request. I'll see her myself and settle this once and for all."

Travis knew how that would go. By tonight he'd have had a second sobbing phone call from his mother. It would almost be easier to intervene himself.

Almost as if he could read Travis's thoughts, his father said, "Don't take her calls today, okay? There are half a dozen men at the club who'd be happy to give her a shoulder to cry on. I'll make sure she turns to one of them for a change."

"You're going to break up with Mom, then set her up on a date?" Travis asked, astonished. Was it any wonder he had a jaded view of relationships?

"Son, I broke up with her years ago. This will just reinforce the message. As for setting her up, she'll never know I'm behind those men calling at an opportune moment. Despite what she thinks, I do care about her. I know I've done my part to make her life miserable, but she's wallowed in that misery for long enough now. Worse, she's used you as her sounding board to keep it alive. That ends today."

Travis didn't honestly believe his father could make good on that promise, but when the day passed without a call from his mother, he began to think that maybe Greg's strategy had worked. When another day went by with no frantic calls, he was sure of it. For the first time in years, he could focus exclusively on his own life and stop worrying about this endless game his mother and father had been playing with him serving as referee.

Mary Vaughn had finally cajoled her doctor into letting her go to The Corner Spa for a facial, a manicure and a pedicure. She took Rory Sue along as a thank-you for her hard work lately, showing real estate to prospective buyers. Rory Sue had made her first official sale on Sunday. Though she still didn't share Mary Vaughn's excitement for the business, the thought of splitting the commission with her mom had stepped up her interest.

"How've you been feeling?" Jeanette asked as she massaged a soothing lotion onto Mary Vaughn's face.

"Frustrated," Mary Vaughn replied. "How about you? You look amazing." She surveyed Jeanette in the mirror, then added with a note of wistfulness in her voice, "You're actually glowing."

She had more of a baby bump than Mary Vaughn did, too. She was already wearing stylish maternity tops that clung to her rounded tummy.

"Where'd you find that top?" Mary Vaughn wanted to know. "I'll have to send Rory Sue shopping for me, since there's no way I can go. I had to plead my case just to come here for a couple of hours. I told the doctor how relaxing it would be."

Jeanette regarded her with concern. "Next time you're feeling in need of some pampering, you don't have to come in here. I'll come to the house, and I can send over the manicurist, too."

Mary Vaughn regarded her gratefully. "You'd do that?"

"Of course, I would. You're a valued customer, aren't you? To say nothing of being my friend. Honestly, I hadn't thought about what it must be like for you to be shut away at home. Why don't I grab some chick flicks from the video store and bring them over one night? We can eat a half-gallon of ice cream and cry off the calories."

"You name the night," Mary Vaughn said eagerly. "I'll make sure Sonny has other plans."

"So, what have you been doing to keep yourself busy?"

"I'm napping too darn much, for one thing. And I'm keeping up with my real estate business as best I can. Rory Sue handles the appointments, but I put the deals together." She grinned. "And you'll never believe this, but Liz and a couple of her friends have been coming over to play cards. Flo Decatur's been by with her twice now."

"Helen's mother?" Jeanette asked incredulously.

"Yep, me and the seniors," Mary Vaughn said jokingly, then sobered. "But you know what? It's been a lot of fun. They're so thoughtful to do it, and I swear I learn something new about this town's history from Liz every single time she stops by. I think she's trying to prepare me to take over for her as an activist, but she's so remarkable, I doubt anyone will ever be able to replace her."

"Travis just adores her," Jeanette said. "He says letting her stay on in the guest house was the best decision he's ever made. He won't admit it, but I think it's because she spoils him rotten by cooking all his favorite dishes and bringing them over to him."

"He's picked her up at the house a couple of times, and it's wonderful to see how he dotes on her," Mary Vaughn said. She glanced up in the mirror to make sure Rory Sue wasn't close by, then added in a low tone, "I wish my own daughter showed that much appreciation for her elders."

"Come on now," Jeanette chided. "She came home to help out, didn't she?"

"And complains bitterly about it whenever things don't suit her. I'd hoped maybe she'd meet someone or at least build a friendship with Sarah, Annie and Raylene, but it hasn't happened. She's too much like me, I think. She won't appreciate the value of friends until later in life. It certainly took me long enough to realize what I was missing by not having the kind of friendships you found with Maddie, Helen and Dana Sue."

"And you," Jeanette told her.

Mary Vaughn felt her eyes sting with tears at Jeanette's declaration. "Come on now. Don't say stuff like that. I'm weepy enough these days. My hormones are on a perpetual roller coaster."

Jeanette gave her shoulder a squeeze. "Tell me about it. Just imagine the kind of sobbing we can do on movie night. It'll be a relief to Tom that for once he won't have to cope with me going all weepy out of the blue."

Mary Vaughn met her gaze in the mirror. "I usually hate messing up my makeup, but it's going to be worth it to cry my eyes out without poor Sonny thinking I'm having a breakdown."

"Amen to that," Jeanette said knowingly. "Tom watches me as if I'm so fragile that one wrong word will unhinge me. Worse, he's right."

"I'll check Sonny's schedule and call you with a date," Mary Vaughn promised. "Hopefully one night next week."

When she left the spa with Rory Sue an hour later, not only did she feel pampered, but making plans with Jeanette had been just the boost her spirits needed. Maybe she'd try one more time to get Rory Sue together with Sarah and the others. Her daughter needed to discover that girlfriends were every bit as important as having the right man in her life.

Though it had been years since she'd actually dated, Sarah recognized that dinner with Travis at his place on a Saturday night was a real milestone. She'd even made arrangements for the kids to spend the night with their dad, so she had all night long for this date. There could be no pretense that she and Travis were getting together tonight strictly for business. Even if he hadn't made his intentions perfectly clear, the sparks these days were all but impossible to ignore.

And if her own impressions weren't enough, half the town seemed to be fully aware of what was going on between them. Expectations were high, especially at Wharton's, where she suspected Grace actually had some kind of pool going. Sarah was scared to ask what the bet was.

She stood at the front door, trying to make herself leave the house. Raylene looked up from the book she'd been pretending to read and feigned shock that she was still there.

"I thought you'd left," she said.

"I can't seem to open the door," Sarah admitted.

"Well, speaking as someone who faces that fear all the time and loses, I'd suggest you just do it fast, or you'll wind up shut away here with me."

"Not amusing," Sarah said. "I don't know

what's wrong with me."

"You have cold feet," Raylene said readily. "You know if you go over to Travis's tonight, it's not just about dinner. And once the two of you do the wild thing, there will be no turning back. You'll have to face the fact that it's serious."

"For me, at least," she conceded. "I fell for him even though I tried so hard not to. He makes me feel . . ." She searched for the right word and came up with one that was both simple and meaningful. "He makes me feel special."

"Because you are."

"I can't stop thinking about his past, though. And about his father. Do men like that ever really change, or are they just masters at making whoever they're with at the time feel special?"

Raylene put down her book and regarded her seriously. "Sweetie, you know as well as I do that life doesn't come with guarantees. Neither does love. You just have to lead with your heart."

"That's the part that's terrifying," Sarah admitted.

"Tell me about it," Raylene empathized. "But you know the good news? You got your heart broken once before and here you are, stronger than ever. You survived and found out just how fabulous you are, and now you have a man who appreciates that. What's not to love about that? I'd say the odds are all in your favor."

Sarah ran across the room and gave her friend a fierce hug. "What would I do without you? You always put things into perspective for me."

"Right back at you," Raylene said. "Now get out of here and have a wonderful evening. Try not to think everything to death."

Sarah grinned. "If Travis has his way, it's much more likely that I won't think at all."

Travis was more nervous than he'd been in years. Liz finally looked at him in disgust.

"You'd think you'd never been on a date before," she chided. "What is wrong with you?"

"I just want this to go well. A lot's riding on it."

"Relationships don't come apart just because one date doesn't go exactly right. Stop putting so much pressure on yourself. The beef Stroganoff will knock her socks off. The asparagus is perfect. The dessert is outstanding, if I do say so myself. I haven't fixed a chocolate decadence cake like that in a while, but people still remember the last one."

"Okay, thanks to you, the food's covered," he said. "I get that, but what about me? There's no guarantee that Sarah's finally going to stop looking at me as if I'm bound to let her down."

"Only time will prove that to her. You're just going to have to give her however much time she needs. There's no magic bullet to get you there faster. Now I'm going to get out of here before she catches me and decides I'm meddling."

"Or invites you to join us," Travis said.

"You could have worse company," Liz teased. "At least I could coach you through these nerves."

"Just how pitiful would that make me look?" he asked, then held up his hand. "Never mind. I already know."

Liz gave his hand a squeeze. "Just remember what a catch you are in anybody's book. You're not going to be the only lucky one tonight. Sarah's darn lucky to have found *you*."

"Maybe I should have you write a testimonial and leave it for her."

"She already knows," Liz assured him. "I see it in her eyes whenever she looks at you. It's time the two of you took a leap of faith."

When Liz had gone, Travis walked through

461

the house one last time. His furniture had come, there were carpets on the floor and curtains at the windows, but there was something missing. The house still didn't feel like a home. He wasn't sure what he'd forgotten.

Then Sarah walked in and, as if the room had suddenly been transformed, somehow it all felt right. She was what the place needed — what *he* needed — and he intended to do everything necessary to make sure she became a permanent part of his life.

The meal, for all the combined effort Travis and Liz had put into it, could have been sawdust for all the attention Sarah paid to it. She studied Travis across the fancy new dining room table and realized he was equally distracted. Unable to ignore her nerves for one more second, she set down her fork.

"This isn't working," she announced.

"Is something wrong with the food?" he asked, immediately looking alarmed.

"The food's great, but I'm a wreck and so are you. Admit it."

"Why would you say that?" he asked, his expression wary.

"We both know what this date is about

and, to be honest, I can't seem to focus on anything else."

"You think I'm going to try to seduce you," he surmised.

"Aren't you?"

A smile tugged at his lips. "It crossed my mind to try. I was thinking I'd at least wait until after dessert, though. I understand that Liz's chocolate decadence cake is quite seductive in its own right."

"Save it," she said decisively, and stood up. "Let's get this over with."

Travis chuckled, but didn't budge. "Now those are words every man dreams of hearing from a woman he's hoping will make love with him."

Sarah studied him with a narrowed gaze. "Are you backing out?"

"Nope, just trying to figure out how to get the romance back into this before it spins out of control into some kind of booty call I'll hear about forever."

"I'm too scared to worry much about romance," she confessed. "Believe it or not, I've never slept with anyone besides Walter, and if you don't make a move soon, I'm probably going to pass out right here."

Finally, Travis was on his feet. "Well, we definitely can't have that," he said, scooping her into his arms and cradling her against his chest. He stood there looking down into her eyes. "We don't have to do this, you know. We could agree to table it for another time, enjoy the rest of the meal, then maybe make out on the sofa all night long. Then we can sit on the patio drinking sweet tea at sunrise before you go home."

"As lovely as that sounds, no. I may never work up this courage again," she said, terrified that he might back down and she'd have to go through this stomach-knotting tension all over again.

"I just wish you didn't look and sound as if this were some kind of chore you need to get out of the way," he told her.

She hesitated, her hand in midair, then rested it against his cheek, her expression softening. "I don't mean to. If you could feel the way my heart is racing, you'd know how much I want this, how much I want you. I just don't want to get it wrong."

"You couldn't possibly get it wrong," he assured her. "There's no way."

"Don't be so sure," she said dryly. "Walter —"

He cut her off. "Walter is not going into this bedroom with us," he said heatedly. "Is that clear? Neither is anyone I've ever been with. Tonight is all about you and me and our first time together." His eyes held hers.

"Can you focus on that?"

Right at that moment, in his arms, with unmistakable desire shining in his eyes, Sarah was pretty sure she'd think of nothing else for the rest of the night . . . and maybe for days to come.

23

Though she'd resolved to live totally in the moment, Sarah grew increasingly self-conscious as Travis removed her clothes. Despite working out for months at The Corner Spa, despite the weight she'd lost, she was still the mother of two, not some slim supermodel. What would he see when he looked at her?

To her regret, instead of making short work of stripping off her clothes, he took his own sweet time about it. Shivering as his fingers skimmed over bare flesh, she kept her gaze pinned on his face, waiting for any hint that he was repulsed by what he saw. Toward the end of their marriage, Walter had insisted on making love in the dark. Sarah had assumed it was because he couldn't bear to look at her overweight body. He'd never said or done anything to dispel that notion, either.

Now, though, as her bra and panties disappeared, leaving her completely vulnerable, and Travis's gaze seemed to be taking her in with a kind of reverence, the last of her nerves evaporated right along with those final scraps of lace.

In that instant her doubts fled. She forgot about months of being conditioned to expect rejection or criticism. She felt unimaginably beautiful, and for that she would always love Travis. In just a few heartbeats, with a few passionate glances and intimate caresses, he'd restored her body image, right along with the missing piece of her self-esteem. She felt whole again, the way she had before Walter and his family had chipped away at her confidence.

After that, she let herself go in Travis's arms, let herself feel . . . everything. Travis took her on the ride of her life, showed her a side of passion she'd only read about in books. He was a thoughtful, generous lover. He turned parts of her she'd never imagined being sensitive into newly discovered erogenous zones.

Even as she lay there, weak and trembling, he looked into her eyes and began to move again, coaxing her to come with him, teaching her that new heights were possible, making her his.

When sensations washed over her like a

tidal wave, tears filled her eyes. "I never . . ." she whispered, her voice catching with the wonder of what she'd experienced.

He touched the dampness on her cheeks, his gaze filled with concern. "Never what?"

"Knew it could be like this. Isn't that amazing, that I could have been married for all that time, and never had any idea sex could be magical?"

He smiled at that. "Sarah Price, you do the most amazing things for my ego," he said.

"Don't get too sure of yourself," she retorted. "It only counts if you can do it again."

Travis laughed at that, which was yet another shock. She'd never known it was okay to laugh in bed, to make fun of yourself or your partner. Walter had never wanted to talk at all. He'd always focused on the end result, not the journey.

"I'll do it again and again, for as long as it takes to convince you," Travis offered.

"Now you're just bragging," she teased, relishing the freedom this night had taught her.

Travis's expression sobered. "Care to test me?"

She cupped his face in her hands and looked into his eyes. "You know, I think I would," she said, then drew his head down until their mouths met.

It was hours before they said another word, but this time the silence was especially sweet.

After confirming one more time with Sarah that she thought she could work with her ex-husband, Travis called Walter back into the station to offer him the sales job. Though his personal distaste for Walter ran deep, he was wise enough to recognize that he was the right man for the job. And if Sarah could put the past behind her for the sake of their kids, Travis certainly ought to be able to.

When Walter showed up for the Monday afternoon meeting, Travis gestured to a chair. He studied the man who'd made such a mess of his marriage to Sarah with something that felt surprisingly like pity.

"Okay, Walter, here's the deal. All of us can agree that you're the most qualified candidate for this job that I'm likely to find in Serenity, but that's not the only thing that matters to me. Sarah means a lot to this station —"

"And to you," Walter said, regarding Travis directly, his gaze unflinching and holding no hint of the animosity Travis had feared.

Travis nodded. "And to me," he agreed. "My point is that she's very anxious for you to stick around because of Tommy and Libby. She thinks you've changed, that the two of you can work together without friction. I want your promise that will be the case."

"You have it," Walter said. "Not to drag you into my personal issues, but back in Alabama, I let my parents run the show. They got in the middle of my marriage. It should never have happened. I should have put a stop to it, but I didn't. I lost Sarah and my kids because I was stupid and weak. Coming here is a fresh start for me, not just with my children, but for my life. I like Serenity. I want to be a part of the town, not just for Tommy and Libby, but for myself. I'm not going to do anything to ruin my chances of staying here."

Travis liked what he heard, not just because Walter was saying all the right words, but because he was looking Travis straight in the eyes when he said it. He figured it took some gumption to be that candid with the man who was now involved with his ex-wife.

"Okay, then, we'll give this a try." He laid out the terms of the job offer. Walter made a couple of modifications that sounded entirely fair. Travis nodded. "Then we have a deal?"

Relief spread across Walter's face. "We have a deal. Thank you, Travis. This means a lot. I won't let you down . . . you or Sarah."

"I'm counting on that. Now why don't you plan to get together with Sarah after her show tomorrow and go over all the current accounts. She's the one who has all that totally organized."

Walter looked surprised. "Sarah? She was never much for organization before."

Travis scowled at the disparaging comment, and Walter immediately got the message.

"No disrespect intended. I just meant it was different when we were married," he said hurriedly.

"Well, now she has this place running like a well-oiled machine," Travis told him. "You'd be wise to take lessons from her."

"Of course. I'll get together with her tomorrow."

Travis watched Walter as he left the station and wondered if he'd done the right thing, after all. But then he thought of how much self-confidence Sarah had gained just in the months he'd known her. If she could handle him — and she did — then she could certainly handle Walter. It might even be fun to watch her putting her ex-husband very firmly in his place.

Sarah regarded Travis with disbelief. "You want me to train Walter to take over the sales?"

"Yep," he said. "You created the system. Teach it to him. I think it will be a good lesson for both of you."

"But maybe it's not the best system," she said, familiar doubts surfacing. "He'll probably have a lot of his own ideas. After all, sales is what he did for his dad's company. It's a much bigger operation and it's been in business for years."

"I think your system suits the station just fine," Travis said, a glint of determination in his eyes.

Sarah studied him suspiciously. "Is this even about the system we use to keep track of advertising accounts?"

"Of course it is," he said. "What else could it be about?"

"Maybe you're thinking I'd enjoy bossing my ex-husband around," she said.

Travis grinned. "Well, that, too. Are you saying you'd rather not?"

"You know he's going to pick everything apart," she said, resigned to getting off on the wrong foot with Walter, just when they'd started to make peace.

"If he does, I'll fire him," Travis replied readily. "There are plenty of people looking for jobs."

Sarah regarded him with surprise. "You really mean that, don't you?"

"Of course. We want team players around here. I'm not saying he can't modify your system as time goes on, but right now he needs to prove to all of us he can fit in. A huge part of that is going to be showing you the proper respect."

She frowned at that. "Are you two going to spend a lot of time around here marking your turf? If so, it's going to get pretty uncomfortable for me and Bill."

Travis gave her an innocent look and beckoned her across the office. "Sit," he said, drawing her into his lap. "You and I, we're together now, right? It's official?"

She didn't deny it, but met his gaze. "What's your point?"

"That I'm not going to waste time staking my claim around a man you divorced."

Though she appreciated him making their relationship perfectly clear, she wouldn't have minded just a tiny hint of jealousy. "You could have at least pretended I'm worth fighting for," she said.

"You are, absolutely," he said at once. "But we both know there's no contest. You don't want Walter."

"Maybe he still wants me," she suggested, just to stir the pot a bit.

A dangerous spark lit in Travis's eyes. "You think so?"

She considered fanning that spark, but decided it was both immature and risky. She and Travis had found something amazing. Why play games with it?

"No," she admitted.

"You were testing me?"

"A little," she conceded.

"Just so we're clear," he said slowly, his gaze locked with hers. "There's not a test you can devise that I won't pass. You're the woman I want and I'm going to do whatever it takes to keep you and make sure you're so happy you'll never even think about looking at another man."

A warm glow filled her, but she tried her best to act nonchalant. She gave him a bright smile, then said casually, "Good to know."

When she would have stood and walked away, he pulled her back and covered her mouth with his in a kiss that was unmistakably meant to stake a claim. She sighed when he released her.

"I love you, Sarah," he declared softly. "Don't ever forget that."

"Very good to know," she said, though this time her voice was a little shaky and her breath seemed to catch in her throat. The first time a man said he loved you was a moment to be savored and held onto for a lifetime.

Walter was amazed as Sarah walked him through the system she'd set up for the station's current accounts.

"And over here are the files for the contacts each of us has made and our notes about why they didn't want to advertise with us now," she said. "If they indicated a willingness to consider it in the future, that's in the file with a target date for getting back to them. I've also made a note about which of us recorded the spots for the current advertisers and included a copy of the scripts. I always ask if they want to make a change when I sign them up for a new series of spots."

"It's a very thorough system," Walter said, genuinely impressed.

Sarah shrugged. "It just seemed to make sense. At first Travis and I were crossing paths with the same people. Something had to be done to make it more organized and professional."

Walter regarded her with newfound appreciation. Sarah had been an excellent student when they'd met, on the dean's list more often than not. Why the hell hadn't he remembered that when his mother was so busy cutting her down because she'd burned a dinner or forgotten to do the ironing?

"I never gave you half enough credit, did I?" he asked, not for the first time.

"You mean for having a brain?" she said wryly. "To be fair, I suppose it was hard to remember that I did when you came home every night to a house that was in chaos."

"Or when my mother was pointing out your housekeeping flaws to me at every turn. It never occurred to me that she'd always had help around the house to keep it spotless. Why didn't you remind me of that?"

"Because I was embarrassed that I wasn't better at it," she admitted. "I wanted so badly to be a good wife, to live up to your expectations, but I just couldn't."

"I should have seen how impossible it was to keep things organized with two little kids. Even now, when I'm with both kids over at the Serenity Inn, I have a hard time keeping the room straight. Two seconds after they walk in the door, it's cluttered with toys and my stuff winds up being strewn every-where."

She smiled at his words. "Now you know I wasn't just making excuses."

"Yeah," he said quietly. "Now I know. I'm sorry I didn't see it sooner."

"Things worked out for the best, Walter. You know they did. If I hadn't moved here and filed for divorce, you'd still be letting your parents run your life. In some ways, I like to think I set you free."

"You did," he admitted, realizing for the first time that it was true. "I couldn't imagine you walking away from me, but when you did, it was a huge wake-up call. I started actually hearing the kind of junk that comes pouring out of my parents' mouths. I hate to sound like I was some kind of victim, because that was you. They made your life hell, and I did nothing to stop them. In fact, I followed their lead. I'll regret that till the day I die. You were my wife. I should have taken your side."

"Let it go. I have."

He regarded her in wonder. "You really have, haven't you? Is that because of Travis?"

"Partly," she said. "Mostly it's because I've figured out who I am and what I'm worth. I don't think Travis would care about me the way he does if I hadn't figured all that out for myself."

"Are you two serious?"

Her cheeks bloomed with color. "I think maybe we are."

"And you're happy?"

Her eyes lit up. "I really am. It scares me sometimes how happy I am."

"Then I'm glad for you."

"You sound as if you really mean that," she said, clearly surprised.

"I do mean it. After all the mistakes I made, you deserve to be with someone who'll treat you right." Despite what he said, there was one thing that nagged at him. "You do know that Travis has a bit of a reputation, right?"

She frowned. "And here it comes . . ." she said sarcastically. "I should have known there'd be a lecture buried somewhere in this conversation."

"I just don't want you to get hurt if it turns out he's not as serious as you think he is."

"You don't need to worry about my relationship with Travis, okay? It's none of your business."

He couldn't seem to make himself shut up. "But what about the kids?"

"They adore him, but they're too little to

understand any of what's going on between Travis and me. It's not as if he's hanging around the house all the time. If things don't work out, they'll be just fine. You're the one they love, Walter. You'll always be their dad."

He should have been reassured, but he wasn't. Not entirely. He feared this was just one more time when Sarah's naiveté was going to cause her heartache. Unfortunately, he recognized that he'd long since lost any right to try to prevent it.

"You look happy," Annie told Sarah as they sat in the bleachers watching the boys play T-ball. She glanced toward the field. "I assume Travis put that glow on your face."

"He did," Sarah said. "He's amazing."

Unfortunately, she didn't miss the little frown that Annie tried to hide. "What? I thought you'd long since stopped worrying about his reputation. You have to admit he's been perfectly straight with me. He hasn't looked at another woman in town. I would certainly have heard about it, if he had. He hasn't been sneaking off to someplace else so he can cheat on me behind my back, either. He hasn't had time."

"That's great," Annie said.

"But? I sense there's a *but* in there."

"I can't help wondering if leopards ever change their spots," she said, her tone oddly despondent.

Of all the people in the world who might have said that to Sarah, she was stunned that it would be Annie. "Excuse me. What about Ty?"

Annie flinched at the direct question. "That's fair. I know Ty and I are solid, okay? I know it with everything in me. It's just that when I saw him the other night, we were out with some of the other players."

"And?" Sarah questioned, knowing there was something more to have put that doubt in Annie's voice.

"One of his teammates, a guy whose wife I've actually gotten to know, was all over this other woman. He wasn't just flirting. It was clear the two of them had something going on, even though he's been married for something like ten years. According to his wife, they'd hit a rough patch early on, but she thinks he's been on the straight and narrow for years now. Now he's with this other woman, not even trying to hide it. I wanted to scream at him. I asked Ty about what was going on, and he didn't even try to deny it. He just said to look the other way, that it was none of our business."

Sarah frowned at the story. "So the moral

is that men like that never change?"

"Not never. I truly believe that Ty has."

"And I think Travis has," Sarah countered. But the truth was, she couldn't be sure. And unlike Annie and Ty, she didn't have years of history as a foundation on which to place her trust. She'd only been getting to know Travis for a few months now. Was that long enough to be sure he was the honorable man she thought he was? If refrigerators and cars came with guarantees, why the heck couldn't men? she wondered in frustration.

"Look, I really don't want to fuel your doubts," Annie said. "But seeing that guy the other night, it made me realize how lucky I am that I can trust Ty now. Even though I have total faith in him, it's still hard. I just want you to be prepared for how hard it can be. You need to understand that before you take the next step with Travis."

Sarah regarded her seriously. "I don't think I have any choice, Annie. I'm in love with him. I don't think I could walk away now if I wanted to."

Less than an hour after her distressing conversation with Annie, Sarah and the kids were with Travis at Rosalina's when Trina turned up there. She was alone and her face was streaked with tears.

"I've been looking for you all over," she told Travis, pulling up a chair from a nearby table and sitting down.

Travis regarded her with the dismay of a man who knew he was about to deal with a messy and potentially embarrassing situation. "What's wrong?"

"I needed somebody to talk to about your father."

Travis stiffened. "I may not be the best person, Trina. I spent most of my life caught between him and my mom. I don't want to get in the middle of your drama with him now."

"But you have to," Trina said, her voice catching on a sob. "I don't know where else to turn. I think he's going to leave me, Travis, and it's all because of you and the stuff you said to him."

"Maybe we should go to the restroom," Sarah suggested, noticing that some of the parents were starting to stare. It would be natural for some of them to assume the issue was between Trina and Travis, rather than with his father. "You can splash some water on your face. You'll feel better."

"Good idea," Travis said at once. "Meantime, I'll try to hurry things along here."

Trina stood and allowed herself to be led to the ladies' room. She took one look in the mirror and did a little yelp of shock. "I look awful. No wonder you wanted to get me out of there. I was just so upset, I got in the car and started driving. I think I cried most of the way. Do you have any makeup with you?"

"No, sorry."

"Well, maybe I can manage to improve things a little," Trina said, suddenly totally focused on her appearance. At least she wasn't sobbing anymore.

When the cool water had lessened the redness in her eyes and reduced at least some of the puffiness, she performed a few magic tricks with her comb and a lipstick. It was an impressive transformation, but there was no mistaking the sadness that lingered in her eyes.

"Do you want to talk to me about what upset you so badly?" Sarah asked hesitantly. "What makes you think Greg is going to leave you, and that Travis had anything to do with it?"

"Look, you're sweet to offer to listen, but only Travis can fix this."

"How?"

"By talking to his father and making things right. He needs to tell him that he

was wrong, that Greg and I belong together."

"What makes you think Travis influenced
Greg to leave you? I thought everything was
on track for you and Greg to get married."

"It was, but now it's all fallen apart. Greg
talked to Travis the other day. I don't know
what Travis said to him exactly, but after
that things between us started changing."

Sarah didn't know Trina well enough to
judge whether she was creating a drama
where none existed or if this was real. "I'm
sure you're mistaken. Greg really loves you."

Trina regarded her with blatant skepticism. "Oh, really? Then why did I catch him
cheating on me with another woman? Less
than two weeks before our wedding, he was
sleeping with somebody else. He would only
do that if he planned to leave me."

Sarah sank down onto one of the chairs
that had been tucked into a corner of the
ladies' room. She felt almost as if Greg's
betrayal was personal.

What kind of man would cheat on the
woman who was carrying his child even
before the wedding? Was it really a precur-
sor to Greg leaving Trina, a last fling, or
had he simply done it because he'd believed
Trina would stay with him no matter what?

Sarah wanted to believe Travis was nothing like his father, but could she really count on that? Greg had been his role model for a lot of years, and for a very long time Travis had seemed to be on a similar path. Would he slip at the first sign of trouble in their relationship? And what if they did eventually marry? Would he turn to another woman to satisfy his ego, especially if Sarah once again gained weight or didn't satisfy him in some way? Would he count on her forgiving him again and again?

Added to everything Annie had said earlier, suddenly it was all too much for Sarah. She needed to get out of here. She needed to think. And she couldn't do that where, with one seductive glance, Travis could make her forget everything that common sense was all but shouting at her.

24

Travis could feel Sarah withdrawing. After weeks of getting closer, weeks of feeling as if he'd found not just the perfect town, but also the perfect woman and business partner, he knew he was losing her. What he didn't understand was why.

When he tried to analyze it, he thought he could trace it to the day Trina had appeared at Rosalina's with the tale of Greg's cheating. By now he understood how Sarah's mind worked well enough to guess that she'd translated his father's behavior into a foreshadowing of how he would treat her, which was utterly absurd, to say nothing of infuriating. He didn't deserve to be judged for something his father had done.

For days he'd been trying to pin Sarah down so they could talk, but she managed to slip away every time, usually with the excuse that she had to get home to the kids.

When she deliberately locked the studio

door one morning in an attempt to keep him out, he came close to losing it. He had his own key, but given his anger, he decided it was best not to use it. He was, however, waiting for her when she emerged.

"We need to talk," he said tightly.

"Sorry. I have an appointment," she said, trying to brush past him.

"Station business?"

She flushed, then shook her head.

"Then it can wait. Let's go."

Alarm filled her eyes. "Where?"

"Someplace where we can talk without the prying eyes of an entire community on us."

"I don't have time . . ." she began, but her voice trailed off when he regarded her with an unyielding expression.

She remained silent in the car. She didn't say another word, in fact, until they reached a waterfront restaurant far enough away from Serenity that they weren't likely to be recognized.

"This was a long way to come just so you can yell at me," she said.

"I'm not going to yell," he said, exasperated. The temptation to yell, however, was so powerful, it was a wonder he didn't give in to it despite his promise.

"You seem angry."

He stared at her incredulously. "You

think?" He snatched up the menu, glanced at it and zeroed in on a shrimp platter. "I'm having the shrimp. How about you?"

"I'm not hungry."

He stared at her until she eventually sighed. "Fine. I'll have the shrimp, too."

Travis placed their orders, then waited until their iced tea arrived before finally meeting her gaze.

"Okay, start talking."

"About?"

He scowled at her. "Don't do this. Don't play games. This is too important. If I've upset you, I want to know how. I can't fix things if you just shut me out."

"You didn't break anything," she admitted, surprising him.

"Then who the hell did? Somebody must have."

"No, I just woke up from the fantasy," she said, her expression bleak.

"What fantasy? You're not making any sense."

"No, Travis, what didn't make sense was us."

"How can you say that? We're perfect together."

"Now, maybe, but not forever."

"That's crazy." He looked deep into her eyes. "Does this have something to do with my father and what he did to Trina?" he asked point-blank.

She looked startled that he'd nailed it. Then her chin set stubbornly. "Does it really matter how I came to this epiphany?"

"I think it does. Dammit, Sarah, you can't blame me for my father's flaws. He has a ton of them, no question about it. So do I, but they're not the same ones, at least not when it comes to the way I treat women. I have always, always, played fair with every woman I ever dated, you included. When I told you the other day that I love you, I meant it, along with all that implies about commitment."

He could see in her eyes how desperately she wanted to believe him, but she shook her head anyway. "Words are too easy, Travis."

More frustrated than he'd ever been, he tried again to get through to her. "I know life doesn't come with guarantees, not the kind you obviously want, but if we both know what we want, we can make it happen."

She obviously remained unconvinced. "I don't think so."

"You don't want it enough?" he asked, scrambling to make sense of her determination to throw away their future.

"I do," she said.

"Well, you can't be talking about me, because you're all I want."

"Now," she said again.

"We're right back to my father again, aren't we? You're convinced I'll cheat on you."

She nodded, looking miserable. "It's bound to happen."

Travis opened his mouth to argue, but how could he? The future might come with well-meant promises, but guarantees? Life just didn't work that way.

"See," she said triumphantly. "You see it, too. You can't deny it."

"Because that's not how relationships work. I can tell you I'm one hundred percent committed to you, but only you can decide whether to believe that or not." Filled with frustration, he met her gaze. "Are you really willing to give up on us because neither of us knows what tomorrow will bring?"

"I have to," she said. "I survived what Walter did to me, but I don't think I could survive losing you."

"Yet you're the one walking away," he said. "That doesn't make any sense."

She shrugged. "It does to me." She shoved aside her untouched plate of food. "I'd like to go home now."

"Come on, Sarah, let's talk this out."

"There's nothing left to say."

Travis might have tried to make her see reason, but it was evident that right this second she believed every defeated word she was uttering. He wanted to call his father and rail at him for setting this into motion, but the truth was Sarah's insecurities had always been there, buried just under the surface. It wasn't only him she'd lost faith in. It was herself and her ability to keep his interest. And that was a battle he had no idea how to fight.

Sarah managed to hold back her tears until she was inside the house. She headed directly for her room, hoping to escape Raylene's probing questions. Unfortunately, the two friends came close to colliding in the hallway. Raylene took one look at her and steered her into the bedroom and urged her to sit on the bed.

"What happened?" she demanded. "You look like death warmed over."

"It's official. I broke up with Travis," Sarah admitted, then let the tears flow.

Raylene, bless her, didn't say a word. She just kept handing her tissues until the waterworks ended.

"Okay, then," Raylene said as Sarah wiped away what she hoped was the last of the tears. "What did the bastard do?"

Sarah frowned at her. "Don't call him that," she said fiercely.

"You're very quick to jump to the defense of a man you've just dumped. Whatever he did can't have been too awful."

"He didn't *do* anything," Sarah admitted. "Splitting up with him had to be done, that's all."

"So, you broke up for no specific reason?" Raylene asked, looking justifiably bewildered.

"Not really. I just looked into the future and saw the inevitable."

Raylene feigned amazement. "Oh, my gosh! You're psychic!"

Sarah frowned at her. "Don't be sarcastic. You know perfectly well it's possible to know when things just aren't going to work."

"Sorry, actually I don't know that. If it were that easy, more people would skip the walk down the aisle."

"More people probably should," Sarah said bitterly. "Look, can we not discuss this? It's too depressing."

"Yes, I imagine walking away from the perfect guy for no good reason would be

492

depressing," Raylene said.

"Travis is hardly perfect."

"He's perfect for you. And until very recently, you thought so, too."

"It's complicated."

"I'm a bright woman. Try me."

Sarah described Trina's visit, Greg's cheating right before their wedding, the whole tawdry mess.

Raylene didn't look impressed with the argument. "So, you're kicking this amazing man to the curb because his father's a jerk. Do I have that right?"

"Like father, like son," Sarah insisted. "Travis says himself that lots of people believe that about the two of them."

"Oh, sweet heaven, will you listen to yourself? Are you sure this isn't a lesson you learned from bitter experience with Walter? He was certainly a chip off the old block, right?"

Sarah couldn't deny anything she was saying. "The genetics certainly held true in that family," she agreed.

"And you've seen no changes in Walter since he got away from their influence?"

"Sure, but . . ."

"But what? You don't trust those changes either?"

Sarah was beginning to lose steam. As

Raylene went on, Sarah was beginning to see just how irrational she'd been. "Something like that," she muttered halfheartedly.

Raylene regarded her with apparent pity. "You know for months now I've thought I was the one in this house with a problem moving on with my life, but, sweetie, you have me beat by a mile. We might just as well lock the door here and throw away the key, because the way I see it, we're both destined to waste the rest of our lives living in the past."

"I'm not doing that," Sarah said defensively.

"Really? Then prove it."

"How?"

"Go after the man you want and do everything you can to hold on to him. If I were in your situation, I couldn't get out of this house fast enough. I'd grab onto Travis and start making wedding plans. Sweetie, surely you know that life doesn't come with guarantees. If you look for problems, you can always find them. Why not opt for hope?"

When Sarah didn't move, Raylene just shook her head, her expression filled with exasperation. "I don't want to hear another word about Greg McDonald or Travis and their flaws, Sarah Price. This is all on you.

You're throwing away your future, and if you ask me, it's a crying shame."

She walked out before Sarah could think of a single way to defend herself. Most worrisome was the nagging sensation that there was no defense.

Mary Vaughn and Sonny stared at the image of the sonogram in wonder.

"That's our baby," she whispered, clinging to Sonny's hand. "Just look at that."

"Can you tell if it's a boy or a girl?" Sonny asked the technician.

She nodded. "Do you both want to know?"

Mary Vaughn met Sonny's gaze. "Do we? Or do we want to be surprised?"

"I think maybe the fact that we're having a baby at all is enough of a surprise," Sonny replied. "Let's find out so we can plan for it. You know you're not going to be happy until you've decorated the nursery and bought about a thousand little outfits."

"You do know me well," she said, turning back to the technician. "Tell us."

"Congratulations, Mom and Dad! It's a boy."

Mary Vaughn saw the delight in Sonny's eyes and nearly cried. "You'll have your son. I know how much you wanted this. And your dad . . ." She shook her head. "He's going to be over the moon when we tell him."

"Rory Sue told me she wouldn't mind having a baby brother, too."

"She just doesn't want to share the spotlight as daddy's little darling," Mary Vaughn said.

"Let's go celebrate," Sonny suggested. "What do you say? I'll get some sparkling cider and pick up some food from Sullivan's."

"I wish we could actually go there," Mary Vaughn said wistfully just as the obstetrician returned.

"If you promise me you'll only stay an hour, I don't see why you can't. Your blood pressure's been better the last few weeks," she said. Her expression turned stern. "But this is not a license for you to start working and running around all over town, you hear me? Bed rest is still necessary, but I don't think one brief meal out will hurt."

Mary Vaughn could have hugged her. "I'll be very careful, I promise." She turned to Sonny. "Call Rory Sue and your dad and have them meet us there. We can celebrate the good news with them."

A half hour later they were seated at Sullivan's when Sonny made the announcement about the baby being a boy.

"I knew it," Howard gloated. "I've been telling those old geezers at Wharton's I was finally going to have a grandson."

"My money was on a boy, too," Rory Sue said. "Here, I'll prove it." She pulled a large envelope from her oversized purse and handed it to Mary Vaughn. It was filled with pictures of nurseries, all of them decorated for little boys. She had fabric swatches as well, all in blue patterns with the occasional hint of yellow or green. There wasn't a shade of pink anywhere.

"You pick what you like, Mom, and I'll take care of the rest. Decorating the nursery is going to be my gift to you."

Mary Vaughn simply stared at her. Rory Sue actually sounded excited about the prospect. "You sure about that?"

"I have the money from my share of the commission on the Simpson house, and I really want to do this for you and Dad. Besides, if I do it, you get to supervise to your heart's content."

Mary Vaughn regarded her with delight. "Now, there's an offer I can't resist."

"Looks as if we're finally destined to be one big happy family," Sonny said enthusiastically.

Mary Vaughn met his gaze. "It's about

time, don't you think?"

"Past time, if you ask me," Howard grumbled.

Sonny scowled at him. "The timing's just the way it's supposed to be."

That's what Mary Vaughn loved most about her husband. For Sonny, the glass was always half full. And she'd finally figured out just how much that kind of optimism really mattered.

Travis spent a couple of miserable weeks nursing the wounds Sarah had inflicted with her unyielding attitude. The tension at the station was so thick it could be cut with a knife, but they were both too stubborn to break the unnatural silence. He hadn't set foot in the studio with her, leaving her to answer the callers who were filled with questions about his absence.

Worse, he had to watch as Walter started hovering around her every darn day. It looked to Travis as if the man had had second thoughts about letting Sarah get away. She didn't seem to be ignoring him the way she once had, either. If those two found their way back to each other, Travis was going to start breaking things, beginning with every piece of expensive equipment in the radio station.

"If you want her back, you're going to have to fight for her," Bill said mildly, when he caught Travis scowling at his two employees laughing in the main office.

"She can't be considering taking Walter back," Travis grumbled. "She has to know what a mistake that would be."

"No worse than you walking away without a fight," Bill said.

"Has she said anything to you?" Travis asked. "Do you know for a fact that her feelings for Walter are changing?"

Bill rolled his eyes. "Forget Walter, you idiot. Sarah's yours unless you decide your pride is more important than getting her back."

"My pride's not the issue. She told me flat out she doesn't want a future with me."

"The way I hear it, she said she's scared to risk a future with you."

"The same thing," Travis said, then frowned. "Where'd you hear that, anyway?"

"Wharton's, of course. Grace is having a field day over this. I think the pool over whether you'll reconcile or not is somewhere around five hundred dollars."

Travis wasn't shocked that there was a pool. Nor was he sure he wanted to know the current odds for a reconciliation.

"Did you place a bet?" he asked Bill.

"Thought about it," Bill admitted. "But I'm not convinced you've got the sense God gave a duck."

"Thanks," Travis said, annoyed.

"Just telling it like I see it."

"It's not as simple as me trying to sweep her off her feet, you know," he said in his own defense.

"You sure about that? Because what I know for sure is that if you do nothing, it's a hundred percent certain you'll lose her."

Bill's words lingered in his head, mocking him for the next few days. By Sunday afternoon he was sick of his own foul mood. He was also determined to make Sarah see the light, that they were the ones who'd determine what kind of future they could have. Not his jerk of a father, that's for sure.

By the time he reached her house, he'd worked up a full head of steam. He was more than ready to state his case for the two of them living happily ever after.

Then he saw Walter in the backyard with the kids. Sarah was nearby. The scene was so darn domestic, he almost turned around and walked away. Some kind of need to torture himself kept him in place. To make matters worse, Walter paused beside Sarah's chair, then leaned down and kissed her like he meant it. She didn't pull away, and

Travis's heart plummeted. Was it possible he was too late, after all?

He stood there, wallowing in his own misery for about sixty seconds, and then his temper kicked in. He was no better than Sarah, leaping to conclusions, ready to give up without a fight. That simply wasn't going to happen. He'd come here to convince her they had a future, and he intended to do just that.

To get his temper under control and solidify his strategy, he made himself go for a walk so he could remind himself just how badly he wanted Sarah in his life. For a man known for glib chatter, this time he wanted to make sure his words were exactly right.

Filled with renewed resolve, he went back, assured himself that Walter had gone, then walked into the kitchen where Sarah was in the middle of dinner preparations.

"He doesn't deserve you, you know," he announced, startling Sarah so badly she dropped the carton of milk she was holding.

Her gaze met his. She didn't even try to pretend she didn't know who he meant. "No, he doesn't," she replied calmly, her eyes sparkling. "What about you? Do you think you deserve me?"

"Damn straight," he said at once. "What I

didn't deserve was to have you blaming me for things I've never done. From the minute we met, I haven't so much as looked at another woman. Rory Sue practically threw herself at me, and was I tempted? Not even a little bit."

She blinked at the ferocity of his words, but she didn't interrupt.

"Keep this in mind. I dated a lot of women, yes, but I was never in love with any of them. Not even close. The only woman I've ever loved is you."

He could see tears welling up in her eyes then, but he needed to hammer his point home, before she started trying to rebut every word he'd said. "If you need more time for me to go on proving it, fine. I'll wait. But I will not let you walk away based on some crazy theory about what might happen down the road. I know exactly what I want, Sarah Price, and what I want is you." He risked taking a step closer and touched her damp cheek with a tender caress, then lowered his voice. "I choose you."

Her lips curved then, the smile lighting up her face. "Okay," she said simply. "I choose you, too."

Travis stared at her in shock. "That's it? Okay?"

She nodded, grinning. "You convinced

me. Well, you and Raylene and even Walter, who surprisingly enough is on your side. If you hadn't come over here today, I'd decided to come looking for you so I could tell you I'd been a fool."

"You could have said something sooner," he murmured, pulling her into his arms.

"And ruin that pretty speech you were making? No way. I wanted to hear every word."

"I have more," he admitted. "Want to hear them?"

"Absolutely," she said, resting her head on his shoulder.

"I will never, ever want you to be less than the best you can be," he promised. "If that means you and I butt heads from time to time, well, at least it will be a fair fight." He caressed her cheek, his voice turning tender. "And we will butt heads, you know. There's not a doubt in my mind about that. Our marriage is going to have enough fireworks to keep the whole town on the edge of their seats."

She faltered as his words registered. "Marriage? Did you just say marriage?"

He nodded. "If you're interested." He shrugged as if her answer didn't matter a bit, even though it meant everything. "Well?"

"For a man who's always been full of sweet talk, words seem to have failed you now," she said.

"I have a whole stockpile of them, if that's what you want to hear. I love you, Sarah Price. You're the best thing that ever happened to me. I want you and the kids to move in with me and fill that big old house with more kids. We'll let Liz spoil them to death as their surrogate grandma. I want to grow old with you and sit side by side on our front porch, still arguing about just about everything." His gaze locked with hers. "How am I doing? If it's not enough, I'll go on the air tonight and tell the world the same thing. That way you can hold me accountable from now to eternity."

She smiled at that. "Not much about this courtship has been private," she said. "I think I'd like your proposal to stay that way, just between you and me."

"Then, will you marry me, Sarah?"

Her smile spread. Her eyes sparkled, but still she said nothing. She just tilted her head and studied him in a way that made his palms sweat.

"You know," she said eventually, "I believe I will."

Travis let out a whoop, then scooped her up and twirled her around the kitchen. "You sure I can't go down to the station and tell the whole darn town?"

She laughed. "Why not? I wanted the proposal private, but I think it would be a shame if Grace wound up scooping our own radio station with the news, and you know she will if we don't do this now."

Which is why Travis McDonald cut off George Strait in midsong to announce that Ms. Sarah Price was going to be his wife. And she interrupted to suggest that he'd taken his own sweet time about asking. Which gave the residents of Serenity even more than usual to talk about first thing in the morning when they arrived at Wharton's.

By the time *Carolina Daybreak* went on the air Monday morning, the whole town was buzzing with the news. The station's phone lines rang off the hook throughout the broadcast. Half the town stood across the street in the square trying to catch a glimpse of Sarah and Travis where they sat in the studio sipping sweet tea and gazing at each other, barely remembering to change the music that was playing.

"We could give them something else to talk about," Travis suggested, pulling Sarah into his arms at the end of her show.

She lifted her face for his kiss, but just as

he was about to claim her mouth, he had second thoughts. He gave a little wave to the crowd, then deliberately pulled down the shade in a gesture meant to declare the show over.

Their future, however, was just beginning.

QUESTIONS FOR DISCUSSION

1. For most of her marriage to Walter Price, Sarah was subjected to a barrage of verbal abuse from him and from his parents. Have you ever been in a situation like that? How did you handle it? Is verbal abuse just as demeaning in its way as physical abuse?
2. Dealing with in-laws can sometimes be difficult. What is your relationship like with yours? If the road has been rocky, has your spouse taken your side?
3. Self-esteem is a huge issue for Sarah. Have you ever struggled with self-doubts? Were they in a particular area like work or relationships? Or were they general, affecting all areas of your life? How did you work this out? Did your friends play a role in making you see yourself in a new light?
4. Travis is the kind of man for whom pretty words come easily. Because of that and her own issues, Sarah has a great deal of

difficulty taking him seriously. Have you ever crossed paths with a flirtatious man and wondered if you dared to trust his sweet talk? What did it take to convince you he meant what he said?

5. Travis's father is marrying a much younger woman and cheating on her only weeks before the wedding. Do you think his marriage to Trina stands even a tiny chance of succeeding? How do you feel about older men marrying younger women? Or older women marrying younger men?

6. Ultimately, Sarah has to take a leap of faith, because there are no guarantees about the future. Have you ever felt you were taking a leap of faith? About what? How did it work out?

ABOUT THE AUTHOR

Sherryl Woods is the author of over one hundred women's fiction, romance, and mystery novels. She has a degree in journalism from Ohio State University, and worked for many years in the newspaper business.

The employees of Thorndike Press hope you have enjoyed this Large Print book. All our Thorndike, Wheeler, and Kennebec Large Print titles are designed for easy reading, and all our books are made to last. Other Thorndike Press Large Print books are available at your library, through selected bookstores, or directly from us.

For information about titles, please call:
  (800) 223-1244

or visit our Web site at:
  http://gale.cengage.com/thorndike

To share your comments, please write:
  Publisher
  Thorndike Press
  295 Kennedy Memorial Drive
  Waterville, ME 04901